THE GIDEON PROTOCOL

Are You Brave Enough To Go Off World?

LC HANSON

ISBN: 0997199512
ISBN: 9780997199512
Cover design by Bioblossom Creative

The only thing necessary for the triumph of evil is that good men do nothing.

Contents

Chapter 1

The boys in the cafeteria of Sector D32 encircled Gideon Wells. Some of them threw food while others pumped their fists in the air shouting, "Fight, fight, fight," followed with "Berserker, Berserker."

"Fight, fight, fight."

"Berserker, Berserker."

Berserker—Gideon knew the name well. It was his nickname. Although he didn't like it he admitted to himself that it suited him and his temper perfectly. He wiped the chunks of potato, bean and kale stew off his grey uniform and glared at the three boys now threatening him. No surprise it was Caleb and his sidekicks Nick and Thomas.

Like the other boys in the Finger Lakes New York Quarantine, Gideon was no stranger to fights. But unlike the others, Gideon won his fights provided it was one against one. He had fought and beaten Caleb twice this year already. But today Caleb had friends with him. Three against one was not easy no matter what level black belt in Krav Jitsui somebody had. Gideon took a deep breath. Today was going to be a bad day.

As the circle of chanting boys closed in around him, Gideon could see the bloodlust in their eyes. He could feel their energy and anger fill the cafeteria. It was contagious, worming its way into him like a virus. He clenched his fists and gritted his teeth.

"Fight, fight, fight."

"Berserker, Berserker."

The situation in Quarantine was always the same for Gideon. The only thing that changed was the name of the bullies. Today it was Caleb telling Gideon that his father was a coward for abandoning him and his mother for the Off World mining colony. With a lazy shrug of his shoulders Gideon let that remark slide. But when Nick and Thomas told him that his mother didn't work fast enough creating the cure for the Virus that killed so many on Earth, that because of her, billions of people died, then the pushing and shoving would start.

Didn't people know that her work in finding the cure for the Virus was what ended her life?

The hands of the other boys pressed into Gideon's back, driving the rough, scratchy material of his Quarantine uniform into his skin. They edged him closer to Caleb, Nick and Thomas. Gideon knew he shouldn't fight them; another fight could hurt his chances of getting into the Galaxy Class Pilot program. He looked for a kind face in the crowd but as usual there were no kind faces in Quarantine, especially in Sector D32. Gideon braced himself for the worst.

"Fight, fight, fight."

"Berserker, Berserker."

Pushed into the center of the circle by the crowd of chanting boys, Gideon unleashed his loudest fighting kiai, a guttural scream of "Eeeee-yah." It froze the other three boys just long enough. Gideon thought of his mother's funeral as he punched Caleb in the nose. The resulting crunch told Gideon he had broken it. Gideon allowed himself a grim smile as Caleb crumpled to the ground, his nose bleeding all over his uniform. The cafeteria erupted with cheers.

"Berserker, Berserker."

"Fight, fight, fight."

Gideon turned to face Nick just as Nick's fist smashed Gideon in the mouth, splitting his lip. The taste of his own blood ran across his tongue, fueling his rage. Gideon spit a mouthful of blood onto the tiled floor.

Nick moved in for another punch but Gideon easily sidestepped him and gave him a spinning sidekick to the stomach driving the air out of him. Nick sank to the floor wheezing. Images of Gideon's father boarding the Off World transport flashed through his mind as Gideon set himself to finish Nick with a round house kick to the head. Then the familiar, shrill voice of the Headmaster cut through the air.

"Enough! Break it up now."

The Headmaster and two Enforcers charged into the circle. The Headmaster was a small man who always wore his tattered blue Skaneateles Lake Country Club blazer and a red tie. The blazer had the country club's insignia – a sailing pennant that looked like the French flag – emblazoned over the Headmaster's heart.

The Enforcers wore black helmets and light blue uniforms. The uniforms were mostly covered by black-tiled body armor. The black body armor was the latest in nanotech shielding. The boys in the Finger Lakes Quarantine joked that the Enforcers looked like turtles. But the electrified batons the Enforcers carried were no joke to the boys in Quarantine. The batons had small orbs on the end that crackled and popped with high-voltage electricity. The boys called these weapons Shockers.

"Gideon, I should have known you were the cause of all this." The Headmaster jabbed his finger into the only potato, bean and kale free spot on Gideon's chest. "It's the third fight this quarter."

Gideon's arms shook from the rush of adrenaline that coursed through him. He slowly unclenched his fists and took a deep breath. Sweat dripped into his eyes, the salt stinging them. He spit another mouthful of blood onto the floor, cleared his throat and tried to speak but the Headmaster cut him off with a wave of his hand. "Save it, boy. Take him to my office now."

As the enforcers grabbed Gideon by both arms, the Headmaster pointed at Caleb and Nick. "Stop mopping the floor with your butts and get to the infirmary. After you've been cleared by medical, report to detention. The rest of you animals clean this place up. It looks like hell in here and stinks even worse."

None of the boys moved. They stood staring in stunned silence at the Headmaster. The only sound was the buzzing of the overhead lights that seemed to cook the mix of blood, beans, potato and kale stew that coated the cafeteria floor. The air was thick with the smell of blood, sweat and potatoes.

Then a glob of the potato, bean and kale stew sailed through the air. It landed on the Headmaster's chest, covering the country club insignia. Instead of a red, white and blue sailing pennant, the insignia was now sticky and green.

It looked like one of the boys shot the Headmaster with a green paintball. The Headmaster gritted his teeth. He slowly wiped the stew off with a flick of his wrist and turned to the Enforcers. "The boys need a lesson."

The Enforcers released Gideon and jammed their Shockers into the boys nearest them. The two boys convulsed violently as the electricity ran through their bodies.

"Stop it," Gideon said. "Those guys didn't even do anything."

The Headmaster turned on Gideon. "Perhaps you want to take their place?"

"No, Sir."

"I didn't think so." The Headmaster calmly watched the boys convulse. When they lost control of their bowels he turned to the Enforcers. "Release them, they've had enough."

The Enforcers withdrew their Shockers.

The boys crumpled to the ground in fetal positions.

"Does anyone else need a lesson?" the Headmaster shouted. "Or are you going to clean this place up like I told you to?"

The boys started cleaning, keeping one eye on the Headmaster and the other on the Enforcers.

Gideon looked for Thomas but the boy had wisely disappeared into the crowd, successfully avoiding the Headmaster. Gideon sighed as the rough hands of the Enforcers dragged him to the Headmaster's office—again.

Gideon stood at attention in front of the Headmaster's desk. The office was chilly, reminding Gideon of why the boys in Quarantine called it the freezer. His wet uniform - soaked with sweat, blood and chunks of green stew pressed against his skin like a cold dirty rag.

"Cadet Gideon Wells, what am I going to do with you?" the Headmaster asked. "You have more demerits than anyone in the history of the Finger Lakes New York Quarantine. Just last month you were kicked off the Krav Jitsui team for fighting and what is it with that crazy nickname they gave you? It's not flattering." The Headmaster's sharp, pinched features and small dark eyes bore into Gideon. Frowning, he looked more rodent than human. It was one of the many reasons why the boys at the Quarantine nicknamed him Weasel.

"No, Sir, most nicknames aren't," Gideon thought of the Headmaster's nickname and tried not to laugh. "My roommate Adrian gave me the Berserker nickname. I can't help that the other guys like calling me that."

"Adrian gave you that nickname? Young man, did he tell you what a Berserker is?"

Gideon gave the Headmaster a blank stare. "Sir?"

"What exactly did Adrian tell you about Berserkers?"

"Adrian said it's a warrior that goes crazy in battle, Sir."

The Headmaster grunted. "That's all? Nothing more? Nothing about Off World?"

"Off World? No, Sir. All Adrian said was that I act crazy like a Berserker sometimes, especially when—."

"Never mind, Cadet. Tell me about the fight in the cafeteria."

"I didn't start it, Sir."

"Nothing's ever your fault is it?"

"Sir, it was three against one. How is that my fault?"

"I saw what happened, Gideon. Like the other fights you've had, you threw the first punch. Not only that, if I hadn't stepped in when I did you would have kicked Nick in the head. You could have caused some serious damage to that boy. You could have killed him."

Gideon shrugged his shoulders. "Then it's lucky for everybody you stepped in when you did, Sir."

"I see." The Headmaster pulled a data pad from off of a nearby table and powered it up. It flashed a file with Gideon's name on it.

Gideon took a deep breath and stared out the window. The autumn sky was grey and overcast. It was a typical autumn day in the Finger Lakes region of western New York State. The waters of Canandaigua Lake mirrored the grey sky reinforcing Gideon's dark mood. He scanned the shoreline and rolling hills, taking in the colorful leaves of the elm, oak, and maple trees of the surrounding forests. The red, yellow and orange leaves reminded him of happier times. It reminded Gideon of a time before the Virus came from Off World to Earth killing billions—before the orphaned survivors of the Virus were forced into quarantines, before his parents left him. Like the changing leaves of the trees, his old life was nothing more than a fading memory. Standing in the Headmaster's office, Gideon never felt so alone. The Headmaster's voice brought Gideon out of his daydream.

"I see you're turning fourteen next month."

"Yes, Sir."

The Headmaster didn't look up from his data pad. He scanned Gideon's file for several minutes and then after a long, heavy sigh shut it down. He frowned at Gideon, giving the pinched features of his face an even sharper, more weasel-like edge. "You're set to leave Quarantine this summer. Any thought about what work assignment you want?"

"Yes, Sir. I've applied for the Galaxy Class Pilot program. It should be in my file." *The Weasel should know that. What's he playing at?*

"The rules at Fort Drum are a lot stricter than the rules here."

Gideon braced himself for what was coming next. His stomach tightened. "Sir?"

"Gideon, there is only one open slot available in the Galaxy Class Pilot program. Your grades are excellent of course. No surprise there since both your parents were scientists. But your behavior - especially the fighting - is a problem. They won't tolerate an angry boy in the pilot program. They only want mature young men."

"Sorry, Sir, but the other boys, especially Caleb, just don't know when to quit. They push and push about my parents, especially about my mother."

"You think you're the only one to have suffered? Everyone lost somebody to the Virus." The Headmaster pointed to the nearby table where a framed photo of his wife and three children sat. "But we don't use it as an excuse to destroy ourselves or hurt others."

Gideon pursed his lips. He forgot about the cracked lip Nick gave him and frowned as the taste of his own blood coated his tongue. He swallowed and looked at the photo of the Headmaster's wife and children aboard a party boat in front of the Skaneateles Lake Country Club. They looked so happy. Gideon could see that the eyes of the Headmaster's wife and children had a slight purple tinge to them. The first sign that the deadly Virus had begun to take hold. Like most that contracted the Virus before Gideon's mother invented the cure, all three of them died. Gideon's eyes welled with tears as he thought of how the Virus killed his mother.

First, the haunting purple eyes.

Then oozing welts.

Then endless coughing fits.

Then a final smile followed by a deep painful sigh as her last breath left her.

Then she was gone—forever.

"Gideon, you're competing against Caleb for the last Galaxy Class Pilot slot. Did you know that?"

Gideon tore his gaze from the photo. "What? No, Sir."

"How do you think it makes your application look when you break the nose of the other guy you're competing against?"

Gideon gasped. "Sir, I swear I had no idea we were competing for the last GCP slot."

"He knew you were competing against him," the Headmaster said in an accusatory tone.

Gideon's face flushed hot. He tried to control his temper. "Sir, did it ever occur to you that maybe Caleb was pushing for this fight? That he wanted me disqualified so he could have the slot for himself? That he's been planning this all along?"

"You better watch your tone with me, Cadet."

Gideon tried to swallow the anger welling up inside him. "Sorry, Sir."

"You want to get that last slot? Then you have to prove you're mature enough to have it. That you can control your temper and follow instructions," the Headmaster said. "Everything you've done here at Finger Lakes Quarantine has demonstrated an unmatched ability to excel as an individual, to look out for yourself—to survive. But you've yet to show us that you can be part of a team."

"Yes, Sir, I promise I'll do better this quarter."

The Headmaster shook his head. He reached for a small silver disc. "We've gone way beyond that."

"Sir?"

"This disc is the first message received from Off World since the Virus. We downloaded the message yesterday morning. Its authenticity has been verified."

Gideon stared blankly at the Headmaster. "Sir, I don't understand how the first message from Off World in three years is important to me."

"It's from your father."

A lump formed in Gideon's throat.

"He needs you Off World."

The news hit Gideon harder than Nick's punch to the face. Gideon's mouth hung open in surprise.

"Doctor Wells wants you to deliver some DNA samples to him for his lab work. The trip should be easy enough. You should be able go Off World and return back to Earth within five days time."

"Sir, I haven't seen or heard from my father in three years. He abandoned my mother and me. I don't want to see him." Gideon's swallowed the bile forming at the back of his throat. "Why can't a droid make the trip?"

"I figured you'd say that." The Headmaster's mouth curled up at the ends revealing a rare smile. It wasn't a kind smile. It was more weasel-like than human. "I can't order you to go. But I do have considerable sway regarding what kind of work assignment you get once you're released from this quarantine."

Gideon looked at the Headmaster with contempt. He didn't like being threatened. It made him feel like he was being bullied. He also didn't want to go Off World. Off World was home to the Virus. It was also home to Shape Shifters and if the rumors were true, strange monsters that ate humans. But as bad as those things were, they were nothing compared to seeing his father.

"So, I offer you this, Cadet Wells," continued the Headmaster. "If you go see your father, deliver the DNA samples to him and return safely, your admission into the Galaxy Class Pilot program is guaranteed."

"If I refuse?" Gideon asked.

"Then Caleb gets the slot and you'll work on a fishing trawler out of Buffalo. Instead of exploring the galaxy, you'll be exploring Lake Erie."

Gideon grit his teeth. His father loved fishing. Gideon hated it.

The Headmaster laughed. "Cheer up, boy. It could be worse, I could put you on a dairy farm outside Batavia repairing milking-bots."

"Do I have to decide right now, Sir?" Gideon chewed on his lower lip, inadvertently re-opening the cut. A trickle of blood tinged the tip of his tongue and ran down his chin.

The Headmaster eyed Gideon's stained uniform and bloodied lip. "Get yourself cleaned up and report to the infirmary, see if they can fix that lip. I will see you back here in my office with your answer tomorrow at 0900. Is that clear?"

"Yes, Sir."

Chapter 2

Gideon pulled a clean uniform from his closet. Despite scrubbing his skin almost raw in the shower, he still felt dirty after his meeting with the Weasel. He inspected the light-skinned face looking back at him from the mirror. Medical fixed his lip using a hand-held laser. The cut was closed and the swelling gone. But the red-rimmed puffiness around his eyes was another matter.

He tried to blink back the tears welling up in his blue eyes but it didn't work. He balled his hands into tight fists and used them to wipe his face and eyes. He dried his hands by running them through his short, brown hair giving himself a spiky hairdo. Satisfied he didn't look like he had been crying, Gideon turned from the mirror and grunted.

He couldn't prove it but Gideon was convinced Caleb had set him up. The thing that really made him mad was that Caleb knew he and Gideon were competing for the last open slot in the Galaxy Class Pilot program. *How did Caleb know? Who told him?* Gideon punched his desk in frustration hurting his hand. As he rubbed the pain from his hand, the words of the Headmaster echoed through Gideon's head. *"You have to prove you're mature enough, that you can control your temper and be part of a team."*

Gideon scanned the dorm room looking for something to break. The room had two twin beds on opposite sides of the room. The beds had metal frames and thin mattresses. There were also two small desks made from lightly stained pressed wood. Each desk had a small computer linked to the net.

The desk used by Gideon's roommate Adrian was covered with family photos, heavy metal music discs, books about drawing and a single sketchpad. Colored pencils were lined up in neat rows.

Gideon's desk had a photo of his mother on it, reggae music discs his mother had given him and books about martial arts. There was also a model of an old-fashioned spy plane, the SR 72. The model SR 72 was given to Gideon by his grandfather on his ninth birthday. It looked like a wormhole jumper so Gideon kept it.

Gideon turned his attention to the hallway when he heard his nickname. Several boys were staring at him and shaking their heads. Gideon slammed the door to his room. The force knocked his family's picture off the wall. Picking it up, Gideon noticed that the glass over his father's face was cracked. Gideon shrugged his shoulders. He had crossed out his father's face leaving a black *X* in its place long ago. After three years of silence what could his father possibly want? The man left Gideon and his mother. He went Off World at the height of the pandemic just when they needed him most. He didn't even have the decency to come back for mom's funeral. *I was all set to leave quarantine this summer and go to flight school. Now this.*

Gideon stared at his mother's picture. He pursed his lips. It wasn't fair. She died creating the cure that saved millions from the Virus. She should be alive. It's not fair.

Gideon tossed the picture on his bunk. He kneeled down and pulled his footlocker out from under his bed and opened it. He rummaged through it until he came across a small wooden box. The box was sanded smooth and had a natural finish applied to it. Gideon ran his fingers across the box slowly, reverently before opening it. He hadn't opened the box since his mother's funeral. He swallowed hard pushing away his anger and loneliness.

A loud knock on the door jarred him. "Go away."

"No can do, I live there too," said an all too familiar voice.

Gideon put the small wooden box down and sighed. His roommate had a terrible sense of timing. "What do you want, Adrian?"

"What do you think I want? I want to come in and make sure you haven't gone completely crazy and wrecked the place like these guys out here say you have."

"Those idiots are lying to you. I've only broken my own things." Gideon looked over at the broken picture frame. "I've left your stuff alone." He paused as a wicked smile crawled across his face, "for now."

"That's nice. I'm coming in now so don't throw anything at me like last time."

"Enter," Gideon said.

The door opened just enough to allow Adrian to peek his head into the room. The two boys couldn't have been more different. Gideon was of medium height with brown hair and blue eyes. Adrian was tall and big boned with platinum blonde hair and bright blue eyes. Of the four roommates Gideon had during the past three years, Gideon liked Adrian the best. Gideon never told Adrian, but he believed the Headmaster chose Adrian to be his roommate because Adrian was the biggest boy in Quarantine. Nobody bullied him and he didn't bully anyone else. During the three years Adrian lived in Quarantine he had never gotten into a fight with anyone.

Gideon envied Adrian. Adrian's older brother and sister were still alive living near Rochester, New York.

Gideon had no one. His grandparents had lived in Eyam, England but died before the Virus. *At least they didn't have to see what the Virus did.*

When the Virus first came to Earth, doctors thought that since parts of Northern England, Russia, and the Scandinavian countries had a higher survivability rate only losing sixty percent of their populations, that cold weather somehow made the Virus less lethal. They were wrong. The Virus wiped out over eighty percent of cities like Montreal, Denver, Anchorage, and Nagano. It ended cities like Miami, Sao Paolo, Cairo, Jakarta and Mumbai.

Adrian scanned the room. His eyes immediately went to his sketchbook and then back to Gideon. After Gideon's last outburst, Adrian had lost some books and music discs so the two boys developed an understanding. Gideon was to never touch Adrian's sketchbook or drawings. Losing a few music discs and books to a temper tantrum was one thing but Gideon knew that damaging Adrian's sketchbook would not only end their friendship it could possibly start a serious fist fight. Gideon was the best fighter in Quarantine, but taking on somebody as big as Adrian wouldn't be smart.

"I hear Berserker appeared in the cafeteria today," Adrian said.

Gideon pretended to be innocent. "Nothing happened in the cafeteria. I have no idea what you're talking about or who this Berserker guy is."

"Are you kidding? Berserker fought three guys at once and even broke Caleb's nose. Everyone's talking about it."

Gideon shrugged his shoulders. He thought back to when Adrian gave him the Berserker nickname. It was on his first day in Quarantine—after his first fight. Gideon had let his temper get the better of him and after screaming at the top of his lungs, had attacked and beaten up a much larger and older red-haired boy that had been picking on him. Adrian had said Gideon looked, sounded and fought like he was in a trance-like fury just like a Berserker. No matter how hard Gideon tried to explain that he was simply unleashing a kia or fighting scream like his father taught him, Adrian would have none of it. He insisted on calling Gideon Berserker. After that, the nickname stuck. Whenever Gideon got mad or into a fight the other boys would start in on him chanting *Berserker*.

"You really are a Berserker taking on three fighters at once. What does it feel like to get all crazy like that? Uh oh, I feel it now." Adrian gave Gideon a mock monster pose flexing his muscles and scrunching up his face.

Gideon laughed. Adrian was tall but too skinny to be able to look fierce. He looked ridiculous. "Stop it, you look like you're taking a dump."

"What's this? Laughter from Berserker?" Adrian struck a new warrior pose as he made fun of Gideon. "Is it possible Berserker is human after all?"

"Ha, ha very funny." Gideon looked past Adrian out into the hallway and his smile disappeared. A crowd of boys had gathered. They were crooning to see Adrian. The last thing Gideon wanted was attention. "Close the door you freak people are staring at you."

"Flattery will get you nowhere." Adrian gave the door a jarring back kick. His gaze fell to the small wooden box on the floor in front of Gideon. "Is that what I think it is?"

Gideon nodded. "It is."

"I've never seen you wear it." Adrian clutched the medallion around his neck. "I always wear mine. It reminds me of my father."

Gideon opened the box and removed the Chain of Remembrance. The silver-chained necklace had a small blue crystal dangling on the end. He watched the crystal spin lazily. Inside was his mother's DNA.

At the height of the global pandemic, families saved the DNA of loved ones in the hope that once a cure to the Virus had been found the dead could be cloned, re-born and given a second chance at life. But after Gideon's mother invented the cure and the Virus was contained, fears of creating a new pandemic forced a halt to all cloning experiments. However, rumors of illegal cloning for the rich and powerful persisted.

"I've never worn mine. It reminds me of her death." Gideon's breath caught in his chest. "It's…it's too painful."

"What gives with you?" Adrian said. "One minute Berserker's busting noses in the cafeteria. The next you're sitting here looking at your Chain of Remembrance. Are you about to do something stupid?"

"Maybe, that's what I'm trying to figure out," Gideon said.

Adrian crossed his long legs and sat on the floor next to Gideon. "We're friends, Gideon. You can tell me. Maybe I can help."

"We're roommates, Adrian."

Adrian shook his head. "You are stone cold. You don't want my help, fine."

Adrian got up and went for the door.

"They want me to go Off World."

Adrian froze, his mouth hung open in surprise.

"Yeah, I had the exact same look on my face when the Weasel told me."

Adrian sat back down "Wow, are you serious?"

"I'm as serious as the Virus calling on a nursery school."

"What's going on, Gideon? Nobody goes Off World anymore except hunters. What are you going to do? Hunt Shape Shifters? If so, let me know so I can change your nickname."

Gideon rolled his eyes. "Yeah, Adrian, that's what I need. A new nickname."

"Oh, I know, how about Berserker the Merciless? That's perfect." Adrian reached for his sketchpad. He quickly drew a caricature of Gideon.

"Adrian, this is serious stop messing around." Gideon grabbed for the sketchbook but his arms were too short. Adrian easily held the sketchpad just out of Gideon's reach.

"Ladies and gentlemen," Adrian said. "I give you Berserker the Merciless, starring in his first graphic novel. Parental discretion advised as some material may be unfit for children under the age of twelve."

The sketch showed Gideon with sharp teeth and long claws. He was gnawing on a bone.

"Nice, very nice. Is this your way of helping me? If it is, maybe you should stop being so helpful," Gideon said, his voice rising in anger.

Chuckling, Adrian set the drawing aside. "Okay, so tell me. Why does the Weasel want you to go Off World?"

"To deliver some lab samples for my father's work."

"Hold on, you have to see your dad?"

"That's what the Weasel said." Gideon stared at the crystal on his Chain of Remembrance. "He said if I made the trip and came back safely I was guaranteed the last spot in flight school. He made it sound so easy. Off World and back in five days time, no big deal."

"If you refuse?"

"Then no flight school. The Weasel told me if I didn't go Off World he would make sure I ended up on a trawler out of Buffalo or on a hydroponics farm in Batavia."

"Fishing's not so bad. My brother ships out of Buffalo. They ship out four months at a time." Adrian started laughing.

"What?" Gideon asked.

"A sailor's life may not be for you. I mean somebody as easy going as you on a ship for four months? I pity the crew."

"You're a funny guy," Gideon said. "If you were any funnier you'd be on the net with your own show."

"Anyway, hydroponics farming in Batavia doesn't sound so bad, Gideon. You get to eat well, at least better than the slop they feed us in here. So what's the problem, you want to be a Galaxy Class Pilot so bad you're willing to risk going Off World?"

"I don't know." Gideon held up his Chain of Remembrance and gently flicked the blue crystal with his finger making it spin. "It's a hard choice."

"What do you think you're going to do up at Fort Drum? Fly fighters and then move on to galaxy class cruisers?" Adrian asked. "It's not like there are any enemy armies left to fight here on Earth. The Virus took care of them as well as us. Don't get me wrong; we'll all get a good shot at getting decent, grown-up work assignments once we get out of Quarantine. I mean they have no choice but to do that because most of the grown-ups are dead. But do you really think they're going to make you a Galaxy Class Pilot?"

Gideon put the Chain of Remembrance around his neck. He frowned at Adrian. "My mother thought they would and so do I. I promised her I would be a Galaxy Class Pilot. I mean she was always telling me how important it is to be a humanitarian, to be generous and help rebuild. We agreed that being a Galaxy Class Pilot was the best way for me to go. You know, I can fly supplies to settlers in the colonies and even bring settlers back to Earth. We made a contract."

Adrian nodded his understanding. "If you made a contract then that's different. But remember, nobody returns from Off World. You go Off World you don't come back. If the Shape Shifters don't kill you then the bone eaters will. You've heard the rumors same as me. Five day trip there and back my eye."

Gideon adjusted his Chain of Remembrance putting the crystal inside his shirt. The crystal was warm. It felt good on his chest.

"No, if it were my choice I would stay here on Earth," Adrian said, stabbing the floor with his finger. "I would work hard at whatever work assignment they gave me, find a nice girl and start a family of my own, that's what's important. That's how we rebuild. We do it one family at a time."

"But what's left of *my* family is Off World." Gideon pulled the broken picture off his bed and pointed at his father. "I want him to tell me why he left and never came back, why he abandoned us."

"You've decided, haven't you?" Adrian shook his head in disbelief. "You're going Off World. You're really doing it."

"Yes, I'm going to see my father, give him the lab samples and ask my questions. There and back in five days time, right? Then it's off to flight school." Gideon touched the crystal on his Chain of Remembrance.

"I will be a Galaxy Class Pilot like I promised."

A long awkward silence filled the room. The two boys stared at each other. Finally, Adrian said, "Can I have your music discs in case you don't come back?"

Gideon laughed and shook his head. "Adrian, you're an idiot."

CHAPTER 3

Gideon powered down the transport's anti-gravity system. He brought the small craft in for a landing just outside the gates of Fort Drum, New York. The computer recorded Gideon's flight score and opened the hatch for him. Its thin metallic voice filled the ship. "Excellent, Sir another perfect flight. You're well on your way to being a Galaxy Class Pilot."

Gideon smiled from ear to ear. He silently congratulated himself for the flawless flight and perfect landing. As much as he liked using the flight simulator in Quarantine, there was nothing better than actual flying. "Beat that, Caleb, you loser," he said. "No way do you get my GCP spot."

Gideon watched the transport lift off and nimbly turn itself in the direction of the Finger Lakes Quarantine. As he admired the computer's flying skill, an odd sadness crept over him. He suddenly felt as if he would never see Adrian or Quarantine again. As bad as Quarantine was at times it had been home for the last three years. A small part of him missed it already.

It had been less than twenty-four hours since the Weasel made his offer to Gideon. But once Gideon accepted, things moved quickly. Gideon had time for a quick breakfast, a brief good-bye with Adrian and barely enough time to grab a warm jacket. Fort Drum was near the Canadian border, hundreds of miles north of the Finger Lakes Quarantine. Before the Virus, Gideon and his parents hiked in the Adirondack Mountains, fished and kayaked in Star, Cranberry and Long Lake. He knew the cold Canadian air would chill him to the bone. He checked his wrist pad. It was only nine-thirty in the morning but his life back in Quarantine seemed like it happened a hundred years ago.

Instinctively, Gideon waved at the transport and then immediately scolded himself. *Stupid, there's nobody onboard.* But to his surprise, the transport wiggled its wings before disappearing into the clouds. He pushed away the sadness and made his way to the main gate. *No worries. I'll be back in five days time.*

Surrounding Fort Drum was a high fence topped with razor wire. At the main gate sat a small brick guardhouse. There was nobody inside, only a sign reading:

All visitors must undergo retinal scanning before entering the base.
Carriers of the Virus will be shot.

A camera hung over the sign. It made a buzzing noise as the lens zoomed in on Gideon. On the side of the guardhouse, just above Gideon's head was the retinal scanner. He cursed. It was too high for him to reach. Gideon stood on his tiptoes but was unable to press his face into the scanner. He looked for something to stand on but finding nothing decided to walk through the gate. *There's nothing I can do about it. They'll just have to understand.*

The November morning air was cold. Gideon closed his mouth and took a deep breath through his nose. The chill bit at the inside of his nostrils. *It smells like pine trees, ice and snow.* When he exhaled, Gideon could see the vapors from his breath. Breathing in and out, he pretended he was a monster breathing icy-fire breath. Laughing quietly to himself Gideon thought of Adrian and how his roommate would probably be making a stupid joke about Berserker breath.

Gideon's hair was still damp from his shower and the ends of his hair started to freeze, making his neck cold. He pulled up the collar of his jacket and set out to explore the base. He kept his eyes open for anyone who might be able to help him find the wormhole jumper that would fly him to Off World. But the base looked deserted. It was eerily quiet. Small buildings that looked like metal cocoons sat in tight rows. Steam rising from piping in the roofs of the buildings made them seem alive as they exhaled into the cold morning air.

As Gideon passed the small buildings, he saw several fighter aircraft neatly arranged on a nearby tarmac. Their sharp-needled noses and tapered wings made them look like deadly insects ready to sting at any moment. Gideon cautiously approached the fighters. He scanned the tarmac for soldiers and guard-bots. He didn't see either. Gideon pursed his lips. *Where is everybody? Why is no one guarding the planes?*

Gideon loved airplanes and had never been so close to a fighter. He slowly reached up to touch the fighter's sharp-edged nose when a siren sounded. It was a guard-bot. The small jeep-like robot raced toward him. On its roof was mounted a camera and a laser targeting system for a blaster.

Gideon cursed himself. *How could I have not seen that guard-bot?*

As the guard-bot approached, it shot a tight beam of red light at Gideon. Gideon looked down at his chest and saw a red circle over his heart. He backed away from the plane and raised his hands above his head.

Then the alarm stopped. Boots stomped on the pavement. A young man not much older than Gideon came alongside the guard-bot. "Don't move, kid. That guard-bot will kill you."

Gideon recognized the uniform as base security. The letters "MP" for military police were on the man's sleeve.

Gideon started to apologize but it was too late. The MP already had his hand on his gun. "Why didn't you use the bio-scanner? Didn't you see the sign?"

Despite the cold morning air, sweat started dripping down Gideon's back. "I couldn't reach it. It's too high for me."

"God help me but I'll order the guard-bot to shoot you right here and now if you're not clean." The guard pulled a mask over his mouth and nose.

"Clean? Of course I'm clean. Do my eyes look purple to you?"

The MP frowned at Gideon. He motioned to the guard-bot. The guard-bot didn't move but Gideon heard a clicking noise followed by a low whistle. "That's the sound of the blaster being charged," the MP said in a deadpan voice. "You say you're clean? Prove it. Give me your Quarantine Release Papers now."

Gideon's hands were shaking. He struggled to open his coat. He put his cold hand inside his coat and reached for his inside pocket but grabbed only sweaty armpit. Finally, he found his papers and slowly offered them to the guard. He made a point of showing the MP the green bio-release form that proved he was not a carrier of the Virus.

The MP took the green form and read through it carefully. "Gideon Wells, Finger Lakes Quarantine," he said. The MP paused. He eyed Gideon with suspicion. "Your last name is Wells and you're from sector D32?"

With his hands still raised above his head, Gideon nodded.

The MP removed his mask and read through the rest of the forms. Gideon noticed small, purplish pockmarks on the MP's face. The pockmarks were faded a bit, but there was no doubt in Gideon's mind. This MP was a survivor of the Virus.

Finally, the MP signaled the guard-bot and the red dot on Gideon's chest disappeared. The guard-bot lowered the blaster, turned itself around and sped away, its motor whining in protest.

The MP returned Gideon's forms. "You can lower your hands. You and your mother saved my life. She was a great lady inventing the cure like that. I'm sorry for your loss."

Gideon was stunned. "Um, thanks."

The MP's mood suddenly darkened. He looked at Gideon disapprovingly. "But why are you going Off World? You're a bit young to hunt Shape Shifters aren't you?"

"I'm not a hunter. I'm going to deliver a package to my father and then come back to Earth. It should all be there in the release papers."

"If you're not a hunter, then what's this?" The MP handed Gideon a drawing of a monster with long teeth and claws. The monster looked like Gideon. The sketch read, "Berserker the Merciless."

Adrian, I'm going to kill you. "Sorry, it's my roommate's idea of a joke."

"I see," replied the MP, his mood slightly improved by the drawing. "Come on, Berserker the Merciless. Let's get you to the maglev launcher. I'm sure the other hunters will be thrilled to meet you."

Gideon put his papers back inside his jacket. He couldn't help but notice the sarcasm in the MP's voice. He watched with fascination as the MP called for a jeep by speaking into a small microphone attached to his wrist. In a matter of minutes a jeep came to a screeching halt right next to Gideon and the MP, forcing them to step back and out of the way. A red-haired driver with freckles poked his head out of the window. "Come on, kid, I'm your ride. Get in."

Gideon couldn't believe it. The driver looked like the red-haired boy Gideon fought three years ago and was the cause for his Berserker nickname.

The door swung open and Gideon jumped into the jeep. He was about to thank the MP when the jeep pulled away throwing Gideon back into his seat. The jeep sped through the base, winding its way past airplane hangars, past a building that smelled like bacon and eggs and several small, squat buildings that Gideon guessed were living quarters for the ground crews. After several minutes they made their way onto a bumpy dirt road lined with trees.

"Put your seat belt on," the driver said as they bounced along the road.

Gideon managed to put on his seat belt just as the jeep hit a large bump. He held on as best he could. The worse the trail became the faster the jeep went and the wider the driver's smile grew. The engine roared as the jeep sailed over another large bump. They landed in a clearing just outside the forest.

"Yeah!" the driver shouted. He gave the jeep more gas, accelerating up a small hill.

"You're supposed to get me there alive and in one piece aren't you?" Gideon shouted over the roar of the engine.

The driver laughed. "Kid, if you can't handle a little joy ride with me, the wormhole jumper is going to be a real killer. Take it easy, we're almost there."

As the jeep finished climbing the hill, the driver stomped on the brake forcing Gideon to brace himself against the dashboard. "We're here."

Gideon jumped out of the jeep. "I hope you fly better than you drive."

"I'm not a pilot."

"That's a relief. Where am I?"

"The launch site is down there, kid."

In front of Gideon lay a long runway. At the far end there was a half-built roller coaster. It had a circular track that led to the steepest ramp Gideon had ever seen. It pointed up toward the sky and simply ended. On the circular portion of the track was a black plane. It had swept wings and a sharp, tapered nose. The plane was covered in heat tiles that shimmered in the morning sun making its skin look reptilian.

Gideon pumped his fist in the air. *Yes, the wormhole jumper. I'm finally flying into space.*

The driver leaned out the jeep window. "That roller coaster-looking thing you're staring at is the maglev launcher. It fires the wormhole jumper into space. You'll be pulling some serious G-forces when you launch."

"This is like a dream come true. I've wanted to fly in outer space since I was a little kid."

"Yeah, you're lucky. The closest I've gotten to riding in a wormhole jumper is when I clean the snow off the maglev. But that's still pretty cool because I just plow it off using an old wormhole jumper rigged with a snowplow and rotating brush. I call it the platypus."

"Sounds like fun." The maglev track made a sudden popping and crackling noise. Gideon jumped at the sound. It reminded him of the bug zapper his parents had kept in the backyard.

"Relax, kid, that's the pre-flight diagnostic check," the driver said. "They want to make sure the magnetic levitation system works and the wormhole jumper floats on the track during takeoff. Check it out."

The wormhole jumper raised and lowered itself on the tracks, levitating every time the tracks buzzed and popped.

"What happens if the wormhole jumper doesn't float? Do they just abort takeoff and start over?"

The driver shook his head. "At those speeds you can't abort anything. If the magnetic levitation system fails during take off, the wormhole jumper will get shredded like cheese on a grater or you wind up a permanent stain on the runway. Either way, your trip will be over before it starts. That's why we have fire-bots but no rescue-bots."

The fire-bots were grouped at the near side of the runway where the tarmac was cratered and burned. The fire-bots looked like small fire trucks and were mounted with cannons that shot white foam. The blackened and cratered portion of the runway was in direct line with the maglev's ramp. The blackened tarmac was not only a landing site for jumpers returning from space but also a final resting place for launches gone wrong.

Gideon was used to takeoffs in regular planes and anti-gravity transports but the risk of getting torn apart on the maglev launcher or being made a permanent stain on the runway made his breakfast churn in his stomach. He swallowed making sure it stayed down.

"You look nervous, kid. Are you okay?"

Gideon lied. "Yeah, I'm good to go."

"Great, nothing worse than a scared passenger. Don't worry. It's usually safe. We've only lost two ships since I've been here."

"Thanks, thanks a lot," Gideon said.

"Chill, kid, the launch is perfectly safe. It's coming out through the wormhole that you need to start saying your prayers."

"What are you talking about?" Gideon asked, but the jeep sped off leaving Gideon in a cloud of dust.

When the dust cloud cleared Gideon saw a large man in army fatigues walking toward him. The man had a shaved head and harsh features. But to Gideon's surprise the man had a warm smile and kind eyes. "You must be Gideon," he said in a deep voice.

Gideon noticed multiple stripes on the man's sleeve meaning he was probably an officer. "Yes, Sir," replied Gideon. He reached inside his coat for his release papers and handed them over.

"Don't call me 'Sir'. Call me Sergeant. I'm the mission commander. You do everything I tell you to do and we'll get along just fine, understand?"

"Yes, Sir," Gideon said, and then corrected himself. "Sorry, okay, Sergeant."

"Good, come this way." The sergeant waved Gideon toward a small grey building. The building looked like a bunker. It had no windows. Its walls were lined with fireproof tiles and its roof covered with several radar dishes and antennae of different lengths. "We'll be getting under way in about an hour. We have just enough time to give you a quick briefing and introduce you to the hunters you'll be traveling with."

Gideon nodded his understanding as the sergeant opened the door to the small building. As soon as Gideon walked in, the room fell silent except for the electronic beeping of the computers that lined the tables. Young men not much older than Gideon manned the computers. They all wore green fatigues similar to the sergeant's. *Mission control technicians.*

On the wall in the front of the mission control technicians, hung three large monitors. The one in the center had a map of Off World. The other two displayed navigational settings. The room smelled like burnt wiring and old coffee.

"Welcome to mission control, Gideon," the sergeant said. "This is the team that will help you get to Off World and back home."

Gideon waved. "Hi, nice to meet you guys."

The technicians gave Gideon a curt nod and turned back to their computers. Gideon shrugged his shoulders. His gaze fell to two men dressed in black flight suits. *They must be the hunters.*

The black-clad men stared back at Gideon eyeing him as if he had stolen something.

A lump formed in the back of Gideon's throat.

"Gideon, these are the hunters who will be going Off World with you," the sergeant said.

"Oh my God, Frankie" said the nearest hunter. He wasn't much taller than Gideon but looked very powerful with muscular arms and a thick neck. He had a thin covering of recently shaved razor stubble on his mostly baldhead. On his pale face, he had stubbly, dark whiskers that matched the black color and thickness of the stubble on his head. "We really are on a babysitting mission."

The other hunter laughed. He also had a thin covering of razor stubble atop his head. But his face was clean-shaven. He was African American and a head taller than the short hunter. Although not as muscular as the shorter hunter, he looked athletic with the lean, chiseled build of a boxer. He nodded at Gideon.

"Stow that nonsense, soldier," the sergeant said. "Call it whatever you want but this boy *is* your mission. You've been briefed so you know that when you bring him back safely to Earth you'll each get a full pardon for whatever crimes you've been convicted of. So let me spell it out for you guys, going Off World is your last chance at redemption so don't screw it up."

Gideon liked that the sergeant said *when* they bring him back to Earth and not *if*.

The sergeant winked at Gideon and walked to the front of the room. He leaned over a computer and started typing on a keyboard.

"Looks like Sarge has a soft spot for the kid, Frankie," the short hunter said.

"Yeah, that figures, V. The kid probably reminds him of his son. Sarge lost the rug-rat to the Virus."

"How do you know?"

"I heard it when I was in the brig, V. The MP was looking for volunteers and started running his mouth."

Gideon had heard the rumors but he never believed they were true. The boys in Quarantine had talked about how the hunters of the Off World Shape Shifters were convicted criminals who agreed to go Off World in order to have their convictions erased. With the Virus creating a population shortage, good soldiers were hard to find so somebody came up with the idea of sending convicted criminals Off World to continue the fight against the Shape Shifters. Gideon remembered his mother telling him that although never proven, Shape Shifters were blamed for sending the Virus to Earth so hunting them was still a priority to many.

"Don't just stand there like it's your first rodeo, introduce yourselves," the sergeant ordered.

"Soft spot for the kid," the short hunter whispered.

The tall hunter extended his hand. It dwarfed Gideon's. "Hi, Gideon, I'm Frank."

The shorter of the two hunters simply nodded at Gideon. "Name's Vince, kid."

Gideon nodded and gave a sheepish wave. "Hi."

"All right, everybody take a seat," the sergeant said. He paced in front of a large computer screen that displayed a picture of Off World.

To Gideon's surprise, the planet was mostly blue like Earth. But unlike Earth, Off World had massive amounts of ice at its northern and southern poles and instead of multiple continents Off World had one large, single land mass centered at the planet's equator. The giant continent was dotted with tens of thousands of lakes and interconnecting rivers. Connecting the northern and southern oceans were several long rivers that lay across the planet's continent like the splayed, bony fingers of a skeleton. As the sergeant spoke, a red flashing dot appeared in the middle of a series of large interconnected lakes. The lakes reminded Gideon of the Great Lakes of Western New York. He smiled, taking comfort with this small familiarity.

"Think of Off World as a lot like prehistoric Earth," the sergeant said. "It's a young planet teeming with life. Many of those life forms are savage and unfriendly to humans so no going off on safari or doing anything else stupid. Stick to the mission and you'll be in and out in five days time. Understand?"

"In and out in five days time, not one day more, right Frankie?" Vince said.

"Amen, V."

There and back in five days. That's what the weasel said.

The sergeant tapped on a nearby keyboard forcing the computer screen to zoom in on the flashing red dot. It was a large island with high mountains and a grassy plain. "You will land here on Smilodon Island. It's named after the saber-toothed cats that live there."

Gideon's eyes widened with surprise.

"Saber-toothed cats?" Vince said. "Are you kidding me, Sarge?"

"Does it look like I'm kidding, soldier? I just said Off World is like prehistoric Earth. Get the wax outta your ears. This island has saber-toothed cats on it, which is why they chose the spot for the lab. Nothing on that planet goes anywhere near the island. We hide in plain sight protected by the planet's worst predator. Get it?"

"Got it, Sarge," Vince said.

"But what protects us from the saber-toothed cats?" Gideon pictured long teeth and claws raking over his skin, slicing it to ribbons. He rubbed his forearms and drew his arms close to his body.

The sergeant held up his hand, signaling for Gideon to wait. "When you land, you will taxi the wormhole jumper to the northern most end of the tarmac. There you will wait until the force field protecting the lab complex is lowered. The cats are very aggressive and don't like humans very much. Unless you want to be cat food, do not leave the protection of the ship until you have confirmed that the force field has been opened for you."

Gideon raised his hand.

"Frankie, the kid raised his hand," Vince said. "Ain't that cute?"

This Vince guy is a jerk.

Frank shook his head. "Come on, V, give the kid a break."

"Agreed, give Gideon a break, soldier," the sergeant said. "Yes, son, what is it?"

"Sergeant, what do we do if the force field can't be lowered?"

Vince shook his head. "Kid, then we need either an old-fashioned nuke or maybe you can daisy chain together about a dozen blaster packs and create an electromagnetic pulse. Otherwise, we're out of luck."

"An EMP? Sounds just like Tehran," Frank said. "Remember that job?"

Vince smiled from ear to ear. "Are you kidding me? That EMP rattled my teeth and shook my bones. Only you would use that many blaster packs. I'm just glad you didn't have a nuke with you."

"Pipe down, soldier," the sergeant said. "There will be no need for an EMP or anything else. Don't worry, Gideon, the force field will be lowered for you. But if there's a problem just follow protocol."

"What's the protocol?"

"You doing what we tell you to do, kid."

"You got that right, V."

Gideon frowned at the hunters.

"Gideon, both Frank and Vince have been trained for all possible contingencies. If the wormhole jumper lands off course or is damaged, they know how to navigate Off World's hostile terrain and get to the nearest mining camp."

Hostile terrain? The map of Smilodon Island stared down at Gideon. The mountains had sharp peaks. *They look just like fangs.*

"If attacked by Shape Shifters, bone eaters or anything else unfriendly, they have the proper training and weapons."

Bone eaters? Adrian's sketch of Gideon as Berserker the Merciless flashed in his mind's eye. *Are there really creatures with long teeth eating humans?*

Gideon started to raise his hand again but stopped himself when he saw Vince watching him. "Excuse me, Sergeant? What's a bone eater?"

"Nothing you need to worry about, son. Both of these soldiers are from elite units of the Corps. They can handle anything coming their way."

"Hooraah," Frank said.

"Damn straight, Frankie. Gonna skin me a Shape Shifter."

Gideon's reached for his Chain of Remembrance and rolled the crystal between his fingers. *Bone eaters? Skin me a Shape Shifter? What have I gotten myself into?*

"Here, Gideon." Frank handed him a data pad with a picture of Off World on the screen. "Why don't you cruise through this?"

"Thanks." Gideon took the data pad and started pressing the screen. He pulled up a map of Smilodon Island and the surrounding area. It reminded Gideon of the nearby Saint Lawrence Seaway and Thousand Islands region of New York State. Smilodon Island was the largest of the many islands that sat in the middle of a large lake. The lake was fed by many smaller waterways. One of them was called Split Rock Rapids. Gideon touched the screen to magnify the rapids. The river looked perfect for white water rafting and it led right to Smilodon Island.

"This is a general resupply mission," the sergeant said."You will be carrying meds and other lab supplies onboard the wormhole jumper. But remember, the primary objective is to escort Gideon and the package into the lab. You will wait twenty-four hours before boarding the wormhole jumper for the return trip to Earth. The lab has a maglev launcher and maintenance-bots so your return trip should be no problem."

"What's in the package?" Frank asked.

"That information is on a need-to-know basis and you don't need-to-know," replied the sergeant.

"I hate that need-to-know nonsense, Sarge. Come on, is it dangerous?" Frank said. "Could it explode if not handled correctly? Is it heavy? What's the situation?"

"All good questions," the sergeant said. "All I can tell you is that under no circumstances should the package be opened outside the lab or given to anyone other than Doctor Wells."

Dad. Gideon sighed. *I'd rather take my chances with a bone eater.*

"If the package gets into the wrong hands, it could have devastating consequences for the entire planet."

Devastating consequences for the planet? The Weasel said it was just some DNA samples.

"Everything's been loaded on the wormhole jumper. You hunters go saddle up and head for the maglev. Gideon, follow me. We'll get you a flight suit and some gear of your own."

"Like I said, Frankie, soft spot for the kid."

Gideon tried to settle comfortably into his seat on the wormhole jumper but it was no use. The jumper's small cabin and hard seat was nothing like the airplane he flew when taking family trips to see his grandparents in Eyam, England. Unlike the passenger airplanes he was used to, the inside of the wormhole jumper was cramped. The walls were lined with blinking panels and beeping computer screens. A small cargo hold in the rear of the craft held the hunters' gear and overhead bins held the medicines and food supplies for the lab. The package for Gideon's father was in the compartment under Gideon's seat. Small round windows on either side of the craft allowed Gideon to peek out but he had to strain against his safety harness.

Gideon tried to adjust his flight suit, pulling at in order to loosen it. The black suit pressed against his legs, stomach and chest. It squeezed him like an anaconda.

"Gideon, don't mess with the suit," Frank said. "It's supposed to be tight. It's designed to make sure your blood continues to flow to your head and your heart during flight. Otherwise you may pass out when the really serious G-forces kick in."

"Yeah, kid, don't mess this up for us by doing something stupid like dying before we get there. You're our meal ticket to a full pardon, so don't blow it."

"My name's Gideon, not kid."

The hunters stared at Gideon with looks of surprise.

Vince shook his head. "Kid, you need to smarten up and change your attitude. I don't care whose son you are, you give me anymore lip I'll feed you to the first Shape Shifter I see."

"Do that and you don't get that pardon, now do you?" Gideon said. "Remember, the sergeant said *I'm* your mission so you better be nice to me."

"What did you say to me?" Vince unfastened his harness and moved toward Gideon. "Kid, I'm gonna teach you—"

Frank grabbed Vince and pulled him back into his seat. "Come on, V, keep your hands off the kid. It ain't worth it."

"Okay, Frankie." Vince turned on Gideon. The hunter's face was red with anger, the veins in his neck bulging. "Alright, kid, if you're so smart, what's a nice boy like you doing going Off World? Nobody goes Off World unless they have to so what's in it for you?"

Gideon continued fidgeting trying to get comfortable. As he squirmed, his flight suit rubbed against the seat making a squeaking noise. "My father runs the lab."

"Yeah, so what?" replied Vince. "I don't believe for a minute you're the type of kid who misses his daddy. A smart-mouthed kid like you couldn't care less."

Gideon stopped squirming. He glared at Vince.

"Come on. Man up, kid. What's in this for you? You know why me and Frankie are going Off World. We want pardons."

"Fine, you want to know why I'm going Off World, I'll tell you." Gideon tried to lean forward as he spoke but the safety harness forced him back into his seat. "When I leave Quarantine this summer I'm guaranteed admission into the Galaxy Class Pilot program."

"Kid, there ain't no such thing in life as a guarantee." Vince pointed toward the cockpit. "Besides, with pilot-bots doin' the work the days of Galaxy Class Pilots are numbered. You'll be obsolete before you even graduate."

Gideon craned his neck so he could see into the cockpit. He grimaced. The pilot-bot looked like a human being whose skin had been melted off and all that remained was a metal skeleton. Its shiny head grazed the ceiling of the cockpit. Its limbs reflected the flashing lights from the control panel. *I bet I could fly this jumper better than any creepy pilot-bot.* Gideon opened his mouth to tell Vince exactly that, but was interrupted.

"Leave Gideon alone and cut the chatter," said a voice over the intercom. It was the sergeant. "Prepare for launch."

"Affirmative," replied the pilot-bot in a metallic voice.

The pilot-bot pressed several buttons on the jumper's control panel. Instantly, the smell of ammonia mixed with gasoline and burnt rubber assaulted Gideon. A low rumble shook the wormhole jumper as the engines powered up. Then the engines surged, pushing the wormhole jumper along the maglev. Gideon grinned from ear to ear. *This is it, space flight.*

"Make sure your seat backs and tray tables are in their upright positions," joked Frank.

The ride was smooth reminding Gideon of the high-speed bullet train he once rode to New York City with his mother. Gideon strained against his harness to look out the window. The forest began to blur as the wormhole jumper picked up speed. He tried to count how many times they went around the maglev track but quickly lost count as the trees outside his window lost all form and shape, blending together to make a warped, melted landscape. As the wormhole jumper accelerated, Gideon felt himself pressed deeper into his seat. His cheeks started to tremble. The smell of burning rocket fuel filled the cabin gagging him. Sweat poured down his face. He tried to lift his arms and legs but couldn't. Then the ship lurched forward, pressing him into his seat as if there were a ton of rocks on his chest. He struggled to breathe against the crushing weight of his own body.

"We are a go for launch," the pilot-bot said.

Gideon fought against the G-forces pressing against him and turned his head to look out the window. He was shocked to see the ground falling away so quickly. Before he knew it the blue sky of Earth gave way to the darkness of space. Then the G-forces pressing on him suddenly eased.

"We have cleared Earth's atmosphere and are preparing to enter the wormhole," announced the pilot-bot.

"Roger that," the sergeant said over the com system.

Gideon took a deep, relaxed breath. "That wasn't so bad. I expected worse."

"Hang on to your hat, Gideon" Frank said. "That was nothing compared to the wormhole."

"Preparing to enter wormhole, all systems go," the pilot-bot said.

"Roger that, good luck," the sergeant said.

Gideon saw the darkness of space replaced by a tunnel that looked as if it were carved from ice. Suddenly the ship shot forward pressing Gideon into his seat and driving his Chain of Remembrance painfully into his chest. He moaned as the air was forced from his body. He struggled to breathe. He fought against the stabbing pain in his chest. His eyes rolled back into his head blurring his vision. Then as suddenly as it began it was over.

Gideon shook his head. He tried to push away the dizziness when a loud clanging noise rocked the ship. Instantly, the wormhole jumper started spinning out of control.

Alarms sounded and lights flashed.

The pilot-bot struggled to regain control of the ship.

Gideon looked at the hunters. The look of terror on their faces said it all. He shuddered when he heard the ship's computer announce the engines were failing and that the ship's hull was breached.

"What's happening?" Gideon shouted.

"Something hit us," replied Frank, "a meteor or something."

Vince looked at Gideon, his eyes wide with fear. "Looks like flight school ain't in the cards, kid, because we're going down and going down hard."

Gideon squeezed his Chain of Remembrance. He remembered what the red-haired driver back at Fort Drum told him. *"Relax, the launch is perfectly safe. It's coming out through the wormhole that you need to start saying your prayers."*

Gideon closed his eyes and started praying.

Chapter 4

Gideon struggled to open his eyes. The inside of the wormhole jumper was filled with grey smoke. Except for the glow of the computer screens, the cabin was dark, adding to his confusion. An acrid burning smell filled his nostrils.

"Hey, Gideon, you okay?"

Gideon groaned.

"Look at the bio-readings, the kid's fine. He's just a little groggy is all." Vince pointed to the small computer screen next to Gideon's seat. It showed Gideon had a strong heartbeat and he wasn't injured.

The sting of a sharp slap ran across Gideon's face. "Gideon, snap out of it."

"What? What happened?"

"We had a hard landing but we're here. We made it to Off World in one piece."

"A hard landing, Frankie? More like a crash landing."

Gideon pulled at the clasp of his safety harness but couldn't unfasten it. He yanked on the harness trying to loosen it but it was no use. "My harness is broken. I can't undo it."

"Frankie, the kid's fine. I'm going up front."

Frank dropped to one knee and pulled at the clasp. "It's jammed. Don't move, Gideon. I need to cut it." Frank pulled a long blade out of his boot and sliced the harness in half with one quick stroke nimbly returning the blade when he was done. "That's it, let's go."

The smell of burnt wiring and smoke caused Gideon's eyes to water. He tried not to cough but the smoke choked him. He squinted trying to see through the smoke when a sharp hissing sound filled the cabin. Instantly, the smoke cleared.

"I vented the smoke, Frankie," said Vince.

"What's the damage, V?" Frank had to stand hunched over; otherwise his head hit the ceiling of the flight cabin.

"The communications system is wrecked but the engines are back online and the main computer seems to be working," said Vince. "But the pilot-bot's fried. Without it we're stuck."

Gideon's head was spinning. He didn't know if it was from the smoke, the ride through the wormhole or the crash landing. He used the wall of the cabin to steady himself. He slowly walked up front to flight control, leaning heavily on the wall as he went. He gasped when he saw the pilot-bot. Its head was torn off. Wires from inside its neck sparked. Its head was rolling on the floor. Above the pilot-bot's seat was a big dent in the ceiling. Gideon shuddered when he thought of the force necessary to decapitate a robot.

"You're right, V. We need a pilot." Frank locked eyes with Vince and nodded his head toward Gideon.

"Are you serious, Frankie? You think the kid can fly us out of here?"

"How about it, Gideon?" Frank asked. "Can you do it? Can you fly this thing?"

Gideon studied the control panel. It was packed with buttons, dials and gauges. There were some similarities to the transports and flight simulators he had flown back in Quarantine, but most of what he saw was confusing and unfamiliar. He swallowed. *I have no idea what half this stuff is.*

Gideon glanced at the hunters. Vince looked anxious and scared. Frank looked calm, but Gideon could sense he was on edge. *I can't let them see I'm scared. It can't be that hard to fly can it?* Gideon took a deep breath and puffed out his chest. "Sure, I can fly it."

"Kid, don't mess around, this ain't a game. Are you qualified or not?" Vince asked.

"Of course I'm qualified. I'm number one in my class at the Finger Lakes Quarantine and I'm joining the Galaxy Class Pilot program when we get back to Earth."

"Good for you, kid. I asked if you could fly not if you were an 'A' student."

"I've flown transports dozens of times and have over one thousand hours in the Quarantine's flight simulator."

"This ain't a simulator, kid. It's the real deal."

"Gideon, me and V are the best grunts you'll ever find. We can shoot, fight and take down anything coming our way. But in the Corps, the grunts do the fighting and the dying. It's the air force pilots that do the flying. If we're getting out of here, we need you to fly. Can you do it?"

I don't want to be stuck here. What choice do I have? "Yeah, I think I can do it."

"Come on, Frankie, don't trust it to the kid. Look at him he's terrified. You flew choppers before the Corps. Can't you fly this?"

"Ain't the same, V. Maybe I can help co-pilot, but I ain't qualified to fly this thing solo. Gideon is the most qualified."

"Frankie, he's just a kid."

Gideon scanned the control panel again while the hunters argued. *There's nobody else to do it but me.* He glanced at the headless pilot-bot. Its lifeless eyes stared at him. Gideon sighed. *Either I man-up or we're stuck here.* "Will you two shut up? I can't think with all that racket."

Frank and Vince just stared at Gideon.

"Listen, this ship isn't all that different from the transports back home," Gideon said. He pointed at the control panel. "Those are the controls for the anti-gravity field. So long as the batteries have juice and the wings aren't damaged, flying her in hover mode will be easy."

"Hooraah! I knew you could do it, Gideon." Frank clapped Gideon on the back so hard he almost fell over.

Gideon swelled with pride.

"What about space flight, kid?" Vince said. "Can you do that?"

Gideon shrugged his shoulders. "Why not? The computer sets the navigation points for the entry and exit through the wormhole. I just need to maintain a straight flight path. So long as the hull isn't cracked I can get us through the wormhole no problem." *Landing her back at Fort Drum is another matter.*

"Yeah, what about the hull? I remember the computer saying something about a hull breach," Frank said. "I'll check it out."

"No, Frankie." Vince stepped in front of the control panel blocking Frank.

"What gives, V?"

Vince stabbed the air with his finger, pointing it like a knife at Gideon's chest. "You say you can fly this thing? Okay, boy-genius, let's see if you can run a diagnostic check first. You do that, maybe I start to buy into this nonsense about you being a Galaxy Class Pilot."

Gideon's eyes narrowed. He kicked the pilot-bot's head out of the way and made for the control panel. Vince was blocking his path. Gideon looked him straight in the eye. *He's a bully. Never show fear to a bully.* Gideon gritted his teeth and swallowed his fear. "Step aside."

Vince moved off letting Gideon access the control panel.

Gideon stared at the tapestry of buttons, knobs and gauges. He pushed a few buttons and waited.

Nothing happened.

Sweat trickled down the small of Gideon's back.

"See, Frankie, the kid's clueless."

"Have some faith, V."

Then, directly in front of Gideon, a picture of the wormhole jumper appeared on a small screen. The screen read, *Diagnostic Complete.* A red light was flashing over the starboard wing. Gideon grinned from ear-to-ear. "What were you saying about clueless?"

"Don't be a wise-guy, kid."

"Nice job, Gideon," Frank said.

Gideon pointed at the screen. "Computer say's there's a crack in the starboard wing."

"Yeah, I see it. Big dent too," Frank said. "Glad that plasma shield worked."

Gideon looked out the small window. Charred plasma sealed the crack and filled the dent. But it looked like the wing was held together with rotted chewing gum. "Oh my God, the wing's wrecked. We're stuck here. I can't believe it."

"Easy, Gideon. Wormhole jumpers are tough little ships. They're designed to take a beating and they're easy to repair. With the right equipment miners can fix it no problem," Frank said.

"The miners can fix that? It looks like we need a whole new wing."

"Kid, pull up the navigation system."

Gideon pressed more buttons on the control panel. A monitor to Gideon's right flashed several times then went dark. "It's broken."

Vince slammed his fist into the control panel making Gideon jump.

"What are you doing?" Gideon said. "You'll break it."

The monitor flashed again and came to life. It showed a map of Off World.

"Works every time, kid."

"Nice, I'll have to remember that."

"Pull up a map of our location, Gideon."

"Okay, Frank." Gideon pressed the map buttons on the control panel. The screen zoomed in on a series of large lakes that looked like they had been clawed out of the planet. The lakes were connected by a series of rivers and canals carved out by construction-bots and miners. At the northern shore of the largest lake flashed a green dot.

"That's us," Gideon said, "near the edge of that big lake." The lake dwarfed any of the Great Lakes Gideon knew. It was dotted with countless islands.

"Great, kid, but we're not going fishing. Find us something useful like your old man's lab or a mining camp. That's what we need to know."

"I'm on it." Gideon's fingers ran over the nav-buttons. He quickly had a red dot flashing on the screen.

"That's Smilodon Island," said Gideon.

"Frankie, it looks like the lab ain't that far south. At least it's on the same lake as us."

"Zoom in on that, Gideon."

Gideon touched the red dot and zoomed in on Smilodon Island. The island and the wormhole jumper were sharing the same lake but were at opposite ends of it. "The computer says its eight hundred miles south of us. What are we going to do?"

"Frankie, the kid's right. We're nowhere near that island."

"Everybody just chill. Gideon, how far to the nearest mining camp?"

"Why are we so far off course? What happened? There has to be a log here somewhere." Gideon scanned the control panel. He quickly found what he was looking for. *Right where it should be, next to system maintenance.* He accessed the log of their flight and waited.

"Gideon, the mining camp coordinates."

"What? Oh, sorry. I wanted to see the flight log."

"Kid, the clock's ticking on this mission. Quit messing around and pay attention to protocol."

"Protocol? What's the protocol for this?"

"The protocol never changes, kid. It's you doing what we tell you to do."

"Sorry, I thought if I could see what happened to the ship—"

"What happened is we crashed and we're way off course. Find the mining camp like Frankie said."

The Headmaster's words ran through Gideon's head. *You have to prove you can be part of a team. That you can follow orders.*

Gideon pursed his lips. "Here comes the flight log. You want me to cancel it?"

"No, let it roll," Frank said. "Gideon, tell me what you see."

The computer screen flashed a video of the ship coming out of the wormhole. There was a white flash and then the ship slowly coalesced appearing as if it had been poured into space. It took shape slowly, the black nano-tiles weaving themselves back into shape after the pulling and pushing of the wormhole.

"So far, looks good. Standard wormhole exit," Gideon said.

Then a crescent-shaped meteor slammed into the starboard wing. The ship ricocheted off the meteor careening into Off World's upper atmosphere. It spun wildly, fire trailing from the wing as if the wormhole jumper had a comet attached to it.

Gideon's breath caught sharply in his chest.

Then a blue liquid covered the fire extinguishing it.

"What is that?"

"The plasma seal, kid. It extinguishes the fire and seals the crack."

Then the wormhole jumper righted itself, the wing somehow holding together. The ship wobbled as it descended toward the planet's surface but its nose was pushed forward. Its wings swept back.

"The pilot-bot put us in the right position for re-entry," Gideon said. "Otherwise we would have been incinerated." He clinched his hands into tight fists squeezing so hard it hurt.

The nose and wings of the wormhole jumper started glowing red. Then the entire ship was glowing, heated by its free fall through the planet's upper atmosphere. The plasma-seal covering the damaged wing turned bright orange before blackening into a crispy, burnt teardrop. The ship dropped through the clouds like a fiery coal through snow. Then the wormhole jumper skipped across the lake in a blast of steam and water until it came to rest in the sand hissing like a wounded animal.

Gideon unclenched his fists; he had deep, red marks from where his nails had bitten into his hands. "I can't believe we're not dead."

"It's obvious we weren't going to make it to the lab, Frankie. Maybe the pilot-bot put us close to a mining camp."

"I hope you're right, V. Gideon, now that we've seen the flight log, punch up the mining camp."

Gideon swallowed. His hands tingled. *What if it's too far? What if we can't get there?* He ran his fingers across the control panel. A green dot flashed on the screen. He took a deep breath and touched the screen. Frank leaned over his shoulder pressing against Gideon's back. The hunter was so close Gideon smelled the hunter's sweat.

"Hooraah!" Frank shouted.

Gideon jumped. "What?"

"It's only four miles east of us. V, that pilot-bot did one hell-of-a-job. He put us close to a mining camp."

Gideon pressed the flashing green dot on the screen. "The computer says it's four and one half miles due east. It's a Muramatsu Mining facility. They used to process fire rock for shipment back to Earth."

"Muramatsu Mining? That's big league, Frankie."

Gideon pointed at the control panel. "Look, it says they have a maglev launcher."

"A maglev? Frankie, that means they have repair-bots."

Frank picked up the pilot-bot's head and kissed it. "I love this guy."

"Outstanding, let's gear up and go." Vince slapped Gideon on the back. "Come on, kid."

"Okay. What?" Gideon tore himself from the computer screen. "We're going out there? We're walking to the mining camp?"

"Frankie, how is it the kid can be a boy-genius one second and an idiot the next?"

Frank laughed. "That's cold, V."

"I'm the idiot? The sergeant said this place is like prehistoric Earth. He also said something about bone eaters. And you want to go out there?"

"Kid, how else are we going to get to the mining camp?"

"We fly there in hover mode."

"Negative," Frank said.

Gideon flinched at the edge to Frank's voice.

"Gideon, we can't risk further damaging the wing. If the miners can't repair the ship, the last thing we want is to be stuck at their camp with a ship we can't fly to your father's lab. I'm not going to risk getting stuck on this rock."

"Amen to that, Frankie. Five days in and out, not one day more."

Gideon craned his neck and looked out the small oval shaped window. The damaged wing was oozing blue plasma. Instead of sealing the crack and filling the dent, the once hardened plasma was becoming soft and squishy. It looked like the wing was dripping blue-colored blood.

Gideon took a deep breath. *I'm going to have to fly this later. There's no way that wing will hold together.* "Hey, guys, something's going on with the plasma seal."

"What's the problem, Gideon?" Frank asked.

"I don't know. It looks weird. You should check it out."

"It ain't good, Frankie. It looks like it's starting to break down."

"How do you know that?"

"See those dark blue lines, Gideon? That's where the nanites are malfunctioning. For some reason, they can't hold the plasma shield in place."

"It looks like it's melting."

"Frankie, ain't that some of the same tech we're packing in the blasters?"

"Weapons check, V. Let's get into it. Gideon, see if the computer can tell you how long the plasma shield will last."

Gideon's fingers ran across the computer buttons. "The computer says the plasma seal will be useless in twenty-four hours."

"That ain't much time, Frankie."

"No worries, V. We'll get us a new wing before that. Gideon, does the computer say why the plasma seal will fail?"

"Not really. It just says the atmosphere is doing something to the nanites. It's like you said, Frank. They're breaking down."

A clicking noise followed by a high-pithed whistle filled the cabin of the wormhole jumper. It reminded Gideon of the guard-bot at Fort Drum.

"At least my blaster works. How about you, Frankie?"

Frank turned on his blaster and charged it. The high-pitched whistle echoed Vince's blaster. "Good to go, V. Hey, Gideon, you need to come away from the computer and gear up."

"Okay, but you need to hear this first," Gideon said.

"Remember the protocol, kid."

"Yeah, I know the protocol, Vince. I do whatever you guys say."

"So what's the problem, kid?"

Gideon hesitated. "Well, you said the plasma shield uses the same tech as the blasters so I ran a quick check. It's . . . It's not good."

"Spit it out, kid. Say your piece."

"The computer says the blasters will stop working in about twelve hours."

"You don't know what you're talking about, kid," said Vince.

Frank's face twisted with doubt. "Gideon, are you sure?"

Gideon pointed at the computer screen. "The computer says once a blaster is charged, the circuitry starts to break down. It's weird, the blaster pack is fine but the circuitry won't work. It won't charge the plasma."

"What does that mean, kid?"

"The weapon won't fire."

"What's going on, Frankie? Why won't the blasters work?"

"It's like the plasma shield, V. The nanites can't hold the shield together and they can't superheat the plasma in the blaster."

"This mission just keeps getting better, Frankie."

"No worries, V. We don't need twelve hours. The mining camp ain't that far."

"Don't you guys have any other weapons? Weapons that don't use charged plasma?"

A wicked smile crept across Vince's face. "Frankie, show the kid the scrambler."

"What's a scrambler?"

"The DNA scrambler," Frank said. "Gideon, come on back here. We'll get you geared up and introduce you to the scrambler."

Gideon shut down the computer and made his way to the rear of the worm-hole jumper. Some of the overhead storage bins had opened during landing spilling packets of vacuum-sealed food, medicine and other supplies onto the floor. Gideon closed the bins and did his best to avoid stepping on the packets.

"This is a DNA scrambler." Frank patted the rifle like it was a trusted friend. "It's the only weapon that is guaranteed to kill a Shape Shifter."

"Frankie, that weapon's as long as the kid is tall."

"How does it work?"

"Gideon, you get hit with this bad boy and it melts you like an old-fashioned candle."

"That's gross."

"Killing is a messy business, Gideon."

"Ain't that the truth, Frankie? Remember Cuba, when you took your knife to the CO? Man the blood—"

"Not now, V. Finish gearing up. The clock's ticking on this mission and on our blasters."

"Okay, Frankie."

Gideon was stunned. *Oh my God. They killed their commanding officer? Can I trust these guys?*

Chapter 5

Gideon eyed the long barrel of the DNA Scrambler. Its end was splayed outward like a blunderbuss. *If they killed their commanding officer, what's stopping them from killing me if I get us stranded here? What if I can't fly the jumper like they want me to?*

Frank charged the DNA Scrambler. Unlike the high pitched whistle of the blasters, the scrambler made a low growl. It sounded like an angry dog.

Gideon jumped back.

"The kid's jumpy, Frankie."

"Is it true, Frank?"

"Is what true, Gideon?"

"You killed your commanding officer?"

Frank slung the DNA Scrambler over his shoulder. He took a deep breath and eyed Gideon. "It's a long story, Gideon but yeah, I did. He got a lot of my men killed. Of the thirteen men in my squad, only me and V survived that mission in Cuba. A lot of good men died that day for nothing. It wasn't right."

"No it wasn't. But you set things right, Frankie."

Gideon crossed his arms over his chest. "But murder—"

Frank shook his head. "It wasn't like that, Gideon. Me and the CO started fighting and it spun out of control is all. He grabbed his knife and I grabbed mine. I won he lost. Okay?"

"Leave it alone, kid. Frankie ain't into talking about it much."

"Going Off World gets you a pardon for that?"

"Damn straight, kid. Gets me and Frankie off death row."

Oh my God, my life is in the hands of death row killers?

"Frankie, the kid just turned pale. Don't worry, kid, we need you alive to get our pardons."

"Can I have a blaster too? I've qualified as a marksman on the shooting range back at Quarantine."

"Kid, that's the funniest thing I've heard all day. Keep those jokes comin'."

"I take it that means no."

"Frankie, the kid's getting smarter all the time." Vince checked what Gideon thought were binoculars.

"Are those binoculars?"

"No, kid, it's a portable bio-scanner. You can never tell when there's a Shape Shifter around unless you're looking through one of these," Vince said. "I spot 'em, Frankie here shoots 'em with the scrambler."

"Heads up, Gideon." Frank tossed Gideon a small black backpack. "You don't get a blaster but you do get a backpack."

Gideon easily caught it. "What's in it?"

"Basic survival gear. Sarge packed it. He said to give it to you if we had to leave the ship for any reason."

"Soft spot for the kid, Frankie."

Gideon bent down and scooped up several packs of food and medicine. He stuffed them into the backpack and slung it over his shoulders. He remembered the early days of the Virus— the dark days, when food and medicine were scarce. He couldn't just let the packets sit there on the floor unused.

"What gives, kid? You don't trust sarge to pack survival gear?"

Gideon shrugged his shoulders. "Yeah, I trust him. It's just you never know when extra food and meds might come in handy."

"Fair enough, kid. As long as you're carrying it, you can stuff as much into that pack as you want."

"Speaking of meds, Gideon. You should check the package before we go. Make sure the seal on the case isn't broken."

"Good idea, Frank." Gideon looked at the scramble of food and med packets on the floor of the wormhole jumper. Using his foot, he shoved aside the packets looking frantically for his father's package. "It's not here. What am I going to do? The Headmaster's going to kill me."

"Kid, chill out. You don't even know what you're looking for."

"It's in the storage bin under your seat, Gideon."

Gideon kept his eyes locked on the floor. He refused to meet Frank's gaze. "Oh, okay, thanks."

The compartment under Gideon's seat easily pulled open. Inside was a small black case. On the cover the words 'Biohazard' were written in bright red letters. Gideon carefully inspected the case. It was undamaged. He breathed a sigh of relief. "It looks okay."

"Good. Put it back, kid, and let's roll. You good to go, Frankie?"

"V, both my weapons are charged up and so am I. I feel mean, bad and ready to go get some."

Vince patted his blaster. "You know it, Frankie. Five days in and out, not one day more."

"Gideon, I almost pity anything that messes with us." Frank said with a quick wink.

Gideon tried to force a smile but only grimaced. His mouth was dry and his throat parched. He was about to explore Off World with two death row inmates that were armed with blasters that might not work and a DNA scrambler.

This wasn't a game.

It wasn't a Quarantine simulation.

This was real.

There were real Shape Shifters out there waiting for him. There were also monsters called bone eaters and who knows what else. Adrian's words echoed in Gideon's head. *You go Off World, you don't come back.*

Gideon licked and pursed his lips. Sweat trickled down his back.

"Let's pop the hatch and get out of here. The clock's ticking," Frank said.

Vince pushed a few buttons above the hatch releasing the door locks. The hatch slowly opened making a hissing sound. "Nothing like exploring new territory."

"New territory? You guys haven't been here before?"

"Gideon, nobody goes Off World a second time. Once we get our pardons, we're done."

"Hey, kid, remember what I said about you getting smarter all the time?" Vince asked.

"Yeah, what about it?"

"I take it back."

Gideon sneered at Vince. "Whatever," he said. But Vince was gone, exiting the wormhole jumper through the open hatch.

"Stay here, Gideon," Frank said. "Don't come out until we secure the area, okay?"

Gideon nodded. "Okay."

After several minutes, Gideon heard Vince's voice. "Come on out, kid, the coast is clear."

Gideon jumped through the hatch and landed on soft, squishy ground. He looked up and gasped. The sky was filled with stars glowing with malice. It reminded Gideon of how the bullies at Quarantine squinted at him only worse. These were hunter eyes studying their prey. Two half moons, one green and one blue hung low in the sky casting an eerie glow over the landscape. It was as if Gideon were looking at Off World through night vision goggles.

Gideon's wormhole jumper sat in a marshy field near the lakeshore. There were tall grasses and odd flowers that looked like small white skulls without eye sockets. The clattered against one another like wooden wind chimes when the wind blew in from the lake. At the edge of the field there was a forest with trees that looked like Adirondack pine. Waves assaulted the shoreline slapping the rocks.

"Welcome to Off World, Gideon," Frank said.

"Smell that, kid? That's the sweet smell of untamed, savage nature. The way only a young planet can smell. It ain't like that hospital smell you get in Quarantine is it?"

Gideon took a deep breath. He tried to identify the smell in the air. The closest thing he could come up with was the sweetness of fresh pine needles from the floor of the deep woods of the Adirondacks. But the Off World air was somehow sweeter. After several more deep breaths he finally decided it smelled like maple syrup.

"That does smell good." Gideon took more deep breaths filling his lungs and holding his breath until his chest hurt. Then he exhaled releasing all the air from his body. He did this several times until his arms and legs tingled with energy.

Then a high-pitched scream cut through the night, making the hairs on the back of Gideon's neck stand on end.

"Let's not hang around and see how savage and untamed this place can be," Frank said as he closed the hatch.

"Right, let's roll," agreed Vince. "I'll take point. The mining camp is this way."

Frank raised the DNA scrambler up to his shoulder and took aim at the tree line, "Stay close, Gideon."

"Wait," Gideon said as the hunters headed for the tree line. "The sergeant told me I had to secure the ship."

The hunters waited while Gideon walked over to the side of the wormhole jumper and pressed several numbers on a keypad. Instantly, a retinal scanner appeared. Gideon placed his face against it. A soft green light bathed his face and eyes. The light was warm and pinching but not uncomfortable. "There, that should do it," he said as the hatch locked and sealed itself shut with a hiss and a loud metallic clang.

"Sarge set it up so only you can lock and unlock the hatch?" Frank asked.

"Sorry, but he said it would prevent you guys from leaving without me."

Frank shook his head. "Unbelievable."

"Like I said, Frankie, a soft spot for the kid."

Gideon fell in with the hunters and the three of them walked in silence heading for the cover of the nearby trees. Each step was squishier than the last and Gideon was glad his flight boots kept his feet dry. A sudden gust of wind rattled the nearby flowers. He reached out to touch one.

"Don't touch that, Gideon," Frank said. "Off World plants aren't like the ones on Earth. Most of the plants here are poisonous and some of them eat meat."

Gideon looked closer at the strange flowers and noticed that instead of petals, they had snapping jaws with small, razor sharp teeth. The jaws opened and shut rapidly, snapping at anything that came close. Gideon picked up a stick and tossed it toward the nearest flower. The flower bit into the stick easily snapping it in half.

Frank motioned for Gideon to keep moving.

"That's something you don't see everyday. You think it would roll over and play dead?" Gideon asked.

"No, but it probably hopes you will," Frank said. "Stay away from those things."

"Where's Vince?"

Frank pressed his finger into his ear and tried to adjust the earpiece to his com unit. "Say again? You're breaking up. I can't hear you." In frustration he yanked it out of his ear. "He should be waiting for us by the tree line."

Gideon squinted, trying to help his eyes adjust to the darkness. "He's over there. I see him."

"Let's jog on over there, Gideon."

As they closed in on Vince, Gideon could see the frustration in his face.

"Is your com unit working, Frankie?" Vince asked in a hushed tone.

Frank shook his head. "No."

"Okay, Frankie, let's go old school and use hand signals."

Frank nodded his approval.

As they drew closer to the forest, Gideon noticed the trees had pinecones on them. "These trees are just like the ones back home."

"You think so, kid?" Vince picked up a large rock and handed it to Gideon. "Throw it at the tree and see what happens."

Gideon eyed Vince with suspicion.

"What's the matter, kid? Don't you trust me?"

"V, we need to keep moving. When you and Gideon are done playing around let me know so we can move out." Frank kept the DNA scrambler leveled at the tree line, scanning it for any possible threat.

The rock was heavy forcing Gideon to heave it at the tree like a shot putter. The short, spiky pine needles extended out of the branches like thin fingers to snatch the rock out of the air. The thin, cord-like vines pulled the rock inside the cover of the branches. Gideon's mouth hung open in surprise. He looked at Vince. "I thought the flowers down by the water were weird but that's just crazy," he said pointing at the tree. "A tree that reaches out and tries to grab things?"

"Yeah, well it tried to grab my blaster so watch yourself," Vince said. "It's lucky I don't have a chain saw."

Gideon saw a series of cuts across the left side of Vince's face. Streaks of dried blood ran across his cheek. "Are you okay? I'm sure the sergeant put a first-aid kit in my pack."

"Thanks, kid, but I'm fine." Vince glanced at his wrist pad. "Navigation says the mining camp is four miles dead ahead. We need to go through these woods so everybody stay close and watch those damn tree branches."

Frank eyed the cuts on Vince's face. "You sure you're good to go, V?"

"I'm good, Frankie." Vince pulled the portable bio scanner over his eyes. "Let's keep our mouths shut and our eyes and ears open. No telling what's in this forest."

Gideon looked up at the imposing trees. He took a deep breath and followed the hunters into the forest. Light from the twin moons filtering through the trees made odd shadows fall on the forest floor.

Following a well-worn path, Gideon and the hunters quietly made their way through the forest for a few hundred yards when Vince froze in place. He held up his hand, signaling Gideon and Frank to stop. Vince stood motionless as he scanned the forest with his bio-scanner. After a few moments, he used two fingers to point at his own eyes and then with the same two fingers pointed up the path.

"Get down, Gideon," Frank whispered.

Gideon crouched low. He held his breath. He thought he heard something up ahead rustling through the forest but couldn't make out what it was. Was it a Shape Shifter? He strained his neck to look further up the path but couldn't see anything except Vince. The hunter was still looking through the bio-scanner.

Frank raised the DNA scrambler and primed it for firing when Vince tore the bio-scanner off his face and aimed his blaster. He started shooting into the trees and yelling at Frank to do the same. "Something bad and ugly is coming and it ain't a shifter! Start blastin', Frankie!"

Gideon had never heard a blaster fire before. It made a nasty ripping sound forcing him to cringe every time it was fired. He watched with horror as the blaster's blue plasma beam carved a hole in the forest burning through several trees at a time.

"Take cover, Gideon." Frank pointed to a spot in the underbrush just off the trail.

Gideon started to make for the underbrush when a long-legged creature with the body of a man, the head of a bat, and angry red eyes charged up the trail. It had wooden darts sticking out of its neck and shoulders and was headed straight for Gideon. Gideon froze with fear. He had seen bears in the Adirondacks and even a cougar but never such a horrible looking thing as the half-man, half-monster now racing straight at him. It closed the last ten feet between them with a mid-air lunge.

"Duck, kid!" Vince shouted.

Gideon fell to his stomach. The heat from the blaster singed his flight suit as the blue plasma beam passed over him.

The creature let out a horrible cry of pain. It whimpered like a dog as it hit the ground.

"Frankie, that thing was stalking you and the kid."

"Nice shot, V. There's probably more of them out there so stay frosty."

Vince scanned the forest, his blaster at the ready. "It's okay, kid. You can get up. Just stay low."

Gideon slowly got to his knees. The smell of burnt flesh made him retch. The creature's skin was still smoking. The darts in its back and shoulder were mostly blasted away with only burnt and bloody shards of wood remaining. The darts in its neck were still intact. Blood stained the trail.

"What is that thing?" Gideon reached down to touch the darts. "Who shot these darts?

"That is a Ripper," said a girl's voice laced with an Irish accent, "and those be my darts. They be full o' poison so don't be toouchin' 'em if ya want to live."

Gideon turned to see a girl not much older than him holding a crossbow. Her eyes were purple. She had the Virus.

Chapter 6

Gideon hadn't seen anybody with the eyes of the Virus in over three years. Before his mother invented the cure, standing so close to someone with the Virus was a death sentence. He backed away from the girl as quickly as he could, forgetting about the dead Ripper behind him. He tripped over it. When he hit the ground there was something wet and sticky on his hands. It was blood. The blood was hot. Too hot, it started to burn. Gideon quickly wiped his hands on his pants.

"Are ya alreet?" the girl asked. She wore brown leggings with matching knee-high boots and a hooded camouflage cloak. She pulled back her hood revealing a freckled face, fair skin and red hair tied into a tight ponytail. She was a pretty girl with a kind smile but her purple eyes haunted Gideon.

Gideon pointed at her, trying to scream for her to back away and leave him alone, but no words came out.

"Drop the crossbow." Frank held his DNA scrambler at the ready as he eyed the girl.

Vince pointed his blaster at her chest. "Do as my partner says, girl."

The girl lowered her crossbow, pointing it toward the ground. "Okay, jist take it easy. I ain't here to hurt nobody."

"Get her away from me!" Gideon scrambled to his feet and grabbed a rock. He threw it at her, narrowly missing her. "Go away. You've got the Virus."

"You need to cop on and stop actin' the maggot," the girl said.

"I don't know what you just said but if you don't drop that crossbow, those are probably your last words," Vince said.

"She told me to get ahold of myself and stop acting stupid." Gideon picked up another rock and drew his arm back preparing to throw.

"Gideon, how do you know what she said?"

"My mother was Irish."

The girl raised her crossbow and gave Gideon a hard stare. "I don't care if yer mum is old Earth's Grace O'Malley or Sister Sarah Clarke, you throw that rock at me, I'll shoot ya in the leg." Her voice was cutting. "And I *never* miss."

Vince and Frank both took a step toward the girl with their weapons raised. "Drop it," they said in unison.

The girl gave Gideon and the hunters an angry, puzzled look. "You still have Earth eyes." She lowered her crossbow and backed away from Gideon. "That means you're new to Off World and judgin' from those flight suits yer wearin' ya probably landed here not too long ago."

"So what do you care?" Gideon asked.

"I don't. But it explains why yer actin' like an eejit. Didn't anyone tell ya before ya came here?"

"Tell me what?" Gideon held the rock above his head ready to throw. He was shaking, filled with a combination of rage and fear.

"Everybody here has Virus Eyes. The Virus don't kill people Off World, ya tool. It only kills people on Earth," she said.

"I don't believe you. How is that possible?"

"How do I know? I ain't no doctur."

Gideon looked at Frank and Vince. "Is it true?"

"Yeah, kid. It's true," Vince said. "Everybody who lives here has Virus eyes without having the Virus."

"Relax, Gideon. It's okay. She's not contagious. Off Worlders have the eyes but not the Virus," Frank said.

Gideon studied the girl's face. It was covered in red freckles but not the telltale purple welts of the Virus. He dropped the rock with a dull thud. "Why didn't you guys tell me before we got here?"

Frank shrugged his shoulders. "Sarge should have told you when he briefed you. Sorry, Gideon, we thought you knew."

"Well, he didn't tell me. Nobody did." Gideon gritted his teeth and crossed his arms over his chest.

"What are ya doin' here anyway? Yer too young to be huntin' Shape Shifters."

"I'm not a hunter."

"Yeah, I suppose not, yer too young and too skinny. Why are ya so skinny? Don't they feed kids on Earth? Ain't there any food left?"

She was born Off World, otherwise she'd remember.

In the early days of the Virus, during the panic, there were runs on the grocery stores and then food riots. But after his mother invented the cure, after things settled down, with so many dead after the Virus took its toll, there was more food than people who could eat it.

"You don't know what you're talking about. If you'd been born on Earth and survived the Virus like me, you wouldn't be saying that."

"Not born on Earth?" Vince put his bio-scanner on and gazed at the girl. "Get ready to blast her, Frankie. I'm getting a funny reading. I think she's a Shape Shifter."

Frank leveled the DNA scrambler at the girl. "Back away from her, Gideon. Is she a shifter or not, V? What's the word?"

"I can't tell, Frankie. This reading ain't so clear."

Gideon stepped away from the girl. He couldn't believe what was happening. "Wait, don't shoot her if you aren't sure if she's a Shape Shifter or not."

The girl grinned at Gideon. "Maybe yer not such a tool after all."

"Shut up and let the grownups talk, kid. Frankie, I say we fry her with the scrambler just in case."

"I'm not shooting a kid, V. Unless that reader tells us she's a shifter, I'm not frying anyone."

The girl looked both hunters up and down and laughed. "Boy, things on Earth must be baad."

"Why do you say that?" Gideon asked.

"Because evlee group of killers that comes here is worse than the last," she said. "I heard ya stompin' through the forest like lost elephants."

"Killers?" Frank said. "Easy, girl. We're not killers."

"Frankie, she has attitude worse than the kid here."

"Well yer not hunters. Hunters give their prey a fair chance. That blaster ain't givin' a fair chance to nothin' and neither is that DNA scrambler yer packin'."

Vince stuck his blaster in the girl's face. "You better watch yourself, girl. No telling what could happen to you out here all alone like you are."

"Oh pleez, that blaster ain't even charged. Go bully somebody else, I've unfinished business with the Ripper." The girl slung her crossbow over her shoulder and took a long blade out of her boot. She pointed the blade at Gideon. "I'm Paige. I need a volunteer. What's yer name?"

"Who me?"

"Do ya see me talkin' to anybowdee else?"

Gideon crossed his arms over his chest. "Gideon. My name's Gideon."

Paige walked toward the monster and waved Gideon over. "You'll have to do…Gideon. Come on then if yer to be helpin' me."

Gideon carefully approached Paige. He kept his eyes locked on the Ripper. "What do I need to do…Paige?"

Paige kneeled down next to the Ripper. Its chest was moving slowly up and down. Its breathing was raspy and labored. The wounds on its back and neck made a sizzling noise. It reminded Gideon of steak on a grill. It even smelled like burnt meat. Steam rose from the wounds.

Gideon blinked several times. He thought his eyes were playing tricks on him. The wounds caused by the wooden darts and Vince's blaster seemed to be healing.

"Paige, the wounds are closing up. They're healing themselves."

Paige gently turned the Ripper's bat-like head to the side. "That they are. Strange, it ain't like a Ripper to heal so fast. It must be a new one. Come on, there ain't a lot of time before its done healin'. Quick, hold its mouth open."

"What? Are you crazy? I'm not sticking my hands in that thing's mouth." Gideon pointed at Frank and Vince. "Why can't one of them do it?"

"I don't trust 'em is why. They would just as soon blast it and be done with it."

"Damn straight." Vince charged his blaster. The weapon made a clicking noise followed by a whistle.

"Amen, V."

"But why don't you just kill it already?" Gideon asked. "Why do you need a trophy?"

"It ain't about gettin' a trophy. This be a new breed of Ripper that she be makin'. By defangin' and declawin' it, it's safe to transport. The docktur said he wants to be examin' these beasties alive not dead."

Gideon's mouth hung open. "Somebody made this thing?"

"Aye, she did exactly that."

"But why would—"

"I can't be explainin' it all to ya. The docktur can do that. Are ya man enough to be helpin' me or not?"

Gideon took a deep breath. He put his hands inside the Ripper's mouth and pulled its jaws open. He had given his dog medicine before but this was nothing like that. The Ripper's saliva was hot and steamy, burning his fingers. Its breath smelled like rotting meat. "Hurry up, its breath is killing me."

Paige leaned over the creature, her knife at the ready. "That's good, keep its jaw open."

"The kid's crazy, Frankie."

"Careful, Gideon," Frank said. "Those teeth look nasty sharp. V, if that thing opens it eyes blast it."

"I'm on it, Frankie."

Gideon licked his lips and swallowed. *If they use a blaster on it this close will I die too?*

"Ya don't need to be blastin' nothin'." Paige put her knife into the Ripper's mouth and leaned her body against its head using her weight to pry out its fangs. There was a sickening snap followed by three more.

"Got 'em." Paige held up the fangs. They were as long as Gideon's forearm. She put them in a black sack.

Gideon let go of the Ripper's jaw and pushed it shut. He wiped his hands on his pants.

"Now the claws," Paige said. "I need you to hold its arm down while I pry 'em out."

Gideon grimaced. *This girl is a piece of work.*

"If ya' can hold its jaws open, holdin' its arm down will be easy."

Gideon placed his hands on the Ripper's arm. Its black skin was slimy and hot. The massive arm was as thick as Gideon's thigh making it impossible for him to grab hold.

Paige gave Gideon a disapproving look. "Kneel on it if ya have to."

Gideon placed his knees on the Ripper's arm and pressed his weight against it.

Paige worked quickly, removing the claws with her blade. There was a nasty crack as she cut away each of the five claws. The claws were as long as Gideon's hand and slightly curved. Some of the claws had a thin sheen of purple on them.

"What's that purple stuff, Paige?"

"Blood, it killed three miners."

Gideon shuddered. *It probably sliced those men to ribbons.*

Paige reached behind her and plucked a large leaf shaped like an elephant's ear from a nearby plant. She used it to wipe the purple blood from the Ripper's claws and shoved them into her black sack.

Purple blood? Everyone here really does have the Virus. How is it they're not dead or dying?

Gideon got up and kneeled on the creature's other arm. "What do you do with the claws and fangs you take?"

The creature began to stir, emitting a low growl as Paige dug the remaining claws out of its hand.

"I make darts out of 'em for the crossbow. Sometimes knives too."

"You need to move faster," Frank said. "That thing is starting to wake up."

"I got it covered, Frankie. If that thing so much as farts, I'm blasting it," Vince said.

"I told ya, ya ain't blastin' nothin'. Now back off. I'm done."

Paige used another elephant ear shaped leaf to clean her knife. "We'll be takin' the creature back to camp now."

"Back to camp? If you expect us to carry that butt-ugly thing to your mining camp, you're crazy," Gideon said.

"Did ya hear me askin' fer yer help?"

"They're arguing like an old married couple already, Frankie."

"Ain't it sweet, V? Nothing brings folks closer together than declawing and defanging a monster."

"What? No, it's not like that at all," Gideon said. "I was just—"

"I don't need yer help. Gus and his crew are here. They'll be takin' it back to camp."

"Who's Gus?"

"I am, boy. I'm Gus."

A bald man with a short brown beard emerged from the cover of the trees. He wore a tattered orange mining uniform. The front of the uniform had *Muramatsu Mining* emblazoned across it. He had an edge to him that only years of hard physical work could give somebody. He was wiry and looked very strong. He held a long staff that at first glance looked like the kind of walking stick Gideon's father used on hiking trips. It was polished to a fine sheen but on the end of it there was a large orb. Small lightning bolts licked the inside of the orb.

Gideon recognized the weapon. It was longer than the ones used by the Enforcers back at Quarantine but there was no doubt in Gideon's mind that it was a Shocker. They were used in the early days of the Virus for crowd control and were supposed to be non-lethal. But when fitted with a power amplifier like the orb flashing in front of Gideon's face, they were deadly.

Behind Gus stood seven other miners armed with Shockers. There was also a group of ten boys about Gideon's age. They carried crossbows like Paige's. Everyone in the group wore orange mining uniforms. They also had the eyes of the Virus. Gideon recoiled at the sight of them. *How is this possible?*

Gus eyed Gideon. His face twisted into a nasty sneer. "What are you staring at, boy? You got some sort of problem?"

"No, it's just... Are you from the mining camp?"

"We ain't from Disney Land, genius."

The miners and boys laughed.

Gideon's face flushed hot. He pursed his lips.

"Whose in charge here?" Vince demanded.

"I'm the one ya' need to be talkin' to," Paige said.

"You're in charge? Are you kidding me?" Vince said.

"Does it look like I'm jokin'?"

"Back on Earth, kids have leadership roles," Gideon said. "Maybe it's the same here."

"Paige is leading this hunting party. Outside the mining camp, she's in charge. Inside the camp, it's me," Gus said.

"I'm Frank, this is Vince and the boy's name is Gideon."

Boy? I'm not a boy. I'm almost fourteen.

"We have orders and it's your job under the Off World Mining Act to help us carry them out," Frank said. "You're required to help us."

"Damn straight. You can start by repairing our ship. The wing is damaged," Vince said.

"Don't tell me the law. I know the law," Gus said.

"Good, then once we get our ship back to your camp you can start working on the repairs," Frank said.

"It ain't that easy. You hunters don't get to come here and order us around. Those days are over," Gus said.

Gideon was shocked. Everybody on Earth knew violations of the Off World Mining Act were dealt with harshly. *Are these guys crazy?*

Vince bristled.

"This is my huntin' party," Paige said. "I'm in charge. Gus, the Ripper's ready to be moved. Take it back to camp. Ya can sort out the details of ship repairs there."

"Shock it," Gus said.

The miners circled the Ripper and pointed their Shockers at it. The large orbs at the end of the Shockers glowed yellow and hummed with electricity. Small bolts of lightning filled the inside of the globes. Paige fell in behind the men. She primed her crossbow and pointed it at the Ripper. The boys in the group followed her lead and aimed their crossbows at the Ripper.

Gideon grimaced as the miners electrocuted the Ripper repeatedly with the fully charged Shockers. He cringed with every howl and convulsion made by the Ripper. Finally, the Ripper stopped writhing and quieted down. Its breathing was shallow and erratic. The smell of burnt flesh filled the air, making Gideon's stomach perform flip-flops. He looked away from the creature only to see Paige watching him. She gave him a curious look.

"Enough," Paige said. "Get the anti-grav pallet and strap the Ripper onto it."

The miners used their Shockers to push the semi-conscious creature onto the anti-grav pallet. They quickly tied it down and turned on the anti-gravity field. To Gideon's amazement the pallet rose several feet in the air. "You use those to transport captured monsters?"

Paige slung her crossbow over her shoulder. "Not at first. Before the Virus, when we were still minin', we used the pallets to carry fire rock. Now we use 'em for this. But at least we no longer have to use the pallets to carry our dead."

"Carry the dead? I thought the Virus didn't kill people here," Gideon said.

"It don't," Paige said. "We lost people to starvation, Shape Shifters and Rippers. After the supply ships stopped comin', the food started runnin' out. We foraged and hunted as best we could but people went hungry, a lot died. But we managed by makin' peace with the Shape Shifters. They taught us how to live off the land so we could feed ourselves. So we could stop starvin'."

Gideon shifted his glance to the Ripper. He couldn't believe how large and powerful looking it was. Its chest slowly rose and fell as it slept tied to the pallet. "Did you surrender to the Shape Shifters?"

"No, it wasn't like that at all," Paige snapped, her accent thickening as her face flushed. "When these creatures started comin' they attacked the Shape Shifters and us. They were eveleewhere. The only way both our clans could survive was to make peace, to work together."

"You said it was a Ripper. What exactly is that?" Gideon said.

"It is a Ripper but this one is different somehow. I don't know how she did it, makin' it stronger and faster and able to heal but the doctur will sure find out." Paige checked the restraints on the anti-grav pallet. Satisfied, she ordered the others in the group to set out for the camp. "We tagged 'em and bagged 'em. Now let's get back to camp before it wakes."

Now that the Ripper was on its back and floating several feet in the air, Gideon could finally get a good look at it. It had slimy, jet black skin that was pockmarked with electrical burns. Its red eyes were partially open as it wavered in and out of consciousness. It had an ominous, bat-like mouth and although its fangs were gone, it still had rows of razor sharp teeth. The Ripper was unlike anything Gideon had ever seen. It repulsed him.

Frank scowled at it. "V, that is one ugly, nasty looking thing. It kinda looks like your ex-wife."

"Ya think so, Frankie? I was thinking it looks more like your sister."

"Let's move out," Paige said.

"Hold on," Vince said. "Nobody's going anywhere."

Gideon stiffened. *Uh oh, here it comes.*

"First things first. What about our ship?" Vince said.

"I said ya can talk about it with Gus when we get to camp," Paige said.

"No, we talk about it now," Vince said.

"We're on borrowed time here," Frank said. "We got five days to finish our mission and get out of here. We can't be wasting time going to your mining camp if you're not going to make the repairs. We need to sort it out now."

"No, we need to be takin' the Ripper back to camp now," Paige said.

Vince leveled his blaster at the Ripper. "I think they need some motivation, Frankie. How about we just fry their little pet so they can focus on what's important to us?"

Frank pointed the DNA scrambler at the creature. "Yeah, you might be right, V."

"Gus, don't let 'em blast it," Paige said. "It's a new breed. The doctur needs to be lookin' at it."

Gus and the miners raised their shockers and slowly spread out encircling Gideon and both hunters. The boys aimed their crossbows. "We got them covered, Paige. They blast it, they die."

Gideon's eyes darted from Vince to the group of miners. He balled his hands into tight fists and gritted his teeth. He had been Off World for only a short time and he hated it.

Chapter 7

"Looks like we got us a regular Mexican standoff, Gus," Vince said.

"Not really. If the Shockers don't kill you the crossbows will."

Frank turned and leveled his DNA scrambler at Gus. "You might be able to kill us but not before I melt some of you with my scrambler. Who wants to be first? You, Gus?"

Gus took a step back, his eyes wide with fear.

"Nobody said we weren't goin' to be fixin' yer ship," Paige said, her Irish accent thickening with her rising anger. "Come to the minin' camp with us. You can plug into our computer and see if we can help ya."

"You don't get to make decisions like that, Paige" Gus said. "I decide what happens back at camp."

"What are ya goin' to do, Gus, kill 'em? Helpin 'em is the decent thing to do. Ya know I'm right."

"I'm not helping them do anything without a contract, Paige. They want our help they need to give us something. That's how it's done."

"Ya don't need a contract to be doin' what's right."

Gideon rolled his Chain of Remembrance between his fingers. Paige had nothing to gain by helping him and the hunters. *She's like my mother. She's willing to help others without getting anything in return.* Gideon shook his head. *She wouldn't last a week in Quarantine.* Gideon had seen it before; a new kid comes to Quarantine and tries to make friends by doing free favors. By the end of their first week, they had nothing left except the uniform on their back. It was even worse during the height of the Virus when people who were once friends and neighbors were killing each other, and those that tried to help—the good Samaritans—wound up dead too. Back on Earth, you had to look out for yourself because only the strong survived. Paige was being stupid.

"What's it gonna be, Gus? Either we make your pet a crispy critter or you're fixing our ship," Vince said.

"You hunters are all the same," Gus said. "You come here bringing nothing we need. You only bring trouble—hunting Shape Shifters and barking orders at us. We don't need hunters stalking after the Shape Shifters that we made peace with. We need doctors, we need medicines and we need the supply ships to come back. *That's* what we need. So unless you've got something to make a contract with in exchange for ship repairs, I say we take our chances and kill the three of you."

Paige leveled her crossbow at Gus. "No, I won't let ya do it. There'll be no killin'. This is my huntin' party."

"Paige, everybody here knows you won't shoot me. You're not a killer."

"I won't kill ya, but I *will* shoot ya, Gus."

"Go ahead, Paige. I ain't worried. The doctor will patch me up no problem."

The miners mumbled their agreement. They primed their Shockers. Lightning bolts crackled and licked the inside of the small orbs. The miners closed the circle around Gideon and the hunters.

Frank charged the DNA scrambler. "Get ready, V. It's going down hard."

"Wait," Gideon said. "I brought medicine. I'll show you."

Gideon ripped off his backpack and pulled out a small bag with a red cross on it. "See, I've got dozens more back on the jumper. I even have antibiotics. I'll trade you meds for ship repairs."

Gus held out his hand. "Let me see it, boy."

Gideon tossed the vacuum-sealed pack to Gus. The miner turned the packet over in his hands examining it.

"Do ya even know what yer lookin' at, Gus?"

"I know enough, Paige. See to the Ripper, this doesn't concern you. It's a mining camp matter."

Paige grunted.

"Well?" Gideon asked.

Gus looked at the miners and nodded. They lowered their Shockers and crossbows and took a step back. "You'll make a contract with me, boy? The meds for ship repairs?"

"Don't give him anything, kid. Those meds aren't yours to give," Vince said. "He should be helping us because the law requires it."

Frank lowered his DNA scrambler. "Let Gideon be, V. If it's our only ticket outta here then let's roll with it."

"Yeah, V. Let the boy speak," Gus said. "If he's old enough to come Off World he's old enough to make a contract."

Gideon glanced at Paige. He rolled his shoulders back and puffed out his chest. "That's right. I'll be fourteen next month."

Vince laughed. "Fourteen? Yeah that makes you a real man."

"Nobody's asking you," Gideon said.

Gus took a step forward. He pointed the shocker at Gideon's chest. "You agree to give us the medicine in exchange for ship repairs? You agree to make a contract with me?"

"Yes."

"Then it's agreed." Gus spit in his hand and extended it to Gideon.

Gideon took a step back. "Gross."

"It's how we do things here, boy. Are we making a contract or not?"

"But in Quarantine we don't exchange spit or anything else that has somebody's germs on it."

The miners laughed.

"You're not in Quarantine anymore, Gideon. It's okay, go ahead," Frank said.

"Don't do it, kid," Vince countered.

"It's our only ticket out of here, V. Let him alone."

Gideon looked at Gus's outstretched hand. It was wet with spit.

"Go on, Gideon, do it," Frank said. "Make the contract."

Gideon swallowed hard. He spit into his own hand and extended it. Gus grabbed it and shook it so hard Gideon was almost lifted off the ground.

"We have a contract," Gus said.

Gideon took his hand back from Gus and wiped it on his pant leg. "Great."

"Can we go now?" Paige said, her voice cutting. She put a fresh set of darts into a circular, drum magazine. Then she put the magazine into the shaft of the crossbow. Satisfied the magazine was loaded properly, she pushed a button just above the trigger. The magazine spun, locked into position and loaded a dart.

"A self-loading crossbow, very cool, I've never seen one of those," Gideon said.

"I'm not surprised. You don't seem to be quite the full shillin'."

"At least I'm not a culchie."

"Don't insult the girl, Gideon. Galaxy Class Pilots don't do that. It ain't nice," Frank said.

"All I said is that she's a country bumpkin."

Paige looked Gideon up and down, studying him. "Nice, your mum taught ya well. There may be hope for ya yet."

"Just maybe?"

Paige tossed Gideon the black pouch.

It jangled when Gideon caught it. He opened it and saw the Ripper fangs and claws. "Gee thanks, and to think I didn't get you a gift."

"It ain't a gift. I need ya to be holdin' that for me until I get back to camp. That way I can keep both hands on my crossbow. Keep 'em from makin' noise when you walk. Can ya handle that?"

Gideon stuffed the pouch of fangs and claws into his backpack. He jammed it toward the bottom so it wouldn't make any noise. "What do you mean when *you* get back to camp? I thought we were all going back together."

"I'm goin' to be scoutin' up ahead. If you can keep up, then ya can come with me."

"Gideon, stay back with me and V," Frank said. "It's our job to protect you."

"Maybe ya need to be listenin' to yer babysitters."

Gideon stiffened.

"Paige is the best tracker and marksman I've ever seen. The boy will be safer with her than either one of you two," Gus said.

"The kid's our responsibility. He stays with us," Vince said.

Babysitters? The boy? The kid?

"I've had it with all of you," Gideon said. "I'm not a kid or a boy and I don't need babysitters. I'm going with Paige."

"Kid, remember the protocol," Vince said.

"How about you and Frank follow me and Paige? Will that make you happy?"

"That's fine, Gideon. Me and V will be right behind you."

"Then let's be on our way," Paige said.

Gideon followed Paige as she jogged up the trail. Her camouflage cloak flowed behind her like a swirl of leaves on a windy day. If not for her red hair, she would have disappeared. She held her crossbow out in front of her, scanning the tree line and potential ambush points. Gideon had hunted with his father and as part of his Galaxy Class Pilot training had led his laser tag team through the forests near the Finger Lakes Quarantine. Gideon's team always won. But he had never seen anyone, not even the instructors at Quarantine, move like Paige. She had the grace of a gymnast mixed with the tenacity of a hardened war veteran. Gideon struggled to keep up with her. He looked back for Frank and Vince. They were nowhere to be seen.

"Wait," Gideon said, grateful for a chance to catch his breath. "We shouldn't get too far ahead of the others."

"Ya seem a bit winded. If ya need a break just say so."

Gideon gasped for a quick breath. "No, it's not that. I just don't want to get too far ahead of Frank and Vince."

"Uh huh," Paige said. "Don't worry about them. They're about a hundred meters behind us."

"How do you know that?"

"I just do."

"Well, let's wait until they can see us."

"Fine."

"Don't you have dogs?" Gideon asked. "When I used to hunt with my father, we always had a dog with us."

"Used to, the Rippers killed 'em all."

"They hunted down and killed all your dogs?"

"That they did. Yer hunter friends will be along in a minute. I can hear 'em stompin' up the trail, especially the short one. He's got heavy feet."

"I don't hear anything."

"That's because ya don't know how to listen to the forest. This ain't Earth, everythin's different here."

Paige extended her hand toward the forest. "Take a look while you catch yer breath."

Gideon took a deep breath and scanned the forest. Streaks of moonlight cut through the forest like claws, exposing tall moss-covered trees with gnarled trunks. The forest floor was covered with dry leaves and small plants. The narrow path leading to the mining camp snaked out before him.

"What's the big deal? It's like any other forest I've ever been in."

Paige clucked her tongue in disappointment. "I said *look* not take a quick glance. Ya can start by lookin' at them mushrooms over thar."

Off the trail about twenty yards, was a cluster of large pink mushrooms with white spots. They were pulsing, moving up and down. Then a gentle breeze blew through the trees. It carried a soft melody. It sounded like someone was playing a harp. It was inviting.

It was the mushrooms. They were playing the music.

A small animal about the size of a housecat cautiously approached the mushrooms. The animal looked like a squirrel except it had horns on its head. Long teeth protruded from its mouth and at the end of its tail were spikes. The animal looked at Paige and seemed to smile. When it looked at Gideon it hissed.

Then one of the mushroom caps changed from pink to red and swallowed the animal whole.

The music stopped, replaced by a sickening sucking and crunching sound. A small purple cloud, which Gideon guessed was the animal's blood, shot out of the mushroom.

Then the mushroom cap raised itself and spit out the animal's skeleton. It was a dissolving, mushy, gelatinous mess.

The mushrooms then emitted a low rumble that sounded like a burp. After a few moments, the mushrooms went back to playing their sweet melody.

"That's one of the grossest things I've ever seen," Gideon said. "Thanks for sharing."

"Ya need to be stayin' here. I'm goin' out there for some of that poison. It's good for takin' down Rippers."

Paige pulled her hood up over her head and waded into the forest. She blended perfectly with the trees and waist-high plants. She crouched and moved cautiously from tree to tree. When she was halfway to the cluster of pink mushrooms, she disappeared.

Gideon drew a sharp breath and held it. Did the forest swallow Paige like the mushrooms did to the small animal? The forest closed in around Gideon. He rolled his Chain of Remembrance between his fingers. *Where is she? Can I trust her? Where are Frank and Vince?*

Then a clump of red hair appeared. The end of Paige's ponytail fell out of her hood.

Gideon exhaled.

Paige moved quickly and silently to the dissolving mass of bones. She removed the circular magazine of darts from her crossbow and emptied it. Then she took the darts and dipped the point of each one into what was left of the small animal. When she was finished, Paige carefully reloaded the magazine and jammed it into her crossbow. She pointed up the trail as she made her way back to Gideon.

Gideon turned. It was Vince and Frank. He was glad to see the hunters until he noticed Vince was red-faced and sweating. The hunter scowled at Gideon.

"Yer friends are here. Ya want to wait for 'em?"

"No. Vince looks mad and I don't want to hear his complaints."

"Okay, Gus and the rest of 'em aren't far behind. We'll push ahead and wait for 'em at the tree line just outside camp. There may be more Rippers about so stay close."

The forest seemed to close in on Gideon. He eyed Paige and her crossbow. Would this girl and her poison darts be enough to stop another Ripper from attacking and killing him? "Maybe we should wait—"

But Paige was gone, bounding up the trail, her red ponytail trailing behind her like a banner.

CHAPTER 8

The humidity in the night air made Gideon's flight suit stick to his body. By the time Paige stopped at the edge of the forest, he was hot, sweaty and thirsty. Gideon was grateful for the drops of water that were dripping onto his head cooling him. Just above him was a broad-leafed plant with large droplets of water hanging from it. He leaned back and opened his mouth. His dry parched throat strained in anticipation.

As a large droplet fell, Paige's hand closed over Gideon's mouth and pulled his head down. The water landed on his forehead.

"That's not water ya eejit. It's plant nectar and it be poisonous. The plant tricks its prey into drinkin', paralyzin' it."

"What happens after that? Do you die?"

"After that? The plant eats ya. It dissolves its prey like the mushrooms ya saw." Paige acted as though her answer was perfectly normal.

Gideon's mouth fell open in surprise.

"Yer welcome."

"Yeah, uh, thanks. What about the stuff on my head?"

Paige's eyes widened. She gasped. "Oh no, it's goin' to melt your noggin."

She put her hand on her chin and looked up as if she were trying to remember something. "Or does it turn yer head into a pumpkin? Hmm, I forget, us culchies ain't too smart."

"Yeah right, and you're calling me a tool?"

Paige wiped the plant nectar off Gideon's forehead with her hand. "It's okay to touch it but don't drink it."

"Hey, kid, nice of you and your girlfriend to wait for us."

"We did, Vince. I made Paige stop until we saw you and Frank…wait, what? She's not my girlfriend."

"We're good, V. The mining camp is dead ahead. The girl steered us right."

"Of course I did. Do ya think I'd do otherwise?"

A searchlight blinded Gideon. He closed his eyes but could still see the orange glare through his eyelids. "That's bright."

"Motion sensors must have activated it," Frank said.

Gideon held his hand in front of his face. "How do you turn it off?"

"Usually a password does it, Gideon," Frank started to say when he was interrupted by a man's deep, booming voice calling out from behind the searchlight.

"Ladybug, ladybug, fly away home, your house is on fire and your children are gone," the voice said.

Paige replied with, "All except one and that's little Ann, for she crept under the fryin' pan."

"Cute password," Vince said. "Are you leading a hunting party or a nursery school?"

"Take it up with Gus. He's arrivin' now."

Gus cupped his hands around his mouth and shouted at the mining camp. "We're coming out. We've got three friendlies." He eyed the Ripper on the anti-gravity pallet and added, "And one prisoner."

"Come out and approach the gate," replied the voice from camp. With a loud metallic snap that echoed in the night air, the searchlight went out as quickly as it had come on.

When Gideon opened his eyes, he had to blink several times to clear his vision of the orange and yellow spots that danced in front of him. When his eyesight returned to normal, he followed Paige to a tall, chain link gate. The gate, like the rest of the fence encircling the camp, had razor wire at the top. The fence buzzed and hummed. "What's that noise?"

"Electric fence, don't be touchin' it," Paige said.

Directly behind the electric fence, tall guard towers rose every ten yards or so. Inside the guard towers stood a miner with a crossbow. Armed with flamethrowers, guard-bots wheeled along the fence's perimeter. Their primed flamethrowers coughed blue fire, making them look like dragons on the prowl.

"This is a mining camp? It looks more like a prison. We didn't even have this kind of security at Quarantine."

"They're not trying to keep people from escaping the camp, Gideon," Frank said.

"Yeah," Vince agreed. "It looks like they're trying to keep something from getting in."

Gideon shuddered at the creature on the pallet. He thought back to what Paige told him about using the anti-gravity pallets to carry the dead. "It must have been awful trying to fight those things off and keep people safe."

"Open the gate," said a voice from one of the guard towers.

Gideon and the hunters followed Paige through the open gate. When Gus and the last of the miners were through, the gate was closed and locked. Wives ran to husbands, mothers to their sons and children embraced their fathers. Gideon reached for his Chain of Remembrance, rolling it between his fingers as he watched the families hug one another. He turned when he heard several children calling after Paige.

Children swarmed her. Gideon counted at least ten of them shouting after her, hugging her. Some of them asked if she brought them any sugar root.

Paige laughed. "Is it really me yer happy to be seein' or do ya just want the sugar root?"

The children unanimously and almost in unison said it was Paige they were happy to see.

"Sure ya are," Paige said with a sarcastic and playful tone. She reached into a small pouch strapped to her waist and pulled out what looked like white candies. Paige gave one to each child but only after they first kissed her on the cheek. When each child had gotten a piece of the sugar root, Paige looked up and saw Gideon watching her.

"These little ones are always wantin' to be fed."

Gideon removed his backpack and pulled out several packets of vacuum-sealed food. He tossed the packets toward Paige. She easily caught them and gave them to the children. The children ripped them open and devoured every morsel.

Paige smiled at Gideon.

Gideon's neck and ears flushed hot. He then tossed her the black pouch of fangs and claws.

"Nice move, Gideon," Frank said.

"The kid's trying to impress the girl is all. Kid, we're leaving in five days so don't get all romantic."

"What are you talking about? I'm just trying to help feed some little kids."

"Paige works in the daycare center here. The kids love her," Gus said.

"What's sugar root?" Gideon asked.

"Something Paige found in the forest. She has a knack for knowing what's safe to eat around here and what isn't. She's an excellent woodsman and tracker."

Gideon nodded. "I noticed."

"You and the hunters follow me. Med-lab is this way."

"Why med-lab?" Frank asked.

Gus pointed at the anti-gravity pallet. "So the doctor can dissect that thing. Paige seems to think it's a new kind of Ripper."

Gideon shuddered. Did he really have to watch somebody dissect the Ripper?

"So long as we can connect to your computer system that's fine," Frank said.

Vince eyed Gus. "Let's roll, time's wasting. I ain't gettin' stuck on this rock and you have a contract to honor."

"Follow me." Gus gave a push against the anti-gravity pallet and made his way through the mining camp.

Gideon and the hunters followed Gus and the floating Ripper through the narrow passages of the mining camp. The moonlight made it easy to see the small squat buildings that housed the miners' families. The houses were made from corrugated metals. They were sturdy and lightweight making them safe to live in and easy to take apart and move if necessary. Gideon recognized them as standard housing units for settlers. As they made their way through the maze of housing units, the sounds of children laughing and playing echoed through the camp. Mothers announced dinnertime. The smell of cooked meats, garlic and other spices wafted through the air making Gideon's stomach rumble. It made Gideon miss his old life.

"Smell that, V?"

"Whatever it is, Frankie, it sure beats the rations we got."

News of Gus and the Ripper on the anti-gravity pallet brought many of the miners out of their houses. Everyone wanted to see the monster. But after a quick glance, parents pulled their children back inside and closed their doors. A few miners stayed and watched the procession giving Gideon the feeling he was part of a macabre parade. Then Gideon realized that everyone they passed was armed with some sort of weapon be it a knife, a crossbow or a club of some kind. *It's weird. Where are the modern weapons?*

Frank noticed it too. "Why such primitive weapons?"

"When the supply ships stopped coming so did the blasters," replied Gus. "Besides, blasters don't work so well here. Something about the Off World atmosphere messes with their circuitry. They stopped working just when we needed them most. A lot of people died holding blasters. We don't use them anymore. I suggest you stop relying on yours."

Vince looked at his wrist pad. "Yeah, we know. I figure we've got about eight hours of juice left in 'em. That about right, Frankie?"

"Sounds right, V."

"We're here." Gus stopped at a building with a red cross on the door. He used the anti-gravity pallet to push the doors open and went inside with the Ripper. Gideon and the hunters followed close behind.

Inside med-lab, was the familiar smell of Quarantine—that antiseptic, artificially clean smell that could only be created with chemicals. Thick curtains divided med-lab creating exam rooms and a sense of privacy for the sick and injured. Gideon knew med-labs well. He spent a lot of time in one watching his mother create the cure for the Virus. He still remembered all the tests she performed on him, all the injections he received, and all the blood samples he gave. The diagnostic computers beeped and flashed at him like he was an old friend. He reached for his Chain of Remembrance and rolled the crystal between his fingers.

Gus turned to the hunters. "I'll be taking the Ripper back to the doctor. You can link up with our main computer over there."

"What about me?" Gideon asked.

"You stay here, boy." Gus and the Ripper disappeared behind the privacy curtains. The curtains closed with a snap.

Boy? Really?

"He left a friend here with us," Vince said.

Gideon turned and saw a guard-bot. It had what looked like an old-fashioned shotgun attached to it.

"Come on, kid. Me and Frankie are going to link up with the camp's main computer. We need to find out if the miners can repair the ship. Maybe you can be useful for a change."

"Gee, thanks."

Gideon and the hunters made their way over to a nearby computer station with the guard-bot closely following them. Vince quickly set up the data link.

"So far it looks pretty good, Frankie. It seems the miners have what we need to repair the jumper."

"Outstanding, V."

Gideon scanned the computer panel. He saw some navigation buttons for the med-lab and started pressing them. Then the conversation between Gus and the doctor came across the speakers. It was barely audible. Gideon looked for the volume control.

"Kid, quit messing around with the system. Me and Frankie got it under control."

"Quiet," Gideon said.

Vince flushed with anger.

Gideon found the volume control and turned up the sound. "Sorry, Vince, but they're talking about the Ripper. I thought you guys should hear it."

"Chill, V. Gideon didn't mean no disrespect. He's right. We need to get the latest intel on the creature feature that they got goin' on here. Turn that up some more, Gideon. I can barely hear it."

"Okay, but not too loud. I don't want Gus to know we're eavesdropping."

⋏

"Doc, I need to know what this thing is," Gus said. "Is it a Berserker? Because I'm tellin' ya it was harder to take down than any Ripper I've ever seen. It killed three of my men."

"It's not a Berserker that's for sure, Gus. If it were, it would have killed all twenty of you.

No, this is a new type of Ripper."

"How can you be so sure, Doc?"

✧

"A Berserker, are you kidding me? I come all the way Off World and still can't escape that stupid nickname?"

"What are you talking about, Gideon?" Frank asked.

"Nothing, just something the morons back at Quarantine like to call me sometimes."

"Berserker? Really?"

"The kid's lost it, Frankie. Less than a full day Off World and he's lost it."

✧

"Gus, this is a new and improved Ripper," the doctor said. "It's been manufactured and bio-engineered beyond the limits of the last Rippers. This creature is designed for battle. If you look closely you can see that it has the remarkable ability to heal its own wounds. It has no digestive system so it doesn't need to eat. It also appears to have two hearts and three lungs. That helps explains the creature's superior stamina and strength. If Gwendolyn can create this type of creature then she's been able to restore most of the lab's computers and other systems. This is a very efficient design and a troubling new development. If she can create Rippers as strong and resilient as Berserkers then we have a serious problem."

✧

"I know that voice," Gideon said.

"Yeah, we all do, Gideon. It's Gus."

"No, Frank, the doctor's voice. I swear I know that voice." Gideon leaned closer to the speaker.

✧

"Doc, you said it was impossible for Gwendolyn to bypass the security protocols you set up. You said the bio-encryption was unbreakable."

"It is," replied the doctor. "As impressive as this creature is, it is still flawed. It may be able to heal itself like a Berserker but its body and other essential functions are burning themselves out. That's why it's so hot to the touch. If battle wounds don't kill it then its own super-charged metabolism eventually will. In my opinion, this creature is incapable of living longer than twelve hours. That tells me Gwendolyn hasn't regained full control of the lab. The only way she can do that is to bypass the bio-encryption and she can only do that if she magically gets my son to appear on this planet."

A

Gideon's drew a quick breath. "No. It can't be."

"Gideon, you okay?" Frank asked.

Gideon disappeared around the corner and headed for med-lab.

"Hey, Gideon, wait up," Frank said.

Gideon ignored Frank and snapped back the privacy curtain. He was met with a blast of noxious air that smelled like sweat and rotting meat. Gideon pulled his flight suit up over his mouth and nose.

The Ripper was lying strapped to the anti-gravity pallet. Its jet-black skin was covered in a fine sheen of sweat. It made the monster look even slimier than when Gideon first saw it. Gus waved a wand over its chest with one hand and pinched his nose shut with the other. The data collected by the wand was transmitted to a computer screen that displayed the creature's internal organs. A man wearing a white lab coat over an orange mining uniform studied the screen.

Gideon stepped around the anti-gravity pallet and locked his eyes onto the man in the white lab coat. *I don't believe it.*

He was older than Gideon remembered. His hair was grey, he had a scar across the left side of his face and his eyes were purple. But there was no doubt. This man was Gideon's father.

CHAPTER 9

Gideon stood with his arms crossed over his chest. He cleared his throat.

Gus continued waving the sensor over the creature while Doctor Wells stared intently at the computer screen. When Gus brought the sensor over the center of the creature's chest, Doctor Wells ordered him to stop.

"Hold it right there, Gus. Yes, this is definitely a second heart. Incredible, it's as big as the other. Move the sensor over to the right. Hold it steady will you? Gus, stop pinching your nose and . . . that's it. Look at that. I was right. It has three massive lungs. Gwendolyn must have added these redundancies so the Ripper could survive an injury to a vital organ and keep fighting. This makes it even harder to kill. With these extra organs, it could survive countless wounds before it finally dies. Tell your men in order to kill this new Ripper, take its head as quickly as possible."

"You should just kill it now, doctor." Gus put down the sensor and handed Doctor Wells a large syringe. It was filled with a blue liquid.

He's ignoring me just like always.

Doctor Wells put the syringe on a metal stand in-between a long bone saw and a row of neatly arranged surgical knives. The blue liquid inside the syringe cast an eerie reflection against the shiny teeth of the bone saw and the blades on the knives. "No, I need to get some more data first. This Ripper will die shortly then I can perform the autopsy. I'll use the neurotoxin only as a last resort. It will kill it instantly."

"I hope so. What's in it, Doctor Wells? Nothing kills these things easy or quick."

"The cure for the Virus."

"The cure? Do you mean to study the Ripper or kill it?"

"We can't just kill it. Not yet. I need the data, Gus. But don't worry. If necessary I'll use the cure. This high of a dosage should kill it."

"Doc, the cure for the Virus could also change the Ripper into something worse. The cure is how you created the Berserkers. If the cure can make a human into a Berserker then who knows what it can do to a Ripper. Don't do it. Just saw the Ripper's head off."

"Don't question my work, Gus."

Gideon filled with rage. *I'm standing right next to him and he doesn't even notice.*

Gideon's anger made him deaf to what his father and Gus were saying. He stared at his father, his eyes narrowing with contempt. *Ripper, Berserker, blah, blah, blah who cares?*

Without looking away from the computer screen Gideon's father said, "I'll be with you in a moment."

I'll be with you in a moment. Gideon heard that phrase too much while growing up. There was always another report to file, another experiment or problem to analyze. Instead of being there when Gideon needed him it was always the same annoying, *I'll be with you in a moment.*

"No, you will listen to me now!"

Doctor Wells and Gus looked up. Doctor Wells blinked several times as if he couldn't believe what he was seeing.

"Quiet, boy can't you see we're busy here?" Gus said.

"How…how can this be?" Doctor Wells' face had a puzzled look, as if he were trying to figure out a complex math problem. "Son, what are you doing here?"

"This is your son?" Shock crawled across Gus' face.

Doctor Wells nodded. "Yes, he's my son. But how—"

"We found him with the two hunters I told you about," Gus said. "Their wormhole jumper crash-landed about four miles due west of here. They walked right into our ambush. The boy almost got himself killed by the Ripper. He claims there are medicines onboard his wormhole jumper so I agreed to repair the ship in exchange for the meds."

Gus eyed Gideon intently. "We have a contract."

Doctor Wells pushed his way past Gus. "My boy, I thought I would never see you again." He reached out for Gideon and tried to hug him.

Gideon backed away from his father. He clinched his fists. "Don't touch me."

"What's wrong, son?"

"What's wrong? I'll tell you what's wrong. You left mom and me when we needed you most. You left and you never came back not even for mom's funeral. Because of you they stuck me in Quarantine."

Doctor Wells' eyes pooled with purple tears. "All transports back to Earth were cancelled, Gideon. I begged them to let me go back. They refused to allow it."

Gideon watched with a mix of sadness and satisfaction as purple tears rolled down his father's cheeks.

Frank put a hand on Gideon's shoulder. "Come on, Gideon. This isn't the time or place for this sort of thing. Let's go back and see what V found out about the ship repairs."

Gideon pulled himself free from Frank. "No, he owes me an apology and I want it. He left us, abandoned us."

"Suit yourself, Gideon." Frank said.

"I'm sorry, Gideon. There was nothing I could do," Doctor Wells said. "Hurting you or your mother was the last thing I ever wanted to do. Please forgive me."

Gideon searched his father's face. The Virus Eyes and the deep scar across his cheek made him look like a shadow of the man Gideon remembered. *He looks old, too old.* Gideon tried to forgive the abandonment, the betrayal he felt. He couldn't do it. Not yet. He reached for his Chain of Remembrance and rolled it between his fingers. The warmth of the crystal relaxed him, easing the tension in his body.

"Excuse me," Gus said. "I don't mean to break up this family reunion but if this is your son, then we have a serious problem don't we?"

Doctor Wells dried his face with his sleeve. "What, what was that?"

Gus pointed at Gideon. "You said the only way Gwendolyn bypasses the bio-encryption settings in the lab is if your son magically appeared. Well abracadabra he's here. What do we do about it?"

"We return him to Earth before Gwendolyn captures him," Doctor Wells said.

"Whoa, hold on. Who is this Gwendolyn you're talking about and why does she want to capture me? Dad, you need to tell me what's going on. You owe me that much."

"Agreed," Frank said. "My mission is to protect your son so if there's a threat to him, I wanna hear about it, Doc."

"Son, Gwendolyn is my former lab assistant. She took over my lab so she could make Rippers."

The Ripper slept on the anti-gravity pallet. Its black slimy skin glistened under the overhead lights of med-lab. Its breathing was soft and rhythmic. The massive chest rose and fell in time to the beeping of the diagnostic computer.

Gideon's eyes narrowed. *I must be tired. There's no way that thing's claws are growing back.*

Frank pointed at the Ripper. "Doc, why would somebody want to make a monster like that?"

"Rippers are Gwendolyn's enforcers. She thinks if she can create enough of them, she can rule this world," Doctor Wells said.

Frank's face twisted with doubt. "Come on, Doc, that's crazy."

"That's exactly what she is, crazy."

"Dad, what does she want with me? Why does she want to capture me?"

Doctor Wells took a deep breath. He walked toward a nearby counter. The counters were jammed with high-powered microscopes and computers. It even had a DNA reader. Gideon recognized it immediately. His mother's lab had several of them only bigger. This one reminded Gideon of an old-fashioned television. The sophisticated equipment looked out of place in the med-lab of a mining camp.

Why does he have all this fancy equipment? Did he take it from the lab?

Doctor Wells opened the door to a small refrigerator. He pulled out several bottles of water. He tossed one to Gideon and Frank. "You must be thirsty after hiking four miles."

Gideon pulled off the cap and took a generous swig.

Frank caught the bottle and drained it in three easy gulps. "Thanks, Doc."

Doctor Wells sat on a wheeled stool. He pushed the other stools toward Gideon and Frank. The stools squeaked as they rolled across the tiled floor. "Have a seat."

Gideon wiped his chin with his sleeve. He kept one eye on the Ripper, the other on his father. "No, I'll stand."

"Son, I'm trying to be nice. Can't you meet me half way?"

Gideon took another sip of water.

"Doc, we don't want to get too comfortable. Not with your little pet so close," Frank said.

"Can't say I blame ya. I say we cut the Ripper's head off and be done with it," Gus said.

"Dad, you're stalling. Are you going to tell me what's going on here or what?"

Doctor Wells took a long pull from his water. "Gideon, you're in great danger. Gwendolyn wants to make an army of Rippers and the only thing stopping her is you."

"Me? What did I do?"

"Right before she took control of my lab, I used your DNA to bio-encrypt the artificial intelligence. So long as she's locked out of the AI she can't perfect her Rippers. She can't create her army. But if she captures you, she'll force you to unlock the system and give her full access to the AI. If that happens this world is finished. She'll be able to make as many Rippers as she wants."

"But how did you that? I haven't seen you in three years. Where did you get my DNA?"

"Before I came Off World, I created two medallions for my Chain of Remembrance. One had your DNA in it. The other had your mother's."

"You broke it open and used it for the bio-encryption?" Gideon said.

"I did. Instead of wearing the Chain of Remembrance like a cheap trinket, I put it to the best use possible. It saved a lot of lives."

Gideon grabbed his Chain of Remembrance and squeezed it as if protecting it from a thief. "A cheap trinket? Is that what you think?"

"No, no, that's not what I meant. It came out wrong."

"What did you do with Mom's medallion?"

Doctor Wells took another drink of water. He refused to meet Gideon's gaze. "Gwendolyn has it."

"You're hiding something, Dad. What aren't you telling me? What did you do?"

"Watch your tone with me, Gideon. I'm still your father."

"Watch my tone? You sound just like the headmaster back at Quarantine. All the guys hate him."

Frank crushed his empty water bottle in his hand. "Doc, your story just doesn't add up. I'm supposed to believe your lab assistant woke up one day and decided to make Rippers so she could conquer this planet?"

"I've told you everything you need to know," Doctor Wells said.

Frank gritted his teeth. "I hate that need-to-know nonsense. If this Gwendolyn took over your lab how did you manage to get all this high-end gear in here? What's really going on?"

Doctor Wells flushed with anger. "Enough questions about my work. We're wasting time. We need to get you and my son out of here."

"Dad, why does everybody Off World have Virus Eyes?"

"Gideon, don't waste my time with silly questions. You know that if you don't leave Off World in five days you'll have Virus Eyes too."

Gideon collapsed onto the stool. "What? I…I didn't…nobody told me *that*."

"Gideon, I thought you knew," Frank said. "It's why me and V keep saying five days in and out not one day more."

Gideon shook his head. Tears rolled down his cheeks. He stared at Gus' and his father's purple eyes. "Dad, are you saying that after five days, I'll have the Virus?"

"Yes, son but the Virus operates differently Off World. It doesn't kill people here. Instead, we become carriers—a type of old-Earth, Typhoid Mary if you will."

"But if I'm a carrier of the Virus, they'll never let me return to Earth."

"That's right, son, it's all the more reason for you to leave Off World as soon as possible. Let's get your ship repaired and get you out of here. The last thing we want is you stuck here hunted by Gwendolyn and her Rippers."

Gideon's head was spinning. Why wasn't he told back on Earth? He rolled his Chain of Remembrance between his fingers and took a deep breath.

"Son, are you okay?"

Gideon locked eyes with his father. The purple Virus Eyes were haunting. They reminded Gideon of the dark days back on Earth—when Virus Eyes meant death.

He shuddered at the thought of being a carrier of the Virus.

Of being stuck Off World.

Of being hunted by Rippers.

Then a shrill beeping cut through the lab. It sounded like an old-fashioned car alarm.

It was the diagnostic computer attached to the Ripper.

Gus shouted. "Doctor Wells, the Ripper!"

Doctor Wells jumped off his stool. He grabbed the syringe filled with the blue anti-Virus serum. But he was too slow. The Ripper tore through the restraints holding it to the anti-gravity pallet. With one swipe of its arm, it sent Doctor Wells flying into Frank and Gus. The three of them collapsed into a heap on the floor.

The Ripper stood behind the anti-gravity pallet and sniffed the room. Then it fixed its gaze on Gideon. Its bat-like face snuffled at him as if it were enjoying the aroma of a good meal before it feasted. Its red eyes widened in anticipation. Saliva dripped from its mouth.

Gideon's blood turned to ice. He tried to move but when he looked into the Ripper's cold, red eyes he froze. Gideon heard his father shouting at him to run, but the Ripper's hypnotic gaze held him. It seemed to draw Gideon in, to hold him in place.

Gideon had never seen anything so horrible as the creature standing in front of him, preparing to eat him. The Ripper opened and closed its mouth several times. It had a multi-hinged jaw that opened not just up and down but side to side as well. As the Ripper gnashed its teeth, Gideon could see that its fangs had grown back. They were razor sharp and designed for ripping flesh. With its jaw fully unhinged and its mouth wide open, Gideon couldn't help but think how easy it would be for the Ripper to take his head off in one bite.

Then the Ripper raised its hand above its head, its regrown claws gashing the ceiling of med-lab. It squeezed its hand into a fist and brought it down against the anti-gravity pallet easily smashing it in half. It reminded Gideon of breaking boards in Krav Jitsui.

Then Gideon was knocked to the floor. Frank was sitting on top of him with his blaster raised and ready to fire. Gideon cringed in anticipation of the blaster shot.

But no blaster shot came.

Instead, the creature started shaking uncontrollably. Its red lifeless eyes rolled back into its head. Then it burst into flames and exploded.

Hot gooey, bloody ash smacked Gideon in the face. It stuck to him like burnt marshmallow and tasted like a combination of sour milk and fried hot-dogs. He spit chunks of the Ripper out of his mouth. "Gross."

Then a fire extinguisher hissed nearby. It was Gus. He sprayed the floor and what was left of the Ripper with white foam.

"Is anybody hurt?" Doctor Wells said. "Gideon, are you okay?"

Gideon slowly rose to his feet. He scooped pieces of the Ripper off himself and flicked it to the floor. "I'm fine, Dad."

Frank brushed the gore from his flight suit. "I'm good to go."

"What the hell happened in here?" Vince had his blaster primed and ready to fire. "I heard an explosion. Where's the Ripper?"

Gideon held out his hands. They were covered with purple sticky goo. "I'm wearing most of it. The rest is on the ceiling, the floors and the walls."

Vince whistled. "Frankie, you did that with the scrambler?"

"Wasn't me, V. The Ripper just exploded like a bug on a windshield."

"What gives, Doc?" Vince asked.

Doctor Wells picked through the pieces of his diagnostic computer. "I don't know. All of my data is gone. The explosion wrecked my computer."

"Dad, you said the Ripper had a twelve-hour life span. Maybe it was just his time."

"Perhaps, Gideon. A violent end nonetheless. It appears Gwendolyn makes them spontaneously combust as their final act."

"At least it's dead and won't be causing us any more problems." Gus picked the blue syringe up off the floor.

Doctor Wells grabbed it from him and placed it on a nearby counter. "Careful with that, Gus."

"Hey, V, what's the word on the jumper?" Frank asked.

"Great, news, Frankie. The miners can repair the ship no problem. The only wrinkle is their maglev is broken. So the boy wonder here has to fly us to his old man's lab if we want to get outta here. It's the only maglev within range of the jumper's battery pack. Any farther out and we run outta juice flying in hover mode."

Gideon scooped pieces of Ripper from under his eyes and flicked them to the floor. "What? Are you kidding me? We have to go the lab? That's the last place I want to go."

"Frankie, what's the kid's problem?"

"V, the doctor here *is* the kid's old man. His lab's been compromised by the lady makin' the Rippers. She's runnin' the show now."

"So we have to take on an army of Rippers to get home?" Vince said.

"Afraid so, V."

Gideon slumped to the floor. He rinsed his mouth with water and spit out the last remaining pieces of the dead Ripper. "I don't believe it. I can either stay Off World hunted by Rippers the rest of my life. Or if I want to return to Earth, go to Gwendolyn's lab—the place where Rippers are made."

Chapter 10

Like stalactites, pieces of the Ripper hung from the ceiling of med-lab. The white privacy curtain was speckled with a reddish purple color. It looked like a paint bomb exploded onto it. The floor was littered with clumps of foamy fire retardant mixed with chunks of bone and meat. A burnt, sulfurous smell permeated the air.

Gideon rolled his Chain of Remembrance between his fingers. "I don't know what to do. Do I run and hide from Gwendolyn or do I fight her and her Rippers so I can get to the maglev?"

Gus set the fire extinguisher down next to the smashed anti-gravity pallet. "It's a big planet, boy. You go far enough away, Gwendolyn may never find you."

"Gus has a point, Gideon. As much as I would like to get you out of here and back to Earth, going to Gwendolyn's for the maglev is suicide." Doctor Wells said.

"You want me to run and hide?"

"No, son. I want you to run and live. The Rippers have a twelve-hour life span. That gives them a limited range. You could live with another mining camp or maybe even the Shape Shifters. I have some influence with them. I'm sure they would take you in."

Gideon looked at Vince and Frank. "What do you guys think?"

"I don't know, kid," Vince said. "We've got two blasters with limited juice and only one scrambler. I don't like running from a fight but these are tough odds. There's no telling how many Rippers this Gwendolyn has. Doc, any idea?"

Doctor Wells shook his head. "It could be dozens, maybe even a hundred or so."

"Home is where you hang your hat, kid. I didn't sign up for the Alamo, Little Big Horn or Outpost Keating," Vince said. "Staying Off World ain't great but it beats dying."

Gideon scooped pieces of the dead Ripper from behind his ears. It was hot and stuck to his fingers like old gum. He flicked it off his hands as best he could. "Hundreds of Rippers?"

"It's your call Gideon. I'll support you either way," Frank said.

Gideon eyed his father. "There's nothing for me here except a life on the run. I say we go to the lab. Gwendolyn will never expect it. Maybe we can take her by surprise. We can act like nothing's wrong and then re-take the lab when she lowers the force field."

"That's not bad, Gideon. You're thinking like a Galaxy Class Pilot," Frank said. "What do you think, V? Are you in?"

"Frankie, you know I would. But this . . .it's—"

"V, don't make me bring up North Korea."

"You just did, Frankie. Don't play that card. Pyongyang was a long time ago."

"I need you, V. So does Gideon."

Vince cursed. "Yeah, I'm in."

Gideon grinned. "Thanks, guys. So now we get the jumper and fly it back here."

"Count me in," Doctor Wells said. "I'm going with you."

"Why, Dad? We can get the ship back here on our own."

"I want to see what kind of supplies you brought Gwendolyn. She's far too clever to have you show up empty handed. I'm sure it's more than just basic medicines."

"You sound like you know her pretty well, Doc," Frank said.

Doctor Wells shrugged. "We worked together for several years. You get to know a person."

"Dad, they told me it was DNA samples for your work."

"I'll wager it's much more than that, son. If it's what I think it is, I may need to destroy it immediately."

"Doctor Wells," Gus said. "I can't let you go out there. You're the only doctor we've got. We can't risk losing you."

"He's got protection," Vince patted his blaster.

Frank cleaned pieces of the Ripper from the DNA Scrambler. "Amen to that, V."

Gideon thought back to the Ripper attack in the forest. Even with Frank and Vince, the Ripper almost got him. His father would just slow them down and make them easier targets. "We need more people out there with us. Gus, can you provide some extra protection for my dad? Maybe Paige can come with us."

"Smooth, kid, real smooth. I told you there's no time to get romantic," Vince said.

"It's not like that. Gus said she's the best tracker and marksman he's ever seen. We need her."

"I saw her move through the woods, V. She is good."

"I want Kaz to come along too," Doctor Wells said.

"It's no coincidence your son's here. If Gwendolyn was able to get your boy sent Off World, she probably knows where the wormhole jumper is. You're walking into a trap," Gus said.

"All the more reason to give us extra protection," countered Doctor Wells.

"I lost three people today. I'm not sending anybody else out there, not with Rippers running around loose. Who knows, there may even be Berserkers out there."

"Frank, how many people can the wormhole jumper carry?" Gideon asked.

"Six, why?"

"I need to fly the jumper back here anyway. If we can have Paige and this Kaz go with us to the jumper, I can fly us all back. Flying back reduces the risk of a Ripper attack by half doesn't it?"

"What do you think, Gus?" Doctor Wells said.

Gus sighed. "Fine, but you leave in the morning. Nobody goes out there after dark. Not even Paige or Kaz."

"There's one more thing, Gus," Gideon said.

"What?"

"We need you to escort us out of the camp."

"Kid, me and Frankie know the way."

"It's not that, Vince. It's the miners. I don't trust them."

"Why do you say that, son? They let you into the camp."

"Dad, if this Gwendolyn is as smart as you say she is, then she probably has people or Rippers out looking for me. Maybe the miners want to turn me over to her. Gus said going to the jumper is probably a trap."

"Son, the people here aren't like that. If they were, you would have been attacked as soon as you walked through the front gate."

"Dad, when I first walked through the front gate nobody here knew who I was. But now that I've been here awhile, I'm sure word has gotten out. If it hasn't, then great but I'm not taking any chances. People act crazy when they're trying to survive. Remember how mom and I were chased down and almost killed after she caught the Virus?"

"Of course I remember, son."

Gideon rubbed his forearms as images of the angry mob chasing after him and his mother flashed through his mind.

Frank raised an eyebrow at Gideon. Gideon suddenly felt self-conscious, aware of everyone's eyes on him. He pulled the sleeves of his flight down past his wrists and put his hands behind his back.

"Gideon, you okay? What's with the arms?" Frank asked.

Doctor Wells took a tentative step toward Gideon.

"Back off, dad. I'm fine. Look, you guys, all I'm saying is that maybe these miners try to turn us over to this psycho Gwendolyn. That's how people are. But Gus is running the camp so maybe if he's with us the people here will leave us alone."

"Gideon's got a point. How about it, Gus?" Frank asked.

"Fine, I'll see you back here in the morning."

"Early," Vince said. "Be here at dawn. As of tomorrow we only have four days left to get off this rock."

"Son, we have showers in the back. Why don't you and your . . . friends get cleaned up and have some food."

"What about you, Dad?"

"I need to clean up in here and prep my equipment for tomorrow. I'll be with you in a moment."

At first light, Gus led Gideon, his father and the hunters out of med-lab and into the glare of the morning sun. Unlike the soft light of the planet's twin moons, the sunlight was blinding. Gideon blinked several times trying to force his eyes to adjust but they refused to cooperate. Even with his eyes closed, the light assaulted him. Tears streamed down his cheeks. "I can't see anything."

"Don't move, Gideon," Frank said. "Let me check your pack for sunglasses. I'm sure Sarge gave you some. They're standard issue."

Frank jammed his hand into the pack and rummaged around forcing Gideon to stumble. "Hey, take it easy back there."

"Quit squirming, Gideon, will you? Here they are."

Gideon lost his balance as Frank pulled hard on the pack, making him feel like a puppet on strings. He righted himself just as the sunglasses were forced into his hand. "Next time why don't you hold me upside down by my ankles and just shake?"

"Good idea, I'll remember that. We're already into day two of this mission and I'm feeling pressed for time."

"Five days in and out not one day more, Frankie. Let's move it, we've got a plane to catch."

Gideon put the sunglasses on. The glare of the twin suns—one orange and one red—was replaced by a soft, orange color that reminded him of sunsets back home. His eyes instantly relaxed. "That's much better, thanks."

"Sorry, son, I should have said something to you about the suns. It's been so long since I've needed sunglasses I forgot about it."

Neither Doctor Wells nor Gus was wearing sunglasses. "Once you get the Eyes of the Virus you don't need the glasses," Gus said.

"We won' be staying long enough to experience that firsthand. Right, V?"

"Amen to that, Frankie."

Both hunters were wearing their sunglasses. They looked at Gideon and nodded their approval. "Looking good, kiddo," Frank said.

Gideon saw his reflection in Frank's mirrored glasses and nodded his agreement.

"If you're done primping and preening follow me." Gus started walking in the opposite direction of the front gate and toward a row of housing units.

"The gate is that way. I can see it from here," Frank said.

"I know where the bloody gate is," snapped Gus. "But it's not smart to go through the center of the camp. It might attract too much of the wrong kind of attention. We'll go through the alleys instead just in case."

"The wrong kind of attention?" asked Frank.

"So the kid was right," said Vince.

Gideon gave his father his best *I told you so look* before falling in with Frank and Vince. With the cover of night now gone and the glare from the suns reduced to a soft orange glow, Gideon could see the true conditions of the mining camp. The small squat buildings housing the miners and their families were held together with a mix of materials brought from Earth and collected from Off World. Some of the houses looked like they were pieced together with a mix of heavy vines, boards and corrugated metals.

Gideon knew that the pre-fab housing units in the other space colonies were not supposed to be permanent, and that other, more durable supplies were supposed to come from Earth. But after the Virus swept across Earth, the supply ships stopped coming so the miners had to make the best of a bad situation. Some of the housing units and other buildings were an odd collection of parts taken from heavy mining equipment, old wormhole jumpers and what looked like boats. Gideon marveled at the odd collection of things the colonists used. He couldn't believe people lived in some of the more dilapidated houses. It made him feel as if he were walking through a refugee camp. *Quarantine isn't so bad after all.*

"Not the best accommodations but the people here have done extremely well for themselves considering the circumstances," Doctor Wells said. "Never underestimate human ingenuity. The housing units may not look like much but if you look closely you'll see that each building has a solar collector on the roof for power generation and some even have a force field on the windows and doors."

"This way." Gus turned into an alley that cut between rows of housing units. The alley was narrow. It allowed for only two of Gideon's group to walk through at a time. Gus and Doctor Wells took the lead followed by Gideon and Frank. Vince brought up the rear.

The orange and red suns were still low in the early morning sky. Sunlight hit only one side of the alley. The darker side of the alley was covered in shadows that hung like ghosts on the walls of the housing units. Wastewater seeped into the alley pooling and mixing with piles of garbage. The soupy mix gave off a sour, noxious smell. Small scaly creatures with long tails, red bulbous eyes and sharp teeth scurried in-between the piles of garbage. Gus kicked one of them causing it to shriek. "Damn rats."

"Those are rats? They look more like armadillos," Gideon said.

"They may not look like the rats back on Earth but they act just like 'em. So that's what we call 'em."

"What the hell is that?" Frank asked.

In the center of the alley was a pile of trash taller than Gideon. At the base of it was an orange mining uniform and a pair of boots.

"What's the big deal, Frank? Somebody threw out a mining uniform and a pair of boots."

"No, Gideon. Look on the other side of the garbage pile. It's what's wearing the uniform and the boots that has me worried."

"Oh, no. I hope Sara didn't do this. I gave her treatment only yesterday. She shouldn't have to feed. It's not necessary," Doctor Wells said.

Gus scanned the rooftops of the housing units. "Some of them like to eat Pure Earth, Doctor Wells. That synthetic stuff you make just doesn't cut it. But if she's already fed, we should be okay."

"Treatments? Already fed? Dad, what are you guys talking about?"

"Nothing, son. It's okay—"

"I don't like this, Frankie. This is a perfect place for an ambush."

"I can't see around the trash pile or you guys." Gideon shoved his way past Gus and his father.

When he saw the corpse, he froze. Gideon had seen dead bodies before. There were plenty of victims of the Virus lying dead in the streets. But he had never seen anything like this. "Oh my God. Did the rats do that?"

The corpse was of a large man about the same age as Doctor Wells. He looked as if he had been strong and powerful but had somehow been instantly aged. His skin was grey and his face puckered. Something had been sucked out of his body, leaving it dried and weathered. The indentations on the head and face made the corpse look more like a raisin than a human.

"That's Larry," Gus said. "When we were mining fire rock, he was one of the best workers. Strong like an ox. But he liked to fight. Get some drinks in 'im and he would go lookin' for trouble. A real backstabber at times."

"It looks like trouble found him," Frank said.

Doctor Wells turned the corpse over. There was a tear in the back of the mining uniform and several large holes in its pelvis. "He's been hollowed out. All of his bone marrow has been removed."

"Dad, did a Shape Shifter do that?"

"No, I did," said a high-pitched voice.

It was a girl about Gideon's age. She had a short blonde ponytail. Her purple eyes were wild and hungry. She was smaller than Gideon. The sleeves of the orange mining uniform she wore hung past her hands.

"Sarah, just calm down. Everything's all right. Let's get you back to med-lab."

"No, Doctor Wells. I don't want anymore of your synthetic Pure Earth." She looked at Gideon and took a step forward. She pointed at him. The hand-less sleeve of the mining uniform hung in mid-air. "I want him. He's Pure Earth and young. He'll be tasty."

"Excuse me? Pure Earth? Tasty? Dad, what is she talking about?"

Sarah looked wide-eyed at Doctor Wells and laughed. "He's your son? That's perfect. Since you're the one who turned me into a monster and stole my life, I'll steal his. He's not like Larry and the other Off Worlders I've fed from. Only their bone marrow was Pure Earth. But every inch of your son is Pure Earth. I can smell it. It's so sweet and coppery. Maybe if I eat him I'll finally be cured. What do you think Doctor Wells? Should I start with his heart or his brain?"

"This girl ain't right in the head, V. Time to lock and load." Frank leveled his DNA scrambler at the girl.

Vince charged his blaster. "Frankie, there ain't nothin' right about this place."

"Dad, is she on drugs or something?"

Sarah's purple eyes bore into Gideon. "Drugs. Yes, that's exactly what it is. Let me show you what your father's drugs did to me. What he turned me into."

"Sarah, don't do it. I can help you. Come back to med-lab. Please don't at-tack my son."

Gideon backed away from Sarah. He stood in between Frank and Vince. "Is she going to do to me the same thing she did to that dead guy?"

"No, something much worse," Sarah said. "I only ate Larry's bone marrow. I left the rest for the rats. But you, I'm going to devour every inch of. There won't be anything left. Not even for the rats."

Gideon got into a fighting stance. "Let's see you try. I've fought worse than you in Quarantine plenty of times."

Then Sarah started changing. Her skin turned a dark, reddish-purple. Her bones popped and cracked as her head elongated. Her jaw grew and unhinged itself from her face. It now opened and closed just like a Ripper's—both vertically and horizontally. She opened her jaw as wide as she could exposing rows of sharp pointy teeth. When she snapped her jaw shut, some of her new teeth protruded like tusks. Then long needle-like claws grew past the sleeves of the mining uniform.

Gideon's throat tightened. "Is . . . is . . . she a Shape Shifter?"

Sarah snarled at Gideon. "No, I'm your father's creation."

"She's a Berserker, son."

"She's a what?"

"We should run." Gus backed into Gideon and knocked him into the trash pile. The dead miner rolled on top of him. The body smelled like garbage and rotting meat. Gideon pushed it off.

Vince leveled his blaster. "Move doc, give me a clear shot."

Doctor Wells jumped in front of Vince, shielding Sarah. "No, don't shoot her. She's my patient."

Then Sarah vaulted twenty feet up onto the roof of a housing unit. The corrugated metal bent underneath her. Vince fired his blaster but Sarah was too fast. Her footfalls sounded like a hammer against the metal roof as she wove her way in between the solar collectors. Then Sarah jumped to the set of roofs on the opposite side of the alley. Vince fired as Sarah sprang across the alley but the blaster shot missed. She landed on the rooftop turned and ducked as another blaster shot passed over her head. Then Sarah opened her jaw from side-to-side and up and down, extended her claws and launched herself at Gideon. Rows of sharp teeth and dagger-like claws raced toward Gideon's head like a missile.

Gideon tried to get to his feet but lost his footing in the wet garbage. Then a low rumble filled the air as a blue beam hit Sarah. It drove her into the wall of a housing unit. When her body dented the metal wall it sounded like a Chinese gong.

The blue beam enveloped Sarah like a cocoon. Her mining uniform disintegrated. Sarah tried to stand but couldn't. She slumped to the ground and tore clumps of hair from her head. Then she screamed. Her body started convulsing. Then her jaw fell off. Her head started to liquefy. The skin on her shoulders and arms began to slide off.

"Nice shot, Frankie. She's melting like an old-fashioned candle."

The DNA scrambler.

"She was fast, V. You set her up nice for me, good teamwork."

Sarah's melting body made Gideon's stomach do flip flops.

"Why did you kill her? I could have helped her," Doctor Wells said.

Sarah slowly got to her feet. Pieces of her arms hung off her like melted wax while the skin on her face slowly grew back. "I'm not dead yet," she said in a guttural voice.

"Her body's healing itself. Shoot her again," Gideon said.

"I told you we should run," Gus said.

"What the hell? Nothing survives the scrambler." Frank leveled the DNA scrambler at Sarah and fired several more blasts into her. Each blast covered her in a blue bubble of energy. Soon there was nothing left of her except a reddish-purple mound of bone and meat.

"Enough! You've killed her. Are you happy?" Doctor Wells said.

Frank shut down the scrambler. "No, doc. I *ain't* happy. I just had to kill a kid because you turned her into a monster. No, I ain't happy at all."

"Me neither, Dad. She said she was going to eat me because of what you did to her. That eating me might cure her. Cure her of what? What did you do here?"

"Nothing. She was . . . sick. I tried to help her."

"Dad, stop lying. She tried to kill me. What are you hiding?"

Vince grabbed Doctor Wells by the collar and slammed him up against the side of a housing unit. It sounded like a rock hit the metal wall. Doctor Wells grunted.

"You need to start talking, Doc. What the hell is goin' on here? That was no shifter. Shifters don't eat humans."

"Let my dad go, Vince."

"Shut up, kid. I'll let him go after he starts talking."

Several miners had gathered at the back of the alley. They pointed at Gideon.

"Let's get to the gate. All that blaster fire is starting to draw a crowd," Gus said.

"Doc, you got sixty seconds to start giving me useful intel or I'm going to let V beat you ugly," Frank said.

Vince slapped Doctor Wells.

"Hey," Gideon said.

"I said shut up, kid."

Doctor Wells rubbed the purple handprint on his cheek. "That isn't necessary. I'll tell you."

"Fifty-five seconds, Doc. And that slap from V was just a love tap to get your attention."

Frank said.

Vince pulled his fist back and prepared to punch Doctor Wells in the face.

"Dad, just tell us."

"The miners and their families were my patients. Sarah was my patient. It was my mission to cure them of the Virus so they could return to Earth. But when I gave them the anti-Virus serum, when I gave them the cure it turned them into . . . what you just saw Sarah become."

"We call 'em Berserkers," Gus said.

Gideon cringed at the sound of his nickname. "Dad, how many patients did you have?"

"Two thousand or so. I can't be sure, the records are at the lab."

"You turned two thousand people into those things? Frankie, let me beat this Doctor Frankenstein jerk to death just for doing those people nasty like that."

"Not yet, V."

"Dad how could you? How could you do such a thing?"

"Keep talking, Doc. Confession is good for the soul and for your health."

"I had no idea the cure for the Virus would work differently here than on Earth. It was several days before the mutations started and by then I had inoculated everybody who volunteered to return to Earth. I tried to cure them, son. I really did. I had some success in reversing and controlling the Berserker mutation. As you just saw, Berserkers can control the mutation with proper treatment. All Sarah wanted was medicine."

Gideon pointed at the corpse. "Is that what Larry was? Medicine? She ate all his bone marrow."

"She ate his Pure Earth. That's all Berserkers ever eat," Gus said.

Doctor Wells nodded. "The Berserker mutation is controlled by human DNA not infected by the Virus. On this planet where everybody like poor Larry, me, and Gus are carriers, the only place to find such DNA is in the bone marrow. The bone marrow produces red blood cells that are not infected by the Virus. It takes five days for newly created blood cells to become infected by the Virus."

"But since I don't have the Virus, every part of me is Pure Earth. Is that why Sarah said eating me would cure her?"

"Precisely, son. But that theory has never been proven. I was working on a cure. But when we ran out of Pure Earth Gwendolyn took the research in a different direction. She created the Rippers and took over the lab. The synthetic Pure Earth I created works. It worked on Sarah but—"

"But some of 'em prefer the authentic Pure Earth, the real stuff. And then there are those Berserkers who simply like to kill," Gus said. "Let's continue the science lesson later. We need to get out of here now."

The crowd at the back of the alley was bigger. It started moving toward Gideon. Some of them carried Shockers.

"Follow me. I know a short cut," Gus said.

Gideon and his group jogged after Gus. The crowd of miners followed them up the alley. Gus made a quick right turn and took off running. Then a left turn and through the back entrance of a housing unit. Gideon chased after Gus through a cramped kitchen that smelled like coffee and onions. A tall, black-haired woman in a yellow robe stood over a hotplate cooking purple eggs.

"Hi, honey, I'm home," Gus said.

"Gus, where have you been?" the woman said. "Who are these people? Oh, hello Doctor Wells."

"Sorry, dear, can't talk now gotta run," Gus said.

Gideon chased Gus out the front door of the housing unit. The front gate to the camp was twenty yards away. Standing in front of the gate was a group of men holding clubs, knives and Shockers. The ball on the ends of the Shockers crackled with electricity.

"Damn," Gus said.

Gideon squeezed his hands into tight fists as one of the men stepped forward and pointed a Shocker at him. "We want the boy, Gus."

Chapter 11

"You can't have him, Marcus," said Gus. "I have a contract with the boy and he needs to leave here in one piece in order to fulfill it."

Marcus was slightly shorter than Gus, had a shaved head and wore an orange mining uniform that was ripped over the right shoulder. He held a Shocker in one hand pointing it at Gus while he spoke. In his other, he held up a small data pad that displayed somebody's picture.

Gideon couldn't see whose picture was on the data pad but he had a pretty good idea it was him. Although the miners blocking the front gate were strangers, Gideon recognized the look on their faces all too well. It was that desperate, scared look that the Virus brought to the faces of his friends and neighbors back on Earth right before they attacked him and his mother. Gideon could tell the miners were gathering their courage, readying themselves to do something that good people wouldn't normally do. Instinctively, he took a step behind Frank and Vince.

"It's no secret Gwendolyn's put a price on the boy's head, Gus." Marcus stabbed the ground with the Shocker causing small lighting bolts to flicker inside the orb on the end. "And we aim to collect it."

"No, Marcus," Gus said. "I've a contract with the boy. He says he has meds on his wormhole jumper. I've agreed to repair his ship in exchange for those meds. You know we need meds here, Marcus."

"Let him go, Marcus. He could tell people back on Earth what's going on here," interrupted Doctor Wells. "They might send help."

Marcus and most of the others in the crowd laughed. "Is that what the good doctor thinks? We should trust in the goodness of others? Is that it? Doc, you really are dumber than they say. Go back to med-lab and let the grownups talk."

Gideon bristled.

"Marcus, you're interfering with my contract," Gus said. "You know how we do things. You've no rights here. "

"Yes, I do, Gus."

"Says who?"

Marcus strode up to Gus and stuck the Shocker into his stomach. The electrical charge sent Gus into convulsions. The smell of burned clothing filled the air. Smoke rose from Gus's body as he fell to the ground.

"Says me and my Shocker," replied Marcus.

Doctor Wells ran to Gus. He tried to take Gus's pulse but pulled his hand back. "Ouch, that's hot."

Gideon held his breath as his father used a small bio-scanner to check Gus. After a few moments, Doctor Wells looked up and shook his head. "He's dead, Marcus. You've killed him."

"Well, that solves the contract problem." Marcus showed his data pad to Vince. "What's it going to be, hunter? There's a reward for the boy and we want it."

Gideon craned his neck to see the picture on the data pad. He gasped. The picture was not only recent but looked like it was taken just after his fight in the cafeteria. Gideon could see chunks of potato, bean and kale on his Quarantine uniform. The caption under the photo read,

Wanted: Berserker the Merciless. Keep your families safe and turn in this Berserker. Kill his bodyguards and turn him over to me alive for treatment. You will receive immunity from all Ripper attacks on your community and $5,000,000 in credits.

"Five million for the kid? He's hardly worth it," Vince said.

Marcus gave a toothless smile. "No, he doesn't look like much at all. I'll grant you that. But who are we to judge? Our garbage is Gwendolyn's treasure."

"Hey," Gideon said.

"Stand down, Gideon. We just might get out of this yet," Frank said.

"I can't give him to you," Vince said. "He's under the protection of me and my partner."

"Then, we'll take him by force," Marcus said.

Gideon squeezed Frank's arm. He hoped his sunglasses hid the fear in his eyes.

"I don't think so." Vince drew his blaster and pointed it at the group of men blocking the gate. "I'm going through that gate and the boy is coming with me. You men can either stand aside or be vaporized. The choice is yours."

Gideon breathed a sigh of relief as several of the men in the front of the group took a few tentative steps backward. Most were still blocking the front gate, but the threat of Vince's blaster seemed to be enough to scare most of the miners into backing off.

"That's it, boys," Vince said. "Now why don't you all part like the Red Sea and give me a nice open path to that front gate."

"What about the others?" Doctor Wells asked. "We're still waiting on Paige and Kaz to join us."

Frank leveled his DNA scrambler at the crowd. "Get real, Doc. Take a look at this mob. They just killed one of their own. We are leaving, and we are doing it now."

"Damn straight." Vince eyed Marcus, leveling his blaster at him. "No matter how many men you've got, you're no match for a fully charged blaster. Now back off and make a hole so we can pass."

"That blaster isn't even charged," Marcus said. "It probably doesn't even work."

"Really, you willing to take that chance?" Vince thrust his blaster into Marcus's face and set the charger.

Gideon waited for the high-pitched sound of the blaster's charger to pierce his ears. But there was only silence. He looked at Vince and his fears were confirmed.

Vince took his eyes off the mob and looked at his blaster. "What the hell?"

"Great, nice poker face, V. And you wonder why I always take your money," Frank said.

"You aren't going anywhere, hunter." A twisted, wicked smile crawled across Marcus' face. "It takes about eight hours for this planet's atmosphere to shut down the circuitry on a blaster. Didn't Gus tell you that? It looks like your time is up and your blaster is no good. We're taking the boy whether you like it or not."

Gideon drew a sharp breath. His mind raced back to when his mother contracted the Virus. Friends and neighbors chased them down and tried to kill them. Now a mob with Virus eyes was about to do the same thing.

Marcus turned to the crowd and ordered them forward. "Take him now!"

The mob surged forward overwhelming Vince. In an instant, he was on the ground being pummeled.

Then rough hands grabbed for Gideon. He got into a fighting stance and swatted them away. He punched several of the miners in the face. He kicked at others.

"Oh no you don't. Not on my watch." Frank fired the DNA scrambler into the crowd. The weapon made a low rumble reminding Gideon of an old fashioned motorcycle.

Several miners screamed as they watched their friends melt into a bloody, gelatinous mess. Then the mob turned on Frank. They grabbed the DNA scrambler and smashed it.

"Wait a minute," Doctor Wells said.

But he was too late. The mob overwhelmed him. The air filled with the grunts and shouts of the mob intermixed with the snapping of bones, cries of pain and the crackling of Shockers.

Gideon tried to duck and spin his way free but there were too many miners. As soon as he spun free from one set of angry hands, there was another. He was dragged to the ground as someone grabbed his backpack.

Gideon slid out of his backpack only to see his Quarantine Release Papers fall to the ground. Turning, he raised his hands readying himself for a fight just in time to see several darts hit the legs and feet of the men around him. The men fell screaming in pain while holding onto the darts lodged in their bodies. After a few more of the men hit the ground, the mob slowed and then stopped.

Gideon knew instantly whom the darts belonged to. "Paige, nice of you to show up."

"Paige, what's the meaning of this?" Marcus grimaced as he tried to pull a dart from his thigh.

"Why don't ya tell me," Paige said, her accent thick and sharp. "Since when do we fight amongst ourselves, killin' our own no less? Not even Berserkers kill their own."

Paige inserted a fresh magazine of darts into the crossbow and raised it. The magazine whirred and spun. It stopped when a new dart was locked into place. "Back off now and let me see Doctur Wells."

"I'm over here, Paige."

Gideon felt a strong hand on his shoulder. The knuckles were bloodied and bruised. He looked up and saw his father. Doctor Wells had an intensity in his eyes that Gideon had never seen before. Both his cheeks were streaked with blood and his forehead was knotted and bruised. Although Gideon had never seen this side of his father before, he recognized the glare in his father's eyes. He knew it well. It was the same one that Gideon had after winning fights in Quarantine. It was a mix of fear, anger and satisfaction. It was why Adrian had nicknamed him Berserker. Looking at his father now, Gideon wondered what happened to the gentle scientist he remembered from his childhood.

"Here's your backpack, son." Doctor Wells dropped the pack at Gideon's feet. "Some papers fell out but it looks like most of your things are still inside."

"Are ya okay, Doctur Wells?" Paige held the crossbow primed and ready to fire.

"Yes, thank you."

"I'm fine too, thanks for asking," Gideon said.

Paige raised an eyebrow at Gideon. "I can see that ya are. I ain't blind."

Gideon scanned the crowd, looking for Frank and Vince. He found them both slightly bloodied about the face but other than that no worse off.

Vince held a fully charged Shocker in each hand and was using them to keep the mob from getting too close. Several miners were on the ground, some with smoke rising from their limp bodies. Vince took the Shocker in his left hand and tossed it to Frank who stood over a pile of no less than ten miners.

Frank easily caught the Shocker with his left hand. In his right hand, he held one of the miners by the throat, suspending the man at least two feet off the ground. The miner wriggled and squirmed until Frank dropped him. He inspected the Shocker and then to Gideon's surprise, started to spin and twirl the Shocker around his back and in front of his body. He then stabbed the ground in front of him. The orb crackled and popped with electricity.

Vince walked over to Frank. "Frankie, you good to go?"

"Good to go? V, I'm just getting started," roared Frank. "You people have no idea who you're messin' with. I've fought elite soldiers on every continent on Earth and every space station orbiting it. One soldier like me is worth fifty of you. Who else wants some?"

Gideon had never seen this side of Frank. It filled him with a mix of fear and jealousy.

"The doctor is fine, Paige," Marcus said. "We've no quarrel with him or you. We just want the boy. He's a Berserker after all."

A look of shock swept across Paige. She moved her crossbow away from the mob and took aim at Gideon. Her purple eyes drilled into him.

Gideon held his hands out in front of him. "That's not true. He's lying. I've only been Off World for a day. How can I be a Berserker?"

"I say we take the boy," said a voice in the mob.

"Yeah, everyone knows Paige doesn't kill," said another.

"You're a good girl, Paige. You won't kill me or any of us no matter what we do," Marcus said. "You're not a killer. Are you?"

Paige moved her crossbow from Gideon to the mob.

"You promised your mother right before she died that you would never kill." Marcus ripped a piece of cloth from his orange mining uniform and used it as a tourniquet around his leg. "Don't break your promise to mommy now."

A streak of purple tears rolled down Paige's face. She lowered the crossbow then wiped her face.

Gideon knew what it was like to be teased about your dead mother. Anger boiled inside of him. "Leave her alone." He started after Marcus but a strong hand held him back.

"Easy, Gideon," whispered Frank. "We've got them thinking twice about attacking us. Don't get stupid. There are too many of them."

Vince gave Gideon a curt nod. "Kid, pick up that Shocker for yourself and give one to your old man."

Gideon picked up the nearest Shocker and gave it to his father. The end of the staff glowed and flickered with electricity. He bent down to pick up another for himself when he noticed his Quarantine Release Papers blowing around. As he reached for the Shocker, he also saw Adrian's drawing of *Berserker the Merciless* floating toward him. He reached for it but a gust of wind blew it away from him and toward Marcus.

The drawing floated lazily toward Marcus on the soft breeze as if it were mocking Gideon. His throat tightened as the drawing hit Marcus squarely in the face. Gideon cursed his bad luck as he picked up the Shocker. It was heavy but not so much so that he couldn't use it. "Get ready, because we are in huge trouble."

"What are you talking about, Gideon?" Frank said.

"That piece of paper is going to be a problem."

"What's this?" Marcus pulled the paper from his face with his bloodied hands.

Gideon's body tensed as Marcus's eyes darted from the drawing to Gideon. Then Gideon's worst fears were realized when Marcus smiled. The smile reminded Gideon of how the Ripper looked as it readied itself to feed on him back in med-lab.

Marcus held up the drawing for all to see. "The boy lies. This paper proves he's a Berserker."

Just my luck to have a roommate that not only likes to draw but is good at it. Gideon gritted his teeth as the drawing made its way through the mob. Gasps and angry mutterings rumbled in waves. As each miner looked at the drawing, Gideon felt himself sinking deeper and deeper into a hole with no bottom.

"Kid, what gives?" Vince asked.

"My roommate back in Quarantine drew a picture of me as a monster. It was his idea of a practical joke. Unfortunately, it looks just like me and has *Berserker the Merciless* written on it."

The hunters both shot Gideon an angry look.

"Berserker was my nickname in Quarantine."

Doctor Wells sighed. "Most unhelpful, son."

"What? I didn't know he slipped it in with my release papers," Gideon said.

"Kid, fear is like the Virus," Vince said. "It's contagious and deadly, especially for a crowd like this. That piece of paper might as well be our death certificate."

"Get ready, V. They'll be coming for us soon," Frank said.

Gideon gripped his Shocker as tight as he could. A surge of energy coursed through his body as he held the weapon in front of him. Was it his own fear, his own anger that drove him or was it simply the electricity of the fully charged

Shocker? Gideon couldn't tell. Through the orange hue of his sunglasses, the angry, contorted faces of the mob didn't look human at all. Instead, the mob looked like a collection of evil puppets driven to cruelty by an evil puppeteer. As the mob moved toward him, Gideon squeezed the Shocker so hard his knuckles hurt.

Several darts landed in front of the mob, some even hitting the miners in the legs and feet. But the mob continued its slow determined push forward.

Paige stood next to Gideon. She aimed her crossbow and prepared to fire but suddenly lowered the bow toward the ground.

Marcus laughed. "That's what I thought you'd do Paige."

Gideon expected Paige to get teary-eyed again. She didn't. Instead, she grinned at Marcus like she had a secret.

"Yer right, I don't kill," Paige said. "But Kaz does. He's baagged over twenty Rippers and a few Berserkers. He's headed this way and he doesn't look too happy with ya at all Marcus. Ya might want to cop on and stop actin' the maggot."

Squinting against the glare of the twin suns, Marcus struggled to see who was approaching. As the figure came into focus, Marcus's shoulders sagged in defeat. Many in the mob simply turned and walked away.

Gideon followed the gaze of the mob to a boy not much older than himself. The boy was only slightly taller than Gideon but looked much stronger through the chest, shoulders and arms. He had dark hair and sharp features. He wore a traditional Japanese hip-length field jacket with tapered sleeves. The hippari jacket was brown and streaked with green and dark yellow. It overlapped in front and tied at the sides. His calf-length field pants were camouflaged like his jacket. His shoes were camouflaged ninja-style boots that were split into two sections at the toes. A bow and a quiver of arrows were slung across his back. But what drew Gideon's eye was the sword. It was long, thin and had a slight curve to it. Sunlight glistened off the blade, cutting into the eyes of some of the miners and blinding them.

Gideon recognized the sword. It was a samurai sword. Standing in front of the miners with his sword drawn, the boy looked like a Japanese prince.

"Kaz," Doctor Wells said. "Thank God you're here. We could use some help."

"Sorry I'm late, Senpai."

"We've no quarrel with you, Kaz." Marcus limped to a nearby Shocker and grimaced as he picked it up. He held the Shocker in his right hand and tightened the tourniquet on his leg with his left.

"If you plan on hurting Senpai then you most definitely have a quarrel with me," Kaz said, a nasty edge sharper than his sword tinged his voice.

"We just want the boy," Marcus said. "He's a Berserker and we intend to give him over to Gwendolyn. She promises a large reward and a halt to all Ripper attacks against this camp."

"You know better than to trust Gwendolyn," Kaz said.

Gideon could see the strength and confidence of Marcus being slowly replaced by fear as the mob broke up. Gideon had seen this type of situation play out with the bullies in Quarantine dozens of times. He lowered his Shocker. *Bullies back down whenever you confront them.*

"Marcus," Kaz said. "You know the doctor adopted me after the Berserkers killed my parents. That makes him and his son family and nobody hurts my family. Those days are over."

Kaz's words hit Gideon like a thunderclap. "What? You abandoned your family on Earth so you could have one here Off World? What's the matter, Dad, we weren't good enough for you?"

Doctor Wells took a deep breath. "As you're finding out, this is a harsh planet, Gideon. Kaz needed help after his parents died. I gave it to him. Your mother would have done the same thing. It doesn't change how I feel about you."

Gideon couldn't help but feel betrayed. Like burning rocket fuel, anger flamed inside him. "Did you get a substitute for Mom also? Maybe cook one up in your lab?"

Doctor Wells flushed with anger. "Be quiet, Gideon. This isn't the time or the place for this conversation."

A loud snap and a sharp crackling noise jolted Gideon.

Kaz stood over Marcus. Marcus' Shocker was sliced neatly in half. Small bolts of electricity danced between Kaz's sword and the now broken Shocker. Slowly the Shocker's electrically charged orb flickered, faded and then darkened.

Kaz eyed the last remaining members of the mob. When the last of them left, clearing the way to the camp's front gate, he sheathed his sword with one quick motion. Kaz bowed his head at Gideon. "Hello, brother."

"I am not your brother."

Chapter 12

Pieces of broken Shockers were scattered in between the dead miners. Gideon counted fifteen bodies. Those killed by Shockers were moved away from the front gate and covered with long grey tarps. They were placed in two neat rows of five. Miners killed by the DNA scrambler were covered with shorter black tarps and left where they fell. Gideon shuddered when he thought of what was underneath the black tarps.

A black-haired woman wearing a yellow bathrobe with a purple egg stain on the front of it knelt over one of the grey tarps. She was sobbing and repeating "why?" over and over. Doctor Wells helped her up and led her away by the hand.

A pang of guilt twisted in Gideon's chest. *Gus's wife.*

"Gus was a good man," Frank said.

Vince agreed. "He did okay by us and the kid. I got no complaints."

Paige sidled up to Gideon and the hunters. A small group of women and children were with her. The women were wearing orange mining uniforms. The children had brown pants and green shirts similar to Paige's. Purple tears ran down their cheeks. Their eyes were transfixed on the tarps. Each of the women and children had a marking stenciled on their cheeks. Some wore the Star of David, some a cross, while others a crescent moon and star. Then they split off into two groups to make way for a tall man dressed in a brown robe. His face was pale and on his forehead he wore each of the three religious symbols worn by the women and children. He carried a small book. Two guard bots followed him. Their flamethrowers hissed a bluish orange flame.

"Paige, what's going on?" Gideon whispered. "Is this a funeral?"

"We call it a flash funeral, Gideon. We have a readin' and then burn the bodies. We can't bury 'em cuz the Berskers dig 'em up and defile 'em."

Gideon thought of Sarah. He pictured her elongated purple head. The way her claws reached for him. How her jaw flashed open wide enough to devour his head in one bite. He swallowed the bile forming in the back of his throat when her words echoed in his mind's eye. *I'll eat every part of you. There won't be anything left of you. Not even for the rats.*

"Gideon," Frank called out. "Let's roll. It's time to head for the jumper."

"Yeah, kid. Come on," Vince said.

"What? Um, okay." Gideon turned to leave but stopped when Paige touched his shoulder.

"Gideon, will ya stand here with me for the readin'?" Paige's eyes welled with purple tears.

"Okay, Paige."

"Kid, what are you doing? There's no time for this."

"This won't take long, Vince. We'll make the time."

Vince reached for Gideon's arm but Frank stopped him. "V, let the funeral be. Stay here and guard Gideon. Make sure the miners don't try anything else stupid. I'll round up the Doc and Kaz. We leave for the jumper in five minutes."

"Okay, Frankie."

Paige took hold of Gideon's hand. She had long delicate fingers and a strong grip. The warmth of her hand spread throughout Gideon's body. She raised her arm and used Gideon's hand to wipe away the purple tears that rolled down her cheeks. The tears were hot.

"Life's a gift," she said. "What a waste to be dyin' like this."

Gideon's mind took him back to the funeral pyres that burned back on Earth. In his hometown, the bodies of those killed by the Virus were placed on makeshift funeral pyres. A skyline that was once lit by homes and office buildings was dotted with the pyres. The nighttime air often smelled like seared flesh. "When the Virus was bad on Earth, we had to burn our dead too."

Paige squeezed Gideon's hand.

The tall miner cleared his throat and started to read. All the women and children grabbed hands and bowed their heads. Gideon bowed his head and closed his eyes. He knew the prayer by heart. It was read at his mother's funeral. *At least she had a proper burial.*

"Even though I walk through the valley of the shadow of death, I will fear no evil, for you are with me; your rod and your staff, they comfort me."

Then the guard-bots rolled in and sprayed the tarps with a mix of fire and liquid fuel. The tarps flashed and ignited. The rush of heat forced Gideon back. The flames burned a bright white. It reminded Gideon of the sparklers his grandfather used to give him on the Fourth of July. Black smoke billowed up into the morning sky. *A quick burn, this is why Paige called it a flash funeral.*

When the last of the miner's bodies were burned, the guard bots shut down their flamethrowers. The tall, pale miner turned to leave. The stenciling on his face had run. The three religious symbols were now blurred together. The women and children followed him. Their crying was drowned out by the crackling of the white flames that now consumed their loved ones.

Paige released Gideon's hand and wiped the purple tears from her freckled face. "We try to burn the dead fast so thar's no smell but sometimes the Rippers still come."

The tarps were quickly reduced to a collection of smoldering, blackened ash piles. Smokey tendrils spiraled up into the sky. A strong breeze carried the smoke out over the forest.

Then a strange howling cut through the air. It sounded like a dog that was hurt, hungry and angry.

"Paige, what was that?" Gideon asked.

"Rippers, but so soon? That never happens."

"Do you know how long before they get here?"

"Thar comin' in from the south so I say maybe forty minutes. The camp defenses should keep 'em busy for awhile but we should leave fer yer ship now, Gideon."

"Hey, kid," Vince said. "Did you hear that? We need to get out of here. Let's go round up your old man so we can leave."

Gideon's father was across the courtyard. He was tending to the wounded miners under the shade provided by the housing units. Frank was leaning over him and pointing at Gideon. Doctor Wells shook his head. Then Kaz ran off toward med-lab.

"Come on, you guys. Frank needs help convincing my dad to leave." Gideon jogged across the courtyard. Paige and Vince were close behind him. There were dozens of wounded miners huddled against the walls of the housing units. Their groans filled the air. Most of the wounded had puncture wounds from Paige's darts. They held makeshift tourniquets while they waited for Gideon's father to tend to them. Others had broken bones that needed setting. Gideon felt their purple eyes on him. Most of the miners had venom in their eyes. Some looked away from him.

Frank leaned over and whispered in Gideon's ear. "Either you talk some sense into your old man, or we go to the jumper without him. We don't have time for his Good Samaritan routine. You read me, Gideon?"

"Yes, I understand, Frank."

"Marcus, you're lucky Paige is a good shot," Doctor Wells said. "She didn't hit anything vital."

"Dad, we need to leave. Paige says Rippers are coming."

"Son, we all heard the Rippers. It will take some time for them to get here. Let me finish treating these people. It shouldn't take long. I'm just waiting for Kaz to bring me a fully charged handheld laser. Look, here he is now."

"No, Dad. We need to leave now. I'm not hanging around here waiting for Rippers or anything else."

"Senpai, here's the handheld laser you asked for. I also brought the med-bot to speed things along," Kaz said.

"Senpai? Dad, why does he call you that?"

"Kaz is just being respectful to me. You should try it sometime."

Gideon grunted. *Respectful? More like a butt kisser.*

The med-bot was an older model. It was white with a red cross emblazoned on its front. The head was shaped like a kind old bear and it had a cartoonish smile on its face. Its small wheels crunched the dirt and grit underneath them as they pushed the robot slowly behind Kaz.

Marcus looked up at Gideon. For a brief moment they locked eyes. Marcus' purple eyes made Gideon recoil. Then Doctor Wells pulled the dart from

Marcus' leg. Marcus closed his eyes and grunted. Doctor Wells tossed the dart in Paige's direction. She picked it up, cleaned it and placed it in an empty magazine.

"Dad, are you coming or not?"

Doctor Wells gipped the handheld laser. It looked like a small pen-sized flashlight. "Marcus, hold still while I cauterize the wound. This is going to hurt."

Marcus grimaced as Doctor Wells sealed the wound shut. The smell of cauterized flesh seared the air. It reminded Gideon of the Lilac Festival—when the mob came for him and his mother. Those medics had a handheld laser too. *They said they had to stop the bleeding or I would die.* The memory of the sharp, burning pain tore through Gideon's forearms.

"Dad, this guy tried to kill me and you're helping him?"

"Of course I'm helping him."

"But why, why help these people after what they just did?"

Doctor Wells gave Gideon a stern look. "I'm helping them because I'm a doctor and because it's the right thing to do. Gideon, no matter how bad things get never lose faith in the capacity of people to do what's right. Deep down people are compassionate; they want to do the right thing. It's what makes us human."

"Dad, how can you say that after what just happened here? These people are no different than the ones back home. Do you remember the riots back home? When people first realized the Virus was out of control? Do you remember the Lilac Festival when Mom and I were attacked? Do you remember how I got these?" Gideon pulled up his sleeves exposing deep, knotted scars on both his forearms. The long scars crisscrossed his forearms like nasty railroad tracks.

"Of course, I remember the attack. Son, I need to tend to the wounded. I'll be with you in a moment."

"Whatever, Dad sometimes I wonder why you—"

The strange howling ripped through the air. Several guard-bots made their way to the front gate of the camp. Dozens of men with crossbows and Shockers followed after them.

Kaz pointed at Gideon. "Senpai, those Rippers were probably sent for him. Paige is right. We should leave."

"My name is Gideon."

"Right, you two haven't been properly introduced. Gideon, this is Kaz. You should consider him a friend and brother," Doctor Wells said.

"Save it, Dad, I know who he is. He's your *other* son. Don't worry, Kaz, I don't plan on staying here long enough to make friends with you or anyone else."

"Gideon, don't be rude," Doctor Wells said.

"After what just happened here you're worried about my manners?"

Kaz ignored Gideon and looked only at Doctor Wells. "Don't worry about the wounded. The med-bot can handle the rest. Come on, Senpai." Kaz then looked directly at Gideon. "Or should I say ... Dad."

"That's it," Gideon said. "It's official. You're a jerk."

Kaz took a step toward Gideon and bumped him with his chest. "Do I look like I care what you think?"

"Bring it, Kaz. I've fought worse than you."

Doctor Wells pulled the two boys apart. "Take it easy, fellas."

Gideon pushed his sleeves back down over his forearms. "Do what you want, Dad. I'm leaving for my jumper. You can have the samples I brought when I get back here."

Doctor Wells raised his eyebrows. "The samples? Yes, of course. I'll come with you right now. The med-bot can handle the rest."

Gideon and Paige jogged out of the front gate of the mining camp followed by Kaz and Doctor Wells. Frank and Vince brought up the rear. Separating the mining camp from the forest was a field about the length of a soccer pitch. It was carpeted with drooping purple, pink and yellow wildflowers that came up to the top of Gideon's flight boots. As Gideon made his way through the field, the flower heads lifted themselves and turned toward him. They opened and closed like blinking eyes and coated Gideon's flight boots with a fine purple powder. The sweet smell of pollen made his nose itch. Gideon fought the urge to sneeze. Intermixed with the flowers, were burnt patches and blackened piles of malformed bones. Gideon guessed the bones were from Rippers who had been set afire by the guard-bots at the mining camp. There were no insects or birds in the field. A tense quiet filled the air. It reminded Gideon of a no-man's land. At the edge of the field, the wildflowers gave way to a line of tall conifer trees.

"Let's stop here and go over the plan, Senpai. The last thing we want to do is to be unprepared in case we run into any Rippers," Kaz said.

"Wait a second. Who put you in charge? Stopping is stupid. It just gives the Rippers time to catch up to us. I say we just keep running until we get to my jumper," Gideon said.

"For once I agree with the kid," Vince said.

"Gideon's right. Me and V have the ship's coordinates right here in our wrist pads. Do you even know where you're going?" Frank asked.

"Of course, the ship is about four miles west of here. It's near the Bone Flowers," Kaz said.

"How do you know where the jumper is?" Gideon asked.

"Everybody in camp was talking about it."

"Well I'm not taking orders from a kid." Vince dug his Shocker into the ground. The orb crackled and popped with electricity.

"Nobody knows how to track Rippers or Berserkers like Kaz and Paige. It's why I asked them to come," Doctor Wells said.

"The girl's proven herself," agreed Frank. "Me and V have seen her in action. We don't know anything about you, Kaz."

"The only thing I've seen him do is slice a Shocker in half," Gideon said.

Kaz grit his teeth and squeezed his sword's hilt so hard the leather squeaked. "Gideon-san, you don't know—"

"If ya trust me, then ya can trust Kaz," Paige said.

Vince walked up to Kaz and stared him straight in the eye. The hunter wasn't much taller than Kaz but he was much thicker and stronger looking. "This ain't Halloween. You dressing like a ninja ain't impressin' me, boy. This mission ain't my first rodeo. What makes you so special that I need to be following you?"

Kaz didn't flinch. "My mother was turned into a Berserker. I tracked her for three weeks. When I found her she begged me to end her shame. I killed her."

Gideon's mouth dropped open. He had lost his mother to the Virus so he knew what it was like to lose a parent—but to have to kill your own mother because she was turned into a monster? Gideon looked at his father as if he had committed an unspeakable crime. *You did this. You turned his mother and others into monsters.*

"So that's it?" Vince said. "That qualifies you to take point on this mission?"

"Since then I've bagged about two dozen Berserkers and about a dozen Rippers. How about you? Judging from those sunglasses and that flight suit, you're a new-comer here. So this is in fact your first rodeo."

Vince bristled. "We know what we're doing. Me and Frankie were both in the Corps. We trained with the best."

"Hoorah, V," Frank said.

"If you guys were in the Corps, then you should have no problem following orders," Kaz said.

Oh no, you did not just say that to Vince.

Vince pointed the Shocker at Kaz's chest. "What did you just say to me? Frankie, can you believe this kid?"

"Disrespectful, no question about it, V."

Kaz took a step back and unsheathed his sword in one fluid motion.

"We don't have time for this. What happened to five days in and out, not one day more? We're already into Day Two of this mission. I don't know about you guys but I don't want to get stuck on this rock. Paige and I are going to the jumper. You guys can stand here and wait for the Rippers to attack the mining camp for all I care." Gideon pushed his way past Kaz and disappeared into the forest.

Paige followed after him. "Gideon, don't be an eejit and go off by yerself."

CHAPTER 13

Inside the forest, a mix of rotting wood, pine needles and dead leaves gave off a dank and musty smell. Rays of intense sunlight stabbed through the tree canopy, allowing Gideon to easily see the path he had taken the night before. The path snaked its way between tall conifer trees that filled the forest. Several small, blue birds fluttered close to a nearby branch. Instantly the branch extended its pine needles into long tentacles. The tentacles grabbed the birds and pulled them into a large hole in the trunk. A sickening crunching sound came from inside the tree. All that remained of the birds were a few blue feathers that floated aimlessly to the ground.

"Paige, did you see that? Do the trees eat people too?"

"Only skinny Earthlin' boys."

"Ha, ha."

"Don't worry, Gideon, not everythin' in the forest is dangerous. Come over here. You look thirsty."

Gideon swallowed. His throat was dry and parched. *How did she know?* "Do we have time for this?"

"This'll take less time than yer friends and Kaz will take arguin' over who's the bigger man." Paige walked to the edge of the path and knelt near a cluster of yellow flowers. She quickly dug at the flowers trying to expose their roots. As she dug, Gideon could see her cleavage.

Suddenly, Paige stopped digging. She looked down at her shirt and glanced up at Gideon. "Yer a bold one aren't ya?"

Gideon's face flushed hot. Sweat trickled down his back. "No, I wasn't, I was just—"

"Uh huh, likely story." Paige pulled several of the flowers out of the ground root and all. Then she plucked off the small plump root balls and handed one to Gideon.

"Um, thanks. What do I do with it?"

"It's called sugar root." Paige took a bite of the root and sucked a yellow liquid into her mouth. "It's better than any lemonade ya ever had." She smiled her whole face lighting up as she did. "Ya do know what lemonade is, don't ya?"

"Lemonade, really?" Gideon broke open the sugar root and drank the yellow liquid. It was sweet and made his tongue tingle. Soon the tingling sensation spread through his body like thousands of little fingers massaging him from the inside out. "That is good."

"Best part is ya won't need to be drinkin' any water for the rest of the day."

"Cool. Now I know why the kids back at the mining camp like it so much."

Paige deftly wove the yellow flowers from the sugar root plant into her red hair using them to secure her long ponytail. Her harsh, tough exterior melted away before Gideon's eyes as she concentrated on arranging the flowers. "Thar, purrfect. The flowers are supposed to bring luck."

A surge of warmth ran through Gideon's body. *She's beautiful.*

"Ya okay, Gideon? Ya don't look so good."

"Fine, fine," Gideon stammered. "Just getting used to the sugar root is all." Eager to change the subject, he pointed back at the mining camp. "Where are the others? Are they coming?"

"It looks like they sorted it out. Here comes Kaz and the rest of 'em now."

"You hunters use the Shockers to keep any Rippers away. The electrical charge will freeze them just long enough for me and Paige to hit them in a vital spot," Kaz said.

"That sounds fine except Paige doesn't shoot to kill," Frank said. "I don't mind setting up a Berserker or a Ripper for a kill shot, but if she's just going to wound them, this plan won't work."

"Gwendolyn's Rippers die in twelve hours," Paige said. "They're already dead but don't know it so I got no problem puttin' 'em down. As for

Berserkers, thar won't be any out in the forest. They stay near the minin' camps so they can eat."

Gideon thought of Sarah. *I'll eat every part of you. There won't be anything left of you. Not even for the rats.* "So we have one less creepy creature to worry about."

"That's the spirit, son. We're going to be fine out here," Doctor Wells said.

A pained, angry howl echoed through the air.

"Not if we don't get a move on. We need to double-time it to the jumper. I don't want to be out here fighting Rippers with just a Shocker, Frankie."

"Damn straight, V. Come on, Gideon let's roll," Frank said.

Gideon's group jogged down the twisting path. Paige and Kaz took the lead, followed by Doctor Wells, and Gideon. Frank and Vince brought up the rear. The morning air was cool. Rays of sunlight sliced through the tree canopy and carved bright holes in the dark shadows created by the trees. The group's footfalls thumped against the hardened, packed dirt of the path. Gideon remembered what Paige said to the hunters just last night when they first met her. *You're stomping through the forest like lost elephants.* Now she was leading him to the jumper. But unlike everyone else, her footfalls were silent. She moved like she was part of the forest. Her crossbow was slung across her back and fastened so it didn't make any noise. Her camouflage cloak flowed around her as she moved. Her red ponytail with the yellow flowers in it waved like a banner.

"We should stop. Senpai needs to rest," Kaz said.

Gideon's father was panting. Sweat poured off him. "No, I'm fine. Just a bit winded is all."

"What about the Rippers?" Gideon asked.

"I don't hear anything, Gideon-san, do you?"

Gideon-san? What a butt kisser. "No, Kaz, I don't. But it doesn't mean we should stop."

"We can stop fer five minutes," Paige said.

"Five minutes?" Gideon looked at Frank and Vince.

Frank looked at his wrist-pad. "We've covered half the distance to the jumper. We can rest for five minutes. Okay, V?"

"If the Doc needs to rest, that's fine, Frankie. But no more stops until we get to the jumper." Vince jabbed his finger at Doctor Wells. "I'll drag you by your hair the last two miles if I have to."

"That won't be necessary. I'm fine really."

Gideon put his Shocker on the ground. It was getting heavy and his arms were tired. A swarm of insects that looked like fireflies buzzed overhead. About thirty yards off the trail, a large six-legged animal that looked like a deer lazily nibbled at some plants with purple flowers. Gideon counted eight horns on its head. It also had small tusks protruding from its mouth.

Kaz squeezed the hilt of his sword then adjusted the quiver of arrows and the bow strapped to his back. He scanned the tree canopy like a nervous animal.

"Hey, Kaz what are you looking at?" Gideon asked.

"The Peelers."

"The what?"

"See those birds? They're stalking us. I don't like them hanging around. It's a bad sign."

Thousands of black birds the size of crows flew overhead. They had one large purple eye in the middle of their head and four wings. They darted and hovered like hummingbirds. Their wings beat so fast they were just a blur. Except for the humming of their four wings, the birds were quiet. Their feet had long talons that looked like grappling hooks.

"Those are the weirdest birds I've ever seen. Kaz, are you saying they think we're going to die out here? That's why they're following us?"

"Like everything else in the forest, Gideon-san, they're looking for a meal."

Gideon picked up his Shocker. "They better stay away from me. I'm not going to be bird food."

"Five minutes are up. Let's move out," Vince said.

"The Peelers only eat new kills. So long as they don't smell fresh blood, thar's no problem," Paige said.

"What happens if they get a whiff of fresh blood?" Gideon asked.

"Ya don't want to be seein' it."

"Let's go," repeated Vince. The hunter had a nasty edge to his voice.

Kaz nocked an arrow and took aim at the horned, deer-like animal. "You want to see what they do to fresh meat? I'll show you."

"No, Kaz, don't be doin' anythin' stupid," Paige said.

"I said, move out," roared Vince. "We don't have time for you to be hunting." He reached for Kaz and spun him around just as Kaz was about to release his arrow. When Kaz turned, the arrowhead sliced Vince across the neck.

Vince touched his neck and looked at his hand. It was covered in blood.

The blood flowed down his neck. It covered the front of his flight suit.

"His blood's red?" Paige asked. "It ain't purple?"

"What did you do, Kaz?" Gideon shouted.

"I'm sorry. It was an accident. He grabbed me when I was about to fire."

Frank shoved Kaz to the ground. "Get the hell outta my way. V, are you okay?"

"I've been sliced worse, Frankie."

Then the forest went dark. The swarm of Peelers blotted out the rays of sunlight that stabbed through the holes in the tree canopy. The thrumming of their wings was so loud it sounded like a plane was flying overhead. Thousands of purple eyes bore into Gideon. Their beaks opened horizontally and vertically exposing rows of sharp teeth. Then the birds dove straight for Vince. Gideon raised his Shocker.

Paige pushed Vince up the trail. "Run or yer dead. The birds will skin ya alive."

Vince took off down the trail. He was running and swinging his Shocker wildly as the Peelers tore at him. Their claws tore at his neck while their beaks bit at his head. He dropped the Shocker and tried to cover his face and head with his arms. He looked like a boxer. Then Vince staggered. His legs gave out and he collapsed onto the trail. Then the flock of Peelers fell on Vince like a school of winged piranha and he disappeared under a cloud of flapping wings snapping beaks and razor sharp talons.

"What . . . what are they doing to him?" Gideon said.

"I'm coming, V." Frank grabbed his Shocker and chased after Vince.

Gideon started after Frank but Paige grabbed him by the arm. "What are you doing? Let me go, Paige."

Paige shook her head. "Thar's nothin to be done for 'em."

"What does that mean? We just let him die?"

"Son, it's already over," Doctor Wells said.

Frank swung his Shocker at the Peelers. When the flock lifted off Vince the only thing left of him was his skeleton. Frank sank to his knees. He dropped the Shocker in the dirt and bowed his head. "Damn, V. Ain't supposed be like this."

Gideon was dumbfounded. "They . . . peeled . . . everything . . . off . . . him."

Paige squeezed Gideon's arm. She pulled him close and whispered into his ear. "I'm sorry about yer friend. The forest can be a harsh place. Right now, I think ya need to be talkin' to Frank so we can get 'em to yer ship. We can't be hangin' around out here."

Gideon glanced at Kaz. *We should have never stopped.* Kaz sat on the trail not far from where Frank shoved him to the ground. His head was in his hands. Doctor Wells was trying to comfort him.

Kaz said, "I just wanted to feed the Peelers so they wouldn't bother us. He shouldn't have grabbed my arm like that when I was trying to shoot."

Gideon rolled his Chain of Remembrance between his fingers. He slowly approached Frank. Vince's bones lay on the trail. They gleamed. His skull had a leering grin. *The Peelers took every part of him.* Gideon took a deep breath. *I hope Vince didn't suffer.* "Frank, I'm sorry about Vince. He was brave and really tough."

"He was more than that, Gideon. He was loyal." Frank pulled the wrist-pad from Vince's skeletal wrist. He wiped the blood from it and handed it to Gideon. "Here, take this. In case we get separated, use this to get to the jumper."

The black wrist-pad looked like an old fashioned watch that Gideon's grandfather once wore. It had a touch screen with several nav-buttons on it—the one for the jumper was a silhouette of a plane. The screen was wiped clean but the black wristband was wet to the touch. "Thanks, Frank. But why would we get separated? The jumper is only two miles from here."

"On this rock, a lot can happen in two miles. Not only that, I ain't convinced this was an accident. Kaz was wrong, your old man didn't need any rest and if Kaz is half as good with a bow as he is with that sword, he should have never sliced V with the arrowhead like that."

At least he trusts Paige.

"And why didn't Paige warn us about those damn Peelers? She's supposed to be some sort of expert woodsman and tracker."

"Frank, what are you saying?" Gideon asked.

Then the strange howling cut through the air. Screams and the snapping and crackling of the mining camp's electrical fence followed.

"I'm saying you need to watch your back," hissed Frank. "I don't trust either one of 'em."

"The Rippers are at the minin' camp. I'm sorry about yer friend but we should go," Paige said.

"I'm sorry as well," Doctor Wells said.

Kaz bowed so low his forehead almost touched the ground. He raised himself back up and said, "I'm truly sorry about your friend. He was a good soldier."

"Save it," Frank said. "Let's roll before the Peelers or the Rippers finish us off. I ain't dyin' on this rock."

Chapter 14

The flock of Peelers stalked Gideon as he jogged up the trail. The birds darted overhead and zigzagged in front of him. The thrumming of their wings buzzed in his ears. Some of the Peelers hovered so close Gideon could see their large purple eye boring into him. He jabbed his Shocker at the closest Peeler but missed. The Peeler was too quick and nimble. It easily dodged the thrust.

"Leave 'em be, Gideon. So long as thar's no blood on ya, the Peelers won't be a problem," Paige said.

Gideon looked at his wrist-pad. His wrist wasn't as thick as Vince's so Frank strapped it to Gideon's forearm so it wouldn't fall off. The face of the wrist-pad was clean. The touch screen was spotless. The nav buttons easy to see. But the strap that held it onto Gideon's forearm was damp. *Is it Vince's blood that makes the strap feel wet? How much blood would it take to attract the Peelers? Can the Peelers smell it?* Gideon held the wrist-pad up to his nose.

"Gideon, what are you doing? The wrist-pad ain't a scratch-n-sniff," Frank said.

"I'm wiping my nose."

"If you say so. Listen, I wiped the wrist-pad clean. There's no blood on it so don't worry."

Gideon thought of Vince. *Don't worry? Are you crazy?*

Then a group of nearby Peelers hovered near Gideon. Their four wings were a blur. Sharp talons hung underneath their bodies like meat hooks. The Peelers studied Gideon with their single purple eye. Each eye moved slowly up and down, taking in every inch of Gideon. *They're doing a diagnostic check like a computer. Are they trying to decide where to bite first?* Then the Peeler's beaks seemed to unfold around their heads. The single purple eye widened and thousands of sharp teeth flashed. The Peelers raised their talons. Gideon swung his Shocker as hard as he could. The impact sounded like a baseball leaving a metal bat. The reverberation shook Gideon's hands and ran up his arms. But he held onto the Shocker as the Peelers rocketed through the air and hit a nearby tree. The tree's branches grabbed the Peelers and stuffed them into the hole in its trunk. "I said I wasn't going to be bird food!"

"That's right. V was enough. No more," Frank's sunglasses hid the hunter's eyes but there were wet streaks in the dirt on his face.

Was he crying?

"Quit actin' like an eejit, Gideon. I told ya the Peelers won't be botherin' ya none," Paige said.

"After what happened to Vince, I'm not taking any chances, Paige."

"Nice shot. But if I were you, I'd get rid of that Shocker, Gideon-san," Kaz said.

The orb on the end of the Shocker was smashed. It was covered with blood and feathers. Gideon raised it like a spear and tossed it into the forest.

"Son, did you . . . get . . . any blood . . . on you?"

Gideon's checked his hands and arms. "No, Dad, I'm okay to go. But you don't look so good."

Doctor Wells was heaving. His face was beat red. Sweat poured from him. "I'm out … of shape." Then he tripped, fell and landed face first onto the trail. When he sat up, there was a cut on his forehead. Purple blood trickled down his face.

"Dad, you're bleeding."

Paige drew a quick breath. "No."

Doctor Wells touched his forehead and looked at his hand. His eyes went wide when he saw the purple stain on his fingers.

"Dad, run before the Peelers come."

"Son, if Vince couldn't outrun them, then neither can I. Take your friends and go. Leave me."

"Dad, I'm not leaving you here for the Peelers. Don't be stupid."

"Neither am I, Senpai." Kaz nocked an arrow and dropped to one knee.

"What the hell are you doing?" Frank said.

"I'm giving the Peelers something else to eat." Kaz scanned the forest and raised his bow. "Leave me alone and let me shoot."

About twenty-five yards off the trail, there was a cluster of broken and felled trees. They were covered in purple fuzz that Gideon guessed was moss.

Overhead, Peelers started to gather.

"There's nothing out there, Kaz. Come on, we need to go," Gideon said.

Doctor Wells wiped the blood from his forehead. "I agree. You should all go before the Peelers come for me."

"Thar's his target. It wants to feed on the moss," Paige said.

Gideon squinted at the purple moss. "I don't see anything."

Then the air near the trees bent and shimmered. A creature like a giant turtle appeared. *It's just like the old holographic games. But this is real.* The turtle was as big as a truck. The shell on its back was covered with thick spikes. As the creature moved closer to the purple moss covered trees, its shell changed colors to match its surroundings. What was once a brown and green shell was now mostly purple. The turtle stuck its thick, veiny neck out from underneath its shell and reached for the moss. When it opened its mouth, a long purple tongue scraped the moss off one of the broken trees. Then in quick succession, three of Kaz's arrows hit a large vein in the turtle's neck. The turtle raised its head and hissed in pain. Purple blood gushed.

The sky overhead grew dark. The thrumming of thousands of wings filled the air. Then the Peelers attacked the giant turtle. The turtle hissed as the Peelers tore at it. It withdrew its head and legs into its shell but the Peelers followed inside. The shell rocked back and forth.

Gideon pulled his father up off the ground. "Let's get out of here before the Peelers finish off that turtle." Then a strangled, angry howl ripped through the air.

"That sounded close," Frank said.

Kaz agreed. "The Rippers got in front of us somehow."

Paige turned on Kaz. "Take 'em to the Bone Flowers. We'll lose the Rippers in thar." She pulled her camouflage cloak up over her head. Her red hair disappeared. She unfastened her crossbow from her back and leveled it front of her. The circular magazine buzzed and whirred as it fed darts into the crossbow.

Then she left the trail and sprinted through the trees. Her cloak flowed around her as she melted into the forest.

Most people run away from Rippers. She chases after them?

Kaz took off down the trail. "Follow me."

Doctor Wells chased after Kaz.

Gideon started to follow but Frank stopped him. "It looks like Kaz can shoot pretty straight when he wants to. Gideon, you and me are going to the jumper and that's all. You copy that?"

"Yes, I understand. But do you really think Kaz killed Vince?"

"I don't trust anybody here but you. Let's get to the jumper. It's only about a mile and a half out. Keep your eye on the wrist-pad and don't go anywhere that doesn't take you to the jumper."

Gideon and Frank easily caught up to Kaz and Doctor Wells. Kaz moved effortlessly across the trail. The black, split toe tabi boots masked his footfalls. His camouflage ninja suit blended with the trees making it difficult to see him. Except for the bow and quiver of arrows bouncing against his back, he would have been nearly invisible.

Doctor Wells was red-faced and panting.

Gideon checked his wrist-pad. *The jumper is now only a mile away.* Then a dog-like yelp echoed through the forest. It was followed by two more. Above him, Gideon saw a surge of Peelers fly by. *Dad.* He raised his Shocker and sprinted toward his father but the Peelers kept on going. *Where are they going?* Then Gideon passed by two large, dog-like skeletons lying by the edge of the trail. Their snouts were elongated and out of proportion to their heads. They each had Paige's darts sticking out of the eye sockets of their skulls. *Paige shot them and the Peelers finished them off.*

At the edge of the forest, Paige was waiting. Gideon checked his wrist-pad. *Jumper is a quarter mile out.* She held out her hands, gesturing for Gideon to stop. "Why are we stopping? What's the problem, Paige?"

"I cleared out most of the Rippers that came from the Raider ship. But we need to be careful goin' out across that open field. Thar may be more."

"A Raider ship? What's that?"

"They're like pirates, Gideon-san, only worse," Kaz said.

"A ship explains how the Rippers got in front of us." Frank pointed his Shocker at Doctor Wells. "Did you know Gwendolyn had a mobile lab?"

Doctor Wells tried to catch his breath. He shook his head. "I didn't know . . . Gwendolyn gave the Raiders . . . Ripper technology."

"So we've got Rippers coming up the trail from the mining camp, some more in front of us and Peelers? What are we going to do?" Gideon asked.

"We're going to run like hell to the jumper before we get boxed in is what we're gonna do," Frank said.

"Frank-san, we'll never make it to the jumper before the Rippers catch us."

"Why are you saying that?" Gideon asked.

Kaz pointed his bow at Doctor Wells. He was doubled over and wheezing.

You're right, Kaz. But I'm not telling you that. Gideon peered out through the trees. There was a grassy field covering the two hundred yards separating the forest and the field of Bone Flowers. Beyond the Bone Flowers was the lakeshore. The white sandy beach was a stark contrast to the black wormhole jumper. The jumper sat on the beach half-buried. The front edge of its wings and part of the nose was covered with sand. It made the ship look like it was burrowing and trying to hide from some predator. Sunlight reflected off the windows of the cockpit. It signaled Gideon like a friend lost in the wilderness. It seemed like a thousand years ago when he last saw his ship. Gideon beamed. "There's my ship. The jumper is just past those weird flowers."

"That's where we make our stand against the Rippers," Paige said. "Inside the Bone Flowers, we can buy enough time to get ya onboard yer ship. Me and Kaz will cover ya while ya make yer way across the field."

"No way," countered Gideon. "I'm not leaving you out here with Rippers and Peelers running around."

"Me and Kaz will be fine."

"We should stick together."

"Gideon's right. We'll make a fire team wedge. Paige can run and shoot with the crossbow so she'll be out front. Kaz will be in the rear with the bow. Me, and the Doc will be on the outside using Shockers. Got it?"

"What about me, Frank?"

"Gideon, you stay in the middle of the formation and clean up anything me or your father miss."

"I can do more than just stand in the middle of the formation."

"I know you can, Gideon. But I need you in one piece so you can fly the jumper," Frank said. "Doc, you good to go?"

Doctor Wells gave a thumbs-up.

Gideon stepped out from the tree line and into the marshy field. The short grass squished under his flight boots as he jogged behind Paige. Paige had her hood pulled up over her head and her crossbow raised. Frank was on Gideon's left; his father was on his right. Kaz brought up the rear of the fire team wedge. Gideon's arms hurt from carrying the Shocker but he gritted his teeth and held it out in front of him.

The dense, heavy air of the forest gave way to a fresh, crisp, salty breeze that blew in from the lake. The lake was a deep blue—white-crested waves crashed onto the sandy shore. Overhead, a large grey bird with four wings dove toward the water with its talons extended. The bird snatched a massive blue and white fish from the lake. The fish had a long sword for a snout. It tried to stab the bird but failed. The fish continued to struggle until the bird tore it in half with its talons. It ate one half of the fish and flew on with the other half gripped firmly in its talons. Just off the horizon was a long ship.

"That must be the Raider ship. It looks like a mining ship," Frank said.

"How can you see that far without binoculars, Frank?"

"On the side of your sunglasses are two buttons, Gideon. One is to increase magnification. The other is for night vision."

Gideon pressed the side of his sunglasses. The sunglasses buzzed and hummed as the lenses increased the magnification. "I see it now."

The ship had a black and red colored hull. The deck was covered with cranes and other equipment. Two large grey parachutes were attached to the bow. The parachutes read, "Muramatsu Mining Corporation."

"What's with the parachutes?"

"They're solar powered sails not parachutes, Gideon-san. We used them to save fuel costs," Kaz said.

"We?"

"My family used to own the mining operations here."

"That Raider ship used to belong to your family?"

"Yes, Gideon-san. Most of the Raiders used to work for us. When mining operations stopped because of the Virus, some of the miners stole what they could and went out on their own. Unfortunately, they continue to steal and worse."

"Losing everything like that must have been rough," Frank said. "Surprised you aren't fighting to get it back."

Kaz didn't answer.

Gideon's Chain of Remembrance bounced against his chest as he jogged. *Everybody lost something or someone to the Virus.*

"We got incoming on the left," announced Frank.

Two large, dog-like creatures charged at them from the lakeshore. The animals were brown and had elongated snouts. *They're like the skeletons in the forest.* "What are those things?"

"Kaz, take them Rippers out," Paige called out.

Kaz stopped and dropped to one knee. He nocked an arrow and fired.

They're at least two hundred yards out. No way does he hit them.

As soon as the first arrow left his bow, Kaz nocked and fired another. Both arrows arched through the air like missiles and hit the Rippers in the neck. The Rippers yelped and collapsed into the marshy field.

Kaz sprinted back to Gideon.

"Nice shooting," Gideon said.

"It looks like you're as good with that bow as you are your katana," Frank said.

Kaz bowed his head. "Thank you, Frank-san."

Then the Rippers got back up. They shook themselves off like wet dogs, which made the arrow in their neck wobble back and forth. Then they broke into a run. The arrow sticking out of their neck bounced up and down as they closed the distance with Gideon. "They're not dead."

"They regenerate," Doctor Wells said.

Kaz dropped to his knee and fired more arrows, hitting the Rippers in the face and neck. But the monsters kept coming.

Gideon was about twenty-five yards from the edge of the Bone Flower field. "We'll never make it to the Bone Flowers before the Rippers catch us." The field of Bone Flowers ran parallel to the lakeshore—seeing it in daylight made the flowers seem larger than Gideon remembered. The tall rows of Bone Flowers reminded him of the sunflowers his mother grew in their backyard before the Virus. *But those aren't flowers. They're eyeless skulls with razor sharp teeth.*

"We stop and fight," Frank said.

The fire team wedge turned and faced the oncoming Rippers. Gideon held the Shocker out in front of his body. The orb on the end bristled with electricity. Adrenaline coursed through his body. It made him lightheaded. Sweat dripped into his eyes. He tightened his grip on his Shocker. The Rippers thundered toward him. Kaz's arrows wobbled back and forth in their face and neck. The Rippers were less than fifty yards away. Then the whir of Paige's crossbow cut through the air.

A volley of darts took the eyes of each Ripper. The Rippers howled and collapsed.

"Come on, Doc. Let's use the Shockers." Frank charged ahead and jammed his Shocker into a Ripper. The Ripper shook violently.

Doctor Wells stood frozen in place. "I . . . can't do it. I'm not a soldier."

Gideon shoved his way past his father ran up to the Ripper and jammed his Shocker into its side. The Ripper convulsed as electricity from the Shocker tore through it. Smoke rose from its body. It struggled to get back up but its legs wobbled and the Ripper sank back into the marshy field.

"Enough, Gideon," Doctor Wells said.

Gideon pulled back his Shocker as Kaz drew his sword. With an easy swipe, Kaz took the heads of each Ripper. He cleaned the purple blood off the sword with a flick of his wrist. The metal blade made a scraping noise against the scabbard as he sheathed his sword. "Let the Peelers have them."

"Are they dead?" asked Gideon.

"Yes. Taking their heads kills them. They can't regenerate from that," Doctor Wells said.

Then the Peelers erupted from the forest. The black flock darted like a school of fish and headed for the dead Rippers.

"Ya need to be gettin' clear of that Peeler food," Paige said.

Gideon, Frank and Kaz ran back to Paige and Doctor Wells. Gideon checked himself for signs of Ripper blood. There wasn't any.

The Peelers descended on the Rippers and quickly went to work peeling the meat from their bones. When the Peelers flew away, two gleaming skeletons were left where the Rippers fell.

"I never thought I'd be happy to see Peelers," Gideon said.

"Let's get to the jumper before more Rippers show up," Frank said.

"Aye, the ones from the minin' camp should be here soon. We need to be gettin' to the Bone Flowers." Paige pulled up her camouflage hood. Only her purple eyes were visible. Like a predator, her eyes narrowed into slits. They radiated anger and hunger.

"Paige? What is it?"

"Listen good to what I'm tellin ya, Gideon. The flowers sleep durin' the day. So long as ya don't wake 'em, they won't bother ya. Do ya understand?"

Gideon thought back to when he threw the stick at the Bone Flower the night before. The flower's razor sharp teeth easily snapped it in half. "Yes, I get it. You want us to walk through a field of flesh-eating flowers."

"That could be worse than facing the Rippers," Frank said.

"Frank-san, Gideon-san, the Rippers will think twice about following us into the Bone Flower field."

"Paige is right, son."

I hope she knows what she's doing.

Frank nodded. "Let's do this."

"Follow me and touch nothin'," Paige said.

Out of the forest, six large dog-like Rippers with elongated snouts came charging toward Gideon. They looked like the Rippers Gideon had just fought. Their jaws snapped vertically and horizontally. Kaz stood and fired a volley of arrows. Three Rippers were hit in the neck. The arrows stuck out of them like porcupine quills. But they kept coming.

"We have to go now," Paige said.

Gideon took a deep breath. He followed Paige and his father into the field of Bone Flowers. Kaz came next followed by Frank. The flowers had long green stems with bony-looking thorns. The flowers were taller than Gideon. But the skull-like flower heads were heavy, causing the stems to bend and droop dangerously close to Gideon's head and neck.

The ground was covered with the bones of small birds and animals. There were skeletons of four winged birds and animals no bigger than squirrels with six legs and long tails. Every step Gideon took crunched underneath his feet. It sounded like he was walking across potato chips.

Gideon wove his way through the maze of Bone Flowers careful not to touch any of them. As he crunched his way deeper into the field, a terrible odor assaulted him. He put his hand over his mouth and nose and tried not to gag. "It smells like something died in here."

Paige pointed toward a clearing in the middle of the field. There were dozens of broken flower stems and crushed flowers. The damaged flower heads looked like smashed skulls. "It looks like something crashed into the field. But the jumper didn't crash here it—" Then Gideon saw it. The half-eaten carcass of a massive bird lay in the middle of the Bone Flower field. It had Bone Flowers stuck to its wings and head. *Even in death, the flowers refused to let go.*

The bird was as big as a car. It could easily carry Gideon. It looked like the same kind of bird Gideon saw pull the fish out of the lake. It had blue-grey feathers, four wings and three eyes. The remains of a large blue and white fish were clutched in its lifeless talons. Sticking through the bird's chest was the fish's long, sword-like snout.

Gideon made a face like he ate something bad tasting. "That's gross."

"It's a dead lake hawk," Paige said.

"The fish impaled the lake hawk," Doctor Wells said.

Kaz examined the corpse. "Yeah, it looks like its dinner killed it."

"That fish had spirit. Just like a soldier in the Corps— no retreat, no surrender."

"Quiet. The Rippers are here," Paige said.

The Rippers were at the edge of the field. Except for the elongated snouts, these Rippers looked like a pack of regular brown dogs. They reminded Gideon of his own dog, Cocoa—the Chocolate Labrador Retriever he used to have back on Earth before the Virus. The Rippers sniffed at the ground and air.

"Dad, I thought there were no dogs here," Gideon whispered.

"Trust me, those aren't dogs. They're Rippers."

"They don't look like the one in med-lab or the ones we just took down. They look like Cocoa," Gideon said. "How did Gwendolyn know to make dogs that look like him?"

"Son, the Ripper you saw in med-lab was a newer, upgraded version of Gwendolyn's combat soldiers. The Rippers out there are primitive creations at best."

"They look lean and fast. They're probably recon units," Frank said.

Gideon's eyes went wide. He realized that what he thought was brown fur was some sort of protective body armor. It looked like the tiles on the wormhole jumper. The Rippers had spikes on their backs and horns where an Earth dog would normally have ears. "Yeah, those are definitely not dogs."

"Shush," hissed Paige.

The Rippers hovered at the edge of the field. They continued snuffling and sniffing. Some of them ran along the border of the Bone Flower field. Gideon recognized the behavior from the hunting trips he had taken with his father and grandfather. *They're trying to catch our scent but can't.* Gideon looked at the dead lake hawk. He slowly made his way toward it and crouched down next to it.

Paige nodded her understanding. She followed close behind Gideon. "The smell of the bird carcass is maskin' our scent."

Kaz crouched next to Gideon. His camouflage hood was pulled up over his head and he had a black mask pulled up over his mouth and nose. Only his intense purple eyes showed. He had an arrow nocked and ready to fire.

He looks like a ninja.

Frank and Doctor Wells kneeled next to the dead bird. Skeletons of small animals crunched under their knees.

Frank winked at Gideon. "Smart, the Rippers can't smell us."

"Look, they're leaving," Gideon said.

The Rippers raced toward the lakeshore. Then Gideon heard a low thrumming. A dark cloud emerged from the forest. It banked left then darted to the right before hovering over Gideon's hiding spot in the Bone Flowers.

"Those damn birds are going to give us away," Kaz said, his voice muffled by his mask.

"Maybe the Peelers want to eat the dead Lake Hawk."

"No, Gideon. Peelers won't be scavengin' and they won't risk comin' in here cuz of the Bone Flowers," Paige said.

The Rippers were back at the edge of the Bone Flower field. Their jaws snapped at the Bone Flowers. They made low, throaty growls at the long, green-stemmed plants. "They're going to come in here," Gideon said.

Then a Ripper bit the stem of a Bone Flower and started chewing on it as if it were a piece of meat. The Bone Flower's jaws flashed open. The plant bent over at the stem and sunk its jaws into the Ripper's hindquarter. The Ripper yelped and let go of the Bone Flower stem. The Bone Flower lifted the Ripper and tossed it high into the air. The Ripper landed in the Bone Flower field with a dull thud. The Bone Flowers nearest to it reared up and sunk their jaws into the Ripper. In a matter of minutes only the Rippers bones were left.

"There as fast as the Peelers," Gideon said.

Then the pack of Rippers charged into the Bone Flowers. They headed straight for Gideon.

Chapter 15

The Rippers zigzagged through the Bone Flowers trying to avoid the snapping jaws of the flowers. Some of the Rippers made it. The Bone Flowers ravaged those that didn't. The flowers worked together, biting, snapping and throwing the Rippers into the air like they were toys.

Gideon squeezed his Shocker. *Oh my God. I'm going to be torn to pieces by either the Rippers or these crazy flowers.*

Paige raised her crossbow. "Gideon, go to yer ship. Me and Kaz will stall 'em."

"What? Just leave you here?"

Paige didn't answer. She moved in between the Bone Flowers while firing volleys of darts at the Rippers. The camouflage cloak flowed around her as she moved. She never fired from the same spot and each volley was answered with a yelp or whimper from the Rippers. Bone Flowers bent and reached for her but she was too fast. She rolled away from a cluster of Bone Flowers and came up firing at the Rippers. Then she disappeared into the Bone Flower field.

"Gideon-san, go now." Kaz unsheathed his sword. He raised it above his head and cut down the Bone Flowers nearest to him. When he finished carving out a circular clearing for himself, he dropped to one knee and nocked an arrow. Bone Flowers snapped at him but he was out of reach. Kaz fired arrows faster than anyone Gideon had ever seen. Each arrow Kaz fired was answered by a high-pitched yelping.

Gideon squeezed his Shocker. *I should be in the fight. I wish I had a blaster or a crossbow like Paige's.*

"Come on, son. We need to get you out of here." Doctor Wells grabbed Gideon by the arm.

Gideon pulled away. "No, we need to help fight the Rippers."

"Gideon, that's not your mission. Your mission is to get to the jumper," roared Frank. "Don't make me carry you outta here."

Gideon turned on Frank when a Bone Flower reared up behind the hunter. Its jaws flashed open. Before Gideon could warn him, the Bone Flower sunk its teeth into Frank's calf. Frank was lifted off the ground by the Bone Flower and waved through the air like a flag.

Gideon raised his Shocker and jabbed it at the Bone Flower.

"No, Son, you'll electrocute him."

Gideon backed off. He jumped out of the way as Frank dropped his Shocker. The hunter pulled a long knife from his boot. He cut the head off the Bone Flower and fell to the ground. He tried to stand but collapsed in a heap at Gideon's feet. The Bone Flower head was still stuck to his calf. Nearby Bone Flowers reached for Frank but Gideon forced them back with his Shocker. Every Bone Flower Gideon jabbed with his Shocker turned black and shriveled like a piece of rotten fruit. "Frank, are you okay?"

Frank gritted his teeth. "Gideon. Get. Me. Outta. Here."

Doctor Wells helped Frank up. The hunter put his arm around Gideon's father and leaned on him. "Son, clear a path to the jumper."

Gideon raised his Shocker and thrust it at a Bone Flower. The Bone Flower dodged Gideon's thrust and bit the Shocker in half. The electricity from the Shocker coursed through the Bone Flower. The Bone Flower convulsed, turned black and fell dead. Tendrils of smoke curled up from its blackened stem. Gideon picked up Frank's Shocker. He charged ahead of Frank and his father. As Bone Flowers reached and snapped at him, Gideon jabbed at them with the Shocker. In a manner of minutes he created a path of withered and dead Bone Flowers for Frank and his father to follow.

Outside the Bone Flower field, the black jumper sat half buried in a sand dune. White capped waves slapped the lakeshore and gently rocked the jumper's stern. Gideon grinned from ear to ear. *I made it.*

"Gideon, open the hatch," Frank said.

Gideon ran across the beach to his jumper. As he climbed up the sand dune, he started to sink. Soon he was up to his knees in sand. His flight boots were filled with it. He used the Shocker as a walking stick and pulled himself the rest of the way to the hatch. He wiped the sandy grit from the jumper's control panel and pressed the keypad. The retinal scanner appeared. Gideon took off his sunglasses. The sunlight made his eyes burn and water. He dried his eyes with his sleeve and pressed his face into the retinal scanner. A warm glow and a green light washed over his face. The air locks on the hatch clicked and hissed. The hatch creaked open and pushed away the sand like a plow. Gideon put his sunglasses back on and turned to face Frank and his father.

The hunter leaned heavily on Doctor Wells as he limped across the beach. A trail of blood followed them to the sand dune. The Bone Flower head was still stuck to Frank's leg. "This is good, Doc. You can set me down here. I'll crawl up the dune."

"Okay," Doctor Wells said. "Tell me where I can find the triage kit."

"What ain't scattered across the floor of the jumper is kept in an overhead bin near the back of the ship," Frank said.

"Dad, is he—"

"He'll be fine, son. Good thing he has those armored combat boots. Otherwise he would have lost his leg."

"I've been hurt worse, Gideon. This is nothing compared to a frag grenade," Frank crawled up the sand dune and toward the jumper, a trail of blood soaked into the sand.

Gideon reached for Frank but the hunter waved him off. "Frank, I'm sorry." *It's my fault. If I hadn't stayed in the Bone Flowers this wouldn't have happened.*

"Gideon, you got nothing to be sorry for. You did one helluva job clearing out those Bone Flowers. I'm proud of you. You're one brave kid."

Gideon swelled with pride.

"I need to get inside the jumper before the Peelers get a whiff of me. Guard the entrance, Gideon. Don't let nothin' in that ain't human."

Once Frank was inside the jumper, Gideon scanned the Bone Flower field. The plants at the center of the Bone Flowers were bent over and snapping. Some of them were flinging Rippers high into the air—the yelping and howling made Gideon cringe. Then a Ripper came running out of the Bone Flowers. Arrows and darts were sticking out of its neck, head and back. Large chunks of its hindquarter were missing and a Bone Flower head was stuck to its back.

The Ripper sniffed the air and then turned toward Gideon. It snapped its jaws several times and then charged straight for him.

Gideon squeezed the Shocker so hard his hands hurt. Despite the arrows, darts and Bone Flower head sticking to it, the Ripper covered the distance between itself and Gideon in no time. Gideon raised the Shocker as the Ripper charged up the sand dune. Halfway up the dune, the Ripper started to sink. The harder the Ripper struggled up the dune, the deeper it sank into the soft sand. Soon its legs were buried in sand. The Ripper's purple eyes were filled with hunger. It snarled at Gideon and opened its jaws both horizontally and vertically. The gaping maw revealed thousands of sharp teeth. Its breath made Gideon gag. It smelled like rotting garbage.

Rage burned inside Gideon like rocket fuel. "You want a piece of me, how about this?" He jammed the Shocker down the Ripper's throat. The Ripper bit the Shocker in half but it was too late. The electrified orb was inside its body. The Ripper howled and convulsed as the electricity burned through its internal organs. Then it fell down in a heap and rolled down the sand dune. Smoke trailed out of its mouth.

Gideon took a deep breath. He filled his lungs with fresh, crisp lake air and held it for as long as he could. When he exhaled, he saw Paige emerge from the Bone Flowers. He pressed the side of his sunglasses and zoomed in on her.

She threw back the hood of her camouflage cloak. Her face was flush. The color masked some of her freckles. Her long red ponytail hung lazily over her shoulder. The yellow sugar root flowers woven into her hair were still perfectly arranged. Gideon bit his lower lip. *Can I trust her? Why didn't she tell us about the Peelers?*

Paige gave Gideon a wry smile. She ran across the beach and stopped at the base of the sand dune. She pointed her crossbow at the smoldering Ripper. "Gideon, are ya hurt? I saw the trail of blood on the beach."

"Me? No, I'm good to go. It's Frank—a Bone Flower bit him in the leg. He's inside the jumper getting it sorted out with my father."

"What happened to the this Ripper?"

"I fed him a Shocker."

Paige's eyes went from the Ripper to the broken Shocker in Gideon's hand. She lowered her crossbow. "I've never seen a Ripper taken down like that."

"Impressed? I thought about using my bare hands but didn't want you to think I was showing off."

Paige rolled her eyes at Gideon. "Have ya seen Kaz?"

Nobody on this rock has a sense of humor.

"No, I haven't—"

"Thar he is."

Kaz jogged out of the Bone Flower field. The camouflage mask was pulled up over his face and his hood covered his head. His bow was slung across his back. The quiver was empty. He looked like a ninja assassin who had just taken out a squad of enemy soldiers. He sprinted across the beach. He stopped next to the Ripper and unsheathed his sword. The scraping of steel against the scabbard rang in Gideon's ears. In one fluid motion Kaz took the Ripper's head. Purple blood coursed from the Ripper's neck and soaked the sand. With a quick flick of his wrist, Kaz cleaned the blood from his sword and sheathed it. He pulled off his hood and mask, and bowed his head.

Show off. Gideon looked out across the water. The Raider ship was now close to shore. Muramatsu Mining was painted on its side. The parachute sails were being reeled in and a massive anchor let loose. Gideon pressed the side of his glasses and zoomed in. The deck was dotted with cranes, men and work-bots. There were several elevated flight decks. Then a dark cloud rose from the ship. Gideon increased the magnification of his glasses again. His breath caught in his chest. Dozens of monsters that looked like a cross between a Peeler and a human were flying across the water. They were headed straight for him. "Hey guys, can Rippers fly?"

"Don't be an eejit."

"No, Gideon-san."

"Then what are those?"

Paige eyed the horizon. "Trouble."

Kaz agreed. "I don't know what those are but they can't be good."

"Let's board the jumper and get out here."

Once inside the jumper, Gideon pressed a large black button located near the hatch. The hatch slowly shut with a hiss. When the hatch closed, the air locks sealed shut with a loud metallic clang. Gideon breathed a sigh of relief. *That should keep out the Rippers and Peelers.*

The floor of the jumper was littered with packets of meds and food. The decapitated Bone Flower head rolled aimlessly on the floor. Its jaws were broken open and covered with blood. In the back of the jumper, Doctor Wells was covering Frank's calf with a blue nanite wrap. Gideon remembered nanite wraps well—he wore them on his forearms for days. Thousands of tiny robots acted like surgeons repairing his torn flesh, severed tendons and ligaments. The pain and itching were awful but the wounds healed quickly. Frank grimaced as Doctor Wells tightened the wrap. Doctor Wells then offered Frank one blue and one red pill. "Don't argue with me, Frank. You need the painkillers. You need to rest."

"Doc, if I take those pain meds I'll be too sleepy to co-pilot the jumper for Gideon. I'm good to go without 'em. The pain will keep me frosty."

Doctor Wells shrugged his shoulders. "Suit yourself."

"I'm going up front to do the pre-flight check," Gideon said. "Everybody take a seat and strap in. Frank, when you're ready come on up to flight control. We need to get out of here fast."

"Son, Frank needs to rest a bit. What's the rush?"

"Dad, we've got incoming."

"Incoming? Incoming what?" Frank asked.

"I think they're flying Rippers. They're coming in from that Raider ship."

"Son, Rippers don't fly."

Gideon opened his backpack and gave his father binoculars. "Oh yeah? Look out the window and tell me what you see, Dad."

"Senpai, I've never seen creatures like this before. Gideon-san may be right."

"Gideon's tellin' it true," Paige said. "Gwendolyn's created a new monster that flies. Thar headed this way."

Doctor Wells put the binoculars up to his face and peered out the window. He gasped. "It looks like she crossed a Peeler with a human. Has she no decency?"

Frank looked out the window. He pressed the side of his glasses and zoomed in on the flock of Rippers. "I don't care what those things are. I don't want to be around when they get here." The hunter hobbled past Gideon and up toward flight control. "Let's roll, Gideon. We need you to get this ship in the air."

"Excuse me. Gideon-san is flying the ship? Not Frank-san?"

Kaz looked pale. Gideon had seen that look many times on nervous passengers. *Kaz, you're afraid to fly.* "You got a problem with me flying the ship?"

"No, it's just . . . Frank-san is the soldier and—"

Frank shoved Kaz into a seat and headed toward flight control. "In the Corps we do the soldiering and the fighting not the flying. So sit down, buckle up and shut up. You read me, boy?"

"Don't worry, Kaz," Gideon said. "It won't be so bad. I'm going to fly us in hover mode back to the mining camp."

"What does that mean?"

"Hover mode is like a controlled fall. I use the thrusters to keep us floating for as long as I can. A bad pilot gives a bumpy ride. The ship can bob and weave worse than an old fashioned anti-grav toy."

Kaz's eyes went wide. He swallowed hard, and muttered something about walking back to camp.

"Son, don't tease Kaz like that. He clearly doesn't like to fly."

Paige looked at Gideon intently. She hung on his every word.

Gideon puffed out his chest. He cleared his throat. "But no worries, I'm a great pilot."

Paige sat in the front of the jumper near a window. She picked up the safety harness and examined it. A puzzled look crept across her face.

"Have you ever flown?" Gideon asked.

Paige shook her head. "Never had a reason to until now. I was born Off World." She held the safety harness out in front of her. "What do I need to be doin'?"

"Let me help you." Gideon kneeled in front of her and reached for the safety harness. He tried pulling it across her hips but the harness had been sliced in half.

Paige gave him a suspicious grin. "What are ya meanin' to do with that?"

"Son. Go up front and prep the ship. I'll handle the passengers. We'll never get out of here with you fawning all over Paige."

"What? Dad, I'm just trying to help her out."

"With a broken safety harness?" Doctor Wells ushered Paige to a different seat. "Son, go up front to flight control."

"Dad, I'm in command here. Not you."

"Then act like it."

Gideon stormed up to the flight deck.

Frank was sitting in the co-pilot seat. "I thought you could use some company."

"Thanks." Gideon took his place in the pilot's seat. The dent in the ceiling left by the pilot-bot was right over his head. He scanned the controls and took a deep breath. He closed his eyes and reached for his Chain of Remembrance. He rolled the crystal between his fingers. *The controls are just like those in the simulator back in quarantine. I can do this.*

"You okay to go, Gideon?" Frank said.

"Absolutely. Other than having four passengers, a cracked wing and a pack of flying Rippers closing in, it's just like the simulator back in Quarantine."

"Gideon, you can do this. No problem."

Let's hope so. Gideon went through his pre-flight check. A picture of the wormhole jumper appeared on a small computer screen. All systems flashed green except one—the starboard wing. It had a flashing red dot. Gideon touched it. The screen zoomed in on the cracked wing. The plasma bubble was still intact but its integrity was down by more than half. The computer flashed a warning—flight status of starboard wing uncertain. *What does that mean?*

"What's wrong, Gideon?" Frank asked.

Gideon pointed at the computer screen. "The starboard wing may not hold together."

"Gideon, there's only one way to find out if the wing will hold. But it's your call. It's your command."

It's my command. "Okay, let's fire up the engines." Gideon's fingers ran across the control panel and the engines roared to life. He checked the systems once more and pulled back on the flight stick. The ship shuddered and lifted itself out of the sand. "We have lift off."

"Roger that," Frank said. "Starboard wing is holding but the ship is going to start to dip unless you compensate."

Suddenly, the wormhole jumper started to pitch heavily.

Kaz groaned.

"Copy that, adjusting the yaw and roll." Gideon quickly adjusted the ship's thrusters so the wormhole jumper would stay level.

Kaz groaned again. "I think I'm going to be sick."

"We're level and ready for more altitude. The wing is holding together," Frank said.

Gideon looked at the approaching tree line. "Right, I'm thinking about one hundred feet above the trees should be good." Gideon slowly fed more power to the engines. The ship wobbled as it climbed. Sweat began to pour down Gideon's back. He adjusted the thrusters. The jumper leveled out.

"You're doing great, Gideon," Frank said. "Just take her nice and easy."

Gideon disagreed. He had flown enough to know how a properly flown ship should feel. This wasn't it. He could feel his hands getting sweaty. The flight stick started to slip from his grasp. He took a deep breath and tried to reassure himself. "Okay, the stabilizers are working. We've leveled off so we can get out of here. It'll be slow going but it beats walking."

"Yeah it does. Especially with those Rippers out there," Frank said.

"I hate going back to the mining camp, Frank."

"Me too, Gideon. But we got nowhere else to go. The lab's too far. Check the batteries. We don't have enough juice to get there."

"But Gus is dead. We don't even know if the miners will fix the ship."

"I'll make sure the camp fixes the ship, Gideon-san," Kaz said. "I know how to run the repair programs. I used to do it for my father's company. Replacing a wing on a jumper isn't a big deal for the repair-bots."

But what's in it for you? As the wormhole jumper gained altitude, Gideon could clearly see the tops of the trees. They swayed gently in the breeze. Their branches moved lazily back and forth. On the port side of the jumper, a flock of Lake Hawks flew past. Their four powerful wings beat slowly up and down. *They make it look so easy. What I wouldn't give to ride one.*

"Somethin' ain't right," Paige said. "Lake Hawks don't fly together like that unless thar's a problem."

"Gideon, we got incoming on the starboard side," Frank said. "Punch it and let's get out of here."

Gideon pushed the flight stick forward and increased power. The jumper shuddered. A warning light on the control panel went red. *The wing.* Gideon eased off the engines. "I can't punch it. Any sudden power increase from the thrusters will tear the wing off."

"Then we got a problem, because here they come and they are ugly," Frank said.

Gideon counted five winged Rippers. There were two on each wing and one on the nose of the jumper. The Ripper on the nose of the jumper sat like a gargoyle and stared at Gideon. It had one purple eye like a Peeler and a long, thin beak. Black slimy skin was wrapped around its humanoid body. Its powerful looking arms hung loosely at its sides just below its four feathered wings. Long, thin talons extended from its feet. Then it launched itself at Gideon. Its powerful wings drove it into the cockpit window. The Ripper hit with a dull thud.

Gideon ducked. When he did, he jerked on the flight stick and the jumper started to dip.

"Gideon, level off," Frank said. "Relax, it can't get through the window."

The window was a blur of feathers. Thousands of sharp teeth gnashed. A dozen gleaming talons scratched.

Is this how it was for Vince? Gideon grit his teeth. He squeezed the flight stick and slowly pulled back. He tried to stabilize the jumper while the Ripper scratched and snapped at the cockpit window. Then the nose of the wormhole jumper rose. The ship straightened. "We're leveling off."

"Nice job, Gideon."

Gideon looked away from the Ripper. He focused on the nav-screen located just below the cockpit window. It showed a three-dimensional picture of the jumper and its surroundings. "I don't need to look out the window. I can fly by instrument."

"How's it going back there, Doc?" Frank asked.

"The Rippers are biting and scratching at the windows. But we're fine. They can't get in."

"Roger that, Doc. Gideon, are we good to go?"

"All systems read green. The wing is stable. All thrusters are working. We are good to go, Frank."

"And where do ya mean to be takin' those Rippers?" Paige said. "Ya can't be bringin' 'em back to the minin' camp. It ain't right."

Gideon looked away from the nav-screen. Frank was staring at him. "She's right. The camp has kids."

"Ya need to do somethin' about the Rippers first, Gideon," Paige said.

"I'm working on it." Gideon scanned the control panel. The jumper had no defense systems.

Then the Ripper from the cockpit window flapped its four wings and flew away.

"Look, Frank, it's leaving."

The Ripper arched high above the jumper. Then it made a sharp turn and dove back for the ship.

"It's coming back, Gideon," Frank said.

"No, it's just—"

The Ripper landed on the damaged starboard wing. It stared at the blackened plasma bubble.

No, please don't. That plasma bubble is all that's holding the wing together.

The Ripper's beak unfolded. It sunk its teeth into the plasma bubble and peeled back the top most layers. Blue plasma erupted like a volcano.

Alarms sounded as the jumper pitched and started dropping out of the sky.

Chapter 16

Gideon fought to stabilize the jumper. He pressed buttons. He twisted knobs. *I need to level us off. We can survive a hard landing so long as we're level.* He pulled back on the flight stick. But nothing stopped the jumper's downward spiral.

"Watch out for those trees."

"I know, Frank. I see them." Gideon turned the jumper so the damaged starboard wing wouldn't hit the trees. Loud crunching and high-pitched scraping noises ran across the portside of the jumper. It sounded like giant claws were scratching to get inside the ship. Branches raked across Gideon's cockpit window. "We need to fly our way out of this. Frank, give me full power to the vertical thrusters."

"You got it, full power to the vertical thrusters."

Gideon pulled back on the flight stick as hard as he could. Branches and tree trunks snapped as the jumper shot up and out of the forest. Broken and crushed trees marked where the jumper collided with the tree line. It looked like a giant fist smashed into the forest. Gideon checked the control panel. He took a deep breath. *The starboard wing is still intact. But we're draining the batteries too fast.*

"Gideon, we ain't makin' it back to the mining camp. The batteries are runnin' out of juice. You need to find someplace safe to land this thing. That means no trees, no rocks and no damn Bone Flowers."

Gideon shook his head. "Frank, I can't set us down with those Winged Rippers out there. I need to get rid of them somehow. Otherwise, they'll be on us as soon as we leave the jumper."

"We can fight them off. Just set us down."

"No, we can't fight them off. You can't walk. Kaz is out of arrows. Paige is almost out of darts and my dad is completely useless with a Shocker."

"I heard that," Doctor Wells said.

Frank pointed at the power display on the control panel. It was flashing red. "In about five minutes this ship is gonna' drop out of the sky like a rock. You can't glide all the way back to the mining camp, Gideon. We need power to fly this crate. Set us down now while you still have enough power to do it."

Gideon looked out the starboard window. The jumper was away from the trees and out over the lake. But the Winged Rippers were eating and tearing at the wing and the plasma bubble. The plasma bubble pumped blue plasma onto the black tiled wing. Instead of holding the damaged wing together, a river of blue plasma ran down the cracks in the wing left by the meteor strike. The hot plasma melted holes in the wing where the heat tiles had been torn off by the Winged Rippers.

The plasma also burned the Winged Rippers. It set their feathers on fire and melted large holes in their beaks. Their black slimy arms were pockmarked and smoking. Some of the Winged Rippers had their skin burned off in places. Bones were exposed. But the Winged Rippers regenerated quickly. Their feathers grew back and the holes in their arms and beaks filled themselves.

Gideon cursed. *Not even the plasma will kill them. But at least it's slowing them down. Otherwise, the wing would have been ripped off by now.*

Then the jumper's computer, using a lady's calm and collected voice announced, "Warning, power failure imminent."

Frank tapped on the power display. The jumper's battery pack was reading dangerously low.

"Isn't there anything on this planet that can kill a Ripper?" Gideon shouted. "I didn't come this far just to be killed by those things."

"The Lake Hawks," Paige said. "They'll be attackin' anythin' that invades thar territory."

Gideon scanned the horizon. A ghostly wall of low hanging clouds floated up and over the lake. Gideon thought back to when Sarge showed him the map of Off World and explained the planet's topography. *There are no oceans Off World, only large inland lakes connected by waterfalls, rivers and locks made by the mining companies.* Several small dots circled high over the lake. "Paige, are those Lake Hawks circling out there?"

"Yes. If ya can fly yer ship out to 'em, the Lake Hawks might be gettin' rid of them Winged Rippers for ya."

"Thanks, Paige. That gives me an idea. Frank, think we can start a fight between the Rippers and the Lake Hawks?"

"Gideon, we need to land this thing. If we hit the water it's game over. The jumper sinks to the bottom of the lake and we're stuck on this rock for good."

"Warning power failure imminent," announced the jumper's computer.

"We can do this," Gideon said. "Prepare to raise the shields."

Frank gave Gideon a raised eyebrow. "Say what?"

"The shields should shock those Winged Rippers enough to get them off the wing. And with any luck, the Lake Hawks will attack them while I circle back for a landing on the lakeshore."

"It's risky but I like it. Preparing to raise the shields," Frank said.

Gideon's throat went dry. *If this doesn't work I have to do a water landing. Then the ship sinks and I'm stuck on this rock.* Gideon pushed the flight stick forward. The jumper quickly closed the distance with the Lake Hawks. The blue-grey feathers of the large birds of prey blended with the sky and lake making them hard to see. There were dozens of them. Some beat their four wings to get away from the jumper. Others held their wings open and lazily rode the air current.

"There's a whole flock of them. Where did they all come from?" Gideon asked.

"The lake yer flyin' over ends at the Whisperin' Rock Falls. The Lake Hawks nest in the cliffs near thar," Paige said.

"Frank, get ready to raise the shields." Gideon maneuvered the jumper into the center of the flock. The Lake Hawks squawked. They turned on the jumper. Their three purple eyes bore into Gideon.

"They look mad," Frank said.

"Good, I'm counting on it." Gideon peered out the starboard window. The Winged Rippers stopped tearing at the starboard wing. They looked up at the Lake Hawks and flashed their teeth. Then a Lake Hawk swooped in and knocked a Ripper off the wing. Another Lake Hawk sunk its talons into a

Ripper, pulled it off the wing and drove it down into the lake. "Look, the Lake Hawks are attacking the Rippers."

"Man those Lake Hawks are tough," Frank said. "Only three more Rippers to go."

A Lake Hawk dove at the jumper. Its claws raked against the cockpit window. Instinctively Gideon ducked and pushed the flight stick forward, sending the jumper toward the water. Gideon pulled back on the flight stick to gain altitude just as a Lake Hawk slammed into the ship. The ship rocked like a meteor hit it. "Now, Frank. Raise the shields."

"Copy that, raising shields." Frank pressed a green switch on the control panel. The jumper shuddered. A green light blanketed the ship. The Winged Rippers leapt from the jumper and were attacked by the flock of Lake Hawks. Outside the cockpit window, there was a blur of snapping beaks, sharp talons, and black and blue-grey feathers.

"Warning, power failure," said the jumper's computer.

Gideon turned the jumper and headed for the lakeshore. The nav screen told him it was ten miles away. "Lower the shields, Frank. We need to conserve what little power we have."

"Copy that, Gideon. Shields lowered."

Gideon pulled back on the flight stick. *I can't stay this low over the lake. When we lose power I'll need altitude so we can maybe glide to shore. Otherwise we drop right into the lake and sink.* The jumper rose high above the lake. The trees lining the lakeshore looked like clumps of broccoli. The lake bubbled and churned with white-capped waves. Off in the distance the Whispering Rock Falls poured over a cliff and into a lower lake basin.

"Warning, power failure," said the jumper's computer. "Warning, failure of starboard wing imminent. Prepare for emergency landing."

The Rippers were gone but the starboard wing was ravaged. Wires snaked everywhere. Heat tiles were missing. The plasma bubble sat in the middle of the wing beating like a dying heart as it pumped the last of the plasma onto the wing. The blue plasma beaded like rainwater on the jumper's heat tiles but burned large smoking holes in the wing where the heat tiles had been chewed off. Black smoke billowed from the wing.

"Warning, power failure," said the jumper's computer. "Warning, starboard wing critical. Warning, prepare for emergency—"

"Frank, will you please shut that thing off?"

"Roger that, Gideon, I'm muting the computer."

Then the jumper shuddered.

Sweat poured down Gideon's back. *We just lost the engines and the thrusters.*

"Gideon, we're losing altitude."

"Raise the flaps, Frank. I need to slow us down."

"Copy that. Wing flaps raised."

As the jumper started falling out of the sky, Gideon pulled back on the flight stick as hard as he could. *Keep the nose up.*

But the jumper fell faster and faster.

The tops of the trees lining the lakeshore disappeared from view. Instead of looking down on the trees, the jumper was now level with them. *We're not going to make it. The beach is too far.*

"Brace yourselves, we're going in hot!" Frank shouted.

The lake rushed up to meet Gideon.

Please, not a water landing. The ship will sink. I'll be stuck here.

Then the jumper smashed into the lake. Water rushed over the cockpit window. Gideon's teeth rattled. He bit his tongue. Blood filled his mouth. His safety harness squeezed the air out of him and drove his Chain of Remembrance painfully into his chest. Gideon looked out the starboard window just as the wing snapped off. The jumper spun wildly out of control. It skimmed across the water and slammed into the lakeshore, carving a deep gouge in the beach. Gideon rocked back and forth in his seat as the jumper slid to a stop and settled in the sand. Silence filled the jumper. Gideon took a deep breath. He was covered in sweat. His hands were still squeezing the flight stick.

"Gideon," Frank said, "you can let go of the flight stick now."

Gideon released the flight stick. His hands trembled as the last remnants of adrenaline coursed through his body.

"Relax, Gideon. Any landing you can walk away from is a good one." Frank clapped him on the shoulder. "Nice job. Is anybody hurt?"

"No injuries back here," Doctor Wells said.

Gideon closed his eyes and took several deep breaths. *It wasn't a water landing. I did it.* When he opened them, Paige was standing over him. Her ponytail was gone. Her red hair was down. It hung loosely over her shoulders. She gave him a sly smile.

"Gideon, is flyin' always this borin'?"

"And you call me a tool?" Gideon tasted blood from the cut on his tongue. He wiped his mouth with the back of his hand. When he pulled his hand away it was blood stained.

Paige leaned in close. Gideon could feel the warmth of her. She touched his face. "You're hurt."

Gideon's ears and neck flushed hot. "No, I'm fine. I… I bit my tongue is all."

Paige reached inside her cloak. She pulled out a small black pouch. "Hold out yer hand."

Gideon outstretched his hand. "Okay, why?"

"Because I'm fixin' to give ya somethin' is why." Paige put a small root in Gideon's hand. It looked like a withered carrot. "Eat this. It'll stop the bleedin'."

The root was dry and cold. "Are you serious, Paige? You expect me to eat this?"

"Did ya hit yer head too? Or are ya' a bein' a tool on purpose? Of course, I'm serious."

Gideon looked at Frank. The hunter nodded his approval. "She was right about the sugar root."

Gideon shrugged his shoulders and popped the root into his mouth. It tasted like an unwashed carrot. "That's awful. Give me some water."

"Hush up and chew," Paige said. "When it's all chewed up, let it sit on yer tongue."

Gideon scrunched up his face and chewed. When the root was a fine paste he let it rest on his tongue. It slowly dissolved. A tingling sensation filled the cut. The taste of blood was gone. The cut healed. "It worked. Thanks, Paige."

"Yer welcome." Paige smiled. Her face seemed to glow.

"Paige, I—"

"Here let me see that wound," Doctor Wells said. "Excuse me, Paige."

Paige turned to leave the flight cabin. When she did, her long hair brushed against Gideon's face. *She smells like strawberries.*

Doctor Wells reached for Gideon's face but Gideon knocked his father's hand away. "I said I'm fine, Dad."

"Son, I'm just trying to help."

"Yeah, well I don't need it. Why don't you help your *other* son? He looks green."

Doctor Wells pursed his lips. He glared at Gideon.

"Senpai, I think I'm . . . going to be . . . sick."

"Not onboard this ship you won't. Get outside before I throw you out." Frank pressed a button on the control panel. The hatch unlocked with a loud metallic clank. It hissed and popped open. Crisp salty air wafted into the jumper. Kaz put his hand over his mouth and ran out the open hatch.

Gideon unfastened his safety harness. "I need to inspect the jumper."

Frank stood on his good leg. He kept his injured leg off the flight deck and leaned heavily on the co-pilot chair for support. The Bone Flower bite left deep gouges and dozens of holes in the hunter's armored boot. Blood was seeping through the blue nanite wrap coiled around his lower leg. "I'm coming with you, Gideon. Doc, you and the girl stay inside the jumper. The jumper's safety systems are working just fine so you're good to go in here."

"Wait a minute," Doctor Wells said. "Who gave you permission to stand on that leg, soldier? That armored boot is the only thing holding your leg together. You're even starting to bleed through the nanite wrap. That tells me you need surgery. You're *my* patient and I *order* you to sit back down."

"My dad's right, Frank. You need to stay off that leg."

Paige reached inside her cloak and pulled out her small black pouch. "I've got more of the root I gave Gideon. It'll numb yer leg good and stop the bleedin' fer sure."

"Everybody just chill," Frank said. "This ain't my first rodeo. I've been wounded before. Priority one is to check the status of the ship. When Gideon and me are done with that, I'll come back inside for some medical. Are we clear, Doc?"

"That's fine. Paige can help me test the DNA samples Gideon brought. If Kaz needs me, let me know."

Gideon pushed his way past his father and headed toward the hatch. "Sure, Dad I'll put that at the top of my list."

Outside the wormhole jumper, Gideon stood in soft white sand. The beach was narrow. The white sand quickly giving way to a hard dense surface covered with dozens of rock formations. Gideon pressed the side of his glasses and zoomed in on them. Other than their grey color, none of the rock formations were the same. Some were huge square blocks that dwarfed the jumper. They were arranged in intricate patterns and looked like a giant must have stabbed them into the ground. Others were massive stone heads with faces carved into them. Each head had a different face—some looked sad some angry. *Wow, Easter Island and Stonehenge combined. I'm glad we made it to the beach. Those rocks would have shredded the jumper.*

Gideon turned his attention to the lake. Despite his sunglasses, he had to squint due to the reflection of the twin suns off the lake. The suns made the blue lake sparkle like someone sprinkled diamonds into the water. The lake was rough and coursing. White capped waves crashed the shoreline. In the distance, the roar of the Whispering Rock Falls cut through the air. Lake Hawks circled overhead. Gideon took several deep breaths. The salt air was invigorating. Energy coursed through his body.

Frank hopped toward Gideon on his good leg. He leaned heavily on the Shocker. "Gideon, what's with the daydreaming? We got work to do."

"What? Sorry, Frank."

"Gideon, listen up. I need you to stay focused on the mission. We've got three days left to repair the ship and get on outta' here so don't get too attached to that girl."

"Frank, I didn't do anything. You're the one who told me eat that weird carrot thing she just gave me."

Frank stabbed Gideon in the chest with his finger. "There's the mission and nothing else. You read me?"

"Yes, Frank, loud and clear."

"Good. One more thing, Gideon, remember what I told you. Her and that Kaz are both hidin' somethin', I feel it in my bones so the faster we can ditch them and this rock the better. You copy that?"

"Yes, Frank."

"You're a good kid, Gideon. Now come on over here and help me walk to the starboard wing. This Shocker ain't much of a crutch."

Gideon put his hand around Frank's waist. He took the hunter's left arm and draped it over his shoulders. Frank leaned heavily on Gideon. The hunter's long muscular frame dwarfed him. Gideon easily bore the hunter's weight. "Damn, Gideon. You're stronger than you look. Last time I had a leg wound it took two medics to help me walk."

"Yeah, it's weird. I thought you'd be heavier."

The black tiled jumper lay on the beach like a wounded bird of prey. Water dripped from the hull. From the back of the ship, steam hissed from the main engines. The starboard wing was gone. Sharp jagged edges outlined where the wing would normally have attached to the hull. Long strands of blue plasma hung from the jumper like stale chewing gum.

"Are you kidding me? Frank, how are we supposed to get this fixed? We'll never make it out of here now."

"Gideon, never say never. One of the first things I learned in the Corps is that what happens to me isn't as important as what I do about it."

Frank removed his arm from around Gideon's shoulder and leaned against the jumper. He checked his wrist pad and nodded. Then he ran his hand over the hull. "We're in luck, Gideon. The hull looks good and the diagnostic confirms no cracks or breaches. I know it looks bad but the miners can replace the wing no problem. They can also re-charge the batteries. The bigger problem is how we get the ship back to the mining camp. Here comes, Kaz. Maybe he has an idea."

Kaz staggered toward Gideon. He held his stomach.

"You still look green, Kaz. Are you feeling okay?"

"Yes, Gideon-san, I was sick before but am better now."

"If you say so but if you were any greener you'd look like your camouflage—"

"Stand down, Gideon. I want to hear if Kaz has any ideas on how to get the jumper back to camp. Maybe we can use mining equipment. What do you think, Kaz?"

Gideon crossed his arms over his chest. "Let's hear it, Kaz."

"We can use anti-gravity pallets, Frank-san. They can lift the jumper no problem and we can use one of the old mining roads to get it back to the camp. Those roads are wide enough for the jumper."

Gideon thought back to the anti-gravity pallet Gus used to carry the half dead Ripper back to the mining camp. "Will that work? The anti-grav pallets I saw aren't that big. They can carry a Ripper and some fire rock but that's about it."

"Gideon-san, we have much larger anti-gravity pallets than the one you saw. The big ones can be easily slipped under the nose of your ship. Once the nose is elevated, we can work backward from there and slip anti-grav pallets underneath the ship's belly. About eight anti-grav pallets should do it."

"The jumper needs a new wing and the batteries need re-charging," Gideon said. "Can you do all that back at the mining camp?"

"Yes, Gideon-san."

Frank nodded his approval. "I say we give it a shot. What do you think, Gideon?"

Gideon checked his wrist pad. Then his gaze fell to Frank's wounded leg. "It's four miles back to the mining camp. You can't walk, Frank. How are you going to make it?"

"I'll stay with the jumper. You go with the others to the mining camp, pick up the anti-grav pallets and bring them back here. It's still early enough in the day for us to get the ship back to the mining camp before nightfall. With any luck, we can be airborne by tomorrow morning."

"I don't know, Frank."

"Gideon, what's the protocol?"

"I know what it is, Frank."

"Then let me hear you say it."

"It's me doing what you and... *don't say Vince...* It's me doing what you tell me to do."

"That's right. Now get your butt inside the jumper and go tell Paige and your old man what's up."

Gideon turned and headed back toward the open hatch before Frank stopped him.

"Gideon, that Raider ship is still out there so double time it back to the mining camp. You read me?"

Gideon scanned the lake. Just off the horizon sat a small dot. Then a black cloud erupted from the ship. *What's with all the smoke? Is there a fire onboard?* Gideon pressed the side of his glasses and zoomed in. It was the Raider ship. Dozens of Winged Rippers were taking off from the deck. They were flying straight for Gideon.

CHAPTER 17

Gideon bounded through the open hatch of the wormhole jumper. Long thin emergency lights ran across the ceiling of the flight cabin, casting a dim blue light. Gideon took off his sunglasses and forced his eyes to adjust from the glare of the twin suns to the darkness that surrounded him. The familiar beeping of computers and flight instruments was gone. A tense quiet filled the jumper. *The ship feels dead. It's like walking into a tomb.*

Doctor Wells kneeled over the black case of DNA samples. He took a deep breath and opened it. Inside were twenty-four vials of a thick, dark red liquid. Each vial was tucked snugly into its own grey-colored foam compartment. Doctor Wells waved a small hand held device over the vials. The device was cylindrical and had a digital display on the bottom.

"Those bottles are tiny," Paige said.

"Dad, we need to leave now. Winged Rippers are headed this way."

"I'll be with you in a moment, son."

Gideon grit his teeth. "Paige, can you talk some sense into him? Winged Rippers are just off the horizon. They'll be here in about five minutes."

"Doctur Wells, Gideon's right. If Rippers are comin' we need to be leavin'."

"Please, I'm almost finished."

"Do what you want, Dad. I'm leaving. Come on, Paige." Gideon grabbed Paige's hand and headed for the hatch. He bumped into Kaz.

"Kaz, what are you—"

"Sorry, Gideon-san. Frank-san told me to hurry you up."

"That's fine because Paige and I were just leaving."

"What about Senpai?"

"My father doesn't listen to me. Maybe he'll listen to you, Kaz."

"Son, wait. You need to hear this. It's as I feared. All of these samples are Pure Earth and they're all from you, Gideon. It's your DNA son. All of it."

Gideon froze. "Oh my God. That means they sent me here just to deliver Pure Earth to Gwendolyn. The whole thing was a lie. But why samples of my DNA?"

"So Gwendolyn could clone you, son."

"Why would she want to do that?"

"In case you refused to access the lab's artificial intelligence for her she could order your clone to do it."

Gideon's mouth hung open in shock.

Paige squeezed Gideon's hand. "I'm sorry, Gideon. It ain't right what they done to ya. Lyin' to ya and violatin' yer body like that."

Kaz pushed past Gideon and reached for one of the vials. "Those are all Pure Earth?"

Dr. Wells snapped the case closed nearly catching Kaz's hand. "Leave it alone, Kaz."

"Sorry, Senpai, it's just . . . so much Pure Earth could maybe cure—"

"Yes, Kaz, I know but now is not the time." Doctor Wells locked the black case. The word Biohazard was stamped on the outside of it.

"Cure who, Kaz?" Gideon asked. Kaz didn't answer.

Paige shrugged her shoulders.

"Dad?"

"Not now, Gideon."

A heavy silence filled the air.

"Gideon, what are you doing in there? Having a party? Get your butt out here!" Frank shouted. "Those Winged Rippers are closing fast."

Gideon put his sunglasses back on and pulled Paige through the open hatch. Dozens of Winged Rippers filled the sky. They flew in one large swarm. *They fly like Peelers. They're quiet like them too.* Gideon pressed the side of his glasses and zoomed in. They were the same type of Winged Rippers that attacked the wormhole jumper. Sunlight glistened off their oily jet-black skin. They pumped their four wings furiously. Their single purple eye stared straight at Gideon.

Some of the Winged Rippers carried cables in their human-like arms. Others carried what looked like long tables with their talons. *What are they carrying?*

"It's about time, Gideon."

"Sorry, Frank. My father was analyzing the DNA samples. They're all—"

"Later, Gideon. Listen up, change of plans. I'm not stayin' with the jumper. If the Rippers know I'm inside it, they'll probably tear it apart just to get to me. I don't want to risk lettin' those monsters further damage the ship. It's our only ticket off this rock. I need you to lock it down before we go find some cover."

Gideon turned toward the open hatch just as Doctor Wells and Kaz exited the jumper.

Doctor Wells held the case of Pure Earth close to his chest. Kaz's eyes never left the case. He pointed toward the lake. "Look, Senpai, Winged Rippers. Gwendolyn sent them for the Pure Earth. We need to get it back to the mining camp."

"Yes, of course. We need to get the Pure Earth out of here."

"Follow me, Senpai. We can hide in the rock formations." Kaz grabbed Doctor Wells by the arm and ran up the beach. His tabi boots left bird-like footprints in the sand. Doctor Wells hugged the case of Pure Earth like it was a baby.

"Dad, wait. You guys are leaving without us?"

"I don't believe what I'm seein'," Paige said.

"Gideon, lock down the jumper like I told you to. I'll deal with Kaz and your old man later."

"Okay, Frank." Gideon reached up and entered the access code on the keypad. The bio scanner appeared. Gideon shielded his eyes from the suns with his hand and took off his sunglasses. The glare from the twin suns instantly made his eyes water. Gideon dried his eyes with the back of his hand. He put his face up against the bio-scanner. A warm green light washed over him. The hatch closed with a hiss and locked with a loud metallic clank. Gideon put his sunglasses back on and turned toward Frank. "Good to go, the jumper's secured."

"Outstanding, now help get me outta here." Frank grimaced as he hobbled toward Gideon. The blue nanite wrap covering his leg was soaked in blood. Frank draped his arm around Gideon and leaned heavily into him.

Paige grabbed Frank's other arm and put it around her shoulders. "Let me help ya too, Frank."

"Thanks, Paige. Let's roll on outta here." Frank launched himself on his good leg, taking long hops.

Gideon and Paige half jogged and half carried him. They made their way quickly across the narrow beach onto the hard dense ground toward the rock formations and large stone heads. The faces carved into the stone heads stared at Gideon. Their eyes seemed to follow him. Each one had a different expression. Some had angry, elongated faces. Others had pained expressions while others looked like giant human skulls that had been polished clean by Peelers. They looked like they would come alive at any moment. The constant roar of the waterfall filled the air. It sounded like the gallery of faces carved into the massive stone heads were groaning.

"Paige, either I'm going crazy or these statues are starting to talk," Gideon said. "It's why this place is called Whisperin' Rock Falls. The waterfalls make it seem like the rocks are talkin'."

Then a Winged Ripper swooped overhead. Its purple eye looked down at Gideon. It snapped its beak several times and made a quick U turn. Three more Winged Rippers followed it. When the first Winged Ripper finished its U turn it dove for Gideon. Its human-like arms reached out for him. Its beak opened wide. Gideon grabbed Frank and dove for the ground. Frank held his leg and screamed in pain. Gideon looked up just as a dozen darts hit the Winged Ripper in the eye and throat. The Winged Ripper slammed into the ground next Gideon. He jumped to his feet and jammed his Shocker into the Winged Ripper's back. Smoke rose from its body as it convulsed. Gideon held his Shocker against the monster until its body went limp. Then he stabbed at the Winged Ripper again and again.

"Gideon, it ain't getting' up anytime soon. Leave it be. We got more of 'em comin' in," Paige said.

The other three Winged Rippers descended on Gideon. Their beaks opened vertically and horizontally exposing rows of pointy, dagger like teeth. Their arms reached for him. *They're going to tear me to pieces. I'm going to die on this rock.* Gideon held the Shocker out in front of him. He glanced at Frank. The hunter was on his back. His face was gripped with pain. But he held his Shocker out in front of him.

Paige raised her crossbow. "I'll shoot 'em down. The two of ya use yer Shockers on 'em like ya just did, Gideon."

A shower of darts filled the sky. Like porcupine quills, Paige's darts stuck out of the Winged Rippers' single purple eye and their throats. The Winged Rippers slammed into the ground one after the other. They used their human-like arms to pull the darts out of their eye. Purple blood washed over their faces and beaks. A bloodied socket in the middle of their forehead was all that was left of their eye.

Gideon jammed his Shocker into the nearest Winged Ripper. It writhed in agony, smoke rose from its body. Its four wings beat furiously. When its body went limp Gideon raised his Shocker and jabbed it at the other Winged Ripper.

But Frank was already using his Shocker. The hunter was up on his knees and jamming his Shocker into the Winged Ripper's neck.

The third Winged Ripper rose to its feet. It had Paige's bloody dart in its hand. Its purple eye was nearly healed. It had a milky purplish hue to it. The monster snapped its beak and lunged for Paige. Paige pulled a foot long wooden dart from her boot and threw it at the Winged Ripper. The dart hit the monster in the eye and disappeared. The sharp pointy end stuck out the back of its head. The Winged Ripper staggered forward and fell face first with a sickening smack.

Frank raised an eyebrow at Paige. "Damn, girl."

"Come on, let's get out of here." Gideon reached down and pulled Frank up off the ground. The hunter slumped into Gideon. Gideon dropped to one knee and slung Frank over his shoulders. He grabbed his Shocker with his free hand and stood up. Gideon grunted as he lifted Frank off the ground.

"Gideon, how the hell are you able to lift me? I'm twice your size."

"I learned the fireman's carry in Quarantine. Survival training is part of the Galaxy Class Pilot program."

"That ain't what I mean and you know it."

Paige stared wide-eyed at Gideon. "It ain't normal that yer able to be liftin' him."

"Can you quit talking about it and just lead us out of here, Paige? He's not getting any lighter you know."

Paige popped a fresh magazine of darts into her crossbow. The magazine buzzed and whirred as it loaded. "Follow me. I see yer Dad and Kaz up ahead."

Gideon walked behind Paige as quickly as he could. Sweat poured down his face and stung his eyes. His back hunched from Frank's weight pressing down on him. His legs trembled with each step. But Gideon grit his teeth and kept going.

Paige kept her crossbow leveled. She scanned the sky for Winged Rippers. Three of the monsters flew past. They quickly turned and hovered above Gideon. They had Paige's darts embedded in their neck. Their single purple eye was bloodied and unfocused. *Are they the same ones we just fought? Could they have healed already?* Paige's crossbow whirred. A volley of darts hit the Winged Rippers in the chest. They snapped their beaks at Paige, pumped their four wings and flew away.

"Nice job, Paige."

"I didn't do nothin' special, Gideon. They'll be back. They just went to get thar friends."

"Then you need to find us some cover," Frank said.

"I already did. It's them rocks up ahead. We can hide in thar with Kaz and Doctur Wells."

Up ahead was a large pyramid shaped rock sculpture. The walls were sagging in on themselves and it looked like the top had been broken off. Each stone of the pyramid was as big as a car. At the pyramid's entrance stood a massive stone slab the size of a school bus. A shocked facial expression was carved into it—the eyes were round and wide, its mouth was gaping. Standing inside the open mouth was Kaz and Doctor Wells. They were waving.

Gideon staggered toward the pyramid. His legs shook from carrying Frank. As he closed in, Doctor Wells and Kaz looked at him in shock. Doctor Wells pointed at Gideon. Then Kaz ran out to meet him.

"Gideon-san, let me help you."

"I don't need any help from you, Kaz. You and my dad left us on the beach."

"Kaz, if I had two good legs, I promise you I'd kick you so hard you'd be wearing your butt for a hat," Frank said.

"I'm sorry, Frank-san. Senpai asked me to protect the Pure Earth. He made me promise to help him. He's waiting for you inside the pyramid."

Gideon shoved his way past Kaz. He swung Frank so that the hunter's good leg hit Kaz in the backside. "Oh, sorry, Kaz, I'm just helping Frank keep his promise."

"That ain't nice, Gideon. Ya ain't impressin' me none." Paige grabbed Kaz by the sleeve and pulled him aside. "Kaz, ya need to be explainin' yerself to me. Get on over here."

"Okay, Paige-san."

The massive stone slab with the face carved into it loomed over Gideon. Its open mouth was an entrance to the inside of the pyramid. Gideon stumbled through the entrance and set Frank down. He lay on his back next to the hunter and took a deep breath. Gideon wiped the sweat from his face. The ground was hard and cold. It helped cool him down. The ceiling was high and vaulted. The stone walls were smooth and polished. Light stabbed through small oval shaped portholes carved in the stone.

Frank held his leg. The blue nanite wrap was soaked with blood. "Thanks, for getting me here, Gideon."

"No problem, Frank. You would have done the same for me."

"Yeah, but *me* carryin' *you* makes sense. What you did for me don't."

"It wasn't that hard. I'm not tired at all just thirsty. When Paige is done chewing out Kaz I need to get some more of that sugar root."

"That's what I'm talkin' about, Gideon. You should be exhausted but you ain't."

Gideon shrugged his shoulders. "It was adrenaline is all, Frank. You know how it is. Sometimes in battle situations humans can do amazing things."

"I ain't buyin' it, Gideon."

"Frank's right, son, I saw what you did and it conerns me."

"Really, Dad, you saw what I did? Well I saw what you did. You abandoned me . . . again."

Doctor Wells took a long deep breath. "Gideon, keeping the Pure Earth away from Gwendolyn is critical. You know this. So with Kaz's help, I did what I thought was best. Besides, I was confident that you could take care of yourself. And I see that I was right."

"Yeah sure, whatever you say, Dad."

"Good, I'm glad you see things my way, son. Now let me have a look at you."

"Why? I feel fine."

"That's the problem. Like our hunter friend just said, you should be exhausted after carrying him. Just take off your sunglasses. I want to see to what extent this planet is affecting you. I want to see if you still have Earth eyes."

"Dad, this is stupid."

"Gideon, do what your old man says," Frank said.

Gideon sat up. He took his sunglasses off. "Fine, are you happy now?"

Doctor Wells peered into Gideon's eyes. Then he grabbed Gideon's wrist and took his pulse. "You still have Earth eyes and your heart rate is normal. So, yes, I'm happy—for now. But I'd like to perform some tests on you back at my lab just make sure this planet isn't changing you somehow."

Gideon put his sunglasses back on. "I don't need any tests. I told you I was fine."

"We'll see, Gideon. Now let's have a look at you, soldier." Doctor Wells took Frank's pulse. "Your heart's racing. You're in a lot pain, aren't you?"

"It sure don't feel like Christmas morning, Doc."

"I'll take that as a yes. Your pain threshold is amazing. Now let me see that leg." Doctor Wells gingerly held Frank's leg. The hunter drew a quick breath. He bit into his lower lip. Doctor Wells sighed. "I'm afraid the nanite wrap has done all it can for you. The bones are crushed. The ligaments and tendons are shredded. If we're to save that leg, you need surgery."

"You got any good news for me, doc?"

"Yes, Paige is here. Perhaps she can give you a natural remedy for the pain. I'm sorry but I've no triage kit with me."

Paige stormed through the entranceway. Her camouflage cloak swirled around her. Her purple eyes narrowed. The freckles on her face blended with the flush of her cheeks. Kaz straggled behind her. His eyes stared at the ground. He sat cross-legged next to the case of Pure Earth and placed his sword across his lap. He never looked up. Doctor Wells sat next to him.

"Frank, it looks like Paige tore Kaz a new one," Gideon whispered.

"Gideon, I'd rather face a Ripper than that girl, especially when she's ticked off."

"If ya need to be talkin' about me, say it loud enough so I can hear it. Otherwise keep yer pie holes shut."

"There's no problem, Paige. We were just wondering if we could get some more sugar root and if you could give Frank something for the pain," Gideon said. "That's all."

Paige reached inside her cloak and pulled out her small black pouch. She tossed a sugar root to Gideon and Frank. Gideon cracked the root open and swallowed the sweet nectar. His whole body started to tingle. *Wow, I feel like I could take on a hundred Rippers.* Paige then turned and offered the small yellow root to Kaz and Doctor Wells. They each thanked her and drank down the nectar.

Then Paige kneeled next to Frank. She looked closely at his leg but never touched it. She put her nose close to it and sniffed several times. Blood continued to seep through the holes in Frank's armored boot and the nanite wrap. She made a disapproving clucking noise with her tongue and reached inside her pouch. She pulled out several small roots. One looked like the withered carrot she gave Gideon. The other two looked like bright blue mushroom caps. She mashed them together into a fine brown powder. She held out her hand and offered it to Frank. "Let this dissolve on yer tongue. Normally I would put it on yer wound but I'm afraid to take yer boot off. It's the only thang holdin' yer leg together."

Frank opened his mouth and let Paige pour the powder onto his tongue. He made a sour face. "Jeez, that's nasty. It's worse than the protein powder rations I got in the Corps."

"Oh hush up and act like a soldier." Paige touched Frank's forehead and cheek. "At least ya got no fever."

A flash of jealously swept through Gideon. He quickly shook it off. *Don't be stupid. I'm leaving this rock.* Then his wrist pad starting beeping. Gideon stared at it wide-eyed in disbelief. "Frank, look at this. The jumper's taking off."

Frank checked his wrist pad. "What the hell? This reads like someone's flying the ship. That's impossible."

Gideon picked up his Shocker and bolted outside.

CHAPTER 18

Winged Rippers swarmed the jumper like vultures fighting over carrion. They snapped at each other as they jockeyed for position near the bow of the ship. Then a small group of the monsters jammed a large anti-grav pallet under the ship's nose, causing the jumper to rise up out of the sand. As the jumper's bow lifted, a second group of Winged Rippers slipped another anti-grav pallet under the hull. The Winged Rippers did this until the entire length of the hull was resting on top of the pallets. Within a matter of minutes, the wormhole jumper was floating several feet off the ground. Then the monsters attached cables to the anti-grav pallets and used their human-like arms to pull the wormhole jumper off the beach and out toward the lake. The jumper slowly turned as the Winged Rippers pumped their four wings furiously.

Gideon squeezed his Shocker so hard his knuckles popped. "Frank, Paige, get out here. I need you. The Rippers are using anti-gravity pallets to steal the jumper. They're flying away with my ship."

Paige ran out of the stone pyramid with her crossbow leveled. She skidded to a stop next to Gideon. "I ain't never seen a Ripper do anythin' like that. I didn't think they had the smarts fer it."

"Nothing I see on this rock surprises me anymore." Frank hopped after Paige on his good leg. He leaned heavily on his Shocker.

"We have to stop them, come on." Gideon took off after the Winged Rippers.

"Gideon, stop. Don't be an eejit. Ya can't be chasin' after 'em like that," Paige shouted.

Frank hopped after Gideon. "That boy is gonna get himself killed. Those ain't pigeons you can just shoo away."

Gideon chased after the jumper as the Winged Rippers pulled it off the beach and toward the lake. Panic seized him. *That's my ticket home. I lose that ship I lose everything.* Gideon stabbed his Shocker wildly at the Winged Rippers. The Shocker popped and crackled as it hit the wings of a nearby Ripper. A cloud of smoke and black feathers filled the air. The Winged Ripper dropped the cable and hit the sand. The other Winged Rippers turned on Gideon. Their single purple eye bore into him. Their beaks flashed open exposing rows of sharp teeth. Then Gideon was surrounded by a sea of snapping beaks, slashing claws and black feathers. Gideon used the Shocker like a fighting staff. He spun and whirled as he swung the Shocker out in front of him. But there were too many Winged Rippers. They bit and clawed at Gideon. Pain tore across his chest as claws raked across his body. Then something grabbed Gideon by the neck and flung him backward. Gideon stumbled to the ground. It was Frank.

"Get the hell outta here, Gideon. Use your wrist pad to track the jumper. Do whatever it takes to get your butt back to Earth. Let them know what's happening on this rock." Frank stood on his good leg and stabbed his Shocker at the Winged Rippers.

Gideon scrambled to his feet. He picked up his Shocker and thrust it at a nearby Winged Ripper. The Ripper dodged the thrust and snapped at him. Then its purple eye filled with darts. The blind monster tore at the darts in its eye and flew in wild circles out over the lake.

"Gideon, thar's nothin' ya can do to stop 'em from takin' yer ship. We got to go." Paige fired volleys of darts at the Winged Rippers. She kept her crossbow leveled at the flock of monsters and fired as they swooped in on her and Gideon.

Then Frank was knocked to the ground. Winged Rippers swarmed him. He thrust his Shocker at them but it was no use. The hunter disappeared under a blur of black feathers and beating wings.

"No, Frank!" Gideon started toward the hunter but Paige held him back.

"Gideon, don't," she said. "Thar ain't nothin' ya can do fer 'im. Thar's too many of 'em."

A loud battle cry echoed from behind Gideon. It was Kaz. He had his camouflage hood pulled over his head and his mask pulled up to his eyes. His sword was raised over his head. He dashed past Gideon and Paige and tore into the Winged Rippers like a buzz saw. He was a blur. Winged Rippers shrieked as Kaz took their arms, wings, and heads. But it was too late. The jumper was pulled off the beach and out over the lake. The Winged Rippers held the cables in their human-like arms and steered the floating jumper toward the waiting Raider ship. A single Winged Ripper pulled Frank's limp body out of the sand. It used its clawed feet to hold Frank by the shoulders and flew away with him. The hunter dangled over the water like a rag doll.

Gideon's eyes welled with tears. He pushed Paige aside and ran for Frank. Gideon jumped and grabbed hold of Frank's leg. The Winged Ripper looked down at Gideon and snapped its beak at him. It swung Frank from side to side like a pendulum. Gideon lost his grip on Frank and hit the lake just as a large wave washed over him. Salt water filled his mouth and nose. Gideon spit the water out and waded after Frank and his wormhole jumper. But both his ship and his friend quickly disappeared over the horizon.

Gideon's shoulders slumped. Waves crashed into him. *I've lost everything. What do I do now?* He turned as someone waded into the surf. It was Kaz. He was covered in purple blood from the Winged Rippers. He closed his eyes and let the waves wash over him. The white-capped waves turned purple. He dunked himself under water. A purple pool bubbled around him. When he re-emerged he was clean. He bowed his head to Gideon.

"I'm sorry about Frank-san and your ship. If I had been earlier, perhaps things could have been different. Senpai was reluctant to let me leave the Pure Earth unguarded."

"None of that makes any difference now, Kaz. Does it?""

"No, I suppose it doesn't." Kaz turned and waded back to the beach.

"Gideon, we got more Rippers comin'," Paige shouted from the beach. "Get outta the water."

Gideon pressed the side of his sunglasses and zoomed in on the horizon. A flock of Winged Rippers was flying low over the water. They were racing straight for Gideon. *Boy they're fast. They'll be here in about two minutes.* A large white-capped wave reared up in front of Gideon. He turned his back on it and rode it to shore. Paige was waiting for him. Her crossbow was slung across her back. She looked at Gideon wide-eyed with concern.

"Are ya okay? Sorry yer ship and yer friend got taken."

Gideon checked his wrist pad. The jumper was about seven miles away and moving east. Frank's words echoed in his mind. *What happens to you isn't as important as what you do about it.* "If I can find my ship, I can find Frank. Come on let's get out of here."

Gideon took Paige by the hand and ran toward the stone pyramid. The beach was covered with smatterings of purple blood, amputated body parts and disembodied heads of Winged Rippers. *Kaz really did a job on those Rippers.* A shriek echoed across the lake. Gideon looked over his shoulder. The Winged Rippers were closing fast. Dozens of single purple eyes narrowed. Beaks snapped open and shut.

"Thar too fast, Gideon. We'll never make it."

The stone pyramid loomed just up ahead. The wide-eyed face carved into the entrance stared at Gideon. Kaz stood in the gaping mouth and waved them forward. The Winged Rippers closed in. Dark shadows covered the ground around Gideon. The air behind him was buffeted by beating wings. The smell of rotting flesh and garbage enveloped him. Outstretched hands grabbed for him. Gideon squeezed Paige's hand and flung her into the stone pyramid. The entranceway seemed to swallow her as she disappeared inside. Claws slashed at Gideon as he dove through the entranceway. He hit the hard stone floor and rolled. A Winged Ripper tried to follow Gideon inside but got stuck in the entranceway. Its wings were bent and the monster was hunched over. It snapped its beak and swung its human-like arms wildly. The more it struggled the more wedged in the entryway it became. It shrieked in frustration.

Winged Rippers stuck their heads through the small oval-shaped portholes carved into the pyramid. Their single purple eye filled the porthole. Paige raised her crossbow and hit each one in quick succession. As she felled one Winged Ripper, another one quickly took its place. Sharp claws scratched at the rocky walls of the pyramid as the Winged Rippers looked for a way inside. It sounded like nails on a chalkboard.

Kaz unsheathed his sword. He stepped toward the Winged Ripper wedged in the entryway. It reached for him with its human-like arms. It shrieked and snapped at him.

"No, Kaz," Doctor Wells said. "It's stuck like a cork in a bottle. It's not going anywhere."

Kaz sheathed his sword and bowed his head toward Doctor Wells. "Senpai, please reconsider. It may be calling to the other Winged Rippers, letting them know where we are."

Gideon shoved Kaz aside and jammed his Shocker into the Winged Ripper's chest. The monster convulsed. Smoke rose from its body. Its single purple eye rolled back into its head. Then it sagged against the walls of the entryway. "That's for Frank you creepy looking freak."

"Gideon, that's enough." Doctor Wells grabbed Gideon by the shoulder and spun him around. His eyes fell to the claw marks raked across the chest of Gideon's torn flight suit. "Gideon, you're hurt. Let me see the wounds on your chest."

"Dad, I'm fine."

"Please open the flight suit, son. Let me see if you're hurt."

Gideon unzipped his flight suit. Across his chest were five faded red stripes. They looked like wounds that were several weeks old. "See, I'm fine."

"Those look like older bruises. Maybe from the jumper's safety harness," Doctor Wells said. "I'll examine you back at med-lab."

Paige gasped. "But I saw the Winged Ripper slash ya good, Gideon. The rips in yer flight suit prove it. How are ya healin' so fast?"

"I don't remember getting hurt, Paige. The fighting…everything…it was so fast." Gideon zipped his flight suit back up. He checked to make sure he hadn't lost his Chain of Remembrance. Gideon breathed a sigh of relief when he closed his hand around it. "Kaz, did you see anything?"

"No, Gideon-san. I only saw Frank-san and your jumper taken away by the Winged Rippers."

"What?" Doctor Wells said. "They have your ship?"

"And Frank too, Dad."

"Yes, yes. I'm sorry about that. I assumed he was dead."

"Well I don't think he's dead!" Gideon shouted. "If he was, the Winged Rippers would have left his body on the beach."

"Son, calm down. I'm sorry about your friend. But the thing we need to focus on is getting your ship back."

"Frank already told me that." Gideon held up his wrist pad. "I can track the jumper with this."

"Good, because under no circumstances can Gwendolyn be allowed to go to Earth. She told me more than once she thought Berserkers were the next step in human evolution. In order to prove her theory correct she wanted to send a stronger strain of the Virus back to Earth with some Berserkers. If she uses your wormhole jumper to do that, she can wipe out humanity with a new pandemic. Then Berserkers like Sara could replace humans as the dominant species on Earth. Promise me you won't let that happen."

"Dad, the jumper's computer can get her through the wormhole but after that she needs a pilot."

"No, she doesn't, Gideon. It doesn't matter if the jumper crashes on Earth. The Virus would be introduced into the atmosphere upon impact and the Berserkers would survive the crash. Remember, they can regenerate."

"Oh, I didn't think of that."

"Son, you need to figure out a way to get your ship back."

Gideon put his hand on his chin and pursed his lips. *What would Frank do?*

"Gideon, when my pa was alive, he ran the comin' and goin' of all the ships flyin' to the minin' camp. I remember him gettin' real mad when the ships didn't stick to the schedule he fixed fer 'em. Or when they flew a path different from the one he gave 'em permission fer. Thar was this one time—"

"That's it. Paige, you're a genius. If Gwendolyn tries to go to Earth with my jumper, she has to follow my pre-approved flight plan. Earth's quarantine rules are strict. If she violates them, she'll get blasted out of the sky as soon as she gets to the other side of the wormhole. That means I know when she's planning on leaving. She has three days to repair my ship and prep it for launch. I'll let her do all the repairs and prep work. Then I'll steal it back and fly out of here."

"Spoken like a true Galaxy Class Pilot, son."

"A very risky plan, Gideon-san. The maglev will be well guarded by Rippers and Berserkers."

"Do you have a better idea, Kaz? If so, I'd like to hear it."

"Gideon-san, giving the jumper to Gwendolyn is a simple business transaction for the Raiders. In order to increase the salvage value of the jumper, they will repair it *before* they give it to her. Their vessel has everything onboard to do this. It used to be a mining ship and is well equipped."

"Kaz, are you saying we can sneak aboard the Raider ship and steal back my jumper without being caught? That sounds crazy."

"Gideon-san, the Raiders have a small crew onboard. They don't have enough men to guard the jumper and man their own ship. We can board their ship at a place along the route to Gwendolyn's when they're most distracted. We can then steal the jumper from them, fly it to the maglev and then you launch for home."

Gideon crossed his arms over his chest. "And you know where this place is? You know where they'll be the most distracted?"

"Yes, Gideon-san, the canal locks. Check the nav points on your wrist-pad. In order to reach Gwendolyn's island with a ship as big as theirs they have to go through the locks. They have no choice. And it will take every single one of the crew to get that ship through because they need to operate the locks and pilot their ship."

A terrible high-pitched shriek filled the stone pyramid. The Winged Ripper trapped inside the entryway regenerated. It clawed and scraped at the blocks of stone. Its beak snapped furiously. As it shrieked, the scratching on the outside of the stone pyramid got louder and more intense. Winged Rippers reached inside the oval portholes. Their clawed hands grabbed the rims of the portholes and pulled and scratched. Then the east wall of the pyramid collapsed. The huge rocks tumbled like an avalanche onto the Winged Rippers. Dust clouds choked Gideon.

"We need to get out of here before the whole thing collapses on us. Come on." Gideon held his Shocker at the ready and scaled the collapsed wall of the pyramid. Beneath him was a mix of purple, blood stained boulders, broken Ripper wings, smashed arms and crushed heads. Winged Rippers circled overhead. Dozens of them filled the sky. A trio of the monsters swooped down at Gideon. Darts hit each of them in their single purple eye. The blinded monsters slammed into the collapsed wall of the pyramid. Gideon jammed his Shocker into them. Then another swarm dove for Gideon.

"I know a way outta here, Gideon. Follow me." Paige kept her crossbow leveled at the Winged Rippers. She fired a salvo of darts at the monsters while nimbly running across the pile of rocks. She never took her eyes off the Winged Rippers while she ran. She hit each of the monsters in the eye and neck. The Winged Rippers grabbed at the darts and veered off.

How does she do that? She moves like a cat.

Doctor Wells struggled to climb over the rocks. He held the case of Pure Earth in one hand and tried to pull himself up with the other. Then Kaz bounded up the rock pile, grabbed Doctor Wells by the collar and dragged him over the rocks. Winged Rippers dove at Kaz. He let go of Doctor Wells unsheathed his sword and took the nearest monster's head in one quick slash. He spun and took the arms of another Winged Ripper and sliced a third in half at the waist. He cleaned the blood off his sword with a quick flick of his wrist, spattering the rocks with purple blood. Kaz sheathed his sword with one fluid motion and grabbed hold of Doctor Wells. The two of them climbed down the rocks and fell in place next to Gideon.

Gideon followed closely behind Paige. Her camouflage cloak billowed around her. Her red ponytail bounced against her back. Gideon ran past several large stone pyramids and smaller stone heads. The faces carved into them stared at him as he ran past. "Paige, what is this place?"

"It's a Shape Shifter burial ground. These are all family tombs yer seein'."

"That's creepy."

The roar of the waterfall grew louder. It echoed in Gideon's ears. It sounded like a giant airplane engine. A wall of mist rose up toward the sky. Water coursed over the cliffs and into the lower lake basin. Then the Winged Rippers came. A swarm of them swooped overhead. They flew past Gideon, pulled up high over the waterfall and disappeared into the mist that rose above the falls.

Gideon squeezed his Shocker so tight his hands hurt. "Paige, those Winged Rippers are preparing to attack. There's too many of them to fight off. We need to find cover now."

"That tomb up thar is what we want. It ain't much further. Come on, we can make it." Paige pointed at a stone head as big as the wormhole jumper. It had a sad, pained face carved into it. The eyes were drooping. On its cheeks, grew patches of purple moss that looked like Off World tears. The lips were pulled back, the mouth downcast.

It's only about fifty yards. We can make it.

Doctor Wells was red faced and wheezing. Sweat poured off him. He hugged the case of Pure Earth close to his chest as Kaz pulled him by the collar.

"Come on, Senpai. Just a little further, you can make it."

From out of the mist, the Winged Rippers appeared. They reminded Gideon of a squadron of fighter jets. The first set of black wings was folded tightly alongside the monster's human torso to allow for a faster dive. The second set of wings were raised and slightly fanned out and looked like a V, allowing the Winged Rippers to steer. They extended their legs forward and splayed their talons. Razor sharp claws reached for Gideon. Beaks flashed open exposing rows of sharp teeth. Their single purple eye was filled with bloodlust.

Gideon held the Shocker down by his waist like a spear. His throat tightened. He ran as fast as he could. His flight boots thumped across the hard rocky ground in time with his heartbeat. He started to pull ahead of Paige. The Winged Rippers closed in. Gideon grabbed Paige by the arm and pulled her after him. Her eyes were wide with fear. *I've never seen her look scared. Only twenty yards to go, it's going to be close. Please, God, let me—"*

"We'll never make it. I have to protect the Pure Earth." Doctor Wells turned away from Gideon and ran for the waterfall. He looked like a man possessed. His face was wild and crazed. Kaz chased after him. His scabbard bounced against his hip as he ran.

The formation of Winged Rippers split. Half veered after Doctor Wells and Kaz. The other half zoomed toward Gideon and Paige.

Then a blur of blue-grey feathers swallowed the Winged Rippers. One by one the Winged Rippers were snatched out of the sky. Gideon pumped his fist in the air. "Yeah, the Lake Hawks!"

"I told ya the Lake Hawks wouldn't like the Rippers invadin' thar nestin' grounds," Paige said.

The Winged Rippers tried to fight back but were no match for the bigger, stronger Lake Hawks. The Lake Hawks sunk their talons into the Winged Rippers, driving them over the cliff and into the waterfall.

Gideon grimaced as a Lake Hawk with white feathers on its head used its talons to tear a Winged Ripper in half. It tossed the two pieces of Winged Ripper over the cliff and turned toward Gideon. It trained its three purple eyes on him and shrieked.

Then it pumped its four wings and headed for the group of Winged Rippers attacking Kaz and Doctor Wells.

Doctor Wells stood at the edge of the cliff. He swung the case of Pure Earth wildly, trying to fend off the Winged Rippers.

Kaz swatted at them with his sword. But the Winged Rippers stayed just out of reach of his katana.

Then the Lake Hawk slammed into the Winged Rippers attacking Kaz and Gideon's father.

Kaz jumped out of the way and rolled.

Doctor Wells stumbled. He dropped the case of Pure Earth. The case bounced off the edge of the cliff overlooking the falls. Doctor Wells grabbed for it but lost his balance and disappeared over the cliff along with the case of Pure Earth.

CHAPTER 19

Gideon ran to the cliff's edge and peered over. The height was dizzying, nausea swept through him. He sank to his knees and took a deep breath to steady himself. *I had no idea we were up so high.* He slowly leaned over the edge. His mouth fell open in surprise. *I thought there was only one waterfall. There must be at least fifty of them.*

Like a staircase for giants, dozens of separate falls were tiered along the mountainside. Some of them reminded Gideon of Niagara Falls while others were much bigger. Water cascaded over the different falls and into the lower lake basin. Mist rose up into the air. The glare from the red and yellow suns made it look like orange smoke. Purple moss carpeted the rock face. Lake Hawks clung to it with their talons. Gideon gasped when a flock of Lake Hawks flew through a cluster of falls, disappearing behind them. Another flock emerged from behind a higher tier of falls, spread their four massive wings and rode the air current. But Doctor Wells was nowhere to be seen.

Gideon grabbed hold his Chain of Remembrance. *How did I mess this up so badly? Frank, Vince, my father, they're all gone. Even my ship's gone. What kind of Galaxy Class Pilot loses his ship, his crew and his father to a bunch of winged freaks? I'm never leaving this rock now.*

A strong hand squeezed Gideon's shoulder. It was Paige. She stood silently next to him. Purple streaks lined her cheeks. She grabbed his hand, pulled him away from the cliff's edge and hugged him. Paige squeezed Gideon so hard he had trouble breathing. She brushed her lips next to his ear. Gideon could smell her hair as her ponytail fell over her shoulder and into his face. *How is it she always smells like strawberries?* Warmth coursed through him. Paige said something that sounded like "I'm so sorry" but her words were lost to the roar of the waterfall. Paige took Gideon's hand and led him to the large head-shaped tomb. The weeping face sculpted into the stone stared at Gideon. Paige dropped to her hands and knees and crawled through the downturned mouth carved into its front.

Gideon followed close behind Paige and entered the tomb.

Streaks of light stabbed through the cracks in the rock, slicing away the darkness. The inside of the tomb was cramped but spacious enough for Gideon to stand. A boxy sarcophagus with Lake Hawks chiseled into it was carved into the far wall. Kaz sat cross-legged next to the sarcophagus. His sword rested across his lap. When Gideon entered, Kaz stood and bowed so low his head nearly touched the ground. When he rose, his eyes welled with tears.

"Gideon-san, I'm sorry for your loss. Senpai was an honorable man. He took me in after Gwendolyn destroyed my family. The miners wanted to banish me but Senpai refused to allow it. I will miss him."

Paige wiped purple tears from her face. "He was the kindest man I ever did know."

Gideon squeezed his Chain of Remembrance so hard his hand hurt.

"I can't believe he's gone, Kaz. We didn't get a chance to say goodbye or nothin'."

Kaz hugged Paige. "I know, Paige-san."

Gideon clinched his jaw and let his Chain of Remembrance fall against his chest. He used his wrist pad to perform a diagnostic check on the jumper. The ship was now fifteen miles away. Its battery was being recharged and a replacement wing was already attached. "Can we focus on getting my ship back? The Raiders have fixed—"

Paige stormed over to Gideon and slapped him so hard he hit the ground.

Gideon rubbed his cheek. Small cartoonish stars flooded his vision. "Hey, what's your problem?"

"Yer my problem."

Gideon blinked away the small stars. *Boy is she strong.*

"Yer father, the kindest man I ever knew just died and all ya can do is worry about yer ship? Are ya dead inside? Have ya forgotten how to feel, how to value life?"

Gideon jumped to his feet. "You don't know the first thing about me, Paige. What do you want me to say, that I'm glad my father looked after you two after he left my mother and me? That I'm happy he was able to do for you guys what he refused to do for me?"

Paige's eyes shot daggers at Gideon.

"Let me tell you something, Paige. I already said goodbye to my father. I did it three years ago. I was ten years old and cried my eyes out every night for a year after he left. It was the height of the Virus. Everybody I knew was dying. Did my father stick around to look after us? No, he left. And you want to know what the really pathetic thing is? I blamed myself for his leaving. But then I smartened up and got mad because after he left us I never heard from him. There was no Christmas message, no birthday message, there was nothing. There wasn't even a message when my mother died. After that I realized I would never see him again, that he was dead to me. But as if that wasn't bad enough, I have to come to this awful place and find that he decided to get himself a new son, that I wasn't good enough for him after all. He never loved my mother or me. He probably even had an Off World wife he never told me about."

"He did love ya, Gideon. He talked about ya all the time."

"Save it, Paige. I don't need your pity party."

Paige lunged at Gideon but was intercepted by Kaz.

"Paige-san, don't."

"But he hasn't even shed one tear fer his own pa. He's stone cold."

Stone cold—the words echoed in Gideon's head. It's what his roommate Adrian called him before he left for Off World. *I do what I need to do to survive. It got me through the Virus. It got me through Quarantine. It'll get me off this rock and back home.* Gideon shrugged his shoulders. "Believe what you want, Paige. I don't care what you think because I'm not staying on this rock long anyway. In three days time, I'm out of here."

"Yer so—"

"Pig headed?" Gideon offered.

"No, that's an insult to pigs." Paige crossed her arms and stared at Gideon as if daring him to say something.

"Everybody, just calm down," Kaz said.

"Calm down? She slapped me. If she weren't a girl, I'd kick her butt."

"Don't let that stop ya, Gideon. I've fought worse then some skinny Earthlin' boy."

Kaz looked at Gideon's cheek. "She didn't hit you that hard, Gideon-san. There's not even a mark on your face."

Gideon held up his sunglasses and looked at his face in the reflective lenses. *No mark? How's that possible? She hit me harder than any of those morons in Quarantine ever did.*

Fast moving shadows blocked the rays of light poking into the tomb, plunging it into darkness. Shrieks pierced Gideon's ears. Sharp claws scratched at the outside of the tomb. Then a Winged Ripper stuck its head and shoulders through the entryway. It looked at Gideon with its single purple eye and snapped its beak at him. Kaz unsheathed his sword and took its head in one fluid motion. The Winged Ripper's head rolled toward Paige. She kicked it away in disgust.

Gideon quickly scanned the inside of the tomb for a way out. There were no windows or doors. The headless Winged Ripper was jammed in the entryway. "Paige, why did you bring us in here? Now we're trapped."

"Ya think I'm an eejit? We ain't trapped, Gideon. This here is the way out." Paige pointed at the sarcophagus. "Don't stand thar gawkin'. Are ya men or not? Help me push the cover off."

Gideon and Kaz stood next to Paige and pushed against the cover. The stone slab grated against the sarcophagus and fell to the floor with a thud. It broke into several pieces. Gideon peered inside. The bottom was broken out and led to a tunnel. A blast of dank air hit Gideon in the face. He stepped back and pulled his flight suit up over his nose.

"That smells terrible, Paige. What's down there? Where does it lead?"

"It's the Shifter catacombs. They'll be takin' us out and down to the lower lake basin."

Gideon took off his backpack and pulled out two long, thin cylinders. He bent them until they made a snapping noise. Then he shook them until they glowed. The red one he gave to Kaz.

"Thank you for the glow stick, Gideon-san. What will you use?"

"My glasses will let me see just fine, Kaz." Gideon gave the green glow stick to Paige and pointed toward the tunnel entrance. "Here, Paige, I'd say ladies first but after that slap you gave me I'm not so sure the word applies to you."

Paige grunted. She snatched the glow stick from Gideon and descended into the catacombs.

Other than the red and green glow sticks, it was pitch black inside the catacombs. It smelled musty and damp like an old basement. The sound of water dripping echoed. Gideon adjusted the settings on his glasses and waited a moment for them to focus. The glasses whirred as the lenses adjusted to the darkness. Gideon gasped. He was standing at the top of a long staircase carved into the rock. It led to a huge cavern. Long, sharp, red stalactites hung from the ceiling. They were met by sharp, pointy red stalagmites rising out of the ground. It looked like the cavern was the mouth of a giant monster that had just fed. Pools of water collected on the ground. Near the walls of the cavern long-stemmed mushrooms grew. As Gideon's group descended the stairs and got closer to the mushrooms, they glowed white.

"Don't touch nothin' down here," Paige said. "The mushrooms be poisonous. They glow to attract thar prey."

"I can't see anything, Paige-san. Can you?"

"Not so good, Kaz. These sticks ain't givin' more than a few feet of light."

"Paige, if you tell me which way to go, I'll take point. I can see just fine with my glasses."

"Thar's only one way, Gideon. Follow the path."

In front of Gideon lay a smooth walkway. On one side was the tunnel wall. It was lined with purple moss and the glowing, long-stemmed mushrooms. On the other side, water flowed down the rocks and in between the stalagmites. Large pools collected where the tunnel's downward slant leveled out. Toads glowing fluorescent green jumped into the pools of water as Gideon's group walked by. Then a squeaking noise echoed through the tunnel. It was followed by a clapping noise. Wind hit Gideon in the face. He stopped walking. Paige and Kaz bumped into him.

"Why are ya stopping'?" Paige asked.

"Something's coming." Gideon held the Shocker out in front of him. Light from the orb on its end flickered against the tunnel walls. Then a white cloud exploded in front of Gideon. It was thousands of white, bat-like creatures. They had one large pink eye and furry antennae sticking out of their heads. Their wings buffeted the air. Gideon fell to his stomach and yelled, "Hit the deck."

Paige and Kaz fell next to Gideon. Paige covered the glow sticks with her cloak. "Gideon, let go yer Shocker."

Gideon took his hands off the Shocker. The light in the orb disappeared, plunging the tunnel into total darkness. Then the swarm of bat-like creatures veered away from Gideon. It flew near the top of the tunnel. It wove in between the stalactites until it finally flew off. Its squeaking echoed after it as it flew back up the tunnel.

"It was the light from the glow sticks and the Shocker that attracted 'em."

"Smart, Paige-san, very smart."

Paige uncovered her cloak. The red and green glow sticks stared at Gideon like two angry eyes.

"Come on, you guys. Let's go." Gideon held his Shocker out in front of him. His flight boots echoed across the smooth stone path. Then the path suddenly dropped off. It sloped at a forty-five degree angle. Gideon started to slide. He grabbed at the wall to try to stop himself but his hand found nothing but wet slippery rock. Then Gideon fell onto his back. He zoomed down the path. Gideon held the Shocker out in front of him and raised his feet. Faster and faster he slid until his flight boots slammed into a wall. The wall moved. It opened slightly to reveal another cavern. Gideon kicked it open and went inside.

The cavern was vast. The walls were pockmarked with thousands of narrow shelves carved into the rock. The shelves ran from the floor to the ceiling. It reminded Gideon of the cramped sleeping quarters he had seen in Galaxy Class Cruisers. *This must be the main catacomb*. Piles of dusty bones littered some of the shelves. Others had decomposed bodies lying in them. A long corridor veered off to the right. It was lined with skulls. Their jaws hung open giving them maniacal smiles. Gideon's throat tightened. His mind flashed back to the darkest days of the Virus. Piles of dead were stacked in the street. Starving dogs tore at their limbs. Nobody took the bodies away. The soldiers that were still alive were too busy shooting the infected. *Is this what I'm going to look like after Gwendolyn gets ahold of me?* Gideon closed his eyes and took several deep breaths.

"Gideon, where are ya?" Paige called out, her voice echoing through the catacomb. "Ya best be waitin' for us."

"Paige, Kaz, I'm in here, you guys."

Paige entered the main catacomb and froze. "Thar's so many of 'em. All of 'em dead Shifters."

"These are Shape Shifters? The bones look human." Gideon walked up to one of the shelves and looked at the skeleton. Its mummified and decomposed face was twisted into a painful expression. Black beetles crawled out of its eye sockets but the facial bones had no abnormalities.

"Gideon, Shifter bones are bendy to allow fer shiftin' to other forms. But other than that, a Shifter's natural form ain't much different than yours."

"Don't you mean ours?"

A low whistle echoed in the catacomb. It was Kaz. "So many dead Yokai. It's bad luck for us to be around all these unpure creatures even if they are dead. We need to leave, Gideon-san."

"Yokai? Kaz, what's a Yokai?"

"Gideon-san, Shape Shifters are impure creatures. I call them Yokai."

"Hush up, Kaz. Don't be sellin' that nonsense again. Shifters ain't monsters and they ain't evil. Ya probably wouldn't know one if it was standin' next to ya."

"Paige-san, the Yokai are cowards. They use their impure blood to hide under the skin of another creature."

"Kaz, I'll hear no more of yer racist talk." Paige stomped off to inspect the skulls lining the walls of the nearby corridor.

"Kaz, what do you mean impure? Are they poisonous?"

"Gideon-san, a Shifter's blood is polluted by a nasty mixture of things that allow them to change into lesser beings. Unlike them, *my* bloodline is pure. I can trace it back centuries to my samurai ancestors. I know who I am. The same cannot be said of the Yokai."

"That's cool your ancestors were samurai. Mine were teachers, scientists and farmers. I remember my grandfather telling me that during the narco wars he'd seen blueblood officers who were some of the worst cowards. But that the poor farmers fighting to protect their land were some of the bravest men he'd ever seen."

"This corridor looks to be the way outta here," Paige said. "If ya all are done pontificatin' we should go."

"Let's roll." Gideon held the Shocker out in front of him and stepped into the narrow corridor. Walls rose up on both sides of him, closing off the main catacomb. The skulls in the wall gaped at Gideon. They looked like they might bite him at any moment. Gideon took a deep breath and tried to focus on the path and not on the skulls in the wall. *They're all dead. They won't bite. They won't come after me.* The corridor zigzagged and sloped downward before it opened into a large cavern. Gideon gasped. Thousands of skeletons were stacked like cords of firewood from the floor to the ceiling. The bones were blackened and charred. They were bent, drooping and twisted. They looked like they were made from melted wax.

Paige grabbed Gideon's hand. "What happened to 'em all?"

"I don't know, Paige. It looks like blasters did this, maybe even DNA scramblers."

"That's exactly what it was, Gideon-san. They attacked my family's mining interests and we defended our property and ourselves. They got what they deserved."

"Kaz, did ya ever think they were defendin' their land and families from yer minin'?"

Gideon took a deep breath. *They were slaughtered. What a terrible way to die. No wonder Shifters hate humans.*

"Gideon, I don't want to be lookin' at this anymore. Can we go?"

Gideon scanned the catacomb. The only exit was a corridor off to the left. He locked fingers with Paige and led her into it. The corridor walls were lined with skulls and other bones. They were arranged in odd shapes and patterns Gideon had never seen before. *What kind of demented art project is this? Why would Shifters do this with their dead?*

"Paige, why are the bones arranged in these weird patterns?"

Paige held her glow stick up against the wall. It cast an eerie green light against the skulls. "The patterns yer seein' are animals. It looks like the Shifters are tryin' to show how they be linked with the creatures of this planet both in life and in death. This one here looks like a Lake Hawk. The Shifters of this clan must be havin' a special bond with the Lake Hawks."

Gideon stepped back and looked at the bony mosaic. The skulls were arranged in an arching pattern that looked like four wings. At the top of the mosaic, the bird of prey's head was outlined. In its center sat three skulls—exactly where a Lake Hawk's eyes would be. "Yeah, I see it now. It's definitely a Lake Hawk."

Kaz gave a disapproving hiss. "It's just a bunch of skulls stuffed into a wall, Gideon-san. It's barbaric. The Yokai don't even bury their dead properly."

"You really don't like Shifters, do you, Kaz?"

"Gideon-san, my father taught me two things about the Yokai. First, the only good Yokai is a dead Yokai. Second, the only thing worse than a Yokai is a half-breed."

"A what, Kaz?"

"A creature that is half-human and half-Yokai. There are rumors that such a creature exists but nobody's ever seen it, Gideon-san."

"Kaz, ya need to cop on and stop actin' the maggot. Nothin' like that exists. Even if it did, it'd be a race between Shifters and humans to see which of 'em could kill it first."

"I'm out of here. You two are starting to make me crazy." Gideon exited the corridor and entered a large cavern. Long purple stalactites stabbed down at him. He wove his way past them. Some of them dripped water into large pools. The sound echoed throughout the tunnel. Other stalactites had dark green vines wrapped around them. Then the vines started to move. Florescent purple eyes stared at Gideon. A hissing sound filled the tunnel. "What are those? Are they—"

"Snakes," screamed Paige. "I hate snakes."

Gideon ducked as a snake snapped at his head. He stabbed his Shocker at it. The snake convulsed and slid off the stalagmite. It dropped to the tunnel floor like offal from a large fang. Smoke rose from its body. The tunnel smelled like burnt meat.

Kaz unsheathed his sword. With one quick motion he decapitated three snakes.

Paige stood wide-eyed. She was frozen in place.

"Paige, you chase after Rippers but are afraid of snakes? Are you kidding me?" Gideon said.

"They got no arms, no legs," Paige shouted. "It ain't right grovelin' and slitherin' like they do."

There were hundreds of snakes on the floor of the cave. Dozens hung from the stalactites. They dropped to the floor in front of Gideon, blocking the tunnel. Gideon used his Shocker to drive them away.

Kaz took the heads of the snakes that reared up to strike.

Paige closed her eyes and screamed. "Get 'em away from me."

Gideon grabbed Paige by the arm and pulled her close to him. He swung and stabbed with his Shocker. The electrified orb on the end of the Shocker flashed and crackled. The snakes closed their purple eyes and hissed at Gideon. They turned and fled back into the darkness of the tunnel. "The light from my Shocker hurts their eyes. Come on, let's get out of here."

Gideon took Paige's hand and ran up the tunnel. Kaz was close behind. Gideon dodged stalagmites and jumped over pools of water. The smell of fresh lake air wafted in. It fought with the musty, dank smell of the tunnel and pushed it aside. Then like a hole in the darkness, light poked its way into the far end of the tunnel. The roar of the waterfall echoed just up ahead.

Gideon emerged from the tunnel into the lower lake basin. A mix of yellow and purple flowers carpeted the ground. Tall conifer trees lined the near shore of the lake. Purple moss covered cliffs bordered the far side. The caves in the cliff face looked like gaping mouths. Lake Hawks entered and exited the caves, while others circled lazily overhead. The roar from dozens of falls filled the air. Water poured over them like an endless tsunami, feeding into the lower lake. A wall of mist rose high into the afternoon sky. Gideon took a deep cleansing breath. The sweet smell of pollen made the inside of his nose itch. He fought the urge to sneeze. "Boy I'm glad to be out of that tunnel. Hey, Paige—"

Paige was hugging Kaz. "The snakes were awful. I can't stand 'em."

"I know, Paige-san. But you got through it."

Gideon stabbed his Shocker into the ground so hard it stuck. *I get her out of the snake infested tunnel and he gets the credit? Okay, just chill. It doesn't matter, I'm leaving this rock.* Gideon checked his wrist pad. The jumper was repaired and moving east toward the locks. *Wow, Kaz was right. Maybe I can trust him after all.* "Hey, Kaz, you were right. My jumper is headed for the locks. But, it's twenty miles from here. Unless you can find us a ride, I don't see how we get there before that Raider ship does."

A Lake Hawk swooped in low. The shadow cast from its four outstretched wings blanketed Gideon. The blue and grey feathered bird of prey landed right in front of him. It towered over Gideon. *It's almost as big as the jumper.* The purple eye in the center of its forehead blinked at him. The eye on the left side of its head looked at Paige. The one on the right rolled toward Kaz.

Gideon pulled his Shocker out of the ground and held it out in front of him. The orb on the end popped and crackled. The massive bird squawked at Gideon. He raised his Shocker. *Maybe if I can stab it in the eye.*

Paige's crossbow buzzed and whirred. Kaz unsheathed his sword. Then the Lake Hawk blurred like an old fashioned hologram and disappeared—in its place stood a purple-skinned humanoid.

Gideon's breath caught in his chest. *A Shape Shifter*

CHAPTER 20

Gideon held his Shocker out in front of him. The orb on the end crackled. The long spear-like weapon thrummed with energy, making his arms vibrate. He grit his teeth and took a fighting stance.

The Shifter wore a dark purple loincloth. He had long white dreadlocks. The unruly coils of hair hung well past his shoulders. He was no taller than Gideon but looked very strong and athletic. He reminded Gideon of a gymnast. The Shifter's purple skin was covered in tattoos—pictures of odd shapes and animals that Gideon had never seen before. The tattoos swirled and flowed like fast moving storm clouds across a purple sky. The animals and shapes constantly changed into new and different forms.

Paige leveled her crossbow at the Shifter. "Stay back. Don't be gettin' no closer."

Kaz crouched into a fighting stance and held his sword at the ready. "He looks like a Yakuza criminal. Why am I not surprised? Gideon-san, the three of us should attack this filthy Yokai before it shifts. Kill it while it's vulnerable."

"Kaz, you and Paige need to stand down and let *me* do the talking."

The Shifter's eyes were a light purple, not as dark as Paige's or Kaz's, with pupils slit like a predator's. "Why were you humans in our burial ground? How did you find your way into our catacombs?" the Shifter said in a deep, gruff voice.

Gideon's hands tightened around his Shocker. Lightning bolts licked the inside of the weapon's orb. "We were trying to escape from Gwendolyn's monsters. If you saw us in your burial ground, then you must have seen the Winged Rippers that were chasing us. I'm sorry. We meant no disrespect."

"You meant no disrespect? Your kind doesn't know the first thing about respect. Even now you point weapons at me."

He's right. If I can get him to trust me, maybe he'll help me get my jumper back. Then I can ditch Kaz and Paige if I need to. Frank was right. I shouldn't trust them. Gideon lowered his Shocker. The orb went dark. "I apologize. You're right. I should not be pointing my weapon at you. Kaz, Paige, lower your weapons. Let's hear what he has to say."

The Shifter's eyes went wide with surprise.

Paige lowered her crossbow. "I hope ya know what yer doin', Gideon."

"Me too, Paige. He probably could have killed me when he was a Lake Hawk. But he didn't. He shifted back to his normal form. Maybe he's not here to fight."

"Gideon-san, this is a bad idea. It's cowardly to surrender. I will not sheath my sword."

"Talking isn't surrendering, Kaz."

"You are brave for one so young," the Shifter said to Gideon. Then he turned to Kaz and scowled. His tattoos whirled and spun. "Why are *you* here, Kazutoshi Muramatsu? You know better than to come here."

Kaz nodded toward Gideon. "I'm taking him to the canal locks so he can get his ship back from the Raiders."

"You know this guy, Kaz?"

"No, Gideon-san. I don't know him. I don't know *any* Yokai."

The Shifter gave Kaz a wicked smile. "You may not know me, but I know who you are. My entire clan knows who you are. You're the heir to the great and mighty Muramatsu Mining fortune. How's that inheritance looking now, boy?"

Kaz raised his sword above his head. "You filthy, Yokai."

"Gideon, ya need to do somethin' before this gets baad," Paige said.

Gideon pushed away his fear of the Shifter and stepped in front of Kaz. "Stand down, Kaz."

Then Gideon wiped his sweaty palm on his pant leg and extended his hand to the Shifter. "Hi, my name's Gideon Wells. It's nice to meet you."

"Are ya an eejit, Gideon? Don't be tellin' 'im yer name."

"Give me a break, Paige. I'm doing the best I can. He's my first alien."

The Shifter recoiled. "Wells? Did you say Wells? Are you the son of the human that created Gwendolyn, the Rippers, the Berserkers, and the Raiders?"

"What? My father didn't create—"

"So it's true. You are his son," the Shifter said.

Gideon took a deep breath. "Yes, it's true."

"As soon as I woke this morning, I knew today was going to be a special day. I felt it in my bones." The Shifter pointed at the sky. "And now, as the twin suns begin to set set and the moons rise, I have the son of the human who infected my planet with monsters. I also have the son of the one who ravaged my planet by digging for rocks."

The Shifter bared his teeth at Gideon. They grew from small humanoid teeth into long, pointy fangs. "Tell me why I shouldn't kill you and your friends now, Gideon Wells."

Gideon raised his Shocker. "Because I'm the only one on this planet that can destroy Gwendolyn is why."

"You're just a little human boy. What could you possibly do to her?" The Shifter studied Gideon with a raised brow. The tattoos on his chest and face spun and swirled.

Gideon squeezed his Shocker. His sweaty palms squeaked against the weapon. "I'm *not* just a little boy. I'm going to be fourteen soon."

"He'll be destroyin' Gwendolyn's lab and takin' her powers so she can't make no more Rippers is what he'll do," Paige said. "It's why she's chasin' 'im down. And it's why I'm helpin' 'im."

"And me," Kaz said.

The Shifter crossed his arms over his chest. "Is this true, Gideon Wells? Can you stop Gwendolyn from making her vile monsters?"

Gideon looked at Paige and Kaz in disbelief. *This is what they think? That I want to lead some war against Gwendolyn? I just want off this rock. But if I say no, they won't help me and the Shifter might kill me. What do I do?*

Gideon checked his wrist pad. The Raider ship was on course for the canal locks. "Look, Sir, if you take me to the canal locks, I'll explain everything to you on the way. Once we get there you'll see that the Raiders have my ship. Then you can judge for yourself if we're telling the truth."

The Shifter turned to Paige. He eyed her suspiciously and then sniffed at her.

Paige took a step behind Gideon. "What's he doin'?"

"How should I know?"

Kaz said, "He sniffs at you like a dog, Paige-san."

The Shifter shook his head back and forth. His white dreadlocks turned the same color as Paige's red hair. He examined his long coils of hair and grunted. "Well, you're right about the hair, young lady. It is a fantastic color. I see why you chose it. Maybe you're right about Gideon Wells."

"Great, so you'll take me to the locks and help me get my ship back?"

"No, Gideon Wells. I will not. Instead I will take all three of you there. And if I find you're lying to me, I will *kill* all three of you there. Do you understand, Gideon Wells?"

Gideon swallowed. "Yes, Sir, I understand. Can you tell me your name?"

"You couldn't pronounce it. But I suppose you should call me something." The Shifter glanced at Kaz. "What was the word you insulted me with, Kazutoshi Muramatsu? That primitive gibberish you speak has so many funny words. Yakuza is what you said I look like but…ah, Yokai. That was it. Call me Yokai."

"That word ain't so nice," Paige whispered to Gideon.

"I'm sure it's not, young lady," Yokai said. "But it keeps our relationship in perspective."

Then Yokai blurred and disappeared; in his place stood a Lake Hawk. The blue and white feathers on its face and head were tinged with red. The Lake Hawk bowed low to the ground. Its three eyes blinked in quick succession. "Climb aboard, children."

The giant bird of prey pumped its four massive wings and took to the air. Its powerful back muscles worked like pistons pushing Gideon up and down like he was riding a horse. In no time, Gideon was hundreds of feet in the air. "This is great. There's nothing better than flying."

Paige sat behind Gideon. Her arms were wrapped around his waist. Her head was buried in his neck. *Strawberries, she always smells like strawberries.*

Kaz sat behind Paige. His eyes were wide with fear, his face was pale. "I hate this, Gideon-san. It's worse than your wormhole jumper. At least the jumper has proper seats and safety harnesses."

"Just hold on tight. You'll be fine."

"Keep yer eyes closed, Kaz," Paige said.

"What? And miss this view? You're crazy, Paige. This is the best." Cold mist from the Whispering Rock Falls dappled Gideon's skin. Below him the dozens of falls that emptied into the lower lake basin roared like a giant jet engine. As the Lake Hawk gained altitude, the falls and the lake fell away. The lake looked like polished glass. Gideon beamed. He filled his lungs with the crisp salt air.

Then Gideon scanned the horizon. His mood sank along with Off World's setting suns. As dusk settled in, the orange and red suns dropped below the horizon, casting an orange hue across the early evening sky. In their place, two full moons—one green and one blue—hung low in the sky. Gideon rolled his Chain of Remembrance between his fingers. *Come morning, I have two days left to get off this rock. I'm running out of time.*

Gideon let go his Chain of Remembrance and checked his wrist pad. "Paige, Kaz, get comfortable you guys. It's going to take awhile to get to the locks."

As Yokai flew toward the locks, stars cut holes in the night sky. A meteor shower slashed overhead. The green and blue full moons continued their climb. The moons followed Gideon like the mismatched eyes of a large monster. Tendrils of bright, greenish-blue light bled into the lake. The waves moved like the undulating body of a green dragon.

The air grew colder. Gideon's teeth started chattering. Paige hugged him close. The warmth of her spread across his back. A hint of strawberries mixed with the salty air.

Gideon and his friends had been in the air over an hour. He checked his wrist pad. His wormhole jumper was only a few miles away. The jumper's wing was repaired and the batteries fully charged. But there was no sign of the Raider ship. Then a ghostly silhouette of yellow, red and green lights appeared on the lake.

Gideon switched to the nighttime setting on his glasses. The dark landscape turned to day. He blinked several times forcing his eyes to adjust. Up ahead, the Raider ship made its way toward the locks. "There it is, Yokai, the Raider ship."

The Lake Hawk bobbed his head up and down. "Yes, Gideon Wells I see it. Is your vessel onboard?"

Gideon increased the magnification on his glasses. They buzzed and whirred. The Raider ship bristled with tall super structures that reminded Gideon of apartment buildings. Piping snaked every which way. All sorts of mining equipment—large drill bits, steel drums, repair-bots and dozer-bots—were scattered haphazardly across the deck. The ship looked more like a floating super factory than a boat. It was bigger than any freighter Gideon had ever seen on the Great Lakes. *How can something that big stay afloat?*

The tallest super structure onboard was the pilothouse. It towered above the deck. Lights blazed inside. Glass wrapped around all sides of it. Gideon zoomed in on it. About a dozen crewmen were inside manning the controls. It bustled with activity.

Gideon zoomed in on his wormhole jumper. It sat on a helipad at the bow of the ship. It was unguarded. A long staircase ran from the helipad down to the ship's deck. There was also a large cargo lift that reminded Gideon of an old-fashioned elevator.

The helipad wasn't as high off the deck as the pilothouse but was still hundreds of feet in the air. Lights flooded the deck and the helipad. Gideon took a deep breath. *Good luck getting all the way up there without getting spotted by the Raiders. This is going to have to be a quick snatch and grab mission.*

Gideon leaned forward and shouted over the whistling wind. "Yokai, that small bird-like thing at the front of the Raider ship is my wormhole jumper."

Yokai spread his four wings and rode an air current high above the Raider ship. He bobbed his head as if agreeing with Gideon. Then he pumped his wings and headed toward the locks, leaving the Raider ship behind. Up ahead, the lake narrowed into a wide man-made tributary. Each bank was outlined by a row of red lights.

"Yokai, those must be the lane locks," Gideon said.

The lights blinked three times then turned yellow.

"Why are them lights blinkin' like that, Gideon? Is it a warnin' fer us to stay clear?"

"It's like a runway for boats, Paige. They're probably signaling the Raider ship, telling them its okay to enter the locks." Gideon looked over his shoulder to check on the Raider ship when something flashed in front of him. Then the air turned hot and sour.

Paige squeezed Gideon's shoulder. "Winged Rippers are comin'."

Three Winged Rippers dove for Gideon and his friends. Each one had a damaged eye socket. Two of the monsters had darts sticking out of their neck. "I don't believe it. They're the same ones we fought earlier. They must have followed us here."

"I can't be holdin' on to Yokai and shootin' my crossbow at the same time," Paige said.

"We need to land, Gideon-san. If we fall from this height we'll die."

Gideon looked down at the lake. They were hundreds of feet in the air. "Yokai, you need to land so we can fight these Winged Rippers."

Yokai folded his four wings and pointed his body toward the lake. Gideon fell forward as Paige slid into him. "Whoa! Yokai, let me know the next time you do something like that."

The wind whistled in Gideon's ears as Yokai dove. He looked over his shoulder. As fast as Yokai was diving, it wasn't enough. The Winged Rippers were gaining. Their black leathery wings were folded back over their human-like torsos. Their single purple eye narrowed. Their arms reached out for Gideon.

Gideon raised his Shocker with his right hand. He tried to extend it out toward the nearest Winged Ripper but the wind was too strong. The Shocker flew out of his hand like a toy sucked out of a car window. The Shocker spun end over end and hit a Winged Ripper. The monster exploded as soon as the Shocker hit it. The explosion almost knocked Gideon off Yokai's back.

"Are ya tryin' to kill us ya eejit?" Paige shouted.

"I had no idea it would explode." Gideon's breath caught in his chest. He thought back to the Ripper that exploded in the mining camp's med-lab. He checked his wrist pad and gasped even more. "It's been twelve hours since these Winged Rippers first attacked us back on the beach. Yokai, you need to get us out of here or we're dead. Those other Winged Rippers are going to explode too."

Yokai pulled up out of his dive and leveled off just above the lake. He skimmed its surface. White-capped waves sprayed Gideon's legs. Yokai pumped his four wings and quickly climbed into the night sky as a loud splash erupted from the lake. One of the Winged Rippers slammed into the water. It flapped its wings and flailed its human-like arms before disappearing under the waves. Then it exploded like a depth charge. Flames and water shot into the air.

But the last Winged Ripper closed in on Gideon. "Lookout, Yokai."

Yokai pulled up as the Winged Ripper shot past his beak. The blast of sour air from the monster made Gideon gag.

Then the Winged Ripper climbed into a tight U-turn and dove again. Gideon's mind raced. He thought back to the flight simulators he trained on back in Quarantine. "Yokai, he's going too fast. You can undercut him and make him fly past us if you bank sharp left when I tell you."

The monster dropped out of the sky like a guided missile. Its wings were folded back and its human-like arms were extended. Long claws reached for Gideon.

"Now, Yokai, bank left!"

Yokai dipped sharp to his left, forcing the Winged Ripper to fly past him. The monster snapped its beak as Yokai flew under it.

"Keep turning, Yokai. Now straighten out and fly for the beach. He's faster than us but we might be able to keep dodging him until you can set us down," Gideon said.

Kaz groaned. "I'm going to be sick."

"Gideon, it's comin' back," Paige said.

The Winged Ripper's four leathery wings sliced through the air. It came within a foot of Gideon. Its eye socket was bloodied. Its single eye was a milky purple. The Winged Ripper opened its beak horizontally and vertically, exposing all of its razor sharp teeth. It extended its arms for Gideon. Every muscle in Gideon's body tensed.

Then the Winged Ripper exploded.

A bright flash blinded Gideon. The night vision setting on his sunglasses overloaded. Searing heat enveloped him. Hot bone fragments from the Winged Ripper bit into Gideon like shrapnel. He lost his grip on Yokai.

CHAPTER 21

Gideon hit the lake like a hammer on an anvil. All the air was punched out of him. Briny water filled his mouth and nose. Pain erupted across his neck, chest, and arms as the salty lake water stabbed at his burns. The pain weighed him down like an anchor.

Gideon kicked and clawed at the water like a caged animal. His lungs screamed for air. His chest was about to explode.

Then Gideon broke the surface of the water. He gulped the sweet salty air. Exhausted, he lay on his back and gulped several deep breaths. White-capped waves pushed him toward shore.

When Gideon's feet touched bottom he struggled to stand. Strong waves slapped him in the back. He stumbled toward shore. His legs felt like they were filled with lead. Each step was harder than the last. When he stepped clear of the surf he sank to his knees and fell face first onto the beach.

Strong hands rolled Gideon onto his back.

Somebody put an ear to his chest.

The smell of strawberries wafted over him.

"Is he dead, Paige-san?"

"No, he's breathin', Kaz. He's alive. But it ain't right."

"What's the problem? You said he's alive."

"That's the problem, Kaz. Gideon shielded me from the blast. He should be burnt to a crisp but he ain't. Look at 'im. He's just got some red spots on 'im like a bad sun burn."

Gideon forced his eye lids open. He leaned onto his side and coughed up lake water. "My…flight suit…is fireproof."

"But what about where ya got no flight suit protectin' ya, Gideon? Yer suit's got rips in the sleeves and the chest but ya got no burns or wounds in them spots from when the Ripper exploded. Ya got none on yer face or neck neither. Ya just got them red spots. How is it that possible?"

"I don't know Paige. That lake water is pretty cold. Maybe that had something to do with it. I've seen guys walk away from much worse."

"Maybe, but I ain't never—"

"Paige-san, he said he's fine."

Gideon scanned the sandy shoreline. "Where's Yokai?"

"We haven't seen or heard nothin'," Paige said. "When that Winged Ripper exploded, the Shifter went down hard and sank. He took the worst of the fall. He saved me and Kaz from gettin' all our bones broke."

Gideon cursed. "He was brave. I hope he made it."

Upriver, a foghorn blew three times. It echoed across the lake. Gideon tried to jump to his feet but his wobbly legs gave out and he fell into the sand. "What was that?"

"It's the Raider ship, Gideon-san. You need to get up if you can."

The Raider ship lit up the night like a badly decorated Christmas tree. Red and green sidelights flashed from its hull. Searchlights from the pilothouse swung back and forth. The helipad and deck were flooded with lights. The ship wallowed into the narrow channel like a whale into a bathtub. As it headed for the lane locks, its churning wake swamped the shoreline. Paige helped Gideon struggle to his feet. Together they made their way up the sandy shoreline as a series of waves swallowed the beach.

The ship was massive. Its hull towered over Gideon like a skyscraper. Its deck bristled with cranes and equipment. Near the bow Gideon's wormhole jumper sat on the helipad. It called to him like an old friend. He checked his wrist pad. The jumper was primed and ready to fly. All it needed was a pilot. Gideon grit his teeth with determination. He tried to shake the effects of hitting the lake but his head was ringing, his legs were like jelly.

Search lights from the Raider ship carved holes in the night. They scanned the shoreline and the lane locks. Gideon ducked as a beam passed over his head. Paige grabbed his hand and pulled him behind a copse of fir trees. "Are ya tryin' to get caught?"

"I'm just excited to see my jumper in one piece is all." Gideon adjusted his glasses to night setting. The wet lenses flashed like an old-fashioned computer re-booting itself. Then the night sky turned to day. He scanned for Winged Rippers and found none.

"That ship's as big as a mountain," Paige said. "We got no way to climb up thar and board 'er."

"We won't have to climb her, Paige. The locks will bring her down to the lower lake basin. Then she'll be low enough for us to jump onboard. Right, Kaz?"

"Yes, Gideon-san, that's right. But our timing has to be perfect. Come on. Let's get to the floodgates."

Gideon's group kept to the fir trees lining the riverbank. They dodged the cutting beams of the Raider ship's searchlights and ran for the floodgates. They stopped at the edge of the floodgates and crouched behind the trees.

Gideon had seen canal locks and floodgates on the Erie Canal in western New York. But the Erie Canal locks seemed like a toy model of what lay before him now. The Off World floodgates were mammoth. They reminded Gideon of the Hoover Dam. They were lit across the top with yellow lights. When the Raider ship entered, the lights flashed green and the floodgate doors closed with a booming metallic clang that sounded like a medieval dungeon. Then an alarm sounded.

Gideon braced himself for an attack. "They found us."

Paige raised her crossbow.

"No, Gideon-san, the alarm is a safety measure only. It's announcing that the upstream floodgate holding the Raider ship is about to empty its water into the downstream floodgate. The ship has to drop over two thousand feet before it enters the lower lake basin, so it will take a few minutes."

"I ain't never seen anythin' like this," Paige said.

Then the floodgate emptied with a roar. The Raider ship began to sink. When it sank about three quarters of the way into the floodgate, Kaz tapped Gideon on the shoulder.

"Gideon-san, Paige-san, there's going to be about a three-foot gap between the ship and the edge of the floodgate," Kaz said. "When you jump, do it as if your life depends on it because it does. If you fall into the floodgate waters, you *will* die."

Gideon slumped against the tree. His breathing was labored. "Okay got it, Kaz. Listen you guys when we land on deck, let's try to get as close to my jumper as possible."

"Ya ain't lookin' too good, Gideon. Can ya be doin' this?"

Gideon gave Paige a thumbs up but he couldn't shake how beaten down he still felt. "Yeah, I'm okay to go."

"Then let's do it, Gideon-san. It's now or never," Kaz said.

Gideon left the cover of the trees and ran for the floodgates. His legs wobbled with every step, his boots felt like they were filled with cement but he pushed himself to close in on the sinking Raider ship. He dodged the searchlights crisscrossing the ground. The alarm blared. The words *Muramatsu Mining* slowly disappeared as the red and black hull sank below the rim of the floodgate.

Gideon's wormhole jumper was still unguarded. It sat perched on the bow's helipad. Seeing the jumper gave Gideon a burst of energy. *This is it, no turning back now.* When he reached the edge of the floodgate, Gideon launched himself into the air like an Olympic long jumper. He swung his arms and legs, trying to propel himself as far as possible.

Gideon flew through the air. Beneath him, water from the upstream floodgate churned and whirlpooled as it was sucked into giant sluices that fed into the lower lake basin. It looked like a giant sink draining.

Then Gideon soared over the deck of the Raider ship. The deck was littered with steel drums, large drill bits, repair and dozer-bots.

I need a clear place to land or I'm done.

Gideon twisted and steered his body.

When he hit the Raider deck, he tucked into a tight somersault. Pain erupted across his body. It was like a dozen knives slashed across his back and right shoulder.

Gideon stumbled to his feet and collapsed behind two robot bulldozers. The dozer-bots were twice the size of Gideon. They had human-looking torsos with large scoops for hands and a rectangular, treaded base. They were the perfect hiding spot while he nursed his throbbing body.

Gideon's right shoulder didn't feel right. He tried raising his arm but his shoulder burned with pain. He reached back and touched it. His left hand came away bloodied.

What did I land on?

Gideon scanned the deck. Nearby was a long drill bit stained with red blood and peppered with shredded pieces of his flight suit.

Paige and Kaz jumped at the same time. They sailed across the deck of the Raider ship. Paige's camouflage cloak billowed behind her like a cape. Her red ponytail flew like a banner. She held her crossbow out in front of her and aimed it at the deck.

Kaz's camouflage hood was pulled up over his head. His mask covered his face. His legs were tucked up into his chest. He held his sheathed sword out in front of him.

They both slammed onto the deck not far from Gideon. Then Kaz collided with Paige, knocking her into a row of steel drums.

The empty steel drums clanged and scattered across the deck. Several rats scurried past Gideon. The small armadillo-like creatures whipped their tails and gnashed their teeth. Their red bulbous eyes squinted against the glare of the searchlights.

Gideon bit into his lower lip. Fear gripped him.

He ducked behind the dozer-bot as the searchlights cut across the deck. Voices rang out.

Sweat poured off Gideon running into his eyes, stinging them.

Paige emerged from underneath the pile of steel drums. Her forehead was bruised. Purple blood trickled out of her nose. "Kaz, yer a tool. I said *I* was jumpin' first."

"So sorry, Paige-san. I thought you said *I* was going first. Are you hurt?"

"Am I hurt? No, I'm bleedin' fer the fun of it, ya eejit."

"You're both eejits." Gideon eyed Paige's bruised forehead and bloody nose. "You're fine, Paige. Now both of you shut up and follow me to my jumper if you want to get out of here in one piece."

Gideon tried to run for the cargo lift but every step felt like a sledgehammer against his shoulder. The pain slowed him to a toddler's pace. Gideon snaked his way between the maze of discarded drill bits, broken down cranes, dozer-bots and steel drums. The cargo lift was empty. Gideon reached to open the cargo lift's gates when pain sliced through his back and shoulder, making him double over. "Help me, Paige. I can't open the gate. My shoulder is all messed up. I landed on a drill bit."

"I ain't steppin' into no cage, Gideon. Once yer in that, ya got nowhere to hide or nowhere to go if the Raiders see ya. Yer trapped."

"Paige, I don't have time for this."

Kaz pushed past Paige and opened the gates. "Gideon-san, we can load those empty steel drums onto the lift and hide behind them as it takes us up to the helipad."

"Will that make you happy, Paige?"

Paige used her sleeve to wipe purple blood from nose. "Gideon, nothin' 'bout this makes me happy, but it'll do. At least we got a place to hide."

"I can't move my arm," Gideon said. "Can you guys do it?"

Paige and Kaz quickly loaded three steel drums onto the lift. Kaz closed the gate and pressed the up button. Gideon slumped behind a steel drum as the lift began to take him to the helipad and his wormhole jumper. The cargo lift whirred and squeaked.

Gideon held his shoulder and groaned. He was covered in sweat.

"Lemme see yer shouder, Gideon." Paige pulled at Gideon's flight suit. "Thar's not much of a cut here. It's just a little scrape."

"But I was bleeding and I can't move my arm."

"Well ya ain't bleedin' no more. The scrape ain't yer problem. Yer shoulder popped out."

"It's dislocated?"

"Yeah, but I can pop it back fer ya."

"Really?"

Kaz let out a low whistle. "That's going to hurt, Gideon-san but at least you'll be able to move your arm again."

"Okay, do it, Paige."

"Wait, Gideon-san." Kaz handed Gideon a black bandanna. "Bite down on this so you don't scream. We don't want the Raiders to hear you."

Gideon put the cloth between his teeth. He took several deep breaths, closed his eyes and grunted. "Let's do this."

Paige held Gideon's arm. She massaged his neck and shoulder. Gideon's body relaxed then Paige jammed Gideon's shoulder back in place.

Pain exploded in Gideon.

His eyes flew open. Small cartoonish stars floated before him. He bit into the bandanna and screamed.

"Are ya okay, Gideon?"

Gideon spit out the bandanna. His breathing was fast and shallow. "That... was...crazy painful, Paige."

The cargo lift whirred and squeaked as it took Gideon upward and closer to his wormhole jumper.

"Kaz, can't you make this crate go any faster?"

"We're almost there, Gideon-san. See for yourself."

Gideon stuck his head above the steel drum he was hiding behind. He was hundreds of feet in the air and eye level with the pilothouse. He increased the magnification on his glasses and peered into the control room. A man in a blue captain's uniform was staring at him through binoculars. *No way does he see anything except these steel drums.* Then a horrible thought crept into Gideon's mind.

"Kaz, is there a master override switch for the cargo lift? Can they shut it down from the bridge?"

"I don't know, Gideon-san."

Then a gravelly voice boomed over the ship's loudspeaker. "I ordered a lockdown on deck while the ship is in the floodgates. When I find out who's operating the cargo lift, there's going to be hell to pay. You all know the penalty for disobedience aboard my ship."

The cargo lift clanged to a stop.

Gideon opened the gate. Pain wormed its way into his shoulder and down his back. He peered over the steel drums. There were no Raiders on the helipad. Gideon's wormhole jumper sat unguarded amongst a mix of discarded equipment—a pile of steel bars and three repair-bots. The repair-bots had human-looking torsos with long gangly arms. Instead of legs, they had treaded rectangular bottoms that also doubled as toolboxes. Their small triangular heads rested against their chests. "Good, no Raiders and the repair-bots are shut down."

Gideon's jumper looked brand new. The starboard wing and the missing heat tiles had been replaced. The sleek, black-tiled ship looked like a bird of prey waiting to be unleashed.

Gideon beamed.

"Come on, let's get out of here." Gideon ran for his jumper.

He reached up for the keypad and was about to enter the code for the retinal scanner when metal clamps slammed onto the jumper's landing gear like bear traps. They locked the jumper onto the helipad.

Chapter 22

Gideon's mouth hung open and his stomach dropped into his flight boots. His head swiveled from left to right. There were no Raiders on the helipad. It was deserted except for Paige and Kaz. Then Gideon saw the camera. It was directly behind Paige and mounted on a pole. It buzzed and whirred as the lens zoomed in on Gideon.

Gideon picked up a metal bar off the deck of the helipad and tried to pry the clamps off the jumper's landing gear. "Come on, you guys, use these metal bars and help me pry these clamps off."

Paige and Kaz each picked up a metal bar and tried to pry the clamps off the jumper's landing gear. But the clamps wouldn't budge.

Gideon grit his teeth and pulled on the metal bar. Hot needles of pain stabbed his shoulder. His muscles burned. But the clamps held fast.

Tears streamed down Gideon's face. He slammed the metal bar onto the helipad and cursed.

"This is Captain Payne," said a voice over the ship's loudspeaker. "Welcome aboard, Kaz. It's been a long time. I see you brought some friends with you. Sit tight. I'll be with you in a moment and give you a proper welcome."

Gideon glared at Kaz. "You know this guy, Payne?"

Kaz's eyes went wide with fear. "He used to work for my father, Gideon-san. There was a time when he was honorable and could be trusted. But now he's ruthless and murderous. We should go while we still can."

"I'm not just leaving my jumper here, Kaz."

"I'm sorry about yer jumper, Gideon. But Kaz is right, we ain't caught yet. Maybe—"

"Save it, Paige. I'm not leaving without my jumper." Gideon picked up the metal bar and stomped across the helipad. He swung the metal bar at the camera. Like a baseball leaving a bat, the camera flew off into the night sky and disappeared.

"That wasn't very nice of you, Gideon Wells," Captain Payne said. "I can still see you with my binoculars. Kaz, you need to keep better company. I expect more from you. Perhaps some babysitters are needed."

"Kaz, how does he know who I am?" Gideon asked.

"Gwendolyn put a ransom out for your capture, Gideon-san. Remember what happened back at the mining camp?"

Paige's eyes went wide with horror. She pointed at the repair-bots behind Gideon. "Gideon, what are them bucket of bolts doin'?"

"What are you talking about, Paige?"

"Gideon-san, Payne's activating the repair-bots."

The small triangular heads of the repair-bots sprang to life. They turned toward Gideon. Their eyes glowed red. Gangly robotic arms reached for him. Vice-like hands snapped like the jaws of a Ripper. Motors revved. The treads on the robot's boxy, rectangular bottoms spun on the helipad until they found purchase. Then the repair-bots raced for Gideon. Their engines squealing like angry hogs.

Gideon swung his metal bar at the head of the nearest repair-bot. The robot's head caved in like a soda can under a car wheel. But the repair-bot kept coming. It grabbed the metal bar from Gideon and snapped it in half like a stick. Then the repair-bot slammed the two halves onto the deck of the helipad.

Paige fired darts at the repair-bot but they bounced harmlessly off its metallic body.

Kaz stabbed his katana into the robot's chest. The repair-bot shook violently and sparks flew from its chest. Then the robot's eyes went dark. Its body went limp.

"Ya killed it, Kaz."

"That's it," Gideon said. "Stab it in the chest, that's where the CPU is located. Kill the chip, we kill the robot." Gideon picked up a broken half of the metal bar and jammed it into the chest of an oncoming repair-bot. The robot sparked and went dead.

The last repair-bot zipped past Gideon and Kaz. It headed straight for Paige. She tried reaching for the other half of the broken metal bar but it was too late. The repair-bot had Paige trapped against the edge of the helipad. Paige fired her crossbow into the robot's red eyes but the repair-bot charged forward.

"It's going to knock her off the edge!" Gideon screamed.

Kaz drew his arm back to throw his sword at the repair-bot.

But as the repair-bot lunged for Paige, she twisted her body and jumped out of the way. The repair-bot drove itself off the edge of the helipad. It smashed onto the deck of the ship hundreds of feet below with a loud clang.

Dozens of men swarmed the deck. They zigzagged their way around the steel drums, stray drill bits, and dozer-bots. They ran for the cargo lift and staircase leading up to the helipad and Gideon. Gideon increased the magnification on his glasses and zoomed in on them.

The Raider crew was a ragtag bunch of men wearing old mining uniforms. Most were waving clubs. Some had makeshift swords. But all of them had an angry, desperate look in their eyes. Gideon recognized the look. He'd seen it many times in the eyes of people back on Earth during the height of the Virus. He saw it in the faces of the miners before they attacked him.

The angry Raiders reminded Gideon of the mob that chased him and his mother after she caught the Virus—when her eyes turned from blue to purple at the Lilac Festival. When a lady pointed at them and screamed. A mob had formed. They chased Gideon and his mother into the greenhouse. They vowed to kill both of them. Rocks flew. Glass shards rained down on them. Gideon rubbed the scars on his forearms.

Gideon peered into the churning, whirlpooling waters of the floodgate. The water was putrid. It smelled like rotten eggs and dead fish. The sluices leading to the lower lake basin acted like gigantic garbage disposals—dead birds, fish, tree branches, and garbage were shredded. *Okay, jumping into that is definitely out.*

Gideon eyed the walls of the floodgate. As the Raider ship sank deeper into the floodgate, high walls rose above him. The walls were covered in a slick black slime. The slime oozed down the walls of the floodgate and into the churning waters below. The walls boxed Gideon in like he was a prisoner in a jail cell. *There's no climbing up those walls and I don't even want to know what that black goo is.*

Gideon was trapped.

His mind raced.

The cargo lift whirred and squeaked. "Kaz, can you cut the cable to the cargo lift?"

"No problem, Gideon-san." Kaz unsheathed his sword. With one quick swipe, he sliced through the cable. Several Raiders screamed as the cargo lift crashed into the deck.

"That'll slow 'em down some," Paige said. "It's a lot of stairs to be climbin'. Maybe they'll be too tired to fight by the time they get up here."

"It's doubtful, Paige-san. Captain Payne is a Berserker. He works for Gwendolyn and will do whatever it takes to get his hands on Gideon-san. We can stall his crew for a while but eventually they'll make it up here. I hate to say it but we're trapped."

Gideon's fear turned to anger. "That's great, Kaz. Thanks a lot. You got me trapped on a Berserker's ship. Why didn't you tell me this guy was a Berserker?"

"I'm sorry, Gideon-san, but I didn't think we'd run into Captain Payne. I thought we could sneak aboard and steal your jumper out from under him. But if I had told you, would it have mattered? You wanted your ship back so badly you would have come aboard anyway."

Gideon clinched his fists so hard it hurt. His knuckles turned white. His nails dug into his palms. "I must be crazy. Without you guys, the Raiders wouldn't have even known I came aboard their ship. I could be flying away right now in my jumper. But no, you idiots had to crash into the steel drums and alert the entire crew."

"Don't be blamin' me none, Gideon. I told Kaz I was jumpin' first. He's the one that knocked me into them steel drums."

"None of that really matters now does it, Paige? The Raiders are coming and we have no place to go. I'm trapped onboard a Berserker's ship. What's next? He eats me?"

The stairs leading up to the helipad shook. Weapons clanged against the metal handrail. Curses and taunts rang out. The Raiders were getting closer.

"Gideon, what do ya want to do?" Paige asked.

A long line of Raiders streamed up the narrow staircase. The staircase was only wide enough to handle two men at a time. Those that got tired from climbing the hundreds of stairs leading to the helipad were shoved out of the way or trampled. The Raiders leading the charge toward Gideon were armed with Shockers, clubs, and swords.

"Let's block the stairs with the repair-bots. Come on, you guys." Gideon got behind a repair-bot. The metal bar he used to disable it was still sticking out of its chest. He steered the repair-bot to the edge of the staircase then gave it a shove.

The repair-bot cartwheeled down the staircase. Its arms flopped and flailed. The metal bar in its chest scraped against the stairs like nails on a chalkboard. The Raiders fell over themselves trying to get out of its way. Some tried to run back down the stairs, others simply jumped over the handrail. Then the repair-bot plowed into the Raiders like a runaway train. It knocked half of them off the stairs and came to a stop near the bottom of the staircase. The metal bar was still wedged in its chest.

The Raiders left on the staircase were furious. They stormed up the stairs, vowing to kill Gideon.

Paige and Kaz struggled to push the last repair-bot to the edge of stairs. Gideon ran over to help. They shoved the repair-bot. It thundered down the stairs.

This time the Raiders were ready. Those armed with Shockers stood at the front of the line. They held the Shockers out in front of their bodies like medieval pikemen waiting to skewer oncoming cavalry. When the repair-bot rolled into them, the Raiders stabbed it with their Shockers then flipped it over the handrail. The repair-bot flew off the stairs like it was flung from a catapult.

Gideon scanned the helipad for weapons. There was nothing except a few steel drums and a stack of long metal bars. No match for men armed with Shockers.

"Paige, do you have any darts left?"

Paige checked her crossbow. "No, nothin'. But they don't need to be knowin' that. I can bluff 'em pretty good."

"My katana is still sharp, Gideon-san."

Gideon's eyes welled with tears. "I don't want you guys getting killed for me. Don't do anything stupid. It's…it's over."

The Raiders swarmed onto the helipad. *Muramatsu Mining* was stitched across the chest of their orange mining uniforms. Their heads were shaved but their faces weren't. They smelled awful and needed baths. But unlike the miners back at the camp, the Raiders looked well fed and strong.

The yellow lights embedded in the deck of the helipad lit the Raiders faces like they were holding flashlights under their chins. The beam sliced across their faces giving them a cruel waxy appearance. The Raiders gave Gideon unkind smiles—like lions looking at their next meal. Most of them had several teeth missing.

The Raiders were armed with clubs, makeshift swords and Shockers—the orbs on the end buzzed and crackled with electricity. One of the Raiders had an old-fashioned shotgun. He had a bandoleer strapped to his chest that was filled with odd shaped shotgun shells. Gideon pressed the side of his glasses and increased the magnification. The shells were made from large nails and bolts typically used in mining equipment. They were deadly and would shred anything they came into contact with.

The Raider leveled the shotgun at Paige.

"Drop that crossbow, girl."

Gideon put his hand on Paige's crossbow and pushed it down toward the deck. "Paige, do as he says."

"Why should I, Gideon? That weapon he's got ain't worth nothin'. He don't even have proper shells fer it."

The Raider pointed the shotgun at a steel drum and pulled the trigger. The weapon boomed. It spit smoke and fire. It punched a hole the size of Gideon's fist into the steel drum.

Then the Raider pumped the shotgun and leveled it at Gideon's head. The barrel was still smoking. It was so close to Gideon's face he could feel the heat radiating from it.

"Drop your crossbow on the deck or I'll blow your boyfriend's head off," the Raider said.

Paige dropped her crossbow on the deck of the helipad.

Gideon raised his hands. "Okay, don't shoot."

The Raider relaxed his grip on the shotgun. He turned and grinned at the crewman next to him. Then Gideon slammed the end of the barrel into the man's face. When the Raider's head snapped back, Gideon jammed the butt of the weapon into his solar plexus and grabbed the gun from him. The Raider slumped to the deck. His face was burned and bloodied. He gasped for air. Gideon pulled the bandoleer off him and leveled the shotgun at him.

A second Raider had moved in with his Shocker. But Kaz was too fast. In one fluid motion, he unsheathed his sword and sliced the Shocker in two. Then he gave the Raider a spinning sidekick to the stomach, sending him careening down the stairs.

Gideon pointed the shotgun at the crew. His arms trembled with a combination of fear and adrenaline. "Everyone back off, real slow."

Paige held her fighting sticks at the ready. "Are ya deaf or just dumb? Ya heard 'im. Back off or I'll beat ya like ya stole somethin' of mine."

Kaz held his sword out in front of him. "I'll take the head of any man that comes near us."

The Raiders backed to the edge of the stairs.

Then a series of clanging noises filled the air. Lights atop the massive downstream floodgates flashed green. The doors leading to the lower lake basin creaked open. The black, slime-covered walls of the floodgate slid past Gideon as the Raider ship moved out of the canal locks.

Hands clapping in mock applause caught Gideon's attention. From behind the Raiders huddled at the top of the staircase emerged a man dressed in a faded blue captain's uniform. He strode onto the helipad. The word Payne was etched across the front of his uniform. He had short black hair and a close-cropped beard to match. Unlike his crew, he looked clean and neat. He had the easy confidence of a man used to being in command.

Gideon pointed the shotgun at Payne. He looked for any signs of the Berserker mutation but found none. Then Gideon thought of Frank. He shuddered. *Did Payne feast on Frank's Pure Earth so he could look human?*

Captain Payne looked at the shotgun and stopped clapping. He gave Gideon a wry smile. The Captain's sparkling white teeth were a stark contrast to his black beard. "In case you haven't guessed who I am, I'm Captain Payne. I must say, Gideon, taking the shotgun away from my crewman like that was very impressive. I haven't seen a move like that since the Academy."

This guy was in the Academy? He trained to be a Galaxy Class Pilot?

"Don't look so surprised, Gideon. Although my Academy days are ancient history, I learned many things there…including how to kill. Killing is a hard thing to learn how to do well." Captain Payne gave Gideon a hard stare. "Are you sure you want to learn on me?"

Gideon gripped the shotgun so hard his hands hurt. "Stay back, Captain."

Captain Payne paced the helipad like a caged animal as he spoke. "Kaz, my young friend, you are always impressive with that sword of yours. It's been a long time. How's the family?"

The crew jeered Kaz.

Gideon gave Payne a look of disgust. Kaz's parents were both dead. His mother killed his father after she became a Berserker. Then Kaz hunted her down and killed her. *This guy Payne is like the jerks back at Quarantine.*

Kaz tightened his grip on the hilt of his sword.

"Have you decided to finally join us, Kaz?" Captain Payne asked. "I could use a guy like you—somebody who knows how to handle the ship and how to salvage mining equipment for Gwendolyn."

Gideon was stunned. *She's using mining equipment to restore the lab? That's how she's been able to make so many Rippers. And that's how she's been able to give Ripper technology to this guy.*

"Me and my friends were thinking about it," Kaz said. "They didn't believe me when I told them I knew you and I could get us onboard."

"Good help is hard to find," Captain Payne said. "That's what your father used to say… before your mom ate him."

The crew laughed.

"He also said once a thief always a thief. He said that after you stole this ship out from under us."

Payne shook his head. He extended his hand toward his crew as he spoke. "Somebody had to feed the workers. Your old man was too busy lining his own pockets and spoiling you rotten to notice how bad things were getting for us."

"You were offered jobs when the mining stopped," Kaz countered.

"Yeah, just like we were offered cures for the Virus," Captain Payne said. He eyed Gideon as he spoke. "It turned me and my son into monsters."

Gideon bit into his lip. *Great, it looks like I get to inherit all my father's enemies.* He looked at the clamps locking his jumper onto the helipad. *I so need to get off this rock.*

"How is your son?" Kaz asked. "I'm sure the little pain is a chip off the old block; stealing, murdering, pirating. You must be proud."

Captain Payne stepped toward Kaz but stopped when Kaz raised his sword above his head. "What should I do with you three? You've snuck aboard my ship uninvited and attempted an act of piracy."

"Piracy, Captain?" Gideon said. "It's not piracy to take back what is rightfully mine. That wormhole jumper is mine and you know it."

Captain Payne feigned surprise. "It is? Young man, under the salvage laws of this planet, that wormhole jumper belongs to whoever salvaged it. Since I salvaged it off the beach and repaired it, I'd say that makes it mine. Isn't that right, boys?"

The crew mumbled their agreement with Captain Payne.

"Besides, you three have no way off this ship. Even with those glasses on, I can tell you're thinking about jumping from the helipad into the lake. I advise against that, Gideon. It's over five hundred feet to the water. You will not survive."

"I say we keep 'em, Captain," a Raider crewman said. The crewman vaulted up the stairs and stood near Paige. He pointed at her and gave a toothless smile. "Especially this one we could use a pretty face around here."

The other Raiders laughed. Some made kissing noises.

Paige's eyes narrowed with contempt.

"How about a kiss, love?" the Raider crewman said.

"Don't touch her," Gideon said.

"You should listen to my friend," Kaz said.

"She's just a little girl, what can she do?" The Raider reached out to grab Paige.

In a flash she brought a fighting stick down hard on his arm. The Raider grabbed his arm as Paige unleashed a flurry of strikes against his legs, arms, and head. She moved so fast Gideon only saw a blur of black sticks and red hair as she overwhelmed the Raider, dropping him to the deck.

"Enough," Captain Payne roared. "He's my crewman, I'll discipline him."

Paige backed off the downed Raider but kept the fighting sticks raised. She glared at the Raiders on the stairs, daring them to attack her. The Raiders stared at her dumbfounded. The downed Raider crewman struggled to get to his feet but failed and fell down hard. He lay on the helipad groaning.

Gideon looked at Paige with awe.

"Don't say we didn't warn you." Kaz shook his head at Captain Payne. "No wonder you're looking for help. With crewmen like that guy you need all the help you can get."

Captain Payne stomped across the deck and stood over the injured Raider. "I had a daughter before the Virus took her and I don't accept anyone aboard *my* ship treating a woman like that. You know the penalty for disobedience."

The Raider looked up at Payne. His eyes were filled with terror. "I'm sorry, Captain Payne. Please, Sir, don't hollow me out."

The crew gasped.

"What does that mean, Paige?"

"Hush up, Gideon. Not now."

Suddenly, Captain Payne started screaming and laughing at the same time. His skin turned a dark, reddish-purple. His bones popped and cracked as his head elongated. His jaw grew and unhinged itself from his face. It now opened and closed both vertically and horizontally, exposing rows of sharp pointy teeth. When he snapped his jaw shut, some of his new teeth protruded like tusks.

Payne's hands were trembling as long, dagger-like claws grew from his fingers. Payne laughed maniacally as he watched the claws grow. Satisfied with his transformation, Payne let out a sharp, bloodcurdling scream.

Gideon's legs wobbled. He tried to swallow but his mouth went dry. His arms started shaking, making it hard to hold the shotgun. The thing standing in front of him was part monster and part human. It sniffed at Gideon several times. Payne and Gideon locked eyes. Bloodlust filled Payne's eyes.

The downed Raider tried to stand but Payne put his boot on the man's back then stomped him into the helipad. Payne fell on the crewman and stabbed his claws into his back. It sounded like a dry stick had snapped. The Raider unleashed a high-pitched scream. Payne's claws sucked the bone marrow from the man's body.

"Getting hollowed out is like banging on the gates of hell ain't it? You just can't die fast enough," Payne said in a guttural, mocking voice.

When Payne removed his claws, the Raider crewman had been reduced to a shriveled raisin. His skin was wrinkled and his body covered with deep indentations.

"Oh...my...God," Gideon said. *The crewman looks like Larry, the miner Sara killed back at the mining camp.* Sara's words blared in Gideon's head like a siren. *"I'll eat every part of you. There won't be anything left, not even for the rats."*

"Kuso kurae no shin, you murderer!" Kaz shouted.

"He's hollowed 'em out for sure," Paige said. "And we're next."

Payne pointed at Gideon, his eyes aglow like a wild animal after a fresh kill. He growled. "I want the Pure Earth."

"Captain, don't," said a Raider crewman. "Gwendolyn wanted the Pure Earth boy unharmed. She said she won't give us any more Rippers if we hurt him."

Captain Payne snarled at the Raider. "Just a little taste is all. She'll never know."

"But Captain—"

Payne removed the crewman's head with one swipe of his clawed hand. The head flew toward Gideon. Gideon ducked as the head bounced off his jumper and landed at his feet. The glassy, dead eyes stared up at Gideon like a zombie. He tried not to retch as he kicked the head back toward Payne.

Payne turned the headless crewman onto his back. Purple blood spewed like a fountain from the decapitated body onto the helipad leaving a viscous pool. Payne stabbed his claws into the body, hollowing it out just like the other crewman. When Captain Payne finished feeding on the dead Raider, he flung the withered body overboard.

Then Payne picked up the disembodied head, tossed it at Gideon and laughed. "I like to play with my food and you're next, Pure Earth."

The head landed at Gideon's feet with a wet smack. The tongue lolled out. Gideon swallowed the bile forming at the back of his throat. His palms were covered in sweat. His arms shook. He fumbled with the shotgun, trying to pump it. "You come near me, I'll shoot."

Payne's eyes went wide with bloodlust and hunger. "Kill them; kill them all except the Pure Earth boy. He's mine. I'm going to eat every piece of him. When I'm finished there won't be anything left—not even for the rats."

Chapter 23

Gideon stared down the length of his shotgun barrel. He placed the gun sight on Payne's chest. *No way do I let this guy hollow us out.* He took a deep breath, braced himself for the weapon's recoil and pulled the trigger. The shotgun erupted with a thunderous explosion of smoke and fire. The recoil knocked him back toward the edge of the helipad.

The blast hit Payne square in the chest, blowing him off his feet. The Berserker lay flat on his back. Purple blood oozed onto the helipad.

The Raider crew surged forward. They ignored Gideon and charged after Paige and Kaz. Angry shouts filled the air. Gideon's hands shook as he pulled a shell from the bandoleer and reloaded the shotgun.

Paige tore into the Raider crew with her fighting sticks. She pummeled their heads, legs, and ribs.

Raider crewmen screamed in pain as their bones shattered. The Raiders tried to use their Shockers on her but they were too slow. Paige ducked, rolled, and twisted her body away from the Shockers.

As Paige hammered the Raider crew, Kaz sliced through their Shockers with his Katana.

The dead Shockers fell to the deck of the helipad like the blackened bones of a defeated monster. Weaponless, the Raider crewmen ran back down the stairs.

To Gideon's horror, Payne stood up. The hole blasted into his chest pumped purple blood for a moment then sealed itself. His jaw flashed open horizontally and vertically. He snapped his long teeth at Gideon and growled. "That the best you can do, Pure Earth? I'll bite your head off, boy."

Gideon pointed his pumped shotgun at Payne. "I'm locked and loaded. Come get me, you freak."

Payne splayed his claws and roared.

Then a dozer-bot dropped from the sky and slammed into the helipad. It shook as if an earthquake had struck.

Gideon stumbled and nearly fell off the helipad. He dropped the shotgun. It cartwheeled out of his hands, then hit the deck of the Raider ship hundreds of feet below and smashed into a dozen pieces.

A second dozer-bot crashed into the helipad. Gideon swung his arms wildly, trying to balance himself. But the helipad buckled and tilted at too steep an angle. Raiders fell off. Their screams echoed in Gideon's ears until they were cut short by sickening smacks on the ship's deck.

Gideon's eyes went wide with horror when a Raider grabbed him to stop himself from falling off the helipad. Gideon wrenched his arm free, but the crewman knocked Gideon off balance.

Gideon's breath caught in his chest.

His feet left the helipad.

Gideon spun his body and grabbed for the helipad. His dislocated shoulder exploded with pain. Gideon bit into his lip so hard he tasted blood. Hundreds of feet below, dead Raiders littered the deck of the ship. Their broken bodies formed a grisly mosaic.

Then the staircase leading to the helipad came unhinged. It fell like a giant tree, taking the rest of the Raider crew with it. Payne rode the staircase down to the deck of the ship and disappeared into a pile of steel drums.

Gideon's grip weakened. A thousand needles stabbed his right shoulder.

He tried to pull himself up but couldn't get enough leverage.

Gideon clung to the helipad by his fingertips.

He closed his eyes.

If I fall I'm dead. Please not like this. I've come too far.

His hands slipped off the helipad.

Gideon screamed.

Then a vice-like grip squeezed his wrists. It was Paige. She gritted her teeth and pulled Gideon up and over the edge of the helipad.

Gideon fell on top of her. His face was so close to Paige's their noses almost touched. Paige's purple eyes were filled with a mix of relief and worry. The smell of strawberries wafted over Gideon.

"Don't be gettin' no ideas, Gideon."

Gideon's neck and face flushed hot. "What? No...I..."

"Git off me, Gideon."

"Okay, sorry. Thanks for saving me, Paige."

Paige loosened a cable from around her waist and dropped it onto the helipad. "Yer welcome. Kaz helped too. He cut some cable from that cargo lift and fastened it 'round yer jumper so I wouldn't fall off while pullin' ya up."

"Thanks, Kaz."

Kaz bowed his head toward Gideon. "Nice to see you, Gideon-san. You had us worried."

The helipad was tilting badly but the wormhole jumper was held in place by the locking clamps.

A crumpled dozer-bot lay nearby. Its head was caved in and one of its arms was broken off. The large scoop it had for a hand was bent backwards.

The staircase leading down to the deck of the ship was gone. The helipad was cut off from the rest of the Raider ship.

"Where did that dozer-bot come from?" Gideon said.

Paige pointed at the sky. "The Lake Hawk."

Gideon increased the magnification on his glasses and zoomed in on the giant bird of prey. A Lake Hawk with red feathers on its head swooped over the deck. Its body was blackened and singed as if it had been burned in an explosion. It picked up another dozer-bot with its talons and flung it at the Raider crew. The crew scattered. But Payne stood defiantly on the deck. His large, purple, Berserker form was easy to identify. He sunk his claws into a steel drum, picked it up and threw it like a football. It spiraled through the air narrowly missing Yokai.

"Is that the best *you* can do, Payne? You're lower than whale crap, you loser!"

"Gideon, don't be provokin' 'im none," Paige said.

"Paige-san is right. We're still on board his ship and he has your wormhole jumper."

Captain Payne picked up a large drill bit and threw it like a spear. It sailed through the air like a missile and headed straight for Gideon. Gideon rolled out of the way just as the drill bit thunked into the helipad. It shook back and forth like a crooked flagpole.

"That was too close," Gideon said.

The Lake Hawk swooped in and landed next to Gideon. "Come on, Gideon Wells. It's time to leave."

"What? I'm not leaving without my jumper, Yokai. I thought you were here to help me get my ship back."

"I cannot remove those clamps from your ship, Gideon Wells. But I can take you and your friends off this Raider vessel before you fall prey to that Berserker."

Kaz climbed onto Yokai's back. "Gideon-san, it's time to go."

"No." Gideon picked up a metal bar and tried to pry the clamps off the jumper's landing gear. He grit his teeth and pulled, screaming against the pain shooting through his right shoulder. The metal bar started to bend but the clamps refused to budge.

Then a soft gentle touch gripped Gideon's wrist. A scent of strawberries washed over him. "Gideon, ya can't do no more. Ya stay here Payne'll hollow ya out fer sure. Ya gotta come with me now."

"But my jumper is right here, Paige."

"I know. But ya can choose to live and fight another day or get hollowed out by Payne."

Gideon cursed. He dropped the metal bar on the helipad.

Paige took Gideon's hand and led him to Yokai. "Ya know Payne is takin yer ship to Gwendolyn. He's probably tradin' it fer more Rippers. Ya can steal yer jumper back from her."

Gideon jumped on the Lake Hawk's back. Paige got behind Gideon and wrapped her arms around his waist.

Several spots on the large bird were blackened and burned. Singed feathers fell off in Gideon's hands making him wonder if riding on Yokai's back was a good idea. "Yokai, are you okay to fly? Can you carry the three of us to Gwendolyn's island?"

"I don't know, Gideon Wells. This Lake Hawk shape drains my energy and the wounds from the Ripper explosion have weakened me."

"Look out, Gideon-san!" Kaz shouted as a steel drum zipped past Gideon's head.

Then a drill bit sailed past. "Go, Yokai!" Gideon shouted.

The Lake Hawk pumped its four wings, lifting them off the helipad. Yokai dodged the barrage of steel drums and drill bits Payne hurled at them. He climbed into the sky and soon the Raider ship was only a small constellation of yellow lights in the lower lake.

"Yokai, that was a nice shot with the dozer-bot," Gideon said.

The Lake Hawk rolled one its three eyes back at Gideon. "Not really. I was aiming for the Berserker."

"Well, thanks for rescuing us. That guy Payne was going to make a meal out of me."

"You're welcome. And yes, those awful creatures your father created do tend to eat other humans."

Great, I'll always be known here as the kid whose father created the monsters. I so need to get off this rock. Gideon checked his wrist pad. His wormhole jumper was still in perfect condition and it was headed for Gwendolyn's lab. Gideon calculated that at Payne's current speed of about eight knots, the Raider ship and his jumper should be at Gwendolyn's in about four hours. *If Yokai can maintain his current speed, we should get there in about one hour. That gives me plenty of time to scout the area and come up with a plan to steal the jumper from her. She'll be expecting me but if I can create a diversion, then maybe I can sneak aboard.*

Gideon squeezed his Chain of Remembrance so hard his hand hurt. *God, I hope this works. It'll be my last chance to get off this rock.*

As Yokai made his way to Gwendolyn's island, the night sky slowly gave way to dawn. The blue and green moons sank below the horizon. The stars disappeared from the sky, pushed aside by the bright orange hue cast by the rising red and orange suns. The lower lake shimmered like an emerald. The chill of the night was replaced by a warm, crisp morning.

A patchwork of odd shaped islands stretched as far as Gideon could see. Some islands were so small they only had one tree on them while others were big enough to host large dense forests and small mountains. It reminded Gideon of the Thousand Islands in northern New York. A deep sadness overwhelmed him. Would he ever see Earth again? He rolled his Chain of Remembrance between his fingers and thought of the promise he made to his mother. Gideon pushed back the sadness. He fought back the tears welling in his eyes. He took a deep breath as Frank's words ran through his mind. *"What happens to you isn't as important as what you do about it."*

Gideon let go his Chain of Remembrance and thumped his chest with his fist several times. "I can do this."

Paige tightened her arms around Gideon's waist. Her head slumped against his shoulder. Her red ponytail fell across Gideon's chest. A hint of strawberries wafted over him. *Is she snoring?*

Gideon was still riding atop Yokai, when the twin suns climbed into the early-morning sky. Jagged mountain peaks bit into the clouds on the horizon. A volcano spewed a column of black smoke and ash, darkening the morning sky. Angry purple lightning bolts clawed at the column of smoke and ash. Orange lava bubbled and flowed down the side of the volcano and into the lake. Steam rose off the water, masking the island in a dense fog.

Gideon checked his wrist pad. Gwendolyn's island was dead ahead. He increased the magnification on his glasses and zoomed in. The fog was too dense. He couldn't see through it. *It's no wonder they choose this island for the lab. It's a perfect place to hide.*

Gideon thought back to his mission briefing at Fort Drum, New York. Sarge told him the animals on the island were savage and unfriendly to humans. It's why the lab had a force field around it. *My Shocker's gone and the Raiders have Paige's crossbow. All we have is Kaz's katana. It's not enough.*

"Yokai, land as close to Gwendolyn's lab as you can. We may not be able to cross the island—"

"No, Gideon Wells. I'm exhausted. I can't make it to the other end of the island. Holding a form as large as a Lake Hawk for so long takes a toll. I need rest and food. If I don't change forms soon, the change will be forced upon me."

The Lake Hawk started molting. Red feathers popped off its head. Gideon swatted them out of his face. Then blue and grey feathers dropped off the Lake Hawk's wings and body. The Lake Hawk struggled to stay aloft. It pumped its four wings furiously but started to drop out of the sky.

Paige screamed in Gideon's ear. Kaz yelled for help.

The lake came rushing up to meet Gideon. "I know you're tired, Yokai, but you can make it. It's just a little further. Open your wings and glide in."

The Lake Hawk bobbed its head up and down. Yokai spread all four wings, stopping the free fall a few feet above the lake. He skimmed the tops of the waves.

"Great job, Yokai. I knew you could do it." Tall white-capped waves sprayed Gideon's legs and face. Then the fog blanketed him. He couldn't see anything except dense white smoke. The smell of sulfur assaulted him. The crash of waves hitting the shore was up ahead.

Then they emerged from the fog bank. The beach was long, narrow and tree-lined. There were very few open places for the massive Lake Hawk to land. But instead of flying for an open, treeless spot of sand, the Lake Hawk glided straight for the trees.

"Yokai, no!"

The Lake Hawk's eyes were rolled back into its head. Instead of dark purple, its eyes were milky white. Its head started sagging forward. "Oh my God, he's passing out!"

Gideon grabbed hold of the Lake Hawk's head and pulled it to the right as hard as he could. "Paige, Kaz, pull Yokai to the right. Steer him away from the trees."

They steered the crippled Lake Hawk to the right. It glided down the narrow coast. But it wasn't enough. Tree branches reached out for Gideon. Then the Lake Hawk shook violently and disappeared.

Gideon fell in the sand with a dull thud. Paige and Kaz landed next to him.

Yokai's purple body lay next to Gideon. The Shape Shifter was barely conscious. His tattoos were dull and faded.

"I…need…rest…food," Yokai stammered.

"What happened to 'im?" Paige said.

Kaz started to unsheath his sword. "The filthy Yokai tried to kill us."

"Stand down, Kaz," Gideon said. "If he wanted us dead he would have left us on Payne's ship. He told me that holding a form for too long is exhausting. His body gave out and he shifted back to his normal form."

"He ain't lookin' so good," Paige said. "His tattoos ain't right."

Gideon pulled Yokai out of the sand. Needles of pain stabbed at his shoulder. "Kaz, help me carry him into the forest. We can't leave him here. If the Raiders find him, they'll kill him."

"Sorry, Gideon-san, but I'm not touching that Yokai."

"You touched him when he saved your life back on that Raider ship—when he allowed you to ride him like a horse. But you won't touch him when he needs your help? What's your problem, Kaz?"

"I'll scout the forest, Gideon-san. We need a good place to hide so we can rest." Kaz gave Gideon a slight bow of his head and disappeared into the forest.

"Yeah, you do that, Kaz."

"Pay him no mind, Gideon. I'll be helpin' ya."

Gideon used the fireman's carry to lift Yokai up onto his shoulders. "I got him, Paige. Thanks anyway. I guess I don't need help after all. He's not as heavy as Frank." Gideon's voice cracked when he said the hunter's name. *I hope he's okay.*

"Yer friend is brave and strong," Paige said. "He'll be fine."

"Lead the way, Paige."

Inside the forest the smell of rotting wood and sulfur filled the air. Dozens of rats swarmed around Gideon's ankles. Gideon kicked one. It squealed in protest. The rest of the rats hurried off into the woods.

"Leave 'em be, Gideon. They mean ya no harm. They only eat dead things off the forest floor."

"That's easy for you to say, Paige." He recalled Captain Payne's words. *"I'll eat every part of you, Pure Earth. There won't be anything left, not even for the rats."*

Volcanic ash fell like snow, dusting the trees and ground. Paige's red hair was spotted with it. Speckles of ash fell into Gideon's mouth. The ashy, burnt taste gagged him. Gideon spit it out.

"It ain't fer eatin', Gideon. Keep yer head down and yer mouth closed."

"Gee thanks, Paige, it's not like I did it on purpose. You have any other words of wisdom for me?"

"Yeah, stay away from them plants unless you want to get coated in ash from yer head to yer toes."

Tall plants with leaves shaped like elephant's ears dotted the forest floor. When a heavy deposit of ash collected on them, the leaves drooped, sending the ash to the ground before righting themselves.

Gideon sidestepped the plants as a pile of ash was nearly dumped on his head.

Clustered throughout the forest were purple mushrooms with bell-shaped tops. The mushrooms were as tall as Gideon and had bat-like wings extending from their white-spotted stalks. The white spots on their stems flashed like neon signs. A small purple creature about the size of a dog, with a frog-like body and the head of an alligator hopped near one of the mushrooms. The mushroom's wings enveloped the creature like a Venus flytrap and squeezed the life out of it.

Gideon turned his head as the frog-like creature died with a sickening crunch. He brushed aside Yokai's long dreadlocks and followed behind Paige.

They followed the odd, bird-like footprints left in the ash by Kaz's tabi boots. The footprints led to a jumble of felled trees. Large root balls jutted into the air. A mix of purple moss and volcanic ash covered the tree trunks. Kaz sat cross-legged underneath a large root ball. His sword rested across his lap.

Gideon set Yokai on the ground underneath one of the upended root balls. The shifter groaned.

Gideon took off his backpack and pulled out a small box of rations. He opened the box and took out two protein pills. He popped them in his mouth and chewed. He waved the pills under Yokai's nose.

"Yokai, eat these. You'll feel better."

The shifter opened his eyes. He sniffed the pills then turned his head away in disgust. "That's not food, Gideon Wells."

Gideon shrugged his shoulders. "It's standard rations for Galaxy Class Pilots and soldiers in the Corps."

"That explains a lot about your species, Gideon Wells."

"Whatever, Yokai, I'm just trying to help." Gideon offered the protein pills to Kaz and Paige.

Kaz took them and bowed his head. Volcano ash dropped onto his lap. "Arigato, Gideon-san."

"Gideon, I ain't eatin' that," Paige said. "Do ya even know what's in it?"

"Nope, all I can tell you, Paige, is that they're better with ketchup."

Paige took her small black pouch out from underneath her cloak. She reached inside and pulled out several small roots. Gideon recognized the sugar root. But Paige also had what looked like a bunch of rotten green grapes and tiny blackened shrunken heads that could have belonged to Medusa. She handed half the roots to Yokai.

Yokai's purple eyes lit up. "Thank you, young lady."

"Gross. That smells as bad as it looks," Gideon said. "You're not seriously going to eat that?"

Paige popped the roots in her mouth and chewed them up. Then she cracked open the sugar root and sucked the juice out of the root ball. She wiped her mouth with her sleeve and gave Gideon a wry smile. "Yummy, just like me mum used to make."

Gideon grimaced. "You like that, Paige?"

"Not so much. It needs ketchup."

Yokai greedily ate the rotten green grapes and shrunken Medusa heads. He eyed Paige suspiciously as he chewed. Then he washed them down with the sugar root nectar. He never took his eyes off Paige. When he finished, his tattoos began to darken and swirl about his chest, neck, and arms. He burped loudly.

"It takes a member of my clan years to learn the ways of the forest. To know which roots sustain life and which ones can take life is a special talent even among my people. Certainly no *human* should have this knowledge. How do you know my clan's ways, young lady? Who exactly was your…mum?"

Paige flushed. "What are ya sayin, ya crazy Shifter?"

Yokai's purple eyes flashed wide with fear. He tried to stand but collapsed. "Run…Gideon Wells…Run." His eyes rolled back into his head. His tattoos faded.

Gideon scanned the forest. There was nothing there except the mushrooms and tall elephant ear plants. "Run from what, Yokai?"

Kaz jumped to his feet and unsheathed his sword. "Something's coming."

"I don't *see* anything," Gideon said.

"Don't look for it, Gideon-san, listen for it."

Paige pulled a long, curved knife from each of her boots. The razor sharp blades were white like ivory. The hilts were wrapped in leather. She handed them to Gideon. "It's them Ripper fangs we took the first day ya got here."

"Why are you giving them to me?"

Paige pulled her camouflage hood up over her red hair. She pointed at the forest with her fighting sticks. "So ya can defend yerself."

Gideon's eyes followed Paige's fighting sticks. He swallowed the lump in his throat. "Oh my God."

Chapter 24

The three Berserkers eyed Gideon like he was a prize ham. They unhinged their jaws and opened them as wide as possible. With their jaws spread both horizontally and vertically, the monsters could take Gideon's head off in one quick bite.

The Berserkers snapped their jaws at Gideon. They made a deep throaty growl that was a mix between a tiger and an old-fashioned motorcycle. They flexed their hands and splayed their long sharp claws. Grey volcanic ash fell on their elongated heads and dusted their purple bodies.

Gideon examined the curvature of the Ripper fang knives Paige gave him. They were as long as his forearms, sharp and deadly but not enough weapon to fend off three Berserkers. He squeezed the leather hilts of the knives so hard his hands hurt. *If a shotgun wasn't enough to take down Payne, what chance do I have with these?*

The Berserkers spread out in a semi-circle and made their way toward Gideon. "Guys, we should take Yokai's advice and run. He was trying to warn us before he passed out."

Kaz pulled his camouflage hood over his head. "I'm not surprised the Yokai said to run, Gideon-san. Running is for cowards. I will stay and fight."

"If I had a katana, I'd stay and fight too, Kaz. But I don't. Neither does Paige. Her fighting sticks will break like toothpicks as soon as she hits a Berserker."

"Gideon, ya can't outrun a Berserker," Paige said.

Gideon eyed the large red mushrooms that had eaten the frog-like creature. Their white-spotted stems flashed. Their bat-like wings snapped at the volcanic ash.

"I don't need to outrun it for long, Paige, just enough to trap it."

"Don't be doin' nothin' stupid, Gideon. Ya need to be—"

Gideon sprinted for the mushrooms. He pumped his arms and legs as hard as he could. The curved Ripper-fang knives he held in his hands sliced through the air as he ran. One of the Berserkers snarled and chased after him.

Gideon's flight boots pounded against the ground.

The Berserker loped after him.

Gideon closed in on the cluster of large mushrooms.

The Berserker's shadow eclipsed Gideon's. The monster's long claws swiped at him. The rush of air caused goose bumps on the back of Gideon's neck.

Gideon dove straight for a winged mushroom. He hit the ground right in front of it, grit his teeth against the pain in his shoulder and rolled out of the way as the mushroom's wings snapped shut.

The Berserker wasn't as lucky. The mushroom's bat-like wings closed like a vice, pinning the monster's arms to its sides.

The mushroom pulsed.

Bones started to crunch.

The Berserker roared in pain.

The white spots on the mushroom's stems flashed deep purple as it sucked the life out of the Berserker.

Gideon grimaced. He raised the Ripper-fang knives and walked over to the Berserker. He thought of Sara. He thought of Captain Payne. *Nobody asked to be a Berserker. I should put it out of its misery. It was human once.*

Then the Berserker broke free of the mushroom's death grip. The monster's arms shot up over its elongated head, shredding the mushroom's wings. It stomped the mushroom into the ground until there was nothing left but a pulpy, squishy mess.

Patches of skin on the Berserker's arms and legs were burned off, exposing the monster's bones. Rivers of purple blood streaked its body. Smoke rose from its wounds. New tissue started growing over the burnt off patches of skin. The monster's crushed bones snapped and popped as they healed themselves.

The Berserker stumbled after Gideon like it was drunk. "Pure Earth, need to eat Pure Earth."

"Then come get some."

Gideon dodged the Berserker's clumsy swipe at his head and stood in front of a mushroom. The mushroom's wings snapped at him. It snagged the back of Gideon's flight suit. The Berserker lunged for Gideon. Gideon easily side-stepped the wounded monster and shoved it into the mushroom's grasp.

"I got you now."

The Berserker roared at Gideon.

Gideon raised his Ripper-fang knives.

Then the Berserker unhinged its jaw, bit into the mushroom and tore it out of the ground. The root ball hung from its mouth like a dying octopus frantically waving its tentacles. The mushroom released its grip on the Berserker. The monster spit the mushroom out of its mouth and grabbed the sleeve of Gideon's flight suit.

It growled at him. "I got *you* now."

Gideon pulled his arm back. The sleeve of his flight suit came off.

The Berserker grabbed Gideon's other arm, tearing that sleeve off as well.

Gideon slashed at the monster with his Ripper-fang knives. The knives left deep gashes in the Berserker's arms. But the wounds sealed themselves quickly.

The Berserker picked Gideon up and slammed him into the ground. The Ripper-fang knives flew out of Gideon's hands. The air was punched out of him. A nearby mushroom snapped at his head. Gideon tried to scramble away from the monster but it was no use.

The Berserker turned him onto his back and sat on him. The monster smelled like a rotting, dead animal. The stench choked Gideon.

The monster snarled in Gideon's ear. "Hollow you out first, Pure Earth. Then I'll eat every part of you. Gwendolyn will never know because there won't be anything left of you, not even for—"

Gideon screamed for help. "Paige! Kaz! Help me!"

Gideon could hear his friends battling the other two Berserkers.

Then the monster sank its claws into Gideon's pelvis.

A tsunami of pain washed over Gideon.

He tried to scream but no sound came out.

Tears streamed down his cheeks.

His whole body shook.

Gideon clawed at the ground. But there was no escape.

The Berserker growled. "Like banging at the gates of hell, ain't it, Pure Earth? You can't die fast enough."

Then the Berserker made a choking noise.

Gideon shuddered as the monster pulled its claws out of him.

The monster flopped on top of Gideon. Its raspy breathing slowed. Then it stopped.

Gideon's body was racked with pain. He wiped the tears from his face and crawled out from underneath the Berserker. He searched for his knives. They were near the stem of a mushroom. The mushroom snapped its wings at Gideon when he reached for them.

"Gideon, we saw everythin'. Are ya okay?" Paige held a hand out for Gideon. Her camouflage cloak was spattered with purple blood. In her left hand was a broken fighting stick, its jagged end stained with purple blood.

Gideon groaned as he stood. Pain shot through his back and down into his legs. He leaned heavily on Paige.

Kaz held his sword at the ready. It was coated with purple blood. He kicked the Berserker. The monster didn't move. Kaz cleaned his sword with a quick flick of his wrist, sending a spattering of purple blood onto a nearby mushroom. The mushroom snapped its wings at it. Kaz sheathed his sword. He pulled off his camouflage hood and mask and gave Gideon a hard stare.

"It's dead, Gideon-san. You killed it."

"I…I didn't do anything to it, Kaz."

"It fed on you and died, Gideon-san. The last time I saw that was at the mining camp back when all this started. A Berserker broke through the fence and attacked a miner. The miner didn't even know she was a Berserker—nobody did. When the Berserker fed from her it dropped dead. Senpai said that when Berserkers feed off each other they get a lethal overdose of the anti-Virus serum that caused the initial mutation. It poisons them and they die."

Gideon's head was swimming. "What are you talking about, Kaz? You're not making any sense."

Paige said, "I remember that, Kaz. It was poor Lucy that got attacked. At least she took a Berserker with 'er when she went. But Gideon ain't a Berserker. With Lucy, she started actin' daft and people were suspectin'. Gideon didn't kill this Berserker. It was them poison mushrooms."

"Paige is right. I didn't kill anybody. How do you even know it's dead, Kaz? Are you a scientist now?"

The Berserker's purple body twitched. They all leaped back. Then the body shook violently. Its bones popped and snapped. Its elongated head shrank. The claws retracted. Its purple color faded. In place of the Berserker was a young man about the same age as Gideon. He had short blond hair and looked like he was sleeping.

"That's how you know, Gideon-san. They change back."

"I need to sit down." Gideon almost passed out. He sat on his haunches. He dropped his head in his hands and covered his face. "This is unbelievable. Off World is a non-stop horror show. I *so* need to get off this rock."

"Gideon, yer arms are all chewed up. Did the Berserker do that to ya?"

Gideon's flight suit was in tatters. His sleeves were shredded, exposing the deep-knotted scars on his forearms. They looked like railroad tracks. He put his arms behind his back and stood. "No, Paige, this happened back on Earth. It was a long time ago."

"It looks painful, Gideon-san."

Gideon checked his wrist pad. Gwendolyn's lab was ten miles away. Captain Payne's ship would arrive in an about an hour. "Why don't you guys check on Yokai? I need a minute."

Kaz turned and walked away.

Paige put a hand on Gideon's shoulder. "Are ya sure yer okay?"

"I'll be fine, Paige, thanks. I'm glad you and Kaz are all right."

"We had a tough time of it but Kaz sure knows how to handle that sword." Paige tossed her broken fighting stick into the trees. "I don't think I would have made it without 'im."

A flash of jealously surged through Gideon. He folded his arms over his chest. When he saw his scars were facing Paige he put his arms behind his back. "I'm glad he was there for you, Paige. Why don't you go make sure he doesn't do anything stupid like cut Yokai's head off?"

"It's true Kaz don't like Shifters none but he ain't crazy, Gideon. I'll let ya alone just the same. Don't be long. It ain't smart to be hangin' 'round out here alone."

Gideon picked up what was left of the winged mushroom the Berserker tore out of the ground. He took the shredded wings and laid them on top of the dead boy's body, making sure he covered the boy's face. He grabbed hold of his Chain of Remembrance. Grief, anger and confusion tore at Gideon. *Did I really kill him? Kaz thinks I'm a Berserker. It can't be possible. My mother gave me the anti-Virus serum three years ago. I remember all the tests, the needles, the DNA sampling. No way am I Berserker. Wouldn't I would have changed by now? Paige is right. The mushroom killed him. Kaz is crazy. There's nothing wrong with me. I feel great.*

Gideon reached for the Ripper-fang knives. He winched in anticipation of pain—pain from his dislocated shoulder and from the Berserker attack. There wasn't any. He picked up the knives as his words hit him like a punch to the face. *"There's nothing wrong with me. I feel great."*

His mouth hung open. He moved his dislocated shoulder up and down and waved his right arm in a circle. There was no pain.

He stretched his lower back. There was no pain from the Berserker attack.

Panic seized him. *Oh my God. Is something happening to me? Paige said I should have died when I hit the lake. But I didn't.*

Gideon pulled back the shredded pieces of his flight suit and examined his chest. *She also said the Ripper on the beach slashed me across the chest. But I have no wounds. And I carried Frank like it was nothing. Am I changing?*

Gideon held his arms out in front of him. His skin wasn't purple. The familiar knotted scars were still there. He inspected his hands. There were no claws. He tried to open his mouth both vertically and horizontally. He couldn't. Gideon shook his head in disbelief. *What am I doing? I'm acting like an idiot. My father examined me in the pyramid before Frank was taken. He said I was fine. Off World is making me crazy. I need to get off this rock.*

A low growl caught Gideon's attention. He crouched below a nearby mushroom and raised his Ripper-fang knives. A large saber tooth cat ambled through the cluster of mushrooms. The great cat was as tall as any horse Gideon had seen but was squat and powerful. Its neck was as wide as Gideon's waist. Its fur had a red tinge to it and was tattooed with swirls and dark spots. The mushrooms shied away from it. Their winged flaps stayed closed despite the cat's proximity to them. The white spotted stems seemed to bow as the cat walked past.

Gideon recognized the tattoos and red hair. He breathed a sigh of relief. "Yokai, what are you doing here? You scared the crap out of me."

The saber tooth cat eyed Gideon's Ripper blades and snarled. It lowered its head and stalked forward.

"Paige and Kaz are looking for you, Yokai."

The cat came within a few inches of Gideon. It sniffed at him.

Gideon swatted the great cat's snout, making it recoil in surprise. "What's your problem, Yokai? Go away, you stink as bad as that Berserker did. Were you eating out of a trash can or what?"

Gideon stared into the cat's yellow eyes. They narrowed with contempt. Then Gideon froze with fear. *This isn't Yokai. His eyes are purple no matter what shape he takes.*

The saber tooth cat opened its mouth, exposing the full length of its fangs. They were as long as Kaz's katana, curved and deadly sharp.

The cat unleashed a deafening roar that shook Gideon to his core.

Please don't eat me.

Chapter 25

The saber-toothed cat's wet, cool nose brushed up against Gideon's cheek as the great cat sniffed him. Its tongue was like sandpaper, its breath fetid.

Gideon held his breath. Every muscle in his body tensed. *Is he tasting me before he eats me?*

The cat's curved fangs were as long as Gideon's arms. They were yellow and jagged. A mix of purple blood and saliva coalesced in the chips and grooves running the length of each of them.

Oh my God, did it just eat Paige, Kaz, and Yokai?

The cat was a head taller than Gideon. It smelled musky and sour.

The cat made a powerful throaty growl and circled Gideon. Its thick muscles rippled making the dark spots on its red tinged fur gyrate. With each step the cat sank several inches into the soft forest floor. Each paw print was the size of a basketball. Each claw mark gouged into the dirt longer than Gideon's foot.

It must be twenty hands tall and at least eight feet long even with that short nubby tail.

The cat sniffed and nudged Gideon. Then to his surprise it spoke. "Your blood smells different from the other humans. Why?"

"You can talk?"

The cat hissed indignantly. Its voice was deep and gravelly. "Of course I can speak. Leave it to human arrogance to think that animals are dumb and only useful as either prey or beasts of burden. Now answer my question, cub."

"I'm new to this planet. My blood is different because I haven't been here long enough for your planet to change me." Frank's and Vince's words ran through Gideon's mind. *"Five days in and out, not one day more."* Gideon checked his wrist pad. *Less than two days left. I'm running out of time.*

"Remove your eye covering," the cat ordered.

"I can't. The glare from the suns hurts my eyes."

"There is shade enough here in the forest. You can return the eye covering after I look into your eyes." The cat growled at Gideon. "You will do as I command."

Gideon's hands trembled as he removed his sunglasses. He squinted against the glare of the suns and looked directly into the great cat's piercing yellow eyes.

The cat's slit pupils widened with surprise. "I've never seen such eyes on a human. So the others of your kind were telling the truth."

Gideon put his sunglasses back on. "Please, I mean you no harm. I'm here to take my ship back from Gwendolyn so I can go home."

The cat snarled and barred its teeth, its fangs two feet long and dripping saliva. "You know the Evil One?"

"No, no not at all." Gideon raised his hands defensively. "She stole my father's lab and has been hunting me since I came to your planet. Now she has my ship."

"You're the Wells Cub?"

Gideon cursed. *I'm so stupid. Why did I have to tell him that?* "Yes, I am."

The cat's yellow eyes narrowed. "Follow me, Wells Cub."

"Why, where are we going?"

"You are my prisoner and my king has business with you."

"Your king wants to see me? Why, what does he—"

A wicked smile crept across the cat's face. "The king wants you to answer for your father's crimes. Now follow me, Wells Cub."

Gideon took a deep breath. "Great. I can hardly wait to meet him."

Gideon followed the cat past the large winged mushrooms. A mushroom opened its wings and snapped at him. Gideon ducked and rolled out of the way. The cat clawed the mushroom to ribbons with a quick easy swipe. Shards of the mushroom's wings landed near the dead boy's body.

The body lay in the dirt. A thin layer of volcanic ash dusted it. Rats sniffed at the body—then the armadillo-like rodents began feeding on the dead boy's toes. Bones cracked like walnuts against their sharp teeth. The rat's red bulbous eyes widened as they fed. Their long thin tails swished back and forth.

Gideon tried shooing away the rats but they simply hissed at him while they fed on the dead boy. Gideon threw a stone at them. The rats squeaked and scattered into the underbrush. Several of them were caught by the bone-crushing, snapping wings of the mushrooms and died.

"Wells Cub, why does your kind insist on disturbing the ways of my world? The little ones fill their bellies with the dead. It's better they feed than let the forest be littered with carrion. It is the way of things. Leave them to it."

"But it's disrespectful to the dead boy."

"He tried to kill you and now you mourn him? Your kind has odd ways."

Gideon and the cat passed where Kaz and Paige fought off the Berserkers. The giant root balls of the felled trees jutted high into the air. Their tangled roots were like petrified snakes. Rats gnawed two disembodied Berserker arms. Purple blood spattered the ground. It mixed with volcanic ash turning the ground into a purplish mush the texture of oatmeal. A broken fighting stick lay on the ground. Paige, Kaz, and Yokai were gone.

A mix of anger and panic squeezed Gideon's throat so tight his voice cracked. "Hey, where are my friends? Are they okay?"

The saber-toothed cat bared its teeth. "Silence, Wells Cub. We are about to leave the forest and enter the gorge. If you make noise, the Tuskers will attack us in numbers far too large for me alone to handle. The beasts are nearly blind but they have excellent hearing and can smell you with their long noses. So you will be silent or you will be dead. Do you understand me?"

Gideon nodded. *What could be fiercer than this guy?*

When Gideon emerged from the forest, he gasped. He stood in the bottom of a gorge rimmed with tall, saw-toothed mountains. Lush green evergreens taller than five-story buildings lined the base of the mountains. The upper reaches gave way to purple rock. Ice topped the peaks of the mountains. Brown and green grasses and purple and yellow flowers carpeted the gorge. Isolated copses of trees dotted the grassland. Water cascaded off a nearby mountain, falling thousands of feet into a river that snaked through the center of the gorge.

About a mile away, hundreds of elephants grazed in the tall grass. Some hosed themselves off with water from the river. The elephants were larger than any Gideon had ever seen. He pressed the side of his glasses and zoomed in. The elephants were covered with brown shaggy hair. They had long curving tusks that came to a sharp pointy end. *Those must be the Tuskers, they look like wooly mammoths. Saber-toothed cats and wooly mammoths?*

Gideon thought back to what Sarge told him during the mission briefing at Fort Drum. *"Off World is like prehistoric Earth, it's young and ferocious."*

The air smelled sweet and fragrant like lilacs. It reminded Gideon of the Lilac Festival when his mother caught the Virus, when the crowd chased him and his mother into the greenhouse. He rubbed the scars on his forearms.

Then Gideon's nose began to itch.

His eyes watered.

He sneezed twice in quick succession.

The sound exploded across the grassland like a double-barreled shotgun blast.

The Tuskers looked up. They stared at Gideon. They raised their trunks and trumpeted. It was deafening.

Gideon covered his ears. Dizziness overwhelmed him. He fell to his knees. Blood trickled out of his nose. Gideon's mind flashed back to the sonic weapons the police used for crowd control when the Virus first burned through the cities back on Earth—before the police used live ammunition.

Then the trumpeting stopped.

The ground shook. It sounded like thunder rolling across the grasslands.

The Tuskers charged directly at Gideon. Their curved, sharp tusks glinted in the sunlight. The Tuskers' massive, circular feet pulverized the brown and green grasses and colorful flowers of the gorge. A copse of trees was flattened like it had been run over by bulldozers.

Gideon struggled to stand. But he couldn't shake the dizziness of the Tuskers' earlier sonic attack. Vertigo seized him and he fell down.

The cat nudged Gideon. It lowered itself to Gideon's eye level. Its shoulders hunched forward as if it were getting ready to pounce on him.

Gideon tried to crab walk away but the cat pinned him to the ground with its paw. The cat pressed on Gideon's chest and stomach making it impossible to breathe. Its sharp, curved claws were inches from Gideon's face. Would the great cat squash him like a bug or shred him with its claws?

"Be calm, Wells Cub. You reek of fear," the cat said. "Climb onto my back and hold on. Do it now or I leave you here to be stomped into the ground by the Tuskers."

Gideon rolled himself onto the cat's back and tried to wrap his arms around its neck. He couldn't. The cat's neck was too thick.

"Grab hold of my fur, Wells Cub."

Gideon sank his fingers into the cat's thick, coarse fur. He squeezed his legs against its ribs as best he could.

The Tuskers closed on them. The ground rumbled like an earthquake had struck. Then a group of Tuskers broke off from the stampeding herd and flanked Gideon. They stopped charging and raised their trunks. "Go, they're going to blast us again."

The cat bounded ahead as the sonic blast hit the ground. Gideon bounced up and down on the cat's back while it zigzagged across the grassy plain, avoiding the barrage of sonic blasts. The trumpeting sound waves pulverized the ground around Gideon—dirt, grasses, rocks and flowers shot into the air. Gideon's vision started to blur. His ears rang.

The cat headed for the base of one of the mountains ringing the gorge. Gideon craned his neck but couldn't see through the clouds masking its peak. He had climbed mountains in the Adirondack Park in Northern New York many times but the size and steep angle of the Off World mountain now standing in front of Gideon made the rounded peaks of the Adirondack Mountains look like parking lot speed bumps.

A sonic blast smashed through a copse of tall evergreens as the cat charged up the forty-five degree slope. Dagger-like wood splinters sliced Gideon's face and arms. Blood and sweat stung his eyes. Long spikes stuck out of the cat's shoulder making him look like a porcupine. Purple blood drizzled down its foreleg.

Gideon ducked low hanging branches as the cat vaulted over large tree roots and surged through the maze of evergreens. Up ahead a large purple rock was pulverized by a sonic blast. The rock exploded into thousands of shrapnel-like projectiles. The cat leapt high into the air as the stone daggers sailed underneath it. Shards of rock sliced into Gideon's flight boots. The air was punched out of him as the cat landed and continued racing up the mountain.

Once clear of the evergreens, the mountain leveled off. The steep slope gave way to a field filled with large purple boulders. The porous volcanic rocks were everywhere. They were bigger than cars. The cat effortlessly jumped atop the nearest rock. Gideon glanced over his shoulder. The Tuskers were crowded near the base of the mountain and heading back to the grassy plains of the gorge.

The cat crouched low. He coiled his muscles then sprang through the air, landing onto the next boulder. The cat repeated this dozens of times. Every time the cat launched itself to the next boulder Gideon was jolted like he was sitting atop a bucking bronco. But each landing was soft, quiet and graceful. The cat's pace never slowed. He was tireless and quickly made his way through the boulder field.

At the end of the field the mountain rose up into a sheer cliff. Gideon tilted his head back as far as he could. The purple rock face had no outcroppings. There were no footholds. *Without anti-gravity boots, there's no way we climb that.*

The cat sat atop a purple boulder at the base of the cliff. He coiled his body and prepared to pounce. Then he jumped and landed with his stomach pressed against the rock face as if he were lying prone on the ground. The cat used his claws like climbing spikes and sank them deep into the rock.

Gideon's legs slipped off the cat. His feet dangled in the air near the cat's hindquarter. Then his hands started slipping. His grip loosened. Gideon fought against the fatigue in his hands and arms and tightened his grip on the cat. "Please tell me you're not going to climb the mountain like this. I don't think I can hold on to you much longer. My hands and arms are getting tired."

"It is the only way, Wells Cub. You must hang onto me or you will fall to your death."

Gideon pressed his chest and stomach against the cat's back. He grit his teeth and squeezed its fur as tight as he could. He pressed his legs against its ribs. "Okay, let's do this."

The cat raced up the mountainside. Its claws crunched into the rock face. Its muscles worked like sinewy jackhammers, its bones like pistons driving Gideon and the cat up the mountain.

A strange bah-bah sound filled the air. Up ahead eight animals with long, shaggy white hair stood prone on the mountain. The animals had two horns that curved up and over their heads like rams. They had suction cups for hooves. Their eyes went wide with fear when they saw Gideon and the saber-toothed cat.

The goat-like creatures galloped down the mountain, their hooves making a sucking sound that echoed off the rock face. Their long shaggy hair changed color from white to purple allowing them to blend perfectly with the rock face. They quickly disappeared.

Those are the weirdest looking mountain goats I've ever seen.

As the cat continued scaling the mountain, Gideon's breath came out in a white, fog-like vapor. Goose bumps mixed with the knotted scars on his sleeveless arms. His hands and arms grew numb. Sweat frosted on his brow. His teeth started to chatter and his breathing became ragged. Pain squeezed his forehead. Waves of nausea swept him.

The air must be thinning. If we go much higher I may pass out.

A thin sheet of ice and snow dotted the rock face. The purple rock was now dusted with slick white icy patches. The wood splinters sticking out of the cat's shoulder were speckled with ice crystals. The purple blood dripping down his foreleg congealed and froze. But the cat continued clawing his way up the mountain crunching through the rock and ice.

A deep crevice in the rock face lay ahead. The cat sidestepped the crevice but as he punched his claws into the ice and rock, a flock of purple and white-feathered birds flew out of their nesting place. The birds were about the size of an eagle. They cawed and flapped their four wings in Gideon's and the cat's face. The cat swiped at the birds. Then he started sliding down the mountain. His claws screeched like nails on a chalkboard—faster and faster he slid.

Gideon squeezed the cat's fur as hard as he could and screamed. "No!"

The cat scrambled against the backward slide. His powerful claws dug deep gouges into the rock and ice. Gideon and the cat began to slow. Then they stopped.

Gideon's hands and arms trembled. He took several deep breaths and tried to slow his heart rate. The white vapor from his exhalations was like steam from a geyser. They had slid about a hundred yards down the rock face. Deep claw marks were carved into the mountainside. "This is crazy. Why can't you guys live underground instead of at the top of the world?"

The cat roared. It echoed off the rock face like thunder. "Stop mewling, Wells Cub."

The cat started climbing again. The rock face crunched like old, dry bones as he gouged and clawed his was up the mountain. A tsunami of muscles rippled and flowed against Gideon's chest and stomach.

The cold bit into Gideon as they climbed. He could no longer feel his hands and fingers. He tried pulling on the cat's fur but had no strength left. Gideon tried squeezing his legs against the cat's ribs but his legs felt powerless and weak. Several hundred yards ahead a rocky outcropping jutted out and over the rock face.

"I feel your grip on me weakening. You must stay strong, Wells Cub," the cat said. "We need only reach that overhang."

Gideon eyed the approaching outcropping and prayed he could hold on long enough. "Climb. Faster. Please."

At one hundred yards away Gideon's teeth started chattering from the cold.

Seventy-five yards away and his arms began to tremble.

At fifty-yards away his entire body started shivering.

Tears streamed down Gideon's face as he started to slide off the cat.

The cat roared and made a final lunge for the rocky shelf. He propelled himself and Gideon high above the rocky outcropping. But as the cat righted itself and prepared to land Gideon fell off.

Gideon was momentarily suspended in the air at the apex of the cat's jump. It reminded him of floating in an anti-gravity chamber—until he started to fall.

The boulder field was thousands of feet below him. How long would it take to fall onto those massive purple boulders? Would it hurt or would death be painless?

Then Gideon was swatted out of the air. His shoulder crunched. The air was punched out of him.

Gideon landed on the outcropping with a thud and rolled. He lay on the frosty cold ground dazed, wheezing and trembling. He struggled to breath. Pain stabbed at his shoulder.

The saber toothed cat stood over him. Its yellow jagged fangs were inches from Gideon's face. "Are you injured, Wells Cub?"

"My shoulder hurts but I think I'm okay."

"Good. The king ordered me to bring you before him unhurt."

"Gee, your concern for me is overwhelming."

"I'm done carrying you, Wells Cub. Get on your feet."

Gideon pushed himself up off the rocky ground. His head spun. His shoulder ached. He rose to his knees and took a deep breath. The air was thin and biting. Goose bumps rose on his sleeveless arms, dappling his knotted scars. He grunted and forced himself to stand.

The saber-toothed cat was licking its wounded shoulder. It tried to pull the bloodied, wooden splinters out with its teeth. But its long fangs made it impossible to grab hold of them.

"Can I help you with that?" Gideon asked.

The cat's eyes narrowed. "You're just a cub. What can you do?"

"I can pull the wood out of your shoulder if you'll let me."

The cat nodded its approval. "You may."

Three wooden splinters were clustered tightly together. They were buried deep into the cat's left shoulder. Gideon reached up over his head and grabbed hold of them with both hands. They were cold and jagged.

"This is going to hurt—"

"Just get on with it, Wells Cub."

"Okay." Gideon took a deep breath and pulled as hard as he could. The cat bared its teeth and growled as the jagged spikes slowly came out. There was a meaty sucking sound. Then the blood soaked spikes were out. Gideon dropped them on the snow-encrusted ground, spattering the snow purple.

Steam rose from the holes in the cat's shoulder. They looked like bullet holes. Purple blood ran down the cat's foreleg. The cat licked its wound with its long black tongue. The faster the cat licked, the faster the holes in its shoulder closed.

"Your wound is almost completely healed."

"Yes, my kind heals quickly. Thank you for your help, Wells Cub. We will move on in a moment. I need to finish cleaning myself before we enter the king's chamber."

Gideon scooped up a handful of snow and washed the cat's blood off his hands. His breath came out in white vapor. He wrapped his arms around himself to try to keep warm.

Gideon scanned the gorge. He was amazed they had climbed so high so fast. The grasslands were a lush brownish-green carpet. The river was a thin blue snake weaving its way through the gorge. The Tuskers were small brown dots.

Large birds flew over the far end of the gorge. Gideon pressed the side of his glasses and zoomed in. He cursed. They were Winged Rippers. He followed the Rippers out to the coast. Payne's ship was moored near a cluster of buildings. The buildings shimmered behind a soft purple light. They were wavy and blurred like they were sitting in a hot desert and not a grassy plain. *That must be the lab complex and the force field.*

Gideon continued scanning the compound until he found the maglev launcher. Like the maglev at Fort Drum, this one also reminded Gideon of a half-finished roller coaster. His wormhole jumper was sitting on it. Workbots tended to it. The force field didn't extend to the maglev. It covered only the compound's main buildings. Gideon checked his wrist pad. The jumper's systems were good to go. The ship was ready. Gideon gave a small fist pump. *Yes!*

"Let's go, Wells Cub. Follow me."

"Wait. What's your name? What do I call you?"

"I am called Nomti."

"Thank you for saving my life, Nomti. Falling from up here would have killed me for sure."

"This way, Wells Cub," Nomti said.

Gideon followed Nomti to the far end of the outcropping. They stopped when they reached the base of a rocky wall. Gideon craned his neck. The mountainside stretched into the clouds. On either side of him were two statues of saber-toothed cats. Nomti roared once and the door rolled open.

Gideon and Nomti walked through the entrance and inside the mountain. Rock grated against rock as the door slid closed. Gideon expected to be enveloped by darkness but holes carved high into the wall allowed rays of light to claw away the darkness. Fresh air wafted in. The cavern had a high vaulted ceiling like an old church with wide pillars extending down into the floor. The floor was made of multicolored stone polished to a fine sheen. There was a mosaic depicting a Tusker hunt with several saber-toothed cats taking down one of the massive creatures.

Nomti nodded at the mosaic. "Before the Evil One, this was used as a welcoming hall. We would receive nobles from all the Shape Shifter clans."

Gideon nodded his understanding. *If the cats were friendly with Shifters maybe Yokai, Paige, and Kaz are okay.*

Gideon left the great hall and followed Nomti down a long corridor. The cat's claws clacked noisily on the stone floor. The air was heavy with the smell of sulfur. To Gideon's relief the walls of the corridor radiated heat. His numb and frigid muscles started to warm and relax.

The walls had intricate carvings of saber-toothed cats fighting Winged Rippers. A man that looked like Gideon's father was kneeling over a large, black saber-toothed cat. In the next frame, the cat rejoined what looked like a major battle involving Winged Rippers, the Tuskers and the cats. Leading the Rippers was a woman with long hair. Gideon froze. Something familiar about the woman struck him. He leaned in closer studying the carving.

Nomti turned and growled. "Keep moving, Wells Cub."

Gideon pulled himself away from the carvings and followed Nomti.

At the end of the corridor a large archway led to an expansive chamber. Two saber-toothed cats guarded it. Roars and high-pitched shrieks echoed in the chamber. Nomti's words ran through Gideon's mind. *"You must answer for your father's crimes."*

Nomti leaned forward and whispered to the nearest guard. The guard eyed Gideon with a raised brow then disappeared into the chamber.

The roars and high-pitched shrieks continued. Gideon tried to peek inside the chamber but the remaining guard stepped in front of him, blocking him. Then the other guard reappeared and nodded at Nomti. The guards parted allowing Gideon to pass.

Nomti walked through the archway. "This way, Wells Cub, the king will speak to you now."

On wobbly legs Gideon followed Nomti into a cavernous chamber. Dozens of saber-toothed cats eyed him. Several showed their long fangs. Sweat poured off Gideon. He felt like a death row inmate walking to his execution. A musky zoo-like smell assaulted him. *Try to be calm. They can smell fear.*

Gideon scanned the ceiling. It was domed and covered with a mosaic of a large saber- toothed cat. The cat's eyes were holes carved into the ceiling. Red and orange light from the twin suns poured through them, making the chamber look like it was painted in blood. The eyes in the ceiling followed Gideon as he walked.

The walls were lined with all sorts of skulls. One-eyed Ripper skulls with the beaks splayed horizontally and vertically—their rows of sharp dagger-like teeth were easy to see. Elongated Berserker skulls with their jaws unhinged and wide open were also on display. There were saber-toothed skulls with long fangs ready to bite and massive Tusker skulls with curved, pointy tusks ready to gore. There were rows of human skulls. Gideon shuddered. *If this is the throne room, I would hate to see the dungeon.*

At the far end of the throne room, a black saber-toothed cat sat on a large, oval stone that was raised high off the ground. A shaggy Tusker hide rug covered most of the stone. On either side of the king two massive, curved tusks pointed up toward the ceiling.

Behind the king was a wall covered with weapons. There were axes, swords, spears, bows, crossbows, blasters and even a few DNA scramblers. Gideon's eye found Kaz's sword. His mind flashed to the Ripper fang knives strapped to his backpack. *Do I tell Nomti about the knives? Would they kill me for bringing weapons before the king?*

To the left of the king, three long chains hung from the ceiling and disappeared into separate pits. From inside the pits, a sour smell wafted up. *I know that smell.*

Gideon peered into the nearest pit.

No! It can't be.

CHAPTER 26

Paige was in a rectangular cage dangling a few feet from the bottom of the pit. The cage hung from a long chain attached to the ceiling of the throne room. A Winged Ripper was in the pit with her. Its wings were chewed off—bloody teeth marks riddled what was left of them. The Ripper tried to jump out of the pit but it was too deep. It shrieked in rage. Then it turned on Paige.

It swatted her cage like a tetherball. The cage clanged against the far wall of the pit. Paige stumbled and fell.

Saber-toothed cats crowded around the edge of the pit and roared their approval.

Gideon ran to the edge of the pit. "Paige, don't worry. I'll save you."

Nomti pulled Gideon back from the edge of the pit. "Do not interfere, Wells Cub."

"But the Ripper will kill her."

"Most likely."

"But she—"

Nomti snarled, his curved fangs inches from Gideon's face. "She is entertainment for the king. You will not interfere."

The Ripper lunged at the cage and reached inside, grabbing for Paige. She deftly moved out of the way but not before the Ripper's claws snagged her camouflage cloak. The Ripper dragged Paige toward its snapping beak.

Paige kicked at the monster's arms but it kept pulling her close.

The Ripper opened its beak horizontally then vertically, exposing its razor sharp teeth.

The saber-toothed cats roared. Bloodlust filled their eyes.

Gideon pushed his way past Nomti and maneuvered back to the edge of the pit. "This is so wrong. You guys are cheering like it's a football game."

Nomti's paw landed hard on Gideon's shoulder. Gideon slumped under the weight of it, his dislocated shoulder still tender. Sharp claws pierced Gideon's flight suit, digging into his skin. He grit his teeth as Nomti pulled him back from the edge of the pit.

"Nomti, do you seriously expect me to stand here and do nothing while my friend dies?"

"Yes. Close your eyes if you must, but do nothing foolish."

Paige slipped out of her cloak and sprang to her feet. The Ripper tumbled backward and slammed into the far wall of the pit. The monster threw Paige's cloak on the ground and charged at her as the cage started swinging back.

The Ripper slammed into the cage. The metal bars bent and caved in.

Paige fell on her stomach.

The Ripper pulled the bars from the cage. There was nothing between it and Paige.

The monster reached in and grabbed for her. Paige scrambled to the far corner of the cage. She kicked at the Ripper. The monster swatted her legs and spun her around. Then it grabbed hold of her red ponytail.

Paige screamed.

The saber-toothed cats roared.

The Ripper pulled Paige close to its gaping beak. A few more inches and it would bite her head off.

Gideon pulled away from Nomti and ran to the edge of the pit. He reached over his shoulder for one of the Ripper-fang knives strapped to his backpack. He squeezed the warm leather handle as hard as he could then threw the knife at the Ripper. The knife sailed through the air end over end and hit the Ripper in the back with a dull smack. The monster shrieked in pain.

The throne room fell quiet. The saber-toothed cats stared at Gideon in disbelief.

Nomti roared. "No, Wells Cub!"

Gideon pulled the other blade. "Hey, ugly, I'm up here."

The Ripper turned to face Gideon. Its single purple eye widened. It released Paige and jumped atop her cage. It reached for the chain attached to the ceiling and started climbing.

Gideon threw the second knife. It hit the monster in the back of the head with a loud crack.

The Ripper fell from the chain and landed face first onto the floor of the pit. Purple blood pooled around the monster's body.

Paige was huddled in the corner of the mangled cage. She peered up at Gideon and mouthed a silent, "Thank you."

Gideon gave Paige a thumbs up.

The saber-toothed cats hissed and spat at Gideon. Nomti growled and stalked forward.

Gideon backed away from the edge of the pit. "Take it easy, Nomti. Uh… nice kitty?"

Then a deafening roar shook the throne room. Nomti and the rest of the cats sat and faced the king. Gideon slowly turned.

The black saber-toothed cat's yellow eyes bore into Gideon. The massive cat nimbly jumped off his throne and stalked toward Gideon. The king's muscles rippled as he came down the steps. The long white fangs were a stark contrast to his black fur. The king was a head taller than Nomti, wider through the neck and broader across the shoulders.

The king made low throaty growls. He came to within inches of Gideon and sniffed at him. The great cat's hot breath fogged Gideon's glasses. It smelled like carrion and death.

Sweat poured off Gideon. He clinched his hands into tight fists to steady himself.

"You aren't like the other humans," the king said in a deep, booming voice that echoed throughout the throne room. "Your blood smells different."

"Yes, great king I've been told that."

"You are the Wells Cub are you not?"

Gideon swallowed. "I am."

"Your father ruined my kingdom by creating the Evil One and allowing her to make these Ripper monsters. Now you ruin my entertainment? What shall I do with you, Wells Cub?"

He blames my father for everything? "Sacrificing the girl is not entertainment worthy for a king as great as you. The Ripper would have killed her too quickly and too easily."

Shrieks from the other two pits filled the throne room. Sharp claws scratched at the walls.

The king's eyes narrowed. "The other Rippers smell you. These monsters seem to be fond of you. Perhaps I should put you in the pit. Then you can answer for your father's crimes and your own disrespect."

Gideon's knees grew weak. He peered down at the dead Ripper. "Great king, I can't answer for my father's crimes if the Rippers kill me."

"You will answer for his crimes by dying at the hands of the monsters he created. Your father's own death has begun to close the circle. When the monsters kill you, the circle will finally be closed and justice will be served."

The saber-toothed cats growled their agreement.

Gideon pointed at the dead Ripper. "Great king, only by destroying Gwendolyn will the circle be closed. Without her, there will be no one to create these monsters. If you let me and my friends live I will help you destroy Gwendolyn."

The king sneered at Gideon. "You can do nothing to the Evil One. You are just a cub."

"Great king, I am dangerous to Gwen...the Evil One. It's why she hunts me."

The Rippers in the pits shrieked. Their claws scratched at the walls.

The king shifted his gaze between Gideon and the pits.

Gideon's mind raced. *There's nothing I can do to stop him from putting me in the pit. Somehow I need to get him to free all of us and help me get my ship back.* Images of Frank being carried away by a Ripper ran through his mind. "Great king, I want to trade my life for the lives of my friends. Free them all and put me in the pit. All I ask in return is that if I survive, you help me destroy the Evil One."

The king growled. "No one survives the pits."

"Then you have nothing to lose by agreeing to the contract."

"I have nothing to gain either, Wells Cub. I can put you in the pit whether you like it or not."

"Great king, you gain the Evil One's destruction and free your kingdom from her monsters once and for all."

Rumbles and growls of agreement echoed in the throne room.

The king bared his teeth at Gideon. "Wells Cub, I agree to your contract. If the Rippers don't tear you apart, my entire pride will help you destroy the Evil One. But only if your battle plans please me."

The throne room erupted with roars. When the throne room quieted, the king eyed Gideon. "You are brave, Wells Cub far braver than your father ever was."

I'm brave only if this works. If it doesn't I'm just plain stupid.

The king's yellow eyes fell to the knotted scars on Gideon's forearms. "I see you were wounded in battle."

"No, great king, I was injured trying to protect my mother from an angry mob."

"These are not battle wounds? Other humans did this to you out of anger?"

Gideon nodded. "Anger and fear."

The king snorted his disapproval. "Typical of your kind. Humans are the cruelest of animals. They kill what they fear or don't understand."

Gideon crossed his arms over his chest. *Weren't you the one who wanted to watch a young girl get torn to pieces?*

The king turned to the other saber-toothed cats and roared. "Free the others and put the Wells Cub in the pit. We'll see if he can die well."

The cats' roars echoed throughout the throne room. Nomti eyed Gideon as if he were a mouse stuck in a trap.

Gideon swallowed the lump in his throat. He squeezed his Chain of Remembrance and closed his eyes. He pictured his mother's face. *Oh my God I hope this works. If not, I'll be seeing you soon, Mom.*

The chains leading from the throne room ceiling to the cages in the pits clanked as they pulled Gideon's friends up. The bars on Kaz's cage were bent—some were missing. But Kaz appeared okay. He sat cross-legged in his battered cage. He gave Gideon a curt nod and slithered out of the cage.

Does anything faze that guy?

Yokai's cage was demolished. The front was missing. He sat huddled in the corner. He was trembling. His back was raked with claw marks. Purple blood stained his red dreadlocks. His tattoos were dull and faded.

A mix of fear and anger swelled inside Gideon. *Will that or even worse happen to me?* "Yokai, you're free to leave the cage."

Yokai turned to face Gideon. His purple eyes were half shut. Gideon draped Yokai's arm over his shoulder. The Shifter was cold to the touch. Gideon helped Yokai from the cage and set him on the ground.

"Thank you, Gideon Wells. If I were at full strength I could have killed that Ripper easily."

"I know, Yokai. But you're free of the pit now."

"Gideon Wells, what foolish thing have you done to secure my release?"

"I did what I had to do, Yokai."

Paige held onto the chain and stood atop her smashed cage as it was raised out of the pit. Purple streaks ran down her cheeks. When the cage cleared the pit she bounded off it and hugged Gideon, squeezing the air out him.

A hint of strawberries wafted over Gideon. His neck and face flushed.

"I can't thank ya enough, Gideon. I thought I was done fer."

"You're welcome, Paige. You saved me back on Payne's ship so—"

Paige pushed Gideon away. "So that's why ya saved me from the Ripper? Cuz ya owed me?"

"Well, yeah but—"

"Yur an eejit *and* a tool." Paige stomped off to Kaz and hugged him.

Jealousy and confusion washed over Gideon. "Yokai, what did I do?"

The Shifter shrugged his shoulders. "You have more pressing concerns, Gideon Wells."

Two saber-toothed cats disconnected the chains from Kaz's and Yokai's cages. The chains swung aimlessly from large pulleys in the ceiling until they were connected to two metal loops in the floor located along the edge of the nearest pit. Once the chains were secured to the metal loops, six cats jumped toward the ceiling and landed on the chains. The cats climbed up near the pulleys and dangled on the chains for a moment. Then the chains grew taught and clanked through the pulleys in the ceiling as the cats used their body weight to ride the chains down toward the floor.

"Yokai, what are they doing?"

"It appears they are lifting something out of the floor, Gideon Wells."

"Whatever it is it must be heavy."

While the great cats rode the chains from the ceiling down toward the floor of the throne room, the chains connected to the metal loops near the edge of the pit pulled a massive portcullis up and out of the floor. The metal door scraped against stone. It separated the pits that once held Kaz and Yokai. When the door was nearly touching the ceiling, three saber-toothed cats jumped into each pit.

Gideon peered into the nearest pit. The three cats cornered the Ripper and prevented it from running through the open doorway leading to the next pit.

In the other pit, the cats swatted, bit, and clawed at the Ripper, driving the monster into the adjacent pit. There were now two Rippers in the same pit.

Then the cats hanging on the chains jumped off. No longer weighed down by the heavy saber-toothed cats, the chains rattled through the pulleys in the ceiling—it sounded like giant steel drums. As the chains went up, the metal door separating the two pits came down. The door slammed into place, jarring Gideon's teeth.

With the door back in place and the two Rippers corralled into the same pit, the cats jumped out of the Ripper pit and sauntered to the king. The king dwarfed the other cats. He turned to Gideon. "It is time, Wells Cub. I will honor your bravery and grant you a final moment with your friends."

Gideon was dizzy and light-headed. *A final moment? Let's hope not.*

"Gideon-san, you're not going in that pit with the Rippers are you?"

"Yeah, Kaz. I made a contract with the king. If I live he'll help us bring down Gwendolyn."

"Gideon-san, don't do it. It's suicide. We need you alive. Think about the people that sacrificed to get you this far—Senpai, Vince, Frank. You die here, their sacrifice was for nothing."

Gideon's chest tightened. Images of his father falling into the waterfall ran through his mind. He thought of Vince being eaten alive by Peelers and Frank carried off by the Ripper. "It's the only way, Kaz."

Paige crossed her arms over her chest. "Ya really are an eejit and a tool. Yer throwin' yer life away. If I knew ya were this stupid I never would of helped ya come this far."

"Thanks, Paige. That's really helpful."

"Gideon Wells, do not let entertainment for these cats become martyrdom for you," Yokai said.

"I'll try Yokai."

The king roared. "It is time, Wells Cub."

Paige grabbed Gideon and hugged him. "Why are ya so stupid?"

Warmth surged through Gideon. "Just lucky I guess."

Nomti nudged Gideon toward a cage at the edge of the pit. "I told you not to interfere, Wells Cub. Look at you now."

Gideon held his Chain of Remembrance. "I know you did, Nomti but I couldn't just stand there and watch my friend die. I was raised better than that."

Gideon stepped inside the cage. The door clanged shut.

The cage swung out over the pit.

The chain clanked as Gideon was lowered into the pit.

The Rippers shrieked. Their beaks snapped.

Panic choked Gideon like a garrote, making it hard to breathe.

Chapter 27

Gideon squeezed the bars of the cage so hard his hands hurt.

The walls of the pit were gouged with claw marks and stained with blood—purple and red. The air was sour and dank.

The Rippers shrieked. They snapped their beaks. Their single purple eye drilled into Gideon. Then they threw themselves at him. Gideon was slammed to the back of the cage. Black slimy arms reached for him through the bars. Gideon dodged the long grey, curving claws.

The Rippers pulled on the metal bars. They bit down on them, breaking their teeth. Their purple eye filled with bloodlust.

Gideon thought of the Rippers back on the beach fighting over his wormhole jumper. *These creeps are all or nothing. I bet they don't like to share.*

Gideon grit his teeth and stuck his arms out toward the nearest monster. The Ripper grabbed Gideon. The monster's claws raked his forearms.

Gideon screamed. Bloody trails cut across the scars on his arms.

The Ripper sank its claws into Gideon's arm and pulled him to the front of the cage, slamming his head into it.

Colored spots swamped Gideon's vision.

The saber-toothed cats roared.

Paige screamed.

The Ripper tried to pull Gideon through the bars. It slammed Gideon's head into the cage again and again. Blood trickled into Gideon's eyes. His vision blurred. His dislocated shoulder burned. Then the Ripper shrieked and let go. Gideon fell into the back of the cage. He wiped the blood from his forehead.

The Rippers circled each other. Their beaks snapped. Claws flashed. Then the monsters tore into each other. They bit, slashed, and punched one another.

Purple blood sprayed out of the neck of one of the Rippers, spattering Gideon. It burned his face and arms. The coppery sour smell gagged him.

The wounded monster sank to its knees.

The other Ripper stood over it and opened its beak horizontally and vertically, flashing rows of razor sharp teeth. It placed its beak over the defeated Ripper's head completely covering it. Then the victorious monster snapped its beak shut with a sickening crunch and bit the defeated Ripper's head off.

The headless body slumped to the ground, spilling a pool of purple blood onto the floor of the pit.

The victorious monster spit the head toward Gideon and shrieked. The head bounced off Gideon's cage with a clang and hit the floor of the pit. The dead Ripper's beak reflexively snapped open and shut like chattering toy teeth.

Gideon recoiled.

The saber-toothed cats roared.

The victorious Ripper staggered like it was drunk. Bite marks in its neck pumped purple blood down its black slimy body. Deep claw marks were gouged across its chest. The monster slumped against the wall of the pit, its breathing ragged.

Gideon eased his way out of the cage. Every step was slow and labored. He felt like he was moving underwater. He sidestepped the decapitated head of the dead monster, making sure to avoid its snapping beak.

The victorious Ripper pushed off the wall and dragged itself toward Gideon.

Gideon froze. *If I don't fight back maybe it won't kill me.*

He raised his hands above his head in mock surrender.

The Ripper stood inches from Gideon. A purple sheen of blood covered its black slimy skin. It smelled of fetid sweat and blood. The monster sniffed at Gideon, then the single purple eye widened. The Ripper tilted its head back, opened its beak vertically and horizontally. Rows of sharp teeth tinged with purple blood and black offal glinted.

Oh my God, it's going to bite my head off.

The Ripper shrieked then grabbed Gideon and tossed him over his shoulder like a sack of potatoes. The monster jumped atop the cage and reached for the chain connecting the cage to the ceiling. It started climbing out of the pit.

The Ripper made its way a few feet up the chain when a saber-toothed cat jumped onto the cage and swatted Gideon and the Ripper onto the floor of the pit.

Gideon hit the floor. Pain stabbed his shoulder as he rolled. He came out of his roll crouching next to the decapitated head of the dead Ripper. Its beak was half open. Purple blood oozed out of its neck. Its dead eye stared at him. Gideon kicked it away in disgust.

The Ripper dragged its battered body across the floor to the far wall of the pit. The monster clawed at the wall, using it as leverage to pull itself to its feet. It pushed away from the wall only to fall back into it with a wet smack. Then the Ripper steadied itself. The monster stood on wobbly legs and came for Gideon.

Two more cats jumped into the pit. All three of the great cats tore into the Ripper. The monster shrieked as it was torn apart.

Gideon closed his eyes. He tried covering his ears but could still hear the shrieks of the dying monster, its bones snapping and the cats relishing their kill. The great cats made quick work of the Ripper.

When Gideon opened his eyes the three saber-toothed cats licked the purple blood from their face and paws. The Ripper was nothing more than a pile of bones.

They're like the Peelers that killed Vince. Gideon tried to stand but his head swam. The coppery sour smell of Ripper blood gagged him. He felt like he was going to faint.

The king roared. "I've seen enough. Remove the Wells Cub from the pit."

Gideon stood dazed and bleary-eyed before the king. His legs wobbled. The room spun. He swayed back and forth. His right shoulder felt like hot needles were stabbing it. Somebody pulled his left arm over their shoulder and stood him up. The smell of strawberries wafted over him.

"Yer the bravest and daftest tool I ever did see."

Gideon leaned into Paige. "Thank God it worked, Paige. I'm no good to Gwendolyn dead. I figured she programmed her Rippers to capture but not kill me."

"A smart gamble, Gideon-san. You would have made a fine Samurai."

"It is nice to see you again, Gideon Wells," Yokai said.

"Thanks, Yokai, Kaz. I'm glad you guys are okay."

Rumblings and growling from the saber-toothed cats filled the throne room.

Then the king roared, silencing them all.

Gideon pushed himself off Paige. He steadied himself then removed his sunglasses and eyed the king.

"Wells Cub, you are brave and cunning. You are worthy to do battle with us against the Evil One."

The throne room erupted with roars of approval.

Gideon swelled with pride.

"I will hear your battle plan now."

Gideon scanned the wall behind the king. It was lined with weapons. His gaze fell to the blasters and DNA scramblers. He thought back to what Vince and Frank said at Fort Drum about an electromagnetic pulse being the only way to lower the force field. *"Get an old fashioned nuke or daisy chain some blaster packs, rig 'em for overload and run like hell."*

"Great King the Evil One hides behind an invisible wall of energy that prevents your warriors from getting to her."

"This is true," the king said. "She is as cowardly as she is evil."

"Those blasters and DNA scramblers behind you on the wall can create an explosion that will interrupt the flow of energy feeding the Evil One's force field. If we can stop the flow of energy we can stop her force field."

The king stared at Gideon with a raised eyebrow. "Wells Cub, if you think you can use those dishonorable weapons to escape from me and my pride you are mistaken. They do not work."

"Yes, Great King, I know. I will not be using them to shoot anything. I will be taking them apart and building a new weapon—the one that will bring down the Evil One's invisible wall."

"You speak as if this energy flows like water."

"It does, Great King. The force field's energy flows like a waterfall. Using the blaster packs from those weapons I can create a pulse that will stop the energy flowing out from the lab. The invisible wall will collapse allowing your warriors to enter the lab and kill the Evil One."

The king eyed Gideon warily. He flashed his long fangs as he spoke. "If you lower the Evil One's invisible wall so that my warriors can enter her lab, you will have your freedom and that of your friends. But hear me well, fail me and I will feast upon you and your friends."

A chill ran through Gideon as images of the great cats tearing the Ripper limb from limb ran through his mind. "Yes, Great King. I understand."

"Give the Wells Cub all that he asks for," the king commanded. "But watch him and his friends carefully. Never let them out of your sight."

Gideon bowed his head. "Thank you, great king."

"When will the weapon be ready, Wells Cub?"

Gideon looked at his wrist pad. He had thirty-six hours left before he became an Off Worlder. Vince's and Frank's words ran through his mind—*"Five days in and out not one day more."*

"The weapon will be ready tonight."

The king purred as he spoke. "See that it is, Wells Cub. We attack at dawn."

Chapter 28

Gideon eyed the collection of blasters and DNA scramblers stacked on the stone table in front of him. The blasters were small pistol-like weapons. The DNA scramblers were long rifle-like weapons with wide mouthed barrels. Gideon had no idea how old the weapons were or if the battery packs still had power. Even if he could use the battery packs to create an electromagnetic pulse big enough to disable the force field around Gwendolyn's lab, would the explosion kill him and his friends? If it didn't, how long would the force field be down?

Gideon glanced over at the cats guarding the arched doorway. Nomti licked his chops, his black tongue running over his long curved fangs. The other saber-toothed cat cleaned his claws. *If this doesn't work will the king order me torn apart and eaten like he did the Ripper?*

He checked his wrist pad. Gideon had thirty-two hours left before he became a carrier of the Virus—before he was stuck Off World and not allowed to return to Earth. He squeezed his Chain of Remembrance and took a deep breath. The guards regarded him suspiciously.

Gideon dumped his backpack onto the stone table. He searched through what was left of his supplies setting aside anything that could be used as a tool. *I'd give anything for a good old-fashioned screwdriver.* Then he saw the red Swiss Army knife, just like his grandfather's.

He set to work taking apart the blasters and removing the battery packs. Using the small screwdriver wasn't easy. The Ripper from the pit left claw marks and gashes in Gideon's scarred forearms. The wounds stabbed at him with every turn of the screwdriver. Paige created a smelly salve to help heal his injuries and told Gideon without his scars his wounds would have been much worse.

Gideon peered at his injuries. *New scars, different monsters.*

He was lost in his work when the smell of strawberries wafted over him.

"Ya look to be strugglin', can I be helpin' ya any, Gideon?"

"Uh, I don't know, Paige, it's complicated—"

"I ain't stupid ya know."

"I never said you were."

"But I ain't smart enough to be helpin' ya. Is that it?"

"Paige, I never said—"

"Gideon Wells, stop talking and just let the girl help you," Yokai said.

"Okay, Paige take this tool and open the weapon's handle like this." Gideon used the small screwdriver in the Swiss Army knife and opened the blaster's handle. Blue plasma glowed inside.

"That be the weapon's ammo clip," Paige said.

"Yes." Gideon removed the blaster pack and handed it to Paige.

Paige squeezed the gel-like pack. "It's warm."

"That's a good sign. They should feel warm. We only want the warm blue ones. If they're cold and yellow, they're no good. Stack the good ones over there, please."

Kaz picked up one of the blue blaster packs and examined it. "Can you really use these to bring down the force field, Gideon-san?"

"Yeah, I think so. Vince and Frank seemed to think it could work."

Kaz set the blaster pack down. "But I thought blasters didn't work Off World."

"Blasters don't work here because firing the weapon somehow fries the circuitry. There's something weird about this planet's atmosphere. It eats away at the circuits when the weapon is fired but the blaster packs go undamaged."

"Yes, thankfully otherwise your kind would have exterminated my people years ago just so they could dig for rocks in our holiest of places." Yokai's eyes narrowed at Kaz.

Kaz bristled. "My family had nothing to do with the massacres."

"Another lie from the Muramatsu Mining boy."

"Filthy Yokai—"

Gideon slammed his fist onto the stone table. "Will you two cut it out? I don't have time for this nonsense."

"These weapons are awful, Gideon Wells. I want nothing to do with them."

"Yokai, I've been in your catacombs. I know what happened to your people and I'm sorry. But I need these weapons. Without them I can't lower Gwendolyn's force field."

"I accept that. But I'm not touching them."

"You don't have to, Yokai."

"Good." Yokai pointed to the far corner of the room. "I'll be over there regaining my strength. Don't disturb me while I'm meditating, Gideon Wells."

"Okay, rest up, Yokai. I need you fresh and strong for tomorrow's attack."

Kaz pointed at Gideon's wrist pad. "Gideon-san, how come your wrist pad works Off World but the blasters don't?"

"I don't know for sure, Kaz. A blaster uses a lot more power than the wrist pad. So it might have something to do with that."

"How do you plan on rigging all these blaster packs to blow?"

Gideon held up his wrist pad. "I'm going to use this to program the packs to overload and then explode."

"Are you sure you can sync your wrist-pad with the blaster packs?"

"How do you know—"

"Don't look so surprised, Gideon-san. I've worked with digital blasting caps and nano-explosives in the mines."

"Cool."

"When the mines were running we did a lot of cool things. You would have liked it, Gideon-san."

"You're okay, Kaz."

"Yeah, *I* am. But *you're* an eejit."

"I've been sayin' that since I met 'im, Kaz." Paige never looked up from her work. She deftly handled the screwdriver and easily removed another blaster pack.

Gideon caught the slightest curl of a smile on Kaz's face. "You told a joke. You even cracked a smile. I don't believe it."

"Gideon-san, you'll find I'm full of surprises." Kaz picked up a DNA scrambler and looked down the gun sight. He scanned the room with the weapon, stopping when the gun sight was trained on Yokai. "Well, it sounds like you've got it all figured out."

Gideon took the DNA scrambler away from Kaz. "Almost, there's one problem. The wrist pad doesn't send that strong a signal so I don't think I can stand too far from the device to detonate it. I think the best I can hope for is a remote detonation from about two hundred yards out. Not only that, once the explosion takes down the force field there are going to be Rippers all over the place. The chances of me getting to the maglev and inside the jumper without getting caught aren't good. It's about a quarter mile away from the lab."

Paige dropped the weapon she was working on. It bounced off the stone table and hit the floor sending the blue blaster pack skittering next to Yokai. The sleeping Shifter grunted but didn't stir.

"Paige, what's your problem? Be careful with those," Gideon said.

"My problem?" Paige asked, her accent thick and biting. "Yer not goin' inside the lab and destroyin' Gwendolyn's computers? Yer just gonna' run home? How selfish are ya that ya won't help us?"

Gideon waved his hand across the table pointing at the collection of disassembled blasters. "Not helping, what do you call this? I'm lowering the force field. The cats will swarm the lab and kill Gwendolyn. Isn't that enough?"

"Gwendolyn's not the problem, ya eejit. Killin' 'er will solve nothin'. It's the lab and them computer systems that need destroyin', not 'er."

"You don't know what you're talking about," Gideon said.

"Really?" Paige crossed her arms over her chest. She looked at Gideon as if he were the dumbest person alive. "Do ya not think they'll send somebody else to replace 'er? Do ya not think they'll be wantin' the work to go on?"

"You're crazy. What work is that, Paige? Creating more Rippers, more Berserkers? Why don't you tell everybody here why you really want me to go into the lab? What are you hiding?"

Paige placed her hands on her hips and leaned in closer to Gideon. Her purple eyes drilled into him. "I'm ain't hidin' nothin'."

"Yeah, right."

"What are you talking about, Gideon-san?" Kaz asked.

"She's working with Gwendolyn," Gideon said. "Why else does she want me to go into the lab so badly?"

Kaz's eyes widened.

Paige stiffened. She clinched her fists.

"Easy, Paige-san, he didn't mean it."

"Yes, I did," Gideon said. "She's hiding something from us. I can feel it. Frank knew it too. He told me not to trust you. What are you hiding?"

"Yer a selfish, stupid little boy," Paige said. "What happens if Gwendolyn ain't in the lab when the cats attack? What then? She lives to fight another day makin' an army of Rippers commanded by Bersererks? What happens to us then?"

"Not my problem," Gideon said with a dismissive wave of his hand. "I've got about thirty hours left and I'm not going to risk getting stranded in this horror show you call home. It's like Frank and Vince said, "Five days in and out not one day more.""

"Ya got plenty of time to get inside the lab, destroy the computers and be on your way. What's the real reason? Is it because thar's nothin' in it fer ya? Is it because there's no contract?"

"But I do have a contract, a contract with the king. If I lower the force field you three gain your freedom and I get to go home. If I fail, he eats *all* of us including *you*. So instead of wasting my time and endangering all our lives with this stupid distraction why don't you either help me or shut up and leave?"

"Selfish, selfish little boy." Paige looked at the scars on Gideon's forearms pointing as she spoke. "Yer no better than the people that did that to ya."

"I never said I was, Paige."

"Yer father was." Paige eyed the Chain of Remembrance dangling from Gideon's neck. "Yer mother too."

"Paige-san, let it alone," Kaz said.

"Yeah, they were, Paige. But what did it get them? Dead, that's what!" Gideon said. "I'm not going out that way. Not for you or anyone else."

"I'm not askin ya to be a martyr, Gideon. I'm askin ya to do what's right."

"I am doing what's right, Paige. It's right for me and its right for you guys." Gideon looked at his wrist pad and flushed. "You're wasting my time. Get out."

Paige shook her head. "I'm not goin' nowhere until ya agree to destroy Gwendolyn's computers."

Gideon signaled for Nomti. "Nomti, would you please have her removed?"

The saber-toothed cat padded toward Gideon. His claws clicked across the stone floor as he approached. "What's going on here, Wells Cub?"

Gideon pointed at Paige. "I was wrong about her. I don't need her help building the king's weapon. Please apologize to the king for me. I think she may be a spy for the Evil One."

Paige's eyes welled with tears. "Gideon, I can't beleive what I'm hearin'."

Nomti nudged her out the door. "Get out."

Kaz let out a low whistle. "That's stone cold, Gideon-san."

"Who cares?"

"I care and so do you. You know you do. She saved your life, remember?"

"Yeah, so she can turn me over to Gwendolyn."

Kaz shook his head. "You know that's not true, Gideon-san."

"I don't trust her, Kaz. Frank was right, she's hiding something."

"Isn't everybody, Gideon-san?"

"Not like her," Gideon said. "She's got something eating at her. I can feel it."

"Sort of reminds me of a kid from Earth who promised his mother he'd be a Galaxy Class Pilot no matter what."

"Yeah, yeah," Gideon said. "Give me that blaster pack will you?"

Kaz handed Gideon the blaster pack but refused to let go when Gideon took hold of it. The two boys locked eyes.

"What?" Gideon asked.

"Let me do it. Let me detonate the EMP bomb for you, Gideon-san. You said you can't be in two places at once so let me do it for you."

Gideon sat back in shock. His grip on the blaster pack loosened, Kaz pulled it out of his hand.

"You would do that for me, Kaz?"

"No, not for you, for Gwendolyn." Kaz squeezed the blaster pack as he spoke. "I owe her."

"Are you sure, Kaz?"

"I'll do this no problem but I want something in return, Gideon-san."

Gideon crossed his arms over his chest.

"Don't act so surprised, Gideon-san. This is how it works with you, right? We need a contract?"

"I'm listening, Kaz."

"I want you to make things right with Paige-san."

"That's the smartest thing I've heard anybody say," Yokai said.

Gideon shot the Shape Shifter a nasty look. "Yokai, I thought you were asleep."

"And miss all that human drama, Gideon Wells? Never."

Kaz gave Gideon a hard stare. His purple eyes were intense and unforgiving. His grip on the blaster pack tightened. "Apologize to Paige-san. Go talk to the king, do whatever it takes because I'm not going out there tomorrow morning without her. She deserves better than this and you know it."

Gideon snatched the blaster pack out of Kaz's hand and set it on the table. "Fine, Kaz, whatever."

Gideon hurried down the corridor, the guard prowling close behind him. Paige was being nudged toward the throne room by Nomti.

"Wait, stop, Nomti. I've made a mistake," Gideon said.

"What's the problem now, Wells Cub?" Nomti said.

"I was wrong. She's not a spy for the Evil One." Gideon took a deep breath. "I...need her."

Purple streaks rimmed Paige's eyes and stained her cheeks. She wiped her face with her sleeve and gave Gideon a guarded look.

Her vulnerability struck Gideon. Standing in front of him wasn't the tough fighter he had come to know. She was just a girl who he had insulted. No, it was more than that. He hurt her—badly. Gideon studied her face, her freckles, and the way her red hair fell down over her shoulders.

Gideon took hold of his Chain of Remembrance and rolled it between his fingers. "I'm...sorry Paige. I said some awful things. I didn't mean it." He let go the Chain of Remembrance and held up the wrist pad. "The time squeeze is making me edgy. I only have about a day left."

She cocked her head to one side and frowned.

"I just want to go home, Paige. Can't you understand that?"

"I understand. Anythin' else?"

"I know you could never be helping Gwendolyn. Please forgive me."

Paige put her hands on her hips. "I bet that was painful to be sayin'. Now will ya be shuttin' down the lab's computer system or not?"

Gideon held up the wrist pad. "No. No time."

Paige took a step towards Gideon.

Gideon felt himself flush.

"Don't worry, I don't bite," Paige said, her accent soft and lilting.

With that she closed her eyes, leaned into Gideon and kissed him softly on the cheek. As she pulled back, she gently caressed his face.

Gideon's face and ears burned. He stared at Paige wide-eyed. "Why…what did you do that for?"

"That's goodbye, Gideon." Paige spun on her heel and headed up the corridor, her red hair bouncing behind her.

Gideon held his hand to his cheek. He could still feel her soft touch. He could still smell a hint of strawberries. "Paige, why are you leaving? Where are you going?"

Paige turned to face Gideon. Her eyes were filled with disappointment. "I've done all I can fer ya, Gideon. I need to get ready fer tomorrow. Kaz will need me watchin' his back and I got no weapons to be doin' it with. I miss my crossbow but the king's trophy wall has a bow that caught my eye and some fine blades."

"Come with me, girl. I will take you," Nomti said.

Paige followed the great cat and disappeared around a bend in the corridor.

Paige expects too much. I can't do it. Gideon held his Chain of Remembrance. The walls of the corridor closed in on him. His chest tightened as the weight of loneliness pressed in on him.

Chapter 29

Gideon's eyes burned with fatigue. He took off his sunglasses and rubbed them with his fists. He had been up late building the EMP bomb. Then he spent most of the night stalking Tuskers in the tall grasses of the gorge. Nomti said it wasn't rare for an early morning hunt so the Evil One wouldn't be suspicious of the great cats approaching so close to the lab's force field. But twice Gideon had to hide underneath Nomti's foreleg as a patrol of Winged Rippers swooped overhead. The Winged Rippers didn't attack and Gideon prayed the monsters hadn't seen him or his friends. The last thing he needed was Rippers reporting his position to Gwendolyn.

The morning air was crisp. It was rich with the smell of grass, flowers and grazing Tuskers. Gideon peered out from the cover of the tall grass. The twin suns pushed away the night sky. As the orange and red suns rose above the horizon, they painted the dawn sky a brilliant coral.

Gideon put his sunglasses back on. The grassy plain of the gorge stretched out before him. It was dotted with several Tusker herds.

The maglev launcher was about a half mile away, silhouetted against the early morning sky. The tracks made a circle then pointed up in a steep incline toward the rising suns. Gideon's wormhole jumper sat perched and ready for takeoff. The sharp nose of the black-tiled ship was pointed for home.

What a beautiful sight.

A quarter mile east of the maglev launcher sat the four buildings of the lab complex. They had thick boxy walls built from purple and black volcanic rock. The roofs were corbelled, making the stone structures look like square beehive huts. They shimmered and bent as the force field's purple energy waves distorted the surrounding air.

"That's it, Gideon Wells?" Yokai asked. "Those small stone dwellings? I expected more from Gwendolyn."

Gideon pressed the side of his sunglasses and zoomed in. Ringing the corbelled roofs of each stone hut was a collection of solar panels. The solar panels were connected to force field projectors that rose up out of the roof like a small satellite dish. Purple light glowed from their center, making the force field projectors look like angry Ripper eyes.

"The lab is underground, Yokai. Those huts are guard posts. Each one guards a tunnel entrance to the lab."

Gideon scanned the lakeshore. He was relieved to see Captain Payne's ship no longer moored. It was far from shore and about to disappear over the horizon.

Gideon checked his backpack making sure the EMP bomb wouldn't fall out. The collection of blue daisy-chained blaster packs reminded Gideon of a rock collection. He slung the pack over his shoulders and grunted. Its weight pressing against his back made him think of life before the Virus when he was doubled over carrying a heavy backpack to school. His mother teased him nearly every morning, *"What do you have in there, honey, a rock collection?"*

All but two of the blaster packs were in good working condition and the larger packs from the DNA scramblers more than made up for their loss. Gideon had twelve usable blaster packs and two working packs from the DNA scramblers. The DNA scramblers even synched with the smaller blaster packs allowing Gideon to create only one overload program for all of the blaster packs instead of having to program fourteen separate ones and then hoping he synchronized their timing perfectly.

It was all so easy.

But would it work?

Gideon's mind filled with thoughts of Vince and Frank. Were they right? Self-doubt stabbed at him.

The plan was simple. The saber-toothed cats would attack the Tuskers causing a stampede. During the stampede, Gideon would place the EMP bomb near the force field and then make his way to the jumper. Kaz and Paige would detonate the EMP bomb allowing Gideon to board the jumper and leave for home.

It seemed so simple.

But would it work?

Gideon eyed the wormhole jumper and squeezed his Chain of Remembrance. *Soon, I'll be home soon.*

Then a dark shadow fell over Gideon. It was followed by a pungent musky odor. Gideon squeezed the handles of the Ripper Fang Knives tucked into the belt of his flight suit.

"You remember our contract, Wells Cub?" The king was so close Gideon could feel his hot breath on his neck. It smelled sour and fishy.

"I do, great king."

"Do you trust the older boy to use the weapon effectively? Your lives depend on his success."

Kaz held up the wrist pad and gave Gideon a thumbs up.

"I do, great king. Kaz has experience using explosives in the mines. He swears he can do it."

"I hope he's right," the king said.

"He can be trusted, great king."

"Wells Cub, I've assigned a guard to you and each of your friends. Do you know why?"

Gideon noted Nomti and other guards standing near him, Kaz, and Paige. Images of the great cats tearing apart the Ripper flashed through his mind. "The guards will kill me and my friends if the weapon fails or if I try to escape before the device is detonated."

"You are smart like your father, Wells Cub. Just don't get too clever like he did. I'm watching you. Be ready to move out. We will attack shortly." The king stalked away from Gideon and disappeared into the tall grass.

Gideon wiped the sweat from his forehead with the back of his hand.

"That was pleasant," Yokai said.

"You're telling me. If I fail, we're all cat food," Gideon said. "The sooner I'm out of here the happier I'll be. You need to get ready. The cats are about to attack."

Yokai's tattoos whirled and spun on his purple body. "I will be ready in a moment, Gideon Wells."

The Shape Shifter closed his eyes. His body shook. His red dreadlocks flew around his head like angry snakes. Then Yokai changed into a red-furred saber-toothed cat with black spots and a long tail. His sleek cat body was leaner than Nomti's. Instead of squat and powerful, Yokai was lean and long. He looked like a saber-toothed cheetah. The Shape Shifter growled and swished his tail. "I am ready, Gideon Wells."

"I'll never get used to seeing you do that, Yokai."

Led by the king, the cats stalked silently past Gideon, closing in on the nearest Tusker herd. Gideon was amazed the great cats—as big as they were—could move so quietly.

Gideon turned his attention to Kaz and Paige. "You guys good to go?"

"Yes, Gideon-san, I know what to do. We've only gone over it a hundred times." Kaz showed Gideon the wrist pad. The overload program for the blaster packs was set as well as the thirty-second timer for the detonator. "The wrist-pad will flash red after you turn on the device. Then I press this button and activate the countdown to overload. After thirty seconds the EMP bomb detonates then the force field comes down."

Gideon extended his hand. "Perfect. Thanks, Kaz. Thanks for everything."

Kaz ignored Gideon's handshake. He bowed at the waist. "No problem, Gideon-san. Now get out of here. You've got a plane to catch."

Paige readied the long black bow she had taken from the king's trophy wall. She pulled four arrows from the quiver on her back and loaded them into the long tube shaped magazine in the center of the bow. She slammed the magazine home and pulled back on the bowstring. The magazine whirred and clicked as it loaded the arrows. "It ain't my crossbow but it'll do."

Gideon reached out to hug Paige. "Goodbye, Paige. Thank you—"

Paige took a step back from Gideon and held up her hand. "Ya know how I feel about what yer doin'. I'll be wishin' ya a safe flight home and that's all, Gideon."

"Paige, why are you being—"

Yokai pawed at Gideon. "It is time, Gideon Wells. Climb onto me." The Shape Shifter bent low so Gideon could climb onto his back.

Then the trumpeting of Tuskers shattered the morning calm as the saber-toothed cats sprang from the tall grass and attacked the herd. Tuskers ran in all directions. The ground shook. It sounded like thunder pounding the sky. Dust clouds billowed up around the stampede making it hard to see anything but the shaggy heads of the Tuskers. Their tusks sliced through the brown dust cloud enveloping them.

The saber-toothed cats chased after the Tuskers and disappeared into the dust cloud. A mix of angry roars and terrified trumpeting filled the air. Then a cat jumped onto the back of a large Tusker. The Tusker reached over its head with its trunk grabbed the cat round the neck and slammed it against the ground. Then with a twist of its massive head, the Tusker flung the cat's limp body through the air. The saber-toothed cat cartwheeled into the force field.

The purple wall of energy crackled and popped as it reduced the great cat to a pile of ash.

Gideon's forearms burned from the Ripper cuts. He fought against the pain and sank his fingers deep into Yokai's fur. "Go, Yokai."

Gideon's head snapped back when Yokai's coiled cat body launched from the cover of the tall grass out into the open plain. They sailed twenty-five feet through the air before the landing rattled Gideon's jaw. Nomti was slow to keep up.

The EMP bomb thumped against Gideon's back as Yokai's sinewy body coiled and uncoiled. The Shape Shifter sliced through the air. His paws rarely touched the ground as he bounded toward the force field in graceful twenty-five foot strides.

Gideon dug his heels into the Shape Shifter's ribs and used them like stirrups. He raised himself off Yokai's back and rode the saber-toothed cheetah like a soldier on a warhorse. Gideon and Yokai shot past the stampeding Tuskers. In ten seconds they would reach the force field.

Then two of the Tuskers broke off from the main stampede and charged at Gideon. Their massive feet cratered the grassy plain. The Tuskers lowered their long curved tusks and gored several saber-toothed cats as they bore down on

Gideon. Dead cats swung from their tusks like rag dolls until the Tuskers shook them off with a hard twist of their neck.

Then the king jumped on the back of one of the Tuskers charging Gideon. The black saber-tooted cat sank his fangs into the back of the Tusker's neck. The Tusker trumpeted once before collapsing, hitting the ground like an avalanche of bone and meat.

The king chased down the second Tusker and attacked its hindquarters but not before the Tusker raised its trunk and unleashed a sonic attack at Gideon.

Gideon sank his hands deep into Yokai's fur and braced himself for the impact or at least a shower of dirt and rocks. There was neither.

The sonic blast slammed into Nomti. The great cat roared in pain. His body bent as if punched by an invisible fist. He twisted and rolled as the energy wave drove him into Yokai.

The Shape Shifter's long sleek legs went out from under him. Yokai tumbled into the ground like he was tackled.

Gideon was less than forty feet from the force field when he catapulted over Yokai's head. He sailed directly for the force field. Then he hit the ground hard. Pain stabbed his shoulder. Gideon rolled. When he came out of his somersault his backpack was bouncing toward the force field.

Gideon ran for the pack. He pumped his arms and legs as fast as he could. He jumped and stretched his body as far as possible. Then his fingers grabbed at the torn shoulder strap. He pulled the pack to his chest. His nose was inches from the force field.

The force field buzzed and crackled. It smelled sweet and pungent like the air right before a summer thunderstorm. The hairs on Gideon's head and arms stood on end.

Gideon said a quick prayer and backed away from the force field. He opened the pack and checked the EMP bomb. None of the blue blaster packs ruptured. The EMP bomb was undamaged.

Yokai staggered to his feet. He shook his body like a wet dog. The Shape Shifter's lean cheetah muscles rippled across his body. He nudged Nomti's limp body. Nomti stirred. He sat up for a moment then lay back down.

A wayward Tusker loped toward Gideon. It had gashes and claw marks on its brown shaggy back and hindquarters. Its long curved tusks were stained with purple blood. It was twenty yards from Gideon. It shook its massive head back and forth.

Gideon froze. The force field hummed and buzzed at his back.

Then the Tusker veered away. It charged Yokai.

Gideon called out. "Yokai, look out!"

The Tusker reared up on its hind legs. It raised both of its front legs high into the air then slammed them into the ground, bringing all its weight to bear. The ground erupted as if hit by two powerful bombs. Enormous craters swelled up and around the Tusker's feet. Yokai and Nomti disappeared in a storm of dirt and rock.

Gideon bounced nearly a foot into the air as the ground rippled outward from the impact craters. He ducked and covered his head against the shower of rocks cascading toward him. The rocks hit the force field above Gideon and disintegrated like a meteor storm hitting the sun. The force field rippled outward as it absorbed the rocks, lashing Gideon's back with searing heat.

Gideon fell to his knees and screamed.

His voice echoed across the prairie.

The Tusker raised its front legs out of the craters. Purple blood and gore stained its left foot.

Then it turned on Gideon.

Chapter 30

Gideon's back sizzled. Smoke rose from his flight suit. He touched the back of his neck and winced. His skin was raw and tacky. He ran his hand through his hair. Singed clumps stuck to his fingers. It smelled awful.

His head spun. His ears pounded. Dizziness overwhelmed him. Gideon fell onto his hands and crawled away from the force field. The backpack was only a few feet in front of him but his arms and legs were heavy and clumsy. Every movement made his body scream. The backpack may as well have been one thousand miles away.

Gideon focused on his pack's torn shoulder strap. It was bent and splayed out toward him like a broken limb. Pain stabbed Gideon's burns as he reached for it. He had the shoulder strap within his grasp when the ground rippled making the pack bounce out of reach.

I must be losing it. The backpack just moved.

Gideon's ears pounded.

Then the ground rippled again.

He snatched the broken shoulder strap before the pack bounced out of reach and pulled it close. Gideon grunted against the pain and rose to his knees.

The brown, shaggy-haired Tusker that killed Nomti and Yokai was twenty yards from Gideon. It stomped its massive legs making the ground ripple. Dust clouds billowed around the Tusker's feet. The constant pounding sounded like a giant bass drum inside Gideon's head.

The Tusker raised its trunk and swung its head back and forth. Its curved tusks were dappled with purple blood and gore.

Nomti's words ran through Gideon's head. *"The beasts are nearly blind. But they have excellent hearing and can smell you with their long noses."*

It heard me scream but it can't see me. It's trying to sniff me out.

Gideon scanned the twin craters created by the Tusker's attack on Nomti and Yokai. He pressed the side of his glasses and peered through the dust cloud. Gideon's glasses caught the infrared heat signature of a humanoid. The human form was outlined in an orange-red silhouette and was slumped against the outer rim of one of the impact craters. The humanoid tried to get up stumbled and then dragged itself onto its hands and knees.

Yokai's alive!

Then the Tusker raised its trunk and turned back toward Yokai.

I need to save Yokai from getting stomped—somehow distract the Tusker.

Gideon peered up at the force field and back at the Tusker. Then he put his fingers in his mouth and let out a piercing whistle.

The Tusker turned back toward Gideon.

Yokai peered around the edge of the crater. His long red dreadlocks were draped over his face. The Shape Shifter crouched on the far side of the crater keeping himself as far from the Tusker as possible.

Gideon whistled again.

The Tusker raised its head, pointed its trunk at Gideon and unleashed a sonic attack.

Gideon grit his teeth and sprinted for Yokai. His burns stabbed hot needles into his back and neck.

The Tusker's sonic wave smashed into the force field, making the purple wall of energy bend in on itself like it swallowed an enormous egg. The force field crackled and popped. Then thick tendrils of the force field erupted outward like a solar flare. The purple flares lashed the Tusker across the top of its head and back like a giant cat o' nine tails.

The Tusker's shaggy hair caught like kindling. Within seconds, the massive creature erupted into a fireball.

The smell of burning hair and flesh made Gideon's stomach turn.

The Tusker trumpeted in fear and pain. It ran in wild circles. Then the Tusker charged the force field. The force field swallowed the massive creature and reduced it to a pile of ash.

Gideon ducked behind the crater next to Yokai. The Shape Shifter was covered in dirt and blood spatters. His tattoos were dull and faded. A gash ran down his right leg. The wound had rock shards and debris sticking out of it.

"Yokai, are you okay? I thought—"

"I am battered but not broken, Gideon Wells. Most of this blood you see belongs to Nomti. He's dead."

"I'm sorry to hear that. He was brave."

"He died a warrior's death. His clan will honor him."

Gideon peered into the next crater. It was too deep for him to see the bottom but the inside walls were spattered with purple blood. Bits of bone and tufts of reddish fur were embedded in the walls. Gideon forced himself to look away.

"Yokai, your leg."

"It will heal in time. But you will have to run the rest of your journey on your own two legs, Gideon Wells."

Gideon's jumper gleamed in the morning sun. It was about a quarter mile away. He squeezed his backpack. *We need cover for when this EMP bomb goes off. Then I can run to my ship.*

Yokai pointed a bloody hand out at the prairie. "Sometimes the dead can help the living, Gideon Wells."

Dead Tuskers dotted the flat prairie like drumlins. Their massive round bodies towered over the saber-toothed cats. The closest Tusker body was about fifty yards from Gideon. Three saber-toothed cats were feeding from it. Giant bones cracked as the great cats sank their long fangs into their kill. The smell of blood and death was thick in the air.

"Yokai, which part of a Tusker has the thickest bones?"

"The creature's skull is armored plated. They use their heads as weapons against one another."

We'll have thirty seconds to get to the other side of that Tusker. But will it be far enough from the blast?

Gideon peered at Yokai's leg. The rock shards sticking out of his thigh were slick with purple blood. *There's no way Yokai can do it.*

"Using the dead Tusker as a shield from that weapon you built is a fine idea, Gideon Wells. But those cats may not want you as a guest to their feast.

"They'll be fine with *our* company, Yokai. We're both going over there and it's not like we'll be stealing their kill. I like my food cooked."

Gideon pressed the side of his glasses and zoomed in on the tall grass bordering the prairie. Kaz and Paige were nowhere. *Kaz knows what to do. He'll start the countdown. Paige probably has them well hidden. Just because I can't see them doesn't mean they're not there.*

Gideon opened his backpack and activated the EMP bomb. He placed it a few feet from the base of the force field. The purple wall of energy crackled. Gideon started counting backward from thirty seconds. He pulled Yokai up by the arm and lifted him off the ground in a fireman's carry. The burns on his neck and back screamed. Gideon growled at the pain and jogged toward the dead Tusker.

Twenty seconds.

Tusker footprints stomped deep into the prairie pockmarked the ground. Gideon wove his way between the craters. Some of them were deep enough to swallow a car. The deepest had bodies of flattened saber-toothed cats inside them. Gideon tried not to think of Nomti.

Purple blood made the grass slippery. The ground squished under Gideon's flight boots. It smelled sweet and coppery. *Fifteen seconds. We're about halfway there. Maybe twenty yards to go.*

Gideon's legs started to wobble. Sweat stung his eyes and blurred his vision. He stepped too close to the soft edge of a deep Tusker footprint and the ground gave way. Gideon grabbed and clawed at the wall of dirt as he fell. He tried to slow his free fall but Yokai's weight drove him down.

Gideon slammed into the ground and fell forward. His head hit the dirt hard as he rolled Yokai off his shoulders and over his head. The cold ground dug into his face. Gideon spit the dirt and grit out of his mouth.

Yokai grabbed his leg. Purple blood ran between his fingers. He barred his teeth and stifled a scream.

Sweat poured off Gideon. His breathing was ragged. *Ten seconds. So this is how I die? Killed by my own EMP bomb?*

Gideon rose to his knees. The walls of the Tusker footprint were over his head. *It's like the trenches they used during the Narco Wars. But is it far enough away from the blast?*

"Yokai, stay down. We should be okay in here." Gideon crouched into a ball. He covered his ears and opened his mouth.

Three, two, one…

There was no blast. Gideon uncovered his ears. The force field buzzed and crackled. "There should have been an explosion, Yokai. Something's wrong—"

Then the force field stopped buzzing and crackling. Gideon peered out of his makeshift foxhole. The force field was gone. "How is the force field down? Yokai, there was no explosion."

Then hundreds of Winged Rippers stormed out of the four corbelled buildings and took to the air. The black swarm of one-eyed monsters filled the morning sky. They circled overhead and went after the saber-toothed cats. Then the force field snapped back into place.

"Oh…My…God, it's a trap, Yokai. I was right about Paige. She must have sabotaged the EMP bomb and told Gwendolyn."

"Go home, Gideon Wells. If the king finds you he'll kill you for sure."

Gideon stared up at his jumper. "But what about you? What will you do?"

Yokai blurred and shook until a small red bird replaced his purple humanoid body. The bird flapped its four wings and buzzed around Gideon's head. "I'll be fine, Gideon Wells. You should run, run as fast you can for your ship. Don't let the cats or Gwendolyn's monsters catch you."

"Thanks for everything, Yokai."

"Good luck, Gideon Wells." The red bird flew off and disappeared into the cover of the tall grass.

Gideon pulled himself up and out of the deep Tusker footprint. His jumper was less than two hundred yards away. Except for the nearby dead Tusker there was no cover. It was all open ground. Gideon cursed Paige's treachery. *I can't believe she betrayed me. Frank was right about her.*

Gideon sprinted for his jumper. He vaulted over the deep Tusker footprints. He ran past the dead Tusker. The three saber-toothed cats feeding on their kill were forced to abandon it and fight off a swarm of Winged Rippers. The cats bit and clawed while the Winged Rippers dove, slashed and snapped at them.

Gideon closed on his jumper. *About one hundred yards to go, maybe twelve seconds.*

A silhouette of a Winged Ripper appeared on the ground in front of Gideon. It grew larger as he ran. The air smelled sour and dank. The shadow blotted out the morning sun. Then the Winged Ripper folded its wings and swooped in on Gideon.

Gideon dove and rolled. The monster's claws tore at his flight suit. Gideon came out of his roll and pulled his Ripper Fang knives from his belt.

The monster hovered just above Gideon. It snapped its beak and reached for Gideon with its slimy black arms. Gideon ducked and sunk his blades deep into the monster's chest and stomach. The Winged Ripper shrieked and fell to the ground. It eased the knife out of its chest and dropped it on the grass. Purple blood gushed down its chest.

More Winged Rippers descended on Gideon. He bolted up the stairs of the maglev launcher and sprinted for his jumper.

He entered the code that opened the bio-scanner for him, tore off his sunglasses and pressed his face into it. A warm green light washed over his face. The hatch opened with a whoosh.

Gideon jumped inside his ship and sealed the hatch. It closed and locked with a loud metallic clank.

Gideon never felt so relieved.

He scanned the controls as he went through his pre-flight checklist. Satisfied that all the systems were working properly, Gideon took a deep breath and hoped the magnetic levitation system was working. If not, the small jumper would simply sit on the track like a stone. It had powerful enough engines for flight but they weren't designed for take-offs.

Gideon placed his hand on the maglev power switch and closed his eyes. "Please, please, please work."

He opened his eyes and flipped the switch. The maglev hummed and powered up. Gideon felt the ship slowly lift itself off the tracks. He checked the control panel and confirmed the ship was levitating. "Yes," he said with a fist pump.

"Now for the risky part." Gideon knew that once the engines were switched on there would be a lot of noise, smoke, and fire. There would be no hiding the fact that he was in the ship and preparing to leave. He sighed. It couldn't be helped. "Computer, prepare for emergency take-off."

"Affirmative," the computer said in a steely voice. "Emergency take-off will commence in three minutes after maglev diagnostic check is complete."

"Good, get it done," Gideon ordered. "As soon as the maglev diagnostic is complete announce the countdown to emergency take-off starting at the sixty second mark."

"Affirmative," replied the ship's computer.

Gideon checked and re-checked the ship's systems. His hands shook and his body raged with nervous energy.

"Maglev diagnostic is complete with all systems green," announced the computer. "Emergency take-off in T-minus sixty seconds, fifty-nine, fifty-eight...."

Gideon sat back in the pilot's chair and took a deep breath. "I made it. I can't wait to see the look on Adrian's face or the Weasel's when I show up at Quarantine. Five days in and out, not one day more."

Then he peered out the cockpit window.

His mouth fell open.

Standing near the maglev launcher was Paige and Kaz. Kaz had hold of Paige by the hair and was twisting it violently. His sword was held up under her neck. A trickle of purple blood stained the sword. Paige's eyes and face were streaked with purple tears.

"T-minus forty-five seconds to emergency take-off," the computer said.

Gideon switched on the intercom. "Kaz, what's going on? Let her go."

"No chance, flyboy. Shut everything down and come out or I take her head."

Gideon was rocked to his core. It was never Paige that was working for Gwendolyn. It was Kaz.

Paige sobbed. "Just kill me and be done with it. He won't come out. He cares for nobody but 'imself.'"

"Shut up." Kaz tugged on Paige's hair nearly lifting her off the ground by it.

"T-minus thirty-five seconds to emergency take-off," announced the computer.

Gideon punched the control panel so hard it hurt. Then a tall woman appeared near Kaz.

It was Gwendolyn.

She was taller than Kaz with long brown hair and purple eyes. But the thing that really struck Gideon was that she looked just like his mother.

Was he hallucinating?

Gideon grabbed his Chain of Remembrance. "It's not possible."

Then she spoke. She sounded just like his mother.

"Gideon, honey," Gwendolyn said. "Please come outside. I think Kaz means to kill this poor girl. I've tried to talk him out of it but he seems pretty committed to it."

"T-minus twenty-five seconds," the computer announced.

The wormhole jumper's engines rumbled to life.

Kaz twisted the sword up under Paige's neck. Gideon watched with horror as purple blood trickled down her neck.

The computer continued the countdown.

"Fifteen, fourteen, thirteen—"

"Gideon, honey, please," Gwendolyn said. "It's been so long since I've held you in my arms. Please help me save this poor girl."

Gideon closed his eyes and shook his head hoping that what he saw before him would disappear when he re-opened them. That it was nothing more than a nightmare born of fatigue and stress.

"Ten, nine, eight—"

Paige's eyes were closed. Purple tears streaked her face. Blood stained her neck.

Gwendolyn held her arms out to Gideon beckoning him to come to her like his mother used to do on so many occasions. She smiled inviting him to join her.

The words of the saber-toothed king ran through Gideon's head. *"Your father created the Evil One."*

The realization hit Gideon like a thunderclap. He cursed his father and punched the control panel again and again. His hand ached and bled. The skin on his knuckles partially tore off.

His father had cloned his mother.

His father was responsible for everything. Creating Gwendolyn, the Berserkers and because he created Gwendolyn, the Rippers. The king's words stung Gideon as they ran through his head again and again. *"If it weren't for your father, there would be no Evil One, no man-made monsters to fight."*

Gideon stared at Paige.

How could he abandon her after all she had done for him?

He peered down at the scars on his forearms. She was right; he was no better than the people who had done this to him.

"Five, four, three—"

The jumper's engines shook the entire ship. They were nearly at full power ready to push Gideon along the maglev and into orbit and then home.

Gideon bit his lip and took a deep breath. "Computer shut down the engines and all flight systems. Abort take-off."

"Affirmative take-off aborted, shutting down all flight systems."

Gideon unfastened his flight harness and raced to the back of the jumper searching it for anything he could use as a weapon. There was nothing. He cursed.

"Gideon, honey, that's a good boy. Now please come outside," Gwendolyn said.

Gideon opened the hatch and walked toward Gwendolyn like he was in a dream— everything seeming to be moving in slow motion.

"Ya came back fer me?" Paige said.

"Let her go, Kaz," Gideon said.

Kaz eyed Gwendolyn. She gave him a curt nod.

Kaz dropped Paige roughly to the ground. He cleaned her blood off his sword with a quick snap of his wrist and sheathed it in one fluid motion.

Gideon strode up to Kaz and gave him a roundhouse kick in the leg, hitting the nerve cluster in his left thigh perfectly.

Kaz dropped to the ground. He grabbed his leg as shock and pain erupted across his face.

Gideon tried a head kick but Kaz dodged it and sprang to his feet. He unsheathed his sword and raised it above his head.

Gideon backed away.

A set of strong hands grabbed him by the hair and nearly lifted him off the ground. Standing on his tiptoes, he was spun around and looking directly into Gwendolyn's face. The resemblance to his mother was unnerving. He couldn't stop staring at her. She was both beautiful and terrible at the same time.

"Now, Gideon, we'll have none of that," Gwendolyn said. "Am I clear?"

Gideon nodded.

"What? I can't hear you."

"Yes." Gideon winced as she twisted his hair.

"Yes, what?"

"Yes, ma'am?"

Gwendolyn yanked Gideon's hair making him do a pirouette. "Try again, dear."

Then her grip slackened allowing Gideon to stand flat-footed.

"You know what I want to hear, Gideon, honey."

Gideon realized what she wanted. It made him sick to think of it. Hatred filled him but he pushed it away. He glanced at Paige. She was being led away by Kaz and two Berserkers. Gideon closed his eyes. "Yes, Mom."

"Good boy." Gwendolyn let go of Gideon's hair and blew the clump she had torn from his head out of her hand.

Gideon rubbed his head with his hand as he watched the clump of brown hair float to the ground.

Then Gwendolyn hugged him. "Gideon, honey, it's so good to finally see you. It's not nice to keep your mother waiting so long."

Gideon went rigid as Gwendolyn pulled him close just like his mother used to.

Gwendolyn's gaze fell to Gideon's injured hand. Blood flowed freely from his bruised knuckles dripping into the dirt and staining it.

"Oh my, Gideon, you're injured. Let's go inside and take care of that. We don't want any of that Pure Earth to go to waste now, do we?"

CHAPTER 31

Gideon and Paige followed Gwendolyn into the stone tunnel that led to the underground lab complex. Kaz and the two Berserkers brought up the rear. The walls and ceiling of the tunnel were scarred with deep lines from the boring machines that carved it. The lines in the stone reminded Gideon of the scars on his forearms and how he got them.

He nearly died trying to protect his mother from a stone-throwing mob. The shattered glass of the greenhouse cut deep gashes into Gideon's arms as he shielded his mother from the falling shards. He saved his mother's life only to lose her when she died creating the cure for the Virus. Now he was a prisoner of her clone.

Gwendolyn was bigger than Gideon's real mother. She was muscular and lithe. She took long confident strides, moving as if nothing could hurt her. Her face was set with grim determination.

Gwendolyn may look like my mother but she's not. She's just a copy. My mother was a brilliant scientist who invented the cure for the Virus. I bet this weirdo uses the cure to make Berserkers. My mother baked me and my friends ginger snap cookies and chocolate potato cake. This nut job cooks up Rippers. I need to get Paige and me out of here somehow.

Gideon reached for his Chain of Remembrance. He made sure it was hidden inside his flight suit. The crystal was warm against his chest.

Motion sensors activated tubular lights in the ceiling. The long tubes snapped on as Gwendolyn led them deeper into the underground lab complex. It created an eerie strobe light effect. Gideon's shadow bled into the Berserker's shadow, creating a ghost-like apparition that skulked along the walls after him.

Gideon pushed his sunglasses up onto his face. *I can't let the Berserkers know I'm Pure Earth. If they find out they'll eat every part of me. I hope to God they can't smell I'm Pure Earth.*

Paige took Gideon's hand. Her grip was strong and reassuring. Gideon interlocked his fingers with hers.

"Are you okay, Paige?"

Paige had a long thin gash across her neck. Purple blood stained her throat. "I ain't hurt none too bad." She leaned into Gideon as they walked and rested her head on his shoulder. "Thank ya fer coming back fer me."

The smell of strawberries wafted over Gideon. His cheeks flushed. "You're welcome."

Paige whispered in Gideon's ear, "Why are ya callin' Gwendolyn mum?"

"She forced me to say it. She's a clone of my mother. My father made her."

Paige recoiled. "Your father made 'er?"

"Yes, he did. She looks and sounds just like my mother. It's starting to creep me out."

"I'm so sorry, Gideon. How awful. I had no ider."

"Don't be sorry for him, young lady," Gwendolyn said. "He has a second chance to reconnect with his mother. All he has to do is give me access to the artificial intelligence and all will be well."

"Don't count on it…Mom."

"Oh but I am, Gideon. All of us are and I've no doubt you'll see things my way soon enough."

Paige squeezed Gideon's hand. "We'll be okay. I know you'll figure somethin' out."

"Ah, we're here at last." Gwendolyn stopped in front of a large grey blast door with a spoke-wheeled handle in the center. It reminded Gideon of a bank vault.

"There's something I want to show you, Gideon. It's a surprise," Gwendolyn said.

"I hate surprises."

Gwendolyn spun the spoke-wheeled handle making it blur like it was a bicycle wheel. Then the handle stopped with a loud clank that echoed in the stone tunnel. Gwendolyn snapped her fingers at one of the Berserkers guarding

Gideon and Paige. The monster pushed its way past Gideon. It grabbed hold of the spoke-wheeled handle and pulled the door open. Metal bars thicker than Gideon's arms ran vertically across the inside of the door.

That door must be three feet thick. What is she hiding?

Humid, sour air hit Gideon in the face. Bright spotlights hung from the ceiling of a large cavern. The floor was lined with power generators as big as cars—the machines buzzed and hummed. Thousands of beehive-like combs were carved into the walls of the cavern. Inside each comb was a birthing pod housing a Ripper waiting to be unleashed.

Gideon's breath caught in his chest. His mouth hung open.

There were dog-like Rippers with multi-hinged jaws like the ones Gideon first saw outside the Bone Flower Field. There were winged, bat-like Rippers identical to the ones fighting the saber-toothed cats. There were also new Rippers Gideon had never seen—creatures with the body of a man but the head and fangs of a saber-toothed cat.

Paige squeezed Gideon's hand so hard his knuckles popped.

Gwendolyn beamed. "Aren't my children beautiful? It's amazing what one can do with discarded mining equipment and a few capable Berserkers. In just a few hours these Rippers will be born and battle ready. They will finish off what's left of those wretched saber-toothed cats."

"Why show this to me?" Gideon said.

"Because I wanted you to see the full extent of my power, Gideon. So you can make the right decision about you and your girlfriend's future." Gwendolyn's purple eyes bore into Gideon. They were wild and crazed. Her face contorted into a hungry grin. "Nobody on this planet can stop me. Now come along, there's no time to dawdle. We don't have much time before you become an Off Worlder and we have a lot of lab work ahead of us."

Gwendolyn spun on her heel and strode across the hall. She stopped in front of a set of thick glass-double doors. The doors slid open with a whoosh and disappeared behind the rocky wall.

The harsh biting smell of disinfectant and nano-sanitizers assaulted Gideon. It smelled like the Finger Lakes Quarantine.

Kaz shoved Gideon into the lab. "You heard the lady. Start walking, fly boy."

"Kaz, when this is over, I'm going to beat you to a pulp."

"Ya need to be gettin' in line fer that, Gideon," Paige said.

"Yeah, yeah shut up, love birds," Kaz said.

The lab was bigger than any Gideon had ever seen. It was bigger than the three hundred-seat cafeteria at the Finger Lakes Quarantine. The lab was smooth walled and oval shaped. Light from thin, claw-like tubes inlaid into the vaulted ceiling reflected off long steel tables arranged in neat parallel rows. The lab was crammed with equipment.

This place is better equipped than anything my mother ever had back on Earth.

High-speed centrifuges whirred. Genetic sequencers beeped and flashed. The glowing nanite farm looked like an aquarium filled with floating green dust motes. There were cell incubators, full body scanners and cryogenic storage tanks. Scanners and laser scalpels shared a table with sharp-edged blades and saws that were better suited for a butcher shop than a medical lab. A chill ran through Gideon.

I don't want to know what she's doing with those saws and blades.

Tall shelves housed translucent jars filled with odd body parts that Gideon guessed were from Off World creatures. There were disembodied wings, legs, arms, and small bat-like heads floating in a thick, clear liquid. White privacy curtains speckled with purple bloodstains cordoned off the rest of this part of the lab.

Oh my God, she's harvesting Off World body parts to make her Rippers.

In the rear of the lab, a purple force field buzzed and crackled. Behind the force field sat a large computer console with multiple flat screen monitors.

"Excellent, Gideon, I see you've found the AI console," Gwendolyn said. "I confess that it's been more than a struggle for me to work without the AI but now that you're here, all that will change. I can finally be rid of this makeshift computer station I've been forced to cobble together."

Gwendolyn's computer station sat atop a steel examination table in the center of the lab. There were four small computers with monitors. Power cords snaked across the table and down its wheeled legs.

Gwendolyn checked her monitors and tapped some keyboard commands. Then she pulled on a crisp, clean white lab coat. She picked up a Shocker and switched it on. The end buzzed and popped with electricity. She strode over to the bloodied privacy curtains and pulled them back, unveiling a birthing pod. Three Berserkers were huddled around it. The purple-skinned monsters snarled at Gideon.

Gideon grabbed Paige and took a step back. He bumped into Kaz.

"Go on, Gideon, take a closer look," Gwendolyn said. "Nobody here will hurt you unless I order it."

"No, thanks, I'm good standing where I am."

"I insist, Gideon. Kaz, please help my son—"

Kaz shoved Gideon forward.

The Berserkers opened their multi-hinged jaws vertically and horizontally. Rows of sharp teeth accentuated by long fangs glistened with saliva. Their jaws snapped at Gideon. Their long needle-like claws splayed outward. The monsters reeked of coppery blood and a vinegar-like body odor.

"What are these, your pets?" Gideon asked.

"Of a sort, Gideon." Gwendolyn snapped her fingers at the Berserkers. "Back off and let my son approach the pod."

The Berserkers stepped back. Each of the monsters gripped a long thin hose that was attached to the birthing pod.

"Gideon, ya need to be careful—"

"It's okay. Stay there, Paige." Gideon pushed his sunglasses up onto the bridge of his nose. He peered inside the pod and gasped. "Is that Frank? Is he dead?"

"It is indeed your hunter friend," Gwendolyn said. "But no, he's not dead— at least not yet."

Frank was in a fetal position. His eyes were closed. His face was drawn and his hair graying. He looked as if he hadn't eaten in weeks. Hoses were attached to his lower back.

Anger boiled inside Gideon. "What are you doing to him?"

"As a member of the Corps it's his job to save people, is it not? Well he's saving people now and he's doing it without having to kill anyone with a blaster or one of those vile DNA scramblers. This is a much more selfless, much more honorable act for a soldier. Don't you think?"

"What are you talking about?"

Gwendolyn pointed at the three Berserkers. "Show my son."

Each Berserker put the end of the hose in its mouth and made a sucking, gurgling sound. It reminded Gideon of how he used to drain the last bits of a milkshake. The hoses attached to Frank pulsed. A pained look crept across the hunter's face. He shifted in his sleep.

"Oh my God, they're feeding from Frank, draining his bone marrow." Gideon dropped to one knee and started to retch.

"Gideon, are ya okay?" Paige pulled Gideon up from the floor.

"Oh come now, Gideon," said Gwendolyn, her voice rising in anger. "Don't be so squeamish."

Gideon removed his sunglasses and rubbed his eyes. As he did, he instantly realized his mistake and cursed himself. He quickly put the glasses back on.

The Berserkers stopped feeding from Frank and stared at Gideon. Their purple eyes widened with anticipation. Their mouths watered—a mix of saliva and Frank's life essence dripped from their fangs. The closest Berserker, a short one with long, dark, unkempt hair pointed a clawed hand at Gideon. "Pure Earth," the monster said in a guttural voice.

Gideon stared at the Berserker in disbelief. In its purely human form it was most likely a petite, perhaps even a pretty woman. But it was more monster than human now. Its purple face was deformed and elongated with a gnarled snout. Long fangs protruded from its face. The Berserker's shoulders hunched forward. Its eyes shifted quickly back and forth from Gideon to Gwendolyn.

Gideon stepped in front of Paige and moved her away from the Berserker.

Suddenly the monster dropped the feeding tube on the ground and launched itself at Gideon like a missile.

Gideon shoved Paige out of the way as the monster knocked him to the floor. The monster stood over Gideon, splayed its claws and roared. "Pure Earth, need Pure Earth."

Gideon tried crab walking away from the Berserker but his flight boots found no purchase on the lab floor. His feet kicked out uselessly in front of him.

Then Gwendolyn's Shocker hit the Berserker in the ribs. The monster dropped to the floor. Gwendolyn jabbed her Shocker into the Berserker again and again. The Berserker shrieked in pain. The smell of burnt hair and flesh assaulted Gideon.

Kaz drew his sword. He shouted at Gwendolyn. "Stop it, you're killing her. Leave my mother alone. She's had enough."

Gideon was stunned. "This...this *thing* is your mother?"

Paige pulled Gideon to his feet. "Is that why ya betrayed us, Kaz, because of yer mum?"

"Shut up, both of you." Kaz sheathed his sword. He kneeled over his mother. She was unconscious and wheezing.

Gideon turned on Gwendolyn. "You said nobody would hurt us unless you ordered it. What's wrong with you? I thought you were in charge here."

"Know your place, Gideon. You will not speak to me like that." Gwendolyn held her Shocker out in front of her like a spear. The end buzzed and popped.

"Then control your pets."

"Gideon, don't be provokin' her none," Paige said.

Mrs. Muramatsu's eyes snapped open. She pushed Kaz away and snarled at him. She struggled to her feet and pointed at Gideon. "Must have Pure Earth."

Gideon grabbed Paige by the hand and pulled her behind him. "Keep that thing away from me."

Gwendolyn pointed her Shocker at Kaz's mother. Small lightning bolts writhed and flickered on the weapon's spear point end. The air around the Shocker smelled of ozone. "Mrs. Muramatsu, you must control yourself. You must fight the hunger. I know you can do it. If the others can, then so can you."

The other two Berserkers stayed by the birthing pod housing Frank. One of the monsters picked up the feeding tube Mrs. Muramatsu dropped and put it in its mouth. The monster was now using two feeding tubes.

Kaz's mother eyed Gwendolyn with contempt. She splayed her claws. She gnashed her teeth. "Need the Pure Earth boy."

"I don't think so." Gideon backed toward the lab's exit, pulling Paige with him. "If that thing comes near me or Paige—"

Kaz's mother lunged for Gideon.

Gwendolyn speared the monster in the stomach with the Shocker. The Berserker snarled and backed away. Smoke rose from its torso. "Mrs. Muramatsu, you need to fight the hunger. Don't let it control you. Soon you will have all the Pure Earth you want."

Kaz's mother swung her clawed hand at the Shocker. She snarled at Gwendolyn.

Paige squeezed Gideon's arm. "Kaz's mum is worse than a miner needin' a fix of crystal rock."

"Kaz, maybe you can reach her," Gwendolyn said. "Your mother is consumed by her hunger for Pure Earth."

"I'll do my best. I've never seen her like this, Gwendolyn-san."

"Do your best? Don't be wishy-washy Kaz. This is her last chance. If you can't control your mother, I *will* kill her. I can't let any harm come to Gideon until he accesses the artificial intelligence for me."

"What?" Gideon said. *Oh my God, is she going to feed me to that thing after I give her the AI? Is that why Gwendolyn told Kaz's mom she'll soon have all the Pure Earth she wants?*

"Mom, *please* stop." Kaz approached the Berserker cautiously. His left hand was extended out in front of him defensively. His right hand was on the hilt of his sword.

"Listen to your son, Mrs. Muramatsu."

"Mom, calm down. It's me Kaz-chan. Don't you remember me?"

The Berserker growled at Kaz. She stared at him with a look of confusion on her face. Then the monster cocked her head to one side and relaxed her body, dropping her arms by her side. She studied Kaz for a moment. "Kaz-chan?" the monster asked in a guttural voice.

"Yes, Mom, it's me. It's your Kaz-chan." Purple tears welled in Kaz's eyes.

The Berserker tried to cover her face with her clawed, misshaped hands. But as she drew her hands up to her face, she stopped and turned them over, examining them. The monster studied her hands as if they belonged to somebody else. Then the Berserker fell to her knees wailing. She tugged at her hair ripping out large fistfuls of it.

Kaz took his hand off his sword and went toward the Berserker. He knelt down beside his mother and hugged her. "I know, I know. I've come to help cure you. I will restore you like I promised. No matter what it takes we will have our honor back."

Paige closed her eyes and shook her head violently back and forth. "It's so awful, Gideon. Got to be the saddest thang I ever did see."

Gideon took hold of Paige and hugged her. "I know, but everything's going to be fine. I won't let anything happen to you."

Gwendolyn said, "You see, you see what your father has done to these poor people, Gideon? Are you going to let me help them by giving me access to the artificial intelligence or will you abandon them like your father did? Like he did to you?"

Gwendolyn's words stung Gideon. "My father came Off World to cure people of the Virus. He didn't mean for any of this to happen."

"Oh come, Gideon. Don't be so naïve. Without your father none of this would have happened."

"The only thing I know is that without him you wouldn't be here," Gideon snapped.

"Nor you, young man."

Rage boiled inside Gideon.

Gwendolyn pointed her Shocker at Kaz's mother. "Gideon, whether intentional or not, your father created the Berserkers and then refused to cure them. If that's not abandonment then please, do tell me what is. They were your father's patients. They needed his help and he refused to give it. It was cruel of him to leave these people to their fate. A fate he created. Then he compounded his cruelty by refusing to allow me to help them. I had to take matters into my own hands. I couldn't let these people suffer. I'm not cruel like him."

"My father felt the cure was worse than the disease. Killing one human to save another? Isn't that cruel? What did Frank ever do to you or the Berserkers?"

Gwendolyn sneered. "Disease? The *Virus* is a disease. The Berserker mutation is not. It is a blessing. With proper study and proper management, two things your father refused to do, the Berserker mutation can and will be the next step in human evolution. Your father was too short sighted, too cowardly to see the mutation for what it truly is."

Kaz's mother was still crying but was now hugging her son.

"A blessing? Tell that to Kaz's mom," Gideon said.

"Oh, but I have. Mrs. Muramatsu understands that the Berserker mutation has made her stronger, stopped the aging process and given her a super-charged immune system. She will never get sick. She will never die from the Virus or any other disease."

Gideon rolled his eyes. "Yeah, she looks real happy about it."

"Only because she hasn't responded fully to my treatments like the other Berserkers have. But Mrs. Muramatsu has made progress, Gideon. Six months ago she would have killed you without a second thought."

"You call this progress? It didn't look to me like Kaz's mother was having *any* second thoughts about eating me."

"That's right," Paige said. "It's like I been sayin'— she's worse than a junkie from a rock house."

Kaz led his mother back to the birthing pod holding Frank. The Berserker using her discarded feeding tube snarled at her.

Gwendolyn snapped her fingers. "Don't be greedy. Give Mrs. Murmatsu her feeding tube back."

The Berserker spit the feeding tube onto the floor with contempt. Kaz's mother picked it up and sucked greedily at it.

"That's much better, Mrs. Muramatsu." Gwendolyn set the Shocker down next to her computer station. "Gideon, the synthetic Pure Earth I make allows most Berserkers to manage the mutation effectively. They can change between their human form and their Berserker form at will."

"Like Captain Payne?" Gideon asked.

"Exactly." Gwendolyn smiled at Gideon like a proud teacher praising her star student. "But some Berserkers like Kaz's mother do not respond to synthetic Pure Earth. They need authentic Pure Earth."

"Why won't she respond? What's wrong with her?" Gideon asked.

"Everyone has a monster raging inside them, Gideon. Some people love giving themselves over to it entirely. Once they taste the power and the freedom, they never want to go back. And then there are those like Mrs. Muramatsu who can't fight the monster at all. Once it's been unleashed, the creature takes over."

Paige inched her way toward Gwendolyn's Shocker.

"Young lady, that Shocker only works for me. In your hands it would be useless."

Paige gave Gwendolyn a sheepish grin. "I was only lookin' at it."

"Oh, please," Gwendolyn said. "Your wiles may work on my son but don't waste them on me."

"What do you want from me?" Gideon asked.

"Isn't it obvious, Gideon? I need you to turn off the bio-encryption that's locked me out of the artificial intelligence. Give me access to the AI so I can clone Pure Earth—so I can cure these people." Gwendolyn pointed at the far corner of the lab. The purple force field buzzed and crackled. Behind it was a large computer console. It sat dust covered and unused. Two skeletons were draped over the control panel.

"Don't be doin' nothin', Gideon," Paige said. "She'll be killin' us after she has what she wants."

"Be quiet, you little harpy. Let my son make up his own mind."

Gideon crossed his arms over his chest. His father's warning ran through his head. *If Gwendolyn gets access to the AI, she can perfect her army of Rippers. Off World is finished.*

"I'm sorry but I can't give you the AI. I don't believe you. I don't think you want to cure anybody," Gideon said. "I think you want the AI so you can make better Rippers—so you can rule Off World."

"What's wrong with wanting to rule this planet, Gideon? Off World is in chaos. It needs order. Stay here with me. Be my son. Help me *rule* this planet. You can be a prince here. Why go back to Earth? It's a disease-ridden world where humans are on the brink of extinction. Stay here and help me create the next stage in human evolution. We can make history together. I'll even give you the young lady who seems to have taken a shine to you."

Paige recoiled. "What? I ain't no prize to be awarded to the winner of this nasty game yer playin."

"You aren't? Then you are of no use to me at all." Gwendolyn snapped her fingers and instantly two Berserkers grabbed Paige. Paige tried to pull free but it was no use.

Gideon grabbed Gwendolyn's Shocker. He pointed it at her throat. "Paige has nothing to do with this. Let her go."

"Really, Gideon?" Gwendolyn grabbed the end of the Shocker and held on to it. Nothing happened.

Gideon stared wide-eyed at the Shocker. "What the —"

Gwendolyn snatched the Shocker from Gideon. She thrust it at his face. The end crackled and popped with electricity, making Gideon's hair stand on end. "The Shocker is bio-encrypted, Gideon. Weren't you listening when I told your lady friend it will only work for me?"

Gideon cursed.

"Gideon, I'll free your lady friend after you give me access to the AI. Otherwise, my Berserkers will tear her in half and suck her bones dry right in front of you. It's a rather unpleasant thing to watch. Trust me I've seen it." Gwendolyn nodded and the Berserkers started pulling on Paige's arms.

That's the problem. I don't trust you.

Paige grimaced in pain. "Don't...do...it."

"Hey, fly boy, you better do what Gwendolyn-san says, otherwise Paige dies," Kaz said.

"Shut up, Kaz. If it weren't for you Paige wouldn't even be here."

Kaz's mother growled at Gideon.

"Kaz, you need to put that thing you call a mother on a leash," Gideon said.

Kaz bristled. He put his hand on his sword.

"What are you going to do, Kaz, buddy? Are you going to cut my head off? Do that and nobody will get access to the AI." Gideon turned toward Gwendolyn. "If you kill Paige I won't help you. I'll die first. But if you let her go I'll do what you ask. I'll give you access to the AI."

Gwendolyn put her hand on her chin. She cocked her head to one side and raised an eyebrow.

Paige's crying grew louder as the Berserkers continued to pull on her arms.

"Please let her go," Gideon said. "Please...Mom, I'll do what you want."

Gwendolyn gave Gideon a shark's smile. "Release the girl. My son will cooperate."

Paige fell to the floor sobbing. She pulled her knees to her chest and hugged herself.

Gideon tried to help Paige to her feet but she pushed him away and turned her back on him.

The hurt and sting of defeat washed over Gideon.

He survived the Virus.

He survived the Finger Lakes Quarantine.

But Off World was rolling over him like a tsunami.

Chapter 32

Gideon cautiously approached the force field protecting the AI console. Behind the force field lay two odd-shaped skeletons. Their heads were elongated and their bones were malformed. They looked like melted statues from a wax museum. Beams of purple light stabbed and probed the bodies.

The lower halves of the skeletons were splayed out on the floor. The top halves were slumped against the AI console, their skeletal arms reaching for the array of dust-covered buttons and switches. The six monitors of the multi-screen computer were black and lifeless.

Gideon turned on Gwendolyn. "That's not a force field like the one outside protecting the lab. If it were, those bodies would be nothing but ash. What is it?"

"It's a DNA scrambler," Gwendolyn said. "Your father bio-encrypted it so that it kills anyone that is not a perfect match for your DNA, Gideon. Unfortunately, your father was devious as well as clever."

Gideon thought back to when Frank used his DNA scrambler on Sara at the mining camp. Frank's words echoed in his mind. *"Nothing survives the scrambler."*

Gideon nodded toward the malformed skeletons. "Those bones don't look human. Who were those guys before the scrambler killed them?"

"They were Berserkers, Gideon. They...*volunteered* to enter the DNA scrambler and died slowly and horribly. It was their ability to regenerate that made their fate worse. They melted like candles."

Gideon couldn't take his eyes off the grisly sight in front of him. "How do I know that won't happen to me?"

Gwendolyn took hold of Gideon's chin and roughly turned his face so that he was now staring at her. "You're still Pure Earth so unless your DNA has changed since your father programmed the bio-encryption you have nothing to fear."

Gideon pointed at the skeletons near the AI console. "That's easy for you to say. You're not the one going in there. At least scan me to make sure the DNA scrambler won't melt me like a stick of butter."

"Don't play games with me, young man. Stalling will not help you."

I need to gain her trust and I need to do it fast. "Please, Mom. I can't help you rule this planet if I'm dead."

"I do see your point." Gwendolyn picked up a small hand-held device from a nearby steel table. The device looked like a miniature telescope. She then snapped her fingers and pointed at Paige. Two Berserkers picked her up off the floor and dragged her toward the DNA scrambler.

"Git yer hands offa me," Paige said.

Gideon squeezed his hands into tight fists, digging his nails painfully into his palms. "What are you doing to her? There's no reason to put Paige in the scrambler. I said I'll do what you ask."

"Gideon, honey, I'm not putting your girlfriend in the DNA scrambler unless you force me to. But I do need her help ensuring you don't change your mind and decide to stay inside the protection of the scrambler. After all, once you enter you will be inaccessible to me. The girl is my guarantee you will be properly incentivized."

"What does that mean?" Gideon asked.

"It means I will give you two minutes to turn off the DNA scrambler. Any longer than that, and I'll send the girl in after you. So if you change your mind and decide not to do as you're told, you can watch this pretty thing melt right before your Pure Earth eyes. Do you understand?"

Gideon's blood boiled. "Yes, perfectly."

Paige's eyes went wide with fear. "Gideon, I'm sorry—"

"You've got nothing to be sorry for, Paige."

Gwendolyn said, "Right, let's make sure you can survive the DNA scrambler, Gideon, shall we?" Gwendolyn ran the hand-held scanner over Gideon's body, stopping at the deep-knotted scars on his arms. The gashes the Ripper in the pit gave him were almost completely healed, as were the bruised knuckles he suffered from punching the wormhole jumper's flight console.

Gwendolyn grabbed Gideon's arms and examined them closely. "What happened to your arms? It looks like old scars interlaced with some relatively fresh wounds."

Gideon winced. He was amazed at how strong Gwendolyn was. "You're right about the scars. I got those helping my…never mind. The cuts are courtesy of your Rippers."

"I see. Well they shouldn't impact the scanning results," Gwendolyn said. "Stay still, Gideon."

Gideon stood rigid while Gwendolyn finished using the hand-held scanner. It hummed as she ran it over his body. Gwendolyn then inserted the scanner into a nearby DNA reader.

"Computer," Gwendolyn said, "scan current readings for compatibility with the Gideon Protocol."

"Gideon Protocol rejected," the computer said in a thin, metallic voice.

"What?" Gideon backed away from the DNA scrambler. "I'm not going in there."

Gwendolyn removed the hand-held scanner from the DNA reader and stomped toward Gideon. "If you aren't who you say you are, if you are one of those vile Shape Shifters, then you are of no use to me. I'll try this once more and that's it. If there's no match I'll have you join your hunter friend and feed you to my Berserkers."

Gideon's knees went weak. "No, don't do that. Check your scanner. Maybe it isn't working properly."

Gwendolyn examined the small hand-held scanner. "Doubtful, but let's try it on your girlfriend to make sure. She can be our control group."

Paige recoiled. "No, I don't want ya toouchin' me with that thang."

"Paige, it won't hurt," Gideon said.

"I ain't carin' how it feels." Paige backed away from Gwendolyn.

"I cannot stand these endless delays." Gwendolyn snapped her fingers and pointed at Paige. The two Berserkers tightened their grip on her. Paige struggled to free herself but it was no use.

"Young lady," Gwendolyn said in a syrupy voice, "it doesn't matter to me if you're whole or in pieces. The DNA scanner will work either way. But my son will be most unhappy if my Berserkers tear you in half."

"Paige, please," Gideon said.

Tears welled in Paige's eyes. Purple streaks ran down her cheeks.

"So squeamish," Gwendolyn said. "Honestly, Gideon, I really don't know what you see in her. You could do so much better."

"She's scared is all. Can you blame her?"

"Well, beauty is in the eye of the beholder." Gwendolyn ran the scanner over Paige and then inserted the device into the DNA reader. She stood over the reader for several minutes. Then her head jerked back in surprise. "These readings can't be right."

"See, I told you," Gideon said. "The scanner is broken."

Gwendolyn re-examined the scanner, adjusted the settings and scanned Paige again. She waited for the DNA reader to process the results then gave Paige a cruel smile. "My dear girl, what kind of creature are *you*?"

"I ain't nobody," Paige said.

"Oh, I disagree. You're barely human. I don't know what you are just yet but if I'm right you're very special—perhaps the first of your kind."

"What are you talking about?" Gideon asked. "She's as human as me or you."

"Your girlfriend never told you her secret? How delicious. A woman does indeed need a bit of mystery to her."

Gideon studied Paige. Her long red hair hung over her shoulders. Her fair-skinned, freckled face was smeared with purple streaks. Gideon knew she had been hiding something from him. Frank felt it too. She looked human but on Off World that meant very little. What was she? Was she a Berserker?

"Paige?" Gideon asked.

Paige refused to meet Gideon's gaze. "This ain't happenin'. This just ain't happenin'."

Then Paige pulled free from the Berserkers holding her and vaulted over a steel table. She ran for the doors and was about to escape into the corridor leading to the surface when a Berserker tackled her. The monster lifted her off the ground by her hair. It snuffed at her. The Berserker opened its mouth vertically and horizontally exposing its long teeth. "She smells good, just a little taste."

"No," Gwendolyn snapped. "Do not eat her unless I order it. Hold her there. Don't let her leave. If she escapes out that door I will punish you."

The Berserker hung its head. It cowered like a dog.

Gideon stood frozen with shock. *Who or what was Paige? What did Gwendolyn mean Paige was barely human?*

"I've adjusted the settings on the DNA scanner for maximum sensitivity so let's try this again, Gideon." Gwendolyn approached Gideon and began scanning him.

Gideon took a deep breath and squeezed his Chain of Remembrance.

Gwendolyn ripped the necklace off Gideon's neck.

"Hey, give it back."

"What is this?"

"It's nothing, just a necklace."

Gwendolyn cocked her head to one side. "Please don't lie to me. It doesn't suit you at all, Gideon."

Gwendolyn scanned the pendant. "A Pure Earth pendant? How nice. This is what must have caused the anomaly in your DNA reading."

"Give it back." Gideon reached for the chain but Gwendolyn was too fast.

"No, I think I'll keep this."

"But it's all I have left of—"

"You said it was just a necklace," Gwendolyn countered.

"There's not enough Pure Earth in there to do you any good."

"I'll be the judge of that, Gideon. Every little bit helps. Now get in there and shut down the DNA scrambler so I can gain access to the AI."

"Don't be doin' it, Gideon. She'll be killin' us anyway," Paige said.

"Young lady, with a DNA reading like yours there are things I can do to you that are far worse than death. Have no illusions. If my son doesn't do as he's told, death will be the least of your concerns."

"Okay, okay, I'm going." Gideon stepped toward the DNA scrambler and swallowed. The purple light buzzed and hummed. He tried not to look at the disfigured skeletons but couldn't help himself. A chill ran down his back. He shook his head in disgust.

"I'm waiting, Gideon," Gwendolyn said.

Gideon closed his eyes. He grimaced and slowly put his hand into the DNA scrambler. It felt like being stuck by a thousand small pinpricks. Gideon opened his eyes and was relieved to find that his hand was still whole and attached to his body. He breathed a sigh of relief.

"Oh get on with it." Gwendolyn snapped her fingers and a Berserker shoved Gideon into the DNA scrambler. Gideon held onto the Berserker and dragged it into the scrambler with him. The DNA scrambler washed over Gideon as he hit the floor. It felt like thousands of ants crawling over his body.

The Berserker started melting like an old-fashioned wax candle. The skin on its purple head, shoulders, and arms sagged like bloody rags. Muscle, tendons and ligaments melted away exposing bone. The Berserker clawed at its face as the monster's eyes oozed out of their sockets. It shrieked in pain. Its skin and muscles tried to grow back but the monster's ability to regenerate was no match for the DNA scrambler.

The Berserker was being melted into a gelatinous blob of bone and meat faster than it could regenerate. The monster staggered toward Gwendolyn. After three steps, it fell with a sickening wet thud. Then the Berserker twitched and died. The purple light of the DNA scrambler continued erasing what was left of it.

Gideon scrambled away from the steaming mass of meat and bone. He checked his own body, examining his hands and arms to make sure he wasn't melting. His breathing was fast and labored. He had trouble catching his breath. Sweat poured down his face and into his eyes, stinging them.

Gwendolyn shook her head and clucked her tongue in disappointment. "Sad, I rather liked that one. He was very loyal and had just started to respond to my treatments. Oh well, your hunter friend will be happy having one less mouth to feed."

"Are ya okay, Gideon?" Paige asked.

"No, I'm completely freaked out!"

"Oh, do grow up," Gwendolyn said. "You're alive and you're uninjured. Remember, I'm giving you two minutes to access the Gideon Protocol, turn off the DNA scrambler and give me access to the AI or I send your girlfriend in after you. The clock is ticking, Gideon, dear, so don't dilly dally."

Gideon struggled to his feet. He tried to breathe through his mouth to avoid the awful smell from the dead Berserker. He sidestepped the monster's body and made his way to the AI console.

The AI console was more advanced than any computer system Gideon had ever seen. There were six large computer screens and a dust-covered control panel with an endless array of keys and colored buttons. Gideon shoved the skeletons away from the control panel. The bones clattered to the floor. He leaned over the AI console and blew on it. Dust swirled around him. Gideon studied the console, trying to figure out what to do first.

"Two minutes, Gideon, starting now," Gwendolyn said.

"Yeah, yeah, why don't you come on in here and help me?"

"Behave yourself, young man."

The DNA scrambler continued probing and pinching Gideon. He took a deep breath and started pressing keys and colored buttons. Nothing happened.

"Ninety seconds, Gideon."

"I've never seen anything like this before. I'm not a computer programmer. I need more time," Gideon ran his hand along the edge of the monitors looking for a power switch. The six screens were dark and lifeless. He pressed more buttons on the control panel.

"Sixty seconds, Gideon, dear. That's all the time your girlfriend has left to live. Hurry up, honey."

Gideon punched the computer console. "I don't know what to do. I need more time, please."

"Time is a luxury you don't have, dear."

"Gideon, I know ya can do it. I trust ya," Paige said. "Try talkin' to it. Yer dad configured it special fer ya to use and nobody else."

"Thirty seconds." Gwendolyn snapped her fingers at the Berserker. The monster lifted Paige off the floor by her neck.

"Gideon, try talkin' to it." Paige pleaded. She punched and kicked at the Berserker but the monster held fast.

Gideon closed his eyes and took a deep breath. "Computer, access Gideon Protocol."

The six screens flashed to life. A green laser shot from the center screen and washed over Gideon's face. Then a thin, metallic voice spoke to him. "Access granted, welcome, Gideon."

"Time's up, Gideon," Gwendolyn said.

The Berserker threw Paige at the DNA scrambler. She flew over the steel tables, hit the ceiling and crashed into a row of tubular lights. Glass rained onto the floor of the lab.

Chapter 33

Gideon grabbed the computer console with both hands and screamed at it. "Initiate emergency shutdown of the DNA scrambler now!"

"Negative," the computer said. "No emergency shutdown procedure was programmed. Shutdown procedure will be complete in three minutes."

Paige bounced off the ceiling and slammed onto a steel table, sending lab equipment crashing to the floor. She jumped to her feet and picked up a long thin surgical blade. She slashed the Berserker several times across the chest. She went for its throat but the monster blocked her attack with its forearm. Purple blood drizzled down the Berserker's chest and arm. The monster grabbed Paige and slammed her against a steel table, sending jars filled with strange body parts crashing to the floor. Disembodied wings, hands, and bat-like heads scattered to the floor like the parts of a jigsaw puzzle.

"Stop using that girl like a wrecking ball. You're destroying my lab," Gwendolyn said. "Put her in the DNA scrambler with my son now or I'll put you in there."

"No, please don't put her in here. The DNA scrambler is shutting down. I did it," Gideon said.

"It doesn't look like it to me, Gideon. I still see that awful purple light."

The Berserker lifted Paige off the table by her neck. It held her several feet off the ground.

Paige's face turned red as the Berserker tightened its grip on her neck. She stabbed at the monster's arm over and over with the surgical blade. Purple blood spattered onto her face and the floor of the lab. But the wounds healed as fast as Paige made them.

The Berserker knocked the blade from Paige's hand and pulled her close to its face. It opened its mouth horizontally and vertically—rows of sharp teeth snapped at Paige. The monster snarled then drew his arm back and prepared to throw her into the DNA scrambler.

"No, don't do it. Put her down!" Gideon shouted.

The purple light from the scrambler buzzed and crackled. It pinched and probed every part of Gideon. "Computer, how long before DNA scrambler shut down?"

"T-minus two minutes," the computer said.

Gideon scanned the floor looking for a weapon. He reached down and grabbed hold of one of the long fangs from the dead Berserker. The fang came out of the monster's skull with a loud snap. Armed with the Berserker fang, he ran for Paige. Gideon drew his arm back and tried stabbing the Berserker in the chest. The monster swatted Gideon back into the DNA scrambler. Gideon grunted as he slammed into the AI console. He sank to floor.

"Noble effort, Gideon but you're too late," Gwendolyn said.

Paige's face went from red to purple. Her eyes rolled back into her head. Her body shook violently.

Gwendolyn turned on the Berserker choking Paige. "Don't break her neck. Throw her into the scrambler like I ordered. "

Gideon struggled to his feet. He picked up the Berserker fang and pointed it at Gwendolyn. "If you put Paige in the DNA scrambler, I won't access the AI or—"

Then Paige blurred like an old-fashioned hologram.

In her place, a red bird appeared. It was the size of a hawk, had four wings, a curved beak and sharp talons. The red bird hovered above the Berserker then attacked. Claws raked over the monster's face. The bird used its beak to tear out one of the Berserker's eyes.

The monster shrieked and fell to the floor. It covered its face with its clawed hand. Purple blood oozed between its fingers.

"Get up, you sniveling idiot, and get after that Shape Shifting girl," Gwendolyn shouted. "You'll grow a new eye soon enough."

Gideon dropped the Berserker fang. His mouth hung open. *Paige is a Shifter?*

The red bird Paige shifted into screeched, spread its four wings and dove at Gwendolyn. Gwendolyn swung her Shocker at the bird but missed. The bird circled the lab once then flew toward the glass double doors. The one-eyed Berserker jumped atop a steel table then launched itself at the red bird. Paige easily veered away from the monster, sending it crashing headfirst into the glass doors. Glass exploded onto the floor of the lab. Then Paige flew out the broken door of the lab and up the corridor.

Why didn't Paige tell me? She could have shifted and saved herself from Kaz and Gwendolyn anytime she wanted.

Betrayal gnawed at Gideon. He could have taken off in his jumper and flown home. Instead he stayed to save Paige and she abandoned him.

"I knew she was unique but half-human and half-shifter? How wonderful," Gwendolyn said. "Fear and rage must have triggered the transformation just like it does in a Berserker." She turned to her Berserkers and snapped her fingers. "I must have her. Bring her back to me *alive*. Go, now!"

All of the Berserkers except Kaz's mother loped after Paige. Kaz stood by his mother's side while she continued feeding from Frank. "She's a filthy Yokai half-breed? I should have taken her head when I had the chance."

Is that why Paige didn't tell me? She thought I was like Kaz?

Then the DNA scrambler shut down. The purple light stopped probing and pinching Gideon.

Gwendolyn beamed. "Ah, the DNA scrambler is down. Well done, Gideon. Computer, open cloning program one."

"Acknowledged, cloning program one activated," the computer said.

Gwendolyn clapped her hands like a child on Christmas morning.

"I'm out of here," Gideon said. "It's time for me to leave this rock and head for home."

"You're not going anywhere." Gwendolyn snapped her fingers and pointed at Gideon.

Kaz's mother snagged him by the collar of his flight suit. Gideon tried to free himself but the Berserker was too strong.

"I gave you the AI. What more do you want from me?"

"Oh, Gideon, my dear boy." Gwendolyn's voice was tinged with disappointment. "Such a smart boy when you take the time to think things through. You only have about six hours left before you turn into an Off Worlder. So in order to make the best use of that time, I'm going to take as much Pure Earth from you as I can. Then I can clone it using the AI system you kindly accessed for me."

"What?" Gideon's eyes went wide with fear.

"Don't be afraid, honey. I won't hollow you out. When you turn into an Off Worlder I'll stop draining you. Then you can help me bring order to this planet."

"Are you out of your—"

"Gwendolyn-san, what about my mother? Did you forget about our contract?"

Gideon turned. It was Kaz.

"I've done all that you asked, Gwendolyn-san. I spied on Doctor Wells for you and I brought you his Pure Earth son. I even brought you that half-human, half-yokai girl."

"She is indeed an added bonus, Kaz. But don't insult my intelligence by taking credit for something you knew nothing about. I know full well you would have taken that girl's head and displayed it like a trophy had you known she was a Shifter."

Kaz squeezed the leather hilt of his sword so hard it made a squeaking noise. "Fair enough, Gwendolyn-san. But it's time to cure my mother like you promised. It's time to honor our contract."

Gwendolyn gave Kaz a thin smile. "Yes, of course." She pointed at Gideon and snapped her fingers. "Mrs. Muramatsu, place my son on the exam table."

Gideon was dragged to an examination table and slammed onto it like a piece of meat. He grunted as the air was driven from his body. Gideon tried to sit up but the Berserker sunk her claws into Gideon's chest and shoved him back onto the table.

"Easy with my son, Mrs. Muramatsu," Gwendolyn said.

Kaz fastened straps around Gideon's wrists, ankles, and mid-section. Gideon had to lift his head off the table in order to see what was happening,

Gideon's examination table slowly raised itself so that it was now vertical. Although he couldn't move, he could see everything going on around him. Kaz's mother stood anxiously next to him with a feeding tube in her hand. Gideon struggled against the straps but it was pointless.

Kaz's mother looked at Gideon with a hungry smile. "Pure Earth."

Tears welled in Gideon's eyes. "Get away from me."

Gwendolyn wheeled a tray of surgical tools next to Gideon. The tray had scissors, a laser scalpel, and a long, very sharp looking needle that reminded Gideon of a Berserker claw. "Gideon, in order to cure Mrs. Muramatsu I need Pure Earth from a young person like yourself. Pure Earth from the young is sweeter and tastier—a real delicacy. It will cure her whereas your hunter friend, Frank, due to his age can only satiate Mrs. Muramatsu's hunger. So, honey, you should be proud that only you can cure Kaz's mother."

Gideon fought against the restraints. "Proud? Are you crazy? I'm a prisoner. Let me go."

"Gwendolyn-san, stop. Don't feed my mother Gideon's Pure Earth," Kaz said. "I need to tell you something first."

"What is it, Kaz?"

"Bruce is dead."

Gwendolyn gave him an empty stare. "Bruce who? So what?"

"He was one of your scouts on the island," Kaz said. "He died right after he tried to feed from Gideon."

"You let a Berserker feed from my son? Kaz, I told you to protect him and bring him here in one piece."

"I did my job," Kaz shot back. "He's here and he's in one piece. What you need to focus on is why Bruce died after he fed from Gideon."

"This is nonsense. I tested Gideon's DNA and it's fine. You saw him go through the DNA scrambler, didn't you, Kaz?"

"Of course I did. It's just—"

"The mushrooms killed him," Gideon said. "I pushed him into a winged mushroom. It trapped him, squeezed him and poisoned him just like Paige said."

"I know these mushrooms," Gwendolyn said. "They're lethal."

"But Gwendolyn-san—"

"Enough of this, Kaz. Leave the science to the scientist. Do you want your mother cured or not?"

"Well, yes, but—"

"Then be quiet and let me work. With every minute that passes, my son gets closer to becoming an Off Worlder and I will lose his Pure Earth." Gwendolyn removed a small panel from the back of the examination table. Then she cut a hole into the back of Gideon's flight suit. The rush of cold air against Gideon's lower back made him a shiver.

"Gideon, I need you to stay still," Gwendolyn said. "This is going to hurt badly enough as it is. Don't make it worse by squirming. The needle needs to be deep enough inside you so it can reach your bone marrow. While every part of you is Pure Earth, it's the bone marrow that really is best for Mrs. Muramatsu. Now take a deep breath, there's going be a pinch." Gwendolyn took a long needle and inserted it into the small of Gideon's back.

Gideon sucked in a quick breath. The taste of salt from his own tears coated his lips and dripped into his mouth.

"Good boy, Gideon, you handled that well. The needle was to prep your body for phase two of the procedure. I'm afraid this next part really hurts," Gwendolyn said. "You're going to hear a drilling sound. Don't be alarmed. It's only the extraction machine drilling a hole into your bones so I can insert the feeding tube for Mrs. Muramatsu. The damage to your body isn't permanent. You'll heal in due course."

A high-pitched drill pierced the air behind Gideon. It reminded him of the old fashioned electric buzz saw his grandfather used to use. Gideon balled his hands into tight fists. "Don't do this, please."

"Be quiet, Gideon. Mrs. Muramatsu, are you ready to feed? I'm about to begin the Pure Earth extraction."

"Yes, please," Kaz's mother said in a guttural voice. She drooled as she spoke, saliva dripping from her long fangs.

Gideon scanned the lab for Paige. His gaze fell to his Chain of Remembrance lying on Gwendolyn's computer station. The blue crystal sparkled. Gideon's mind flooded with images of his mother and his life on Earth. Sadness and guilt swamped him. *She always told me life was precious. That I should cherish every day. I was a moron not to listen. She was right. I wish I would have hugged her more, told her I loved her more often. Now I'm Berserker meat.*

Gideon bucked against the restraints. "Let me out of here!"

"Gideon, honey, take deep breaths and try to relax. I'm sorry there's no anesthesia," Gwendolyn said. "When the re-supply ships stopped coming so did the anesthesia and I simply can't waste resources making more of it."

Kaz waved a wooden tongue depressor in front of Gideon.

"What am I supposed to do with that, beat you with it?" Gideon asked.

"Bite down on it. It will help with the pain."

"Go to hell. I don't want anything from you."

Kaz shrugged his shoulders. "Suit yourself."

Then pain exploded in Gideon's back as Gwendolyn inserted the drill. It rocked Gideon to his core.

Gideon opened his mouth to scream but no sound came out.

His arms and legs stiffened.

His bones rattled from the vibration of the drill inside his body.

A burning smell assaulted him.

Tears streamed down his cheeks. Colored spots and stars floated in front of his face. Then the drilling stopped. The drill was removed from Gideon's back. Then a snake-like tube wormed its way inside him.

"The feeding tube is in place, Mrs. Muramatsu. You may begin."

Gideon felt a sucking sensation in his lower back. There was a slurping noise, like someone struggling to drink the last of a thick milkshake.

"Easy, Mrs. Muramatsu. Take it slowly, please," Gwendolyn said.

Kaz's mother greedily drank from the tube connected to Gideon's back.

Gideon swallowed the bile in the back of his throat. He felt like his arms and legs were filled with sand. He struggled to lift his head. Tears blurred his vision.

Then Kaz screamed. "Mom, get up, get up."

The sucking sensation and the pain in Gideon's back stopped. It was replaced by a dull ache. The colored spots and floating stars faded away.

Gideon turned toward Kaz. The older boy was holding his mother's head in his lap. She was slumped on the floor. Her breathing was labored and raspy.

"Mom, are you okay? It's your Kaz-chan."

Kaz's mother raised her purple arm and pointed a shaky clawed hand at Gwendolyn. Then the arm dropped to the floor with a dull thud.

"No!" Kaz turned on Gwendolyn. "You killed her."

Gwendolyn hurried over to Kaz's mother and took her pulse. She then used a hand-held scanner and waved it over her body. Gwendolyn shook her head. "She's not dead but she's very weak, Kaz. I told you the Berserker mutation was too much for her to handle. I tried to help her. It's not my fault she didn't respond to my treatments. Blame the man that turned her into a Berserker, not me."

Gideon scanned the lab. He searched for Paige. *Please come back. I need you.*

Kaz said, "I told you what happened to Bruce. You should have tested Gideon's Pure Earth before you gave it to my mother."

Gwendolyn walked over to Gideon and removed the feeding tube from his back. Gideon grunted as it snaked out of his body. "There, there, Gideon. We'll take a little break until I can sort out what happened to poor Mrs. Muramatsu. Then I'll need to take just a little more of your Pure Earth for cloning purposes."

Gideon shook his head. "No more, please stop."

"You just rest for a bit." Gwendolyn took the feeding tube and walked toward an examination table that had a flat, thin panel resting a few feet above it. The panel was connected to a large diagnostic computer.

It was a DNA decoder. Gideon had seen them many times before. His mother's lab had several of them. She used them to test Gideon's DNA and the anti-virus serum.

"What are you doing?" Kaz demanded. "What about my mother?"

"I'm trying to find out what happened to her." Gwendolyn placed the feeding tube on the table and sliced it open. The inside of the tube was coated with Gideon's bone marrow.

Gideon grimaced as he watched Gwendolyn examining his pinkish, spongy marrow.

Gwendolyn lowered the flat panel just a few inches over the feeding tube. She stepped back and turned on the machine. A soft white light emanated from the flat panel. It bathed the feeding tube in light as Gideon's bone marrow was scanned and the results fed into the DNA decoder. Gwendolyn stood in front of the decoder. She stared into a monitor for several minutes.

"Well? What happened?" Kaz's hand was on his sword.

Gwendolyn held up a hand signaling for quiet. She leaned in close to the monitor, frozen in place as she studied the results. Then her head jerked back in surprise. Her face contorted with rage. "What's this? You have a mutated CCR5 delta 32 gene? Gideon, why didn't you tell me you had a mutated gene?"

Gideon shrugged his shoulders against the restraints. "How was I supposed to know that? My mother said I helped her create the cure for the Virus. She said she couldn't have done it without me. That's all I know."

"Gideon, you didn't *help* her create the cure," Gwendolyn roared. "You *are* the cure."

Gideon was stunned. "What?"

"Why is my mother dying?" Kaz asked.

"Don't you see, Kaz?" Gwendolyn said. "Without Gideon there's no cure for the Virus. His DNA is the building block for the cure."

"So you poisoned my mother by feeding her Gideon's Pure Earth," Kaz said.

Gwendolyn's eyes hardened. "Gideon, in what section of the Finger Lakes Quarantine were you housed?"

"Delta 32."

"So you knew. How could you not?"

"I'm just a kid, not a scientist. You should have listened to Kaz and tested my Pure Earth."

"I have a better idea. Why not just hollow you out and be done with you?" Gwendolyn picked up a fresh feeding tube and connected it to a tall, thin black box. It looked like a coffin. She wheeled the box toward Gideon. "This extraction machine will hollow you out in less than two minutes. When it's finished, you'll look like a dried prune."

Gwendolyn turned on the machine. It buzzed and whirred.

"No, don't. I'm sorry." Gideon thought of what Larry from the mining camp looked like after Sara hollowed him out and what Captain Payne's crewman looked like. Both bodies were wrinkled and riddled with indentations making them look like raisins.

"Wait. My mother's trying to tell me something. Turn off that damn machine so I can hear her," Kaz said.

Gwendolyn snapped off the extraction machine.

Gideon glanced at Kaz's mother. Her eyes were barely open. Her body quaked. She was bleary-eyed. She frowned at Kaz.

She pointed at Gwendolyn. "You let her dishonor me and yourself, Kaz-chan. You betrayed your friends and dishonored our family."

Kaz bowed his head. He nodded agreement as his mother spoke. Purple tears streamed down his cheeks.

Kaz's mother reached for his sword. She tried to take it from him but lacked the strength. "You are no longer worthy to carry this sword. I may not look human but it is *you* who are the monster."

Kaz used the back of his hand to wipe away his tears. "What would you have me do? What is your final wish?"

"Kill...her." Kaz's mother closed her eyes as her final breath left her body. She stared wide-eyed at Kaz. Then her body quaked. Her bones snapped and contorted back into their human form. Her skin changed from purple to a light olive color.

Kaz closed his mother's eyes and kissed her on the forehead. His face was pinched with pain. His eyes welled with purple tears. He slowly rose and unsheathed his sword. The sound of the steel blade scraping against its leather scabbard rang out, echoing throughout the lab. He pointed the sword at Gwendolyn. "You have forced me to dishonor myself and my family. It's time for you to die."

"Calm down, Kaz." Gwendolyn turned on the extraction machine. "If your mother were stronger, we wouldn't have been in this situation in the first place."

Gideon stiffened at the sound of the extraction machine. He struggled against the restraints. "No, please don't hollow me out."

Kaz scowled. "Now you blame my mother for your failures?"

"It's not my fault," Gwendolyn said. "You want to punish someone, punish Gideon. He should have told me about his gene mutation."

Kaz raised his sword above his head and brought it down onto the extraction machine, cutting it in half. The machine sparked, then its two halves clunked to the floor. "Enough of your lies, kono ama!"

Gideon slumped against his restraints. *Thank God.*

"Kaz, you need to calm down," Gwendolyn said. "Calling me vile names won't accomplish anything."

"Calm down?" Kaz said in a mocking tone. "If I were you I would choose my next words more carefully. They will be your last."

Gwendolyn scanned the lab for Berserkers but found none to help her. They were out looking for Paige. "Damn that girl."

"Kaz, I'm sorry about your mom. Help me, please," Gideon said.

Kaz shot Gideon a hard stare. He raised his sword above Gideon's head.

Gideon shouted, "No!"

CHAPTER 34

K az's sword sliced through Gideon's restraints. With the restraints cut in half, there was nothing holding Gideon onto the vertically inclined examination table. He slid to the floor like he was poured out of a bottle.

Gideon tried to stand but searing pain bit into his back and clawed at his legs, forcing him back down to the floor. He grit his teeth and used his arms to pull himself across the floor of the lab and toward the AI console. His back muscles twisted like there were snakes inside his body biting him. Sweat poured down his face. His arms shook.

The AI console was at the other end of the lab, about twenty yards away. The skeletal remains of the dead Berserkers stared at Gideon with their empty eye sockets. Their skulls gave him a mocking smile, but Gideon needed the protection of the DNA scrambler. If he could reactivate the scrambler he would be safe from Gwendolyn and her monsters.

Gideon was drenched in sweat. He struggled to catch his breath as he dragged himself toward the AI console. Shards of glass from the broken ceiling lights cut into his arms. But he pressed on until he finally made it to the AI console. He pushed the Berserker skeletons out of the way. Their skulls rolled across the floor.

Then the sound of breaking glass focused Gideon's attention to the front of the lab. Gwendolyn pushed a steel table between herself and Kaz as she tried to make her way to the broken doors of the lab.

Kaz vaulted atop the table. He kicked the equipment onto the floor. Then he jumped in front of the doors, blocking Gwendolyn's path. He pointed his sword at her chest.

"Kaz, calm down. I didn't make you do anything you didn't want to do. Don't blame me for your mother's death." Gwendolyn held her Shocker out in front of her. The end buzzed and crackled.

Kaz cornered Gwendolyn near a nanite farm at the front of the lab. He sliced her Shocker in half and pointed his sword at her throat.

Gideon tried to stand but his legs gave out and he slumped back down to the floor. The impact jarred him, sending waves of pain through his back. Then a terrible shriek pierced the lab.

It was Gwendolyn. She was changing. The woman that looked exactly like his mother screamed as her head elongated. Her skin turned purple. Her jaw unhinged. It snapped both vertically and horizontally. Long teeth hung down from her mouth. Her hands sprouted claws.

Gwendolyn was a Berserker.

Fear squeezed Gideon's throat like a cold fist.

With her transformation complete, she flexed her hands and examined her claws. She snapped her jaws exposing rows of sharp teeth. She growled at Kaz. "I'm going to tear you apart limb from limb and eat your bones."

For the first time, Gideon saw fear in Kaz's eyes. The older boy stood frozen with his sword raised above his head. Kaz took a deep breath, his eyes narrowed. "Try it," he said, "and I'll cut you in half."

Gwendolyn let out a roar that echoed throughout the lab. She lunged for Kaz who sidestepped the attack, barely getting out of the way in time.

Gwendolyn lunged for Kaz again but this time he was ready. He spun out of the way and brought his sword down in a slashing move across Gwendolyn's back, leaving a deep gash. She shrieked with a mixture of pain and anger. Purple blood coated Kaz's sword. But the wound quickly healed itself.

Gideon leaned heavily against the AI console for support. His head swam as he tried to focus on the control panel in front of him. "Computer, confirm user authentication."

"User authentication verified, welcome back, Gideon," said the AI.

"Computer, give control of all systems to me alone. Restrict access to my voice command only and nobody else."

"Acknowledged," said the AI. "All systems are now under your voice command."

"Computer, deactivate outside force field."

"Acknowledged," said the AI. "Outside force field deactivated. Are you aware intruders are now able to enter the lab facility?"

"Yes, I'm counting on it," Gideon said.

"Would you like me to shut down the intruder alert system?" asked the AI.

Gideon eyed the battle at the front of the lab. Kaz was exhausted. He was on his back and struggling to catch his breath. Blood ran down his face from a deep gash that ran across his cheek. Another deep gash ran across his right arm and shoulder. He could barely hold his sword.

Kaz doesn't deserve it but he needs help with Gwendolyn.

"Computer, have intruders entered the lab?" Gideon asked.

"Affirmative, they are quickly approaching this area," said the AI. "I have released Winged Rippers to intercept the intruders."

"Computer, deactivate the Winged Rippers. Call them back," Gideon said.

"Negative, the Winged Rippers cannot be recalled."

"Let me see what's happening. On screen," Gideon said.

Gideon counted ten saber-toothed cats. Paige was with them. Her red hair was tied in a tight ponytail. She had a bow with her.

Paige didn't abandon me. She went for help.

Then a squad of Winged Rippers flew up the corridor to meet Paige and the cats. Gideon counted twenty of the monsters.

Paige and the cats should be able to handle those Rippers but just in case—

"Computer, shut down all birthing pods except the one here in med-lab housing the human. Do not release any more Rippers."

"Affirmative, birthing pods shut down," the AI said.

"Computer," Gideon said, "prepare to announce intruder alert on my command."

Gwendolyn was laughing at Kaz—toying with him. "I have ten times your strength and quickness. I heal instantly and will never tire. You don't stand a chance against me, boy." She raised her clawed hand above her head preparing to give Kaz a killing blow.

"Now," Gideon said. "Announce intruder alert."

An alarm blared, lights flashed. It reminded Gideon of the fire drills back at Quarantine. "Intruder alert, intruder alert," announced the AI.

Gideon cringed. It was deafening.

Gwendolyn froze, her hand still raised above her head. "Impossible, no one can breach the force field." She eyed Gideon standing in front of the AI console and snarled. "What did you do?"

Then Kaz sat up and stabbed Gwendolyn in the stomach, jamming his sword so deep Gideon could see the end of it sticking out of her back. The blade was coated in purple blood.

Gwendolyn shrieked in pain. She backhanded Kaz sending him flying across the lab. Then she dropped to one knee and locked eyes with Gideon. She never left his gaze as she placed her clawed hands over the hilt of Kaz's sword and pulled the sword out of her stomach.

Gwendolyn dropped the sword on the floor with contempt and staggered to her feet.

Gideon watched in horror as the hole in Gwendolyn's stomach closed.

Gwendolyn splayed her claws and roared. She picked up a steel table blocking her path and flung it across the lab. It hit the wall above Gideon's head with a clang. She flashed her teeth and snapped her jaws. "I'm going to crack open your skull and dance in your blood, boy."

Gwendolyn stomped across the lab toward Gideon. She smashed everything in her way.

Fear strangled Gideon.

His vision blurred.

His breathes became short and choppy.

His body shook.

Sweat poured off him.

"Computer," Gideon said, in a strange guttural voice he didn't recognize. "Re-engage Gideon Protocol."

"Negative," said the AI. "User authentication required."

A wave of pain clawed at Gideon, doubling him over. Gideon growled at the AI console. "Negative? Computer, it's Gideon Wells."

"Negative, voice authentication not recognized."

Gideon's bones popped.

His ligaments and tendons stretched.

What's happening to me?

Gideon caught sight of his reflection in the multi-screened AI console. He nearly fainted.

His head was starting to elongate.

His jaw popped and snapped as it unhinged itself.

Gideon screamed in pain.

He held his hands out in front of him. They were purple. Long claws for feeding on humans cracked through his fingertips.

No please, not this.

Gideon gazed at himself in the computer screen. There was no denying it. He was a Berserker.

A combination of power, fear, and rage coursed through his body. The smell of coppery blood assaulted him. His body tingled with danger. Gideon ducked as Gwendolyn's claws sliced through the computer screens.

Gideon opened his jaws horizontally and vertically. He clamped his teeth into Gwendolyn's arm, biting down to the bone. Hot blood coated his tongue, fueling his Berserker rage. Gideon snapped his head back, taking a large chunk of meat from Gwendolyn's forearm. He spit it on the floor of the lab.

Gwendolyn shrieked in pain. She grabbed her arm, covering the exposed bone.

Gideon sank his claws into her throat, chest, and stomach. Gwendolyn's blood rained down on him. The more Gideon hurt her, the stronger and angrier he felt. A strange euphoria washed over him.

Gideon stabbed and clawed Gwendolyn over and over. Deep gashes opened across her body. But Gwendolyn's wounds healed as fast as Gideon made them. Even the exposed bone in her arm now had a thin covering of muscle and purple skin on it.

Gwendolyn laughed. "You stupid little boy, there are only two ways to kill a Berserker. Either take its head or force it to change back to its human form— then you can kill it any number of ways. Since you're new to this game, let me show you what I mean."

Gwendolyn picked Gideon up and slammed him onto the floor of the lab.

She turned him onto his stomach and placed one arm around his neck and the other behind his head. Then she squeezed, making it impossible for Gideon to breath. "First, I'll choke you until you start to pass out. As you approach unconsciousness, your fear and rage will be extinguished. Without those, you will revert back to the weak, stupid little boy that you are. But don't worry; I won't let you pass out. I don't want to kill you in your sleep. I want you awake so you can feel me slowly crack open your skull like a pistachio shell."

Gideon clawed at Gwendolyn's arms.

He snapped his jaws at her.

But it was no use. Gwendolyn was squeezing the air out of him.

Gideon's arms grew weak. His eyes became bleary and unfocused. Darkness closed in on him. His body quaked. His bones started popping. He held his hands out in front of him. His claws began to disappear back into his body. His skin was no longer purple. He was becoming human again.

Gwendolyn stood over Gideon. Her jaws snapped at him. Then she bent down and put her face only inches from his. Saliva dripped from her long teeth. Her purple eyes were glazed with rage. They bore into him. Her breath was fetid. It smelled like death. Gwendolyn dragged a claw across Gideon's cheek, slicing deep. "That's much better, Gideon. In your human form your skin is so tender and easy to slice."

Gideon sucked in a quick breath as warm blood ran down his face. *I won't give her the satisfaction of screaming.*

"It's time to die, Gideon."

Gwendolyn lifted Gideon off the ground by his neck and held him several feet in the air. His legs swung back and forth like a puppet's.

Every breath was a struggle against Gwendolyn's powerful grip. Sharp claws dug into Gideon's throat. Then Gwendolyn pulled Gideon close to her and drove her claws into his forehead an inch at a time.

Blood ran into Gideon's eyes, blurring his vision. He grunted against the pain. *I refuse to scream. I'm not going out like that.*

"What's that, Gideon? You have some last words before I crack open your skull?"

Gideon nodded. He tried to speak but only managed a croaking noise.

Gwendolyn loosened her grip on Gideon's throat. "Let's hear it, boy."

"Computer, activate Gideon Protocol now!" Gideon shouted.

"Acknowledged, Gideon Protocol activated."

The DNA scrambler snapped on like a searchlight. Its purple light pinched and probed Gideon.

Gwendolyn's eyes went wide with fear. The skin on her face started to melt as the DNA scrambler washed over her. She dropped Gideon to the floor and staggered, trying to make her way out of the DNA scrambler and toward the safety of the lab.

Gideon held his neck and coughed. His throat was ragged and sore. Every breath was painful. His skin crawled with thousands of small pin-pricks from the DNA scrambler.

Gwendolyn growled and gnashed her teeth at the purple light. It reminded Gideon of a dog snapping at a housefly. She shrieked as her skin and muscles melted, exposing her skull, ribs, leg, and arm bones. Thin layers of new skin and muscle struggled to grow back only to be erased by the DNA scrambler.

Gwendolyn continued to fight her way out of the DNA scrambler and make her way toward the lab. In another five feet she would be clear of the scrambler and able to heal herself completely.

No way does she escape. Gideon launched himself at Gwendolyn's legs and tackled her.

They hit the floor hard, their bodies a jumbled mess of twisted arms, legs, and melting flesh and sinew.

Gwendolyn's viscous body felt wet and sticky on Gideon. Her blood spattered Gideon's face and arms. It was scalding. It tasted salty, tinged with a rancid vinegar-like bitterness.

Gwendolyn tried to stand but Gideon refused to let go of her legs.

Then Gwendolyn tried to jump out of Gideon's grasp. But Gideon held tight and pulled the skin and muscles off Gwendolyn's legs like they were oversized snow pants. She roared in pain.

Gideon threw the sinewy leggings across the floor.

The DNA scrambler dissolved the skin and muscle.

Gideon jammed his fingers into the gap between Gwendolyn's tibia and fibula. Her leg bones were slick with blood. Gideon held onto her like an anchor.

Gwendolyn tried raking her claws across Gideon's arms but her claws broke off. Gwendolyn held up her clawless hand and stared at it. As she did, the skin on her hand melted away to the bone. She opened her jaw vertically and horizontally, exposing her fangs and teeth. She tried to bite Gideon but the lower half of her jaw dropped off, the muscles and ligaments holding it in place melted by the DNA scrambler.

Then Gwendolyn's eyes melted.

She collapsed onto the floor with a wet thud. She made raspy gurgling sounds as she fought to breathe.

Gideon felt the last breath leave Gwendolyn. He pushed her partially de-composed body away in disgust and staggered to his feet. He stood over her remains like a victorious gladiator. *You were wrong. There are three ways to kill a Berserker.*

Gideon was covered with blood and pieces of Gwendolyn. He wiped his face with his hands and flicked away the gore.

The DNA scrambler continued to wash over him—its pinprick-like probing replaced by a stinging and burning sensation. Smoke rose from Gideon's body.

Panic gripped him. He held his hands out in front of him. His skin was still intact but the pieces of Gwendolyn that were stuck to him were being burned off. Gideon outstretched his arms. He let the DNA scrambler erase every last bit of Gwendolyn from his body.

Gideon eyed the AI's security monitor. The saber-toothed cats finished off the last of the Winged Rippers. The cats raced past the dead monsters down the corridor and toward the lab. There was no sign of Paige. *I hope she's okay.*

Gideon scanned the lab for any sign of Kaz, Rippers or Berserkers. The lab was deserted. Even Mrs. Muramatsu's body was gone. Then Gideon strode out of the DNA scrambler.

Kaz took his mother's body. I wonder how much he saw before he left.

On the floor where Kaz's mother died was a crudely written message scrawled in purple blood. *I know what you are, Gideon.*

Gideon smeared the message with his boot, making it unreadable. *I don't know what I am, Kaz. But you better hope I never see you again.*

Gideon reached for his Chain of Remembrance. It was gone. He scanned Gwendolyn's main computer console and found it next to the DNA reader. The clasp was broken but the blue crystal was intact. He grabbed a handheld laser from the floor and soldered the clasp back together. After it cooled, he hung the Chain of Remembrance around his neck. The crystal was warm against his chest.

Gideon made his way to the birthing pod holding Frank. He checked Frank's vital signs on the small computer located on the side of the pod. The hunter was alive. Gideon pressed the release button. The tubes in Frank's back fell away. The pod opened with a click and a hiss. A white gas that smelled like almonds wafted over Gideon.

Frank stirred. His eyes opened. "Gideon? Is that you?"

"Hi, Frank."

"*You're* saving *me?*"

"I guess so, yeah."

"Ain't that a kick in the head?" The hunter rubbed the sleep from his eyes. "Where's the queen bee at?"

"Gwendolyn's dead. I killed her."

"She was the queen Berserker. How did you manage that, Gideon?"

"I'll tell you on the flight home. We don't have much time before we turn into Off Worlders. Can you walk, Frank?"

Frank tried to sit up. He groaned and sat back in the birthing pod. "I don't think so."

Gideon grabbed Frank's arm and draped it over his shoulder. He pulled the hunter up and out of the birthing tube. Frank's leg showed no signs of the Bone Flower bite except some light scarring.

At least Gwendolyn repaired his leg.

Frank started shivering. Goose bumps sprouted on his bare arms and legs. "Damn, this floor's cold."

"We need to get you dressed. Your flight suit will warm you up." Gideon led Frank to a nearby examination table and laid him on top of it. He grabbed the hunter's flight suit from underneath the exam table.

Gideon slipped Frank's legs, arms, and torso into the flight suit and zipped it up. In a pocket on the suit's left shoulder was a hand-sized triage kit. The small computer could diagnose Frank's condition and administer enough na-nite-meds to stabilize him provided he wasn't in critical condition.

Gideon pulled open Frank's shoulder pocket and withdrew the triage kit. He inserted the kit's nasal tubes in Frank's nose, and activated the small computer. The triage kit beeped and flashed Frank's condition in red—dehydration, malnutrition, hypothermia, and anemia. Gideon pressed the dispense button. The nasal tubes glowed green as the nanite-meds flowed into Frank's body.

"Give the nanite-meds a few minutes to start working," Gideon said. "After that you should be okay to fly. Are you getting any warmer?"

Frank's flight suit buzzed and hummed as heat ran through it. "Don't give me them puppy-dog eyes, Gideon, I've been hurt worse than this. And yeah, the suit's warming me up nice. After I chew some of these red stim pills I'll have energy to be able to walk. It's bad enough you had to dress me. You ain't gonna carry me to the jumper too."

"Okay, Frank."

Frank eyed the lab. "Looks like I missed the party, Gideon. This place is trashed."

"What? Oh, yeah. One of the Berserkers tossed Paige around the lab. It broke a lot of the equipment."

"Where is that girl, Gideon? I thought I heard her voice when I was asleep. Is she okay?"

Worry strangled Gideon. Words caught in his throat. "I...I don't know."

Chapter 35

G ideon wove his way between overturned steel tables and smashed lab equipment. He stepped over disembodied wings, clawed hands and bat-like heads. Shards of broken glass crunched under his feet. Power cords sparked and snapped. Long tubular lights jutted from the ceiling like broken bones. They flickered like emergency beacons.

Gideon eyed the purple, blood-smeared message Kaz left for him on the floor of the lab. *I know what you are, Gideon.*

Like a nightmare that couldn't be remembered upon waking, disjointed images of Gideon as a Berserker flashed through his mind. Vague memories of rage, raw power, and fear ran through him. Gideon clinched his fists as the memory of his bones popping, his claws stabbing, and his jaws tearing into Gwendolyn clouded his thinking. It was like looking through someone else's eyes.

Gideon's mouth watered at the thought of hot steaming blood bathing his tongue. He wiped his mouth with the back of his hand and swallowed. *What's wrong with me?*

Gideon pushed the images from his mind as he approached the lab's AI console. Only two of the six monitors were working. The other four were smashed in the fight with Gwendolyn. *Paige was right. I need to destroy the computer files.*

"Computer, prepare to engage auto destruct of all system files including secondary storage systems. I want all data from Gwendolyn and Dr. Wells' experiments destroyed."

"Negative, secondary storage systems cannot be destroyed," the computer replied.

"Why not?"

"Secondary systems are not located in this facility."

"Where are they?"

"Onboard Captain Payne's vessel," the computer said.

Gideon cursed. "Computer, engage auto destruct in T-minus five minutes. I want a silent countdown only."

"Affirmative, auto destruct sequence engaged. All files will be destroyed in T-minus five minutes."

Frank sidled up to Gideon.

The smell of Frank's blood made Gideon's skin tingle with anticipation. He salivated. *What is going on with me?*

"Gideon, the meds are kickin' in. I'm good to go. Let's get off this rock. The clock's ticking," Frank said.

Tremors shook Gideon. His hands began to quake. Sweat poured off him. The sound of Frank's heartbeat hammered in Gideon's ears.

"Gideon, you don't look so good. You're shaking like a junkie."

"I don't know, Frank. I think I might be…sick." Gideon glanced at the purple, blood-smeared message on the floor.

I know what you are, Gideon.

"Gideon, look at me. Let me see your eyes."

Gideon stared into Frank's eyes. An insatiable hunger squeezed him like a fist. Gideon pictured himself tearing Frank to pieces, feeding on his broken body.

I know what you are, Gideon.

The smell of Frank's blood was sweet and intoxicating. Gideon squeezed his fists together. *Am I monster? Am I human? Am I both?*

"Gideon, you've still got Pure Earth eyes. You're good to go. Let's man-up and roll on outta here."

What happens to me when I go back home? Will I crave human flesh? Will I be able to control myself or will I kill everyone?

Gideon pictured himself killing the Headmaster of Quarantine. *The Weasel deserves it.*

He pictured himself eating the bones of Caleb, Nick, and Thomas. *Those guys are bullies and jerks.*

Euphoria surged through Gideon. *I could kill everyone in Quarantine. They called me Berserker for years. Let them see what a real one is.*

Fight, Fight, Fight.

Berserker, Berserker.

Gideon reached for his Chain of Remembrance. *No, I'm not a monster. I can fight this. I can beat this.*

Frank waved his hand in Gideon's face. "Earth to Gideon, come in, Gideon."

"Frank, I can't go back."

"What, you think you're in love with that girl? Is that it? Come on, Gideon. I've known lots of girls. Forget about her."

"Frank, that's not it. I think I'm a—"

"Gideon, our mission is to return to Earth before we turn into Off Worlders—five days in and out, not one day more, remember? Staying here is not a mission parameter. This is day five and I'm leaving this rock with or without you. Don't give me that look, Gideon."

"Frank you need to listen to me."

"No, Gideon, you need to listen to me. You're going to open the jumper for me and show me how to engage the autopilot and anything else I need. I'd rather take my chances crashing and burning on Earth than staying on this rock."

"You can't go back either, Frank. Take a look at your eyes."

Frank ripped his sunglasses off. He held the mirrored lenses up to his face. His purple eyes went wide. He slammed his fist onto the table. "Damn, man. So now I'm a carrier of the Virus? How come your eyes didn't change, Gideon?"

"Gwendolyn did tests on me, Frank. She said I'm immune to the Virus and that my mother used my DNA to create the cure."

"But your old man said the cure turns people into Berserkers."

Tears welled in Gideon's eyes. "I know."

"Gideon, are you telling me you're a Berserker?"

"I don't know, Frank. Something happened to me when I was fighting Gwendolyn. I can't remember everything, just bits and pieces. But it's why I can't go back. I need to figure this out."

Frank put his hand on Gideon's shoulder and squeezed. "Gideon, I ain't goin' anywhere. You saved my life. Whatever you need, I'm here. You read me?"

"Thanks, Frank."

"Remember what I told you, Gideon. What happens to you isn't as important as what you do about it."

"I remember."

"Who else knows about this, Gideon?"

"Kaz knows. I think he saw me change into a Berserker. But I'm still not sure what happened to me."

"Then we do two things, Gideon. First, we find Kaz and we make sure he stays quiet about you and what he thinks he saw here today. We don't need him blabbin' that you're a Berserker. Then we're going to get us some payback for him setting up Vince to be eaten by those Peelers and for betraying us to Gwendolyn. He was working for her the whole time. He's gonna get his."

"How do you know Kaz was working for Gwendolyn?"

"She told me."

"What's number two?"

"Number two, we find you a cure. Hell, my mother used to say home is where you hang your hat. Maybe Off World won't be so bad."

The smell of strawberries wafted over Gideon.

Paige was standing in the doorway of the lab. A small group of saber-toothed cats was with her. She dropped her bow on the floor, ran to Gideon and threw her arms around his neck. "I knew ya would make it. Yer the bravest, smartest eejit I ever did know."

Gideon's face flushed. "You might be right, Frank. Maybe Off World won't be so bad after all."

Acknowledgments

Writing a novel is a tough and rewarding journey best taken with friends and loved ones. I'm blessed to have had the support of both for *The Gideon Protocol*.

I want to thank the Writing Center at the University of Wisconsin – Madison, especially my writing coach who has asked to remain anonymous. Without my coach's support this book would not have been possible. Enough said.

I also want to thank The Bethesda Writer's Workshop for the excellent workshops that laid the foundation for this book.

A special thanks to my first readers, AKA, the Literary Focus Group; a great collection of brave individuals whose feedback made this book better—Andrew, Ari, Anna, Jeffrey, Heidi, Christine, Julia, Jake, Amy, Samantha and especially my Alpha reader, Cristina.

And of course my family, their love and understanding never wavered despite the steep hills and deep valleys of the novel writing process.

ABOUT THE AUTHOR

LC Hanson lives in Bethesda, Maryland with his wife, two daughters, and Labrador Retriever. He has worked as a regulatory lawyer specializing in U.S. export control law and is an avid martial artist. He loves Science Fiction thrillers, Westerns and martial arts. What happens when you combine all three? You get *The Gideon Protocol*!

Please visit TheGideonProtocol.com for more information and follow me on Twitter for the release date of the sequel to *The Gideon Protocol*.

www.ingramcontent.com/pod-product-compliance
Lightning Source LLC
Chambersburg PA
CBHW061326170626
46817CB00001B/334